*Meet the lords and ladies of London's ton,
Bath society and Regency
country house parties*
in

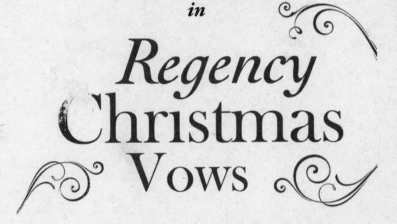

Regency
Christmas
Vows

**Two vivid, festive novels
by reader favourites
Nicola Cornick and Anne Herries**

Regency Christmas Vows

NICOLA CORNICK

ANNE HERRIES

MILLS & BOON

Published in Great Britain 2014
by Mills & Boon, an imprint of Harlequin (UK) Limited,
Eton House, 18-24 Paradise Road, Richmond, Surrey, TW9 1SR

REGENCY CHRISTMAS VOWS © 2014 Harlequin Books S.A.

The Blanchland Secret © 2000 Nicola Cornick
The Mistress of Hanover Square © 2009 Anne Herries

ISBN: 978-0-263-25097-8

012-1114

Harlequin (UK) Limited's policy is to use papers that are natural, renewable and recyclable products and made from wood grown in sustainable forests. The logging and manufacturing processes conform to the legal environmental regulations of the country of origin.

Printed and bound by
CPI Group (UK) Ltd, Croydon, CR0 4YY

The Blanchland Secret

Nicola Cornick

For the first eighteen years of her life **Nicola Cornick** lived in Yorkshire, within a stone's throw of the moors that had inspired the Brontë sisters to write *Jane Eyre* and *Wuthering Heights*. One of her grandfathers was a poet and her family contained teachers and avid readers who filled the house with books. With such a background it was impossible for Nicola not to become a bookworm.

Nicola met her future husband while she was at university, although it took her four years to realise that he was special and more than just a friend. Her husband, being so much more perceptive, had worked this out much sooner, but eventually an understanding was reached.

This lack of perception also meant that Nicola did not realise for years that she was meant to be a writer. She wrote bits and pieces of novels in her spare time, but never finished any of them. Eventually, she sent in the first three chapters of a Regency romance to Mills & Boon and, although they were rejected, she found she had become so addicted to writing that she could not stop. Happily, her third attempt was accepted and she has never looked back.

Nicola loves to hear from her readers and can be contacted by e-mail or via her website, www.nicolacornick.co.uk.

Chapter One

Mr Julius Churchward, representative of the famously discreet London lawyers of the same name, had a variety of facial expressions he could draw upon, depending on the nature of the news he was imparting to his aristocratic clients. There was sympathetic but grave, used when breaking the news that an inheritance was substantially smaller than expected; there was sympathetic but rueful, for unsatisfactory offspring and breach of promise; finally, there was an all-purpose dolefulness, for when the precise nature of the problem was in doubt. It was this third alternative that he adopted now, as he stood on the doorstep of Lady Amelia Fenton's trim house in Bath, for if the truth were told, he knew nothing of the contents of the letter he was about to deliver.

Mr Churchward had travelled from London the previous day, stopped overnight at the Star and Garter in Newbury and resumed his journey at first light. To undertake such a journey in winter, with Christmas pressing close upon them, argued some urgency. The morning sun was warming the creamy Bath stone of Brock Street but the winter air was chill. Mr Churchward shiv-

ered inside his overcoat and hoped that Miss Sarah
Sheridan, Lady Amelia's companion, was not still at
breakfast.

A neat maid showed him into a parlour that he remembered from a visit three years before, a visit during
which he had conveyed to Miss Sheridan the disap-
pointing news that her brother Frank had left no estate
to speak of. At the back of his mind was an occasion
some two years before that, when he had had to proffer
the even more depressing intelligence that Lord Sheridan had left only a small competence to keep his daughter from penury. Miss Sheridan had borne the news with
fortitude, explained that she had very few material
needs and gained Mr Churchward's admiration in the
process.

He still felt the inequity of her situation keenly. A
lady of Miss Sheridan's breeding should not, he felt, be
reduced to acting as companion, even to so benevolent
a relative as her cousin, Lady Amelia. He was sure that
Lady Amelia was too generous ever to make Miss Sheridan feel a poor relation, but it was simply not fitting.
For several years Mr Churchward's chivalrous heart had
hoped that Miss Sheridan would make a suitable match,
for she was young and looked well to a pass, but three
years had gone by and she was now firmly on the shelf.

Mr Churchward shook his head sadly as he waited in
Lady Amelia's airy drawing-room. He tried hard not to
have favourites; it would have been quite inappropriate
when he had so many esteemed clients, but he made an
exception in the case of Miss Sarah Sheridan.

The door opened and Sarah came towards him, hand
outstretched as though he was a great friend rather than
the bearer of doubtful news.

'Dear Mr Churchward! How do you do, sir? This is an unexpected pleasure!'

Mr Churchward was not so sure. The letter he carried seemed to weigh down his document case. But such misgivings seemed foolish in the light of day. The parlour was bright with winter sunlight; it shone full on Miss Sheridan, but she was a lady whose face and figure could withstand the harshest of morning light. Indeed, her cream and rose complexion seemed dazzlingly fresh and fair and her slender figure was set off to advantage by a simple dress of jonquil muslin.

'How do you do, Miss Sheridan? I hope I find you well?'

Mr Churchward took the proffered seat and cleared his throat. He was astonished to find that he was nervous, too nervous to indulge in talk of the weather or the journey. He bent to unbuckle his case and extracted a letter in a plain white envelope.

'Madam, forgive my abruptness, but I have been asked to deliver this letter to you. The manner in which the request came about is quite extraordinary, but perhaps you would wish to read the letter first, before I explain...' Mr Churchward was unhappily aware that he was rambling. Sarah's wide and beautiful hazel eyes were fixed on his face with an expression of vague puzzlement. She took the letter and gave a slight gasp.

'But this is—'

'From your late brother. Yes, ma'am.' Mr Churchward groped for his all-purpose solemn expression, but was sure he was only achieving the anxious look of a man who was not in complete control of the situation. 'Perhaps if you were to read what Lord Sheridan has written...'

Miss Sheridan made no immediate attempt to open

the letter. Her head was bent as she examined the familiar black writing and the sunlight picked out strands of gold and amber in the hair that escaped her cap.

'Are you aware of the contents of the letter, Mr Churchward?'

'No, madam, I am not.' The lawyer sounded slightly reproachful, as though Francis Sheridan had committed a decided *faux pas* by leaving him in ignorance.

Miss Sheridan scanned his face for a moment, then walked slowly over to the walnut desk. Mr Churchward heard the sound of the letter-opener slicing through paper and felt relief wash over him. Soon they would know the worst…

There was silence in the little room. Mr Churchward could hear the chink of china from the kitchens, the sound of voices raised in question and answer. He looked around at the neat bookshelves laden with works he remembered from Blanchland; books that Sir Ralph Covell had dismissively thrown out of the house he had inherited from his second cousin, Lord Sheridan; books that Sarah had gladly retrieved for her new home.

Miss Sheridan did not speak at all. Eventually she crossed to the wing chair that mirrored Mr Churchward's on the other side of the fireplace and sat down. The letter fell to her lap; she looked him straight in the eye.

'Mr Churchward, I think I should read you the contents of Frank's letter.'

'Very well, madam.' Mr Churchward looked apprehensive.

'Dear Sal,' Miss Sheridan read, in a dry tone, 'if you get this letter I shall be dead and in need of a favour. Sorry to have to ask this of you, old girl—fact is, I'd rather trust you than anyone else. So here goes. I have a daughter. I know that will surprise you and I'm sorry I never told you before, but to tell the truth, I hoped you'd never need to know. Father knew, of course— made all the usual arrangements, all right and tight. But if he is gone and I'm gone, then the child needs someone to turn to for help, and that's where you come in. Churchward will tell you the rest. All I can say is thank you and God bless you.

'Your loving brother, Frank.'

Miss Sheridan sighed. Mr Churchward sighed. Both were thinking in their different ways of the insouciant Frank Sheridan who would have fathered a child so lightly, made cheerful provision for her future perhaps, but not really given the matter the thought it deserved. Mr Churchward could imagine him dashing off such a letter before he went off to join the East India Company on yet another mad attempt to make his fortune…

Sarah's voice broke into Mr Churchward's thoughts. 'Well, Mr Churchward, can you, as Frank suggests, throw any more light on this mystery?'

Mr Churchward sighed for a second time. 'I confess, madam, that I did know of Miss Meredith's existence. Your late father…' He hesitated. 'Lord Sheridan came to me seventeen years ago to ask me to make arrangements for a certain child. I thought…'

'You thought that the child was his own?' Sarah said calmly. For a moment, Mr Churchward could have sworn that there was a twinkle in Miss Sheridan's eye, a look that was surely inappropriate for a young lady when confronted with the evidence of some improper connection of her family.

'Well, I assumed—' Mr Churchward broke off unhappily, aware that it was dangerous for lawyers to make assumptions.

'It was a natural supposition,' Sarah said kindly, 'especially since Frank could have been little more than eighteen himself at the time.'

'Young men...wild oats...' Mr Churchward made a vague gesture. He suddenly realised the impropriety of discussing such a matter with a young, unmarried lady, cleared his throat purposefully and pushed his glasses up his nose. He deplored the necessity of giving Miss Sheridan this information, but there was nothing for it. Best to be as businesslike as possible.

'The child was placed with a family in a village near Blanchland, I believe, madam. The late Lord Sheridan paid an annuity to a Dr John Meredith each year during his lifetime and...' he hesitated '...left a sum to him in his will. Dr Meredith died last year, at which time his widow and daughter were still resident near Blanchland.'

'I remember Dr Meredith,' Sarah said thoughtfully. 'He was a kindly man. He attended me when I had the measles. And I do believe he had a daughter—a pretty little girl some seven or eight years younger than I. She went away to school. I remember everyone saying that the doctor must have some private income—' She broke off, a rueful smile on her lips as she realised that the mystery of the doctor's finances was now solved.

The arrival of some refreshments—a pot of coffee for Mr Churchward and a strong cup of tea for Miss Sheridan—created a natural break in the conversation and gave the lawyer the opportunity to move smoothly forward.

'I do apologise for springing such a surprise on you, Miss Sheridan—'

'Pray do not, Mr Churchward.' Sarah smiled warmly. 'This is none of your doing. But I understand from

Frank's letter that you were to contact me if Miss Meredith was in need of help. In what way may I assist her?'

Mr Churchward looked unhappy. He reached for his bag again and extracted a second letter. It was smaller than the first, the paper of inferior quality, the hand round and childish. 'I received this three days ago, Miss Sheridan. Please…'

Once again, Sarah read aloud.

Dear Sir,

I am writing to you because I am in desperate need of help and do not know where to turn. I understand from my mother that the late Lord Sheridan gave her your direction, instructing her to contact you should either of us ever be in dire need. Please come to me at Blanchland, so that I may acquaint you with our difficulties and seek your advice.

I am, Sir, your most obedient servant,
Miss Olivia Meredith.

There was a silence. Mr Churchward was aware that he should have felt more at ease, for provision for illegitimate children and difficulties raised by said children was very much a part of Churchward and Churchward's business. Never before, however, had he been confronted by the situation in which an errant brother had asked his younger sister to offer help to his byblow. Frank Sheridan had been a likeable man, but thoughtless and devil-may-care. He had indubitably put his sister in a very awkward situation.

'Miss Meredith makes no mention of the precise nature of her difficulties,' Sarah said thoughtfully. 'And

when Frank wrote his letter he would have had no notion of the sort of help she would need—'

'Very difficult for him, I am sure, madam.' Mr
Churchward still looked disapproving. 'He wished to do
the right thing by the child without knowing what that
would be.'

Sarah wrinkled up her nose. 'I fear I am becoming
confused, Mr Churchward. May we go over this once
again? I shall call for more coffee and tea.'

The pot was replenished, Sarah's cup refilled, then
the maid withdrew once again.

'Now,' Sarah said, in her most businesslike voice, 'let
us recapitulate. My late brother left a letter with you to
be despatched to me in the event of a plea for help from
his natural daughter, Miss Meredith. Frank was, I suppose, trying to guard against my niece being left friend-
less in the event of his death.'

'I assume that to be correct, madam.'

'And there has never been any request for help until
three days ago, when you received this letter from Miss
Meredith?'

Mr Churchward inclined his head. 'All contact with
Dr Meredith and his family ceased on your father's
death, ma'am. I believe that Lord Sheridan left them a
sum of money—' Mr Churchward's lips primmed as he
remembered that it was a not-inconsiderable sum of
money '—in order that the child should want for nothing in the future. Why she has seen fit to contact us
now...'

'The help Miss Meredith needs may not be of a financial nature,' Sarah observed quietly, 'and she is still
my niece, Mr Churchward, despite the circumstances of
her birth.'

'Very true, madam.' Mr Churchward sighed, feeling

reproved. 'This is all most irregular and I am not at all happy about it. For you to have to return to Blanchland is the most unfortunate thing imaginable!'

Once again, the lawyer thought that he detected a twinkle in Miss Sheridan's eye. 'Certainly, Frank asks a great deal, Mr Churchward.'

'He does indeed, ma'am,' Mr Churchward said fervently. He shuddered, thinking of Sir Ralph Covell, the late Lord Sheridan's cousin, who had inherited Blanchland Court upon Frank's death. In the following three years Covell had turned the place into a notorious den of iniquity. Gambling, drunken revels, licentious orgies... The tales had been wilder each year. It seemed impossible to believe that Miss Sarah Sheridan, respectable spinster and pillar of Bath society, would ever set foot in the place.

'Your cousin, Sir Ralph Covell, is still in residence at Blanchland, Miss Sheridan?' Mr Churchward asked, fearing that he already knew the answer.

'I believe so.' The warmth had gone from Sarah's voice. 'It grieves me to hear the tales of depravity at Blanchland, Mr Churchward. It is such a gracious house to be despoiled by such evil.'

Churchward cleared his throat. 'For that reason, Miss Sheridan, it would be most inappropriate for you to return there. If your brother had known what Covell would do to your home, he would never have suggested it. Besides...' Churchward brightened '...he has not actually asked you to go to see Miss Meredith yourself! You may advise her through an agent, perhaps—'

Churchward broke off as Sarah rose to her feet and crossed to the window. She gazed into the distance. The bare trees that lined the Circus were casting shifting shadows onto the pavements. A carriage rattled past.

'Perhaps someone could represent your interests at Blanchland,' Churchward repeated, when Sarah did not speak. He was desperately hoping that she would not ask him to be that person. His wife would never stand for it. But Sarah was shaking her head.

'No, Mr Churchward. I fear that Frank has laid this charge on me alone and I must honour it. I shall, of course, gratefully accept your advice when I have ascertained the nature of Miss Meredith's problem. I imagine that it should be easy enough to find the girl and see how I may help her.'

Mr Churchward was ashamed at the relief that flooded through him. There was an air of decision about Miss Sheridan that made it difficult to argue with her, despite her relative youth, but he still felt absurdly guilty. He made a business of shuffling his papers together and as he did so he remembered the piece of news that he had still to impart. His face fell still further.

'I should tell you, ma'am, that I took the liberty of sending a message to Miss Meredith to reassure her that I had received her letter. By chance I passed my messenger on the road as I made my way here. He had been to Blanchland and was on his way back to London.'

There was a pause. Sarah raised her eyebrows. 'And?'

Mr Churchward looked unhappy. 'I fear that he was unable to find Miss Meredith, ma'am. The young lady was last seen approaching the front door of Blanchland Court two days ago. She has not been seen since. Miss Meredith has disappeared.'

Later, as he was driving back to London, Mr Churchward remembered that he had forgotten to tell Miss Sheridan about the third letter, the one that Francis

Sheridan had requested be despatched to the Earl of Woodallan. His spirits, which had been depressingly low since leaving Bath, revived a little. Woodallan was Sarah's godfather and a man of sound sense into the bargain. It was a pity that Mr Sheridan had ever thought to involve his sister in such an undignified situation, but at least he appeared to have had the sense to apply to a man of Woodallan's stature to support her. Mr Churchward sat forward for a moment, debating whether to ask the driver to turn back to Bath, then he caught sight of a signpost for Maidenhead and sat back against the cushions with a sigh. He was tired and nearing home, and, after all, Miss Sheridan would learn of Lord Woodallan's involvement soon enough.

Lady Amelia had already left for her morning engagements by the time Mr Churchward departed for London, so Sarah had no chance to confide in her cousin. She thought that this was probably a good thing, for her natural inclination had been to rush and tell Amelia all, when perhaps it would be better to think a little. Frank had not laid any strictures of secrecy on her, but Amelia was the least discreet of people and no doubt the tale of Sarah's niece would be all over Bath in a morning were Amelia to be made party to the story.

Sarah sat on the edge of her bed and thought of Frank and of her father, paying for his granddaughter's upkeep, and of neither of them breathing a word to her. She suspected that neither of them had ever intended that she should know. But perhaps Frank had had some premonition of his own end when he was about to set sail for India that last time. At least it would have been some comfort to him to think, as he lay racked by fever so far from home, that he had made some provision, hasty and thoughtless as it was, for Olivia's future...

Sarah stirred herself. She could sit here thinking of it all day, but she had errands of her own to attend to— some ribbons to match at the haberdasher's and bouquets to collect from the florist for the ball Amelia was holding the following night. Sarah replaced her lace cap with a plain bonnet, donned a sensible dark pelisse, and hurried down the stairs.

Mrs Anderson, Lady Amelia's housekeeper, was lurking in the stairwell, a look of slightly anxious eagerness on her homely face. She started forward as Sarah reached the bottom step.

'Was there...did the gentleman bring any good news, Miss Sarah?'

Sarah, adjusting her bonnet slightly before the pier glass, smiled slightly. News travelled quickly and a visit from the family lawyer was bound to cause speculation.

'No one has left me a fortune I fear, Annie!' she said cheerfully. 'Mr Churchward came only to tell me of a request my brother Frank made a few years ago. Nothing exciting, I am sorry to say!'

Mrs Anderson's face fell. In common with all the other servants in the house, she thought it a crying shame that Miss Sheridan should be the poor relation, and her a real lady, so pretty-behaved and well bred. Not that Lady Amelia ever treated her cousin as though she was a charity case, but it was Miss Sarah herself who insisted on running errands and doing work that was beneath her. She was doing it now.

'Would you like me to collect the vegetables whilst I am out?' Sarah was saying. 'It is only a step from the florists to the greengrocer's—'

'No, ma'am,' Mrs Anderson said firmly. It was one

thing for Miss Sheridan to carry home a bouquet of hot-house roses and quite another for her to be weighed down with cauliflower and lettuce. She moved to open the door for Sarah and espied the portly figure of a gentleman just passing the gate. 'Why, ma'am, 'tis Mr Tilbury! If you are quick to catch him up, he may escort you to the shops!'

'Thank you for warning me, Annie,' Sarah said serenely. 'If I walk very slowly, I am persuaded he will lose himself ahead of me! I just pray that he does not turn around!'

Mrs Anderson shook her head as she watched Sarah's trim figure descend the steps and set off slowly up Brock Street towards the Circus. There was no accounting for taste, but to her mind a marriage to a rich gentleman like Mr Tilbury was far preferable to being a poor spinster. Unfortunately, Miss Sheridan seemed too particular to settle for a marriage of convenience. Mr Tilbury was older, a widower with grown-up children, and if he were a little dull and set in his ways, well…

Mrs Anderson closed the door, noticing in the process that the housemaid had left a smear on the polished step. She walked slowly back towards the kitchens, still thinking of Miss Sheridan's suitors. Bath was a staid place and could not offer much in the way of excitement, but there had been several retired army officers who would have been only too happy to offer for Miss Sheridan if she had given them the least encouragement. And then there was Sir Edmund Place—an invalid, with a weak chest, but a rich one! And there had been young Lord Grantley—very young, Mrs Anderson admitted to herself, barely off the leading reins, in fact, but infatuated with Miss Sheridan and no mistake! Old Lady Grantley had soon whisked her lamb out of harm's way, declaring to all and sundry that Miss Sheridan was a designing female! Mrs Anderson bridled. Miss Sarah was more of a lady than Augusta Grantley would ever be!

Still, there was always hope. Cook's sister, who was Lady Allerton's housekeeper, had overheard her ladyship mention that a number of new visitors had been listed in the *Bath Register*, chief amongst whom was Viscount Renshaw, son of the Earl of Woodallan. Not just that, but his lordship was rumoured to be staying with his good friend Greville Baynham, one of Lady Amelia's beaux... Still plotting, Mrs Anderson called for the housemaid and made some pungent remarks about the slovenliness of her cleaning.

The subject of these musings, completely unaware that her cousin's matchmaking staff had plans for her, had purchased two very pretty pink ribbons for the bodice of Amelia's ballgown and was just leaving the florist with her arms full of specially cultivated roses. No matter how she tried to avoid it, the events of the past hour kept flooding back into Sarah's mind. A niece of seventeen! And she was only four and twenty herself! Frank, her senior by eleven years, had begun his womanising young. He had always been one with an eye for the prettiest maids. And who had been Olivia's mother? Sarah paused on the street corner. Surely it had not been the doctor's prim little wife? Mrs Meredith had been so very proper...

Aware that she was speculating in a most ill-bred manner, Sarah smiled a little. She was certain that Churchward had been shocked by her lack of sensibility when acquainted with the news! Engrossed in her thoughts, she stepped off the pavement and someone bumped into her, knocking all the breath out of her body. The roses went flying across the cobblestones. Sarah lost her balance and would have fallen were it not for an arm that went hard around her waist, steadying her.

'I beg your pardon, ma'am!' a masculine voice exclaimed. 'Devilish clumsy of me!'

The gentleman set Sarah gently on her feet and removed his arm from about her with what she considered to be unnecessary slowness. He turned to gather up the scattered flowers, but he was too late. A carriage, bowling along at a smart pace, neatly severed the heads of half of them.

'Oh, no!' Sarah went down on her knees again to try to rescue those that were left, but even they were bruised, their petals drooping. Amelia would be furious. The red roses were the centrepiece of her decoration the following night and the florist had grown them especially for the event. With all her heart Sarah wished she had left the roses to be brought round later on the cart with the other flowers, but she had been looking forward to walking through the winter streets with such a splash of colour. She sat back on her heels, holding the sad bouquet in her hand.

'Pray have some sense, madam! You are likely to be squashed flat if you remain in the road!'

The gentleman took Sarah firmly by the elbow and hauled her to her feet again. There was considerably less courtesy in his voice this time.

Sarah stepped back and glared at him furiously. 'I thank you for your concern, sir! A pity you did not think of the danger before you consigned my roses to precisely that fate!'

The gentleman did not answer at once, merely raising

one dark eyebrow in a somewhat quizzical fashion. His thoughtful gaze, very dark and direct, considered Sarah from her skewed bonnet to her sensible shoes, pausing on her flushed face and lingering on the curves of her figure beneath the practical pelisse. Sarah raised her chin angrily. Her experience of gentlemen was indisputably small, but she had no trouble in recognising this one as a rake—nor in reading the expression in his eyes.

His was a tall and athletic figure, set off to perfection by an elegance of tailoring seldom found in conservative Bath society. London polish, Sarah thought immediately, remembering Amelia's description of her years in the capital and the intimidatingly handsome gentlemen who had flocked to her balls and soirées. This gentleman had thick fair hair ruffled by the winter breeze, its lightness a striking contrast to the dark brown eyes that were appraising her so thoroughly. A slight smile was starting to curl his firm mouth as he took in the angry sparkle in Sarah's eyes, the outraged blush rising to her cheeks.

'I can only apologise again, madam,' the gentleman said smoothly. 'I was so taken in admiring the beauties of this city—' the amusement in his eyes deepened '—that I was utterly engrossed!'

Sarah felt an answering smile starting and repressed it ruthlessly. There was something here that was surprisingly hard to resist; some indefinable charm, perhaps, or, more dangerously, an affinity that was as disturbing as it was unexpected. The gentleman exuded a careless confidence and a vitality that seemed to set him apart. Bath was full of invalids, Sarah realised, and it was almost shocking to meet someone who seemed so very alive.

The strangest thing of all was that he seemed vaguely

familiar. The combination of fair hair and dark eyes was very unusual and definitely stirred her memory. She paused, unaware that she was staring and that the quizzical twinkle in the gentleman's eyes had changed to thoughtful speculation.

'I beg your pardon, but have we met before, sir?' Sarah frowned slightly. 'There is something familiar—'

Too late, she realised just how he might misinterpret her question. She had been thinking aloud and bit her lip, vexed with herself.

The gentleman's dark eyebrows rose fractionally and there was a certain cynicism in his drawl as he said, 'You flatter me, ma'am! I should say that we could be very good friends if you so choose.'

The colour flooded into Sarah's cheeks. She stopped dead, regardless of curious glances from the other shoppers in Milsom Street.

'That was hardly my intention, sir! I would scarcely attempt to scrape an acquaintance in so ramshackle a manner, particularly with a gentleman who is an undoubted rake! Your assumptions do you no credit! Good day to you, sir!'

He was already before her as she turned on her heel to leave him standing there.

'Wait!' He put out a hand to detain her. 'Forgive me, ma'am! It was not my intention to offend you!'

Sarah looked pointedly down at his hand on her arm, and he removed it at once. 'I should have thought that that was precisely what you intended, sir!'

'No, indeed!' He would have seemed genuinely contrite were it not for the glint of amused admiration she could see lurking in his eyes. 'I intended quite otherwise—' He broke off at the furious light in Sarah's eyes. 'You must allow me to apologise for my deplorable manners, ma'am! And for the roses…' He gave a wry smile to see the drooping posy in Sarah's hand. 'I hope it is a simple matter to procure some more?'

It was said in the tones of someone who had never had any difficulty in finding—or paying for—two dozen red roses for his latest *inamorata*. Sarah, who was finding it extraordinarily difficult to remain angry with him, managed a severity she was proud of.

'I fear that these were the last roses to be had, sir,' she said frostily. 'They were grown especially. And even if they were not, I can scarce afford to go around Bath buying up flowers in an abandoned fashion! Now, you will excuse me, I am sure!'

The gentleman appeared not to have heard his dismissal, although Sarah suspected that he had, in fact, chosen to ignore it. He fell into step beside her as though by mutual consent.

'I trust that you were not injured at all in the accident, ma'am?' The undertone of amusement was still in his voice. 'It was remiss of me not to enquire before. Perhaps I should escort you home to reassure myself that you are quite well?'

Sarah raised her eyebrows at such flagrant presumption. She wondered just how blunt she was going to have to be to dismiss him. It was difficult when a part of her was drawn to him in such a contrary fashion, but she was not accustomed to striking up a conversation with strange gentlemen in the street. Besides, no matter what her errant senses were telling her, such behaviour was dangerous. This man was definitely a rake and had already shown that he would take advantage.

'It is quite unnecessary for you to accompany me, sir. I am indeed well and will be home directly!'

'But it is not at all the done thing for a lady to wander

around unattended, you know,' the gentleman said conversationally. 'I am sure that Bath cannot be so fast as London; even so, the worthy matrons would not approve of such behaviour!'

Once again, Sarah was almost betrayed into a smile. He was outrageous, but surprisingly difficult to resist.

'I am sure that *you* are aware, sir, that it causes less speculation to walk around unchaperoned than to be seen in company with a complete stranger! That being the case, I shall continue alone and wish you a pleasant stay in our city!'

So saying, she gave him a cool nod and walked away, every line of her body defying him to follow her.

Guy, Viscount Renshaw, watched the slender figure walk purposefully away from him. A faint, rueful smile curved his lips. He saw the lady reach the corner of the street, saw her pause to exchange greetings with a gentleman coming the other way and noted with quickened interest that the gentleman was his good friend, Greville Baynham. Reflecting that it was fortunate that Bath society was proving to be so close-knit, Guy strolled across the street just as Greville took his leave of the lady.

'Sorry I was so long, old fellow!' Greville gave his friend an amiable grin. 'Saw a pair of Purdeys that took my fancy. I hope that you found enough to amuse you in my absence!'

'Oh, I was well entertained,' Guy said lazily, watching Sarah disappear out of sight. She had a very trim figure, he thought, good enough to challenge any of the accredited London beauties. Those hazel eyes, set in the wide, pure oval of her face, were magnificent... He real-

ised that Greville had addressed another remark to him
and was waiting patiently for his response.

'I merely asked whether you would care to take the
spa waters?' his friend said with a quizzical look.
'Though perhaps you have found other attractions more
to your liking? Bath is a slow place these days, especially out of season, but—'

'But not as slow as all that!' Guy turned a thoughtful
look on his friend. 'Tell me, Grev, who is the lady to
whom you were speaking just now?'

Greville frowned, pushing a hand through his ruffled
brown hair. 'The lady?' His brow cleared. 'Oh, you
mean Miss Sheridan? Save yourself the trouble if you
thought to strike up a flirtation there, Guy! She don't
give rakes the time of day!'

Guy laughed. 'I believe you, although she did claim
an acquaintance with me! Thought I had mistaken her
quality until she gave me the coolest set-down I've ever
experienced!' Guy frowned a little. 'Sheridan, did you
say? The name *is* familiar… Why, yes, I remember her!
Well, I'll be damned!'

Greville burst out laughing. 'Doing it too brown,
Guy! I don't believe you've ever met the lady before!'

'No, I assure you!' Guy looked triumphant. 'Miss
Sheridan is the sister of the late Lord Sheridan, is she
not? She is also my father's goddaughter and, though I
have not seen her for an age, it must be the same girl!
We were practically childhood friends!'

Greville's shoulders slumped. 'Devil take it, Guy! Of
all the cursed luck!'

Guy gave his friend a pained look. 'Surely you mean
it is a charming coincidence! And, as you evidently
know the lady, you will be able to furnish me with her
direction—'

Greville groaned. 'Don't do it, Guy! Miss Sheridan is Lady Amelia Fenton's cousin and Amelia will string me up if you try to get up a flirtation with Sarah!'

Guy smiled. He had heard quite a lot about Greville's hopeless passion for Lady Amelia only the previous night, when his friend had been in his cups and musing on the cruelty of womankind. Guy had imagined that Bath would prove very shabby genteel now that it had passed its heyday as a fashionable spa, yet the staid society was promising several intriguing possibilities. Greville had made no secret of the fact that he intended to press his suit with the lovely Lady Amelia and now there was Miss Sheridan...

Remembering the flash in those beautiful hazel eyes as Sarah had administered her set-down, Guy was forced into a reluctant grin. He had noticed her as soon as she had come out of the florist with those wretched roses in her arms. Beneath the prim bonnet, her hair had been the colour of autumn leaves; not brown or gold or amber, but a mixture of all three. She had held herself with an unconscious grace, slender and straight; despite her demure appearance, she was far from priggish. There had been a hint of laughter in her eyes and a smile on those pretty lips, and he had known that, for all her propriety, she had been attracted to him.

It was a shame that his father was also Sarah Sheridan's godfather. Guy acknowledged that that would preclude the sort of relationship that had sprung to mind on first seeing her. Nevertheless, it gave him the perfect excuse to pursue the acquaintance and that was a thought that held definite appeal. He drove his hands into his coat pockets.

'Has Miss Sheridan never wished to marry?' he asked, still following a train of thought of his own.

'No money,' Greville said succinctly, watching his friend with deep misgiving. 'Here in Bath everyone is looking to marry a fortune. Sarah goes about with Lady Amelia, writes her letters and so on—' He broke off at the look of distaste on Guy's face.

'Miss Sheridan a lady's companion? Surely not!'

'It is hardly like that,' Greville said, leaping to Amelia's defence. 'Lady Amelia is most sincerely attached to her cousin—they are friends rather than employer and employee! Why, Amelia is the sweetest-natured creature—'

Guy held up a hand in mock surrender. 'No need for such heat, old fellow! You'll be calling me out next! I had no intention of casting doubt on Lady Amelia's generosity, but it seems...' he hesitated '...incongruous to think of Miss Sheridan in such a situation. I wonder if my father knows? At the very least he would offer her a dowry...'

Greville's mouth twisted wryly. 'Thought it was something else you had in mind to offer Miss Sheridan, Guy!'

'I won't deny it crossed my mind,' the Viscount murmured, ' but m'father wouldn't like it! Tell me, Grev, if all the roses in Bath had been sold, where would you go to buy a posy for a lady?'

Greville stared at him as though he had taken leave of his senses. 'Don't know what the devil you're talking about, old chap! Roses in winter?'

'It is very late for them, I suppose. Would I be able to send someone to purchase red roses in Bristol, perhaps?'

'You can buy anything with your sort of money,' Greville said, without rancour. 'Though why you would wish to go to the trouble—'

'A favour for a lady,' Guy explained.

'I collect you mean to win a lady's favour!' Greville said glumly. 'Well, I can't stop you! But be warned, Guy—Miss Sheridan is no fool! She will see through your schemes! And as for Lady Amelia, well, I would not like to be in your shoes if she takes you in dislike!' His gaze fell on the one red rose that Guy had rescued from the street and which he still held in one hand.

'Must you walk round carrying that thing?' he besought. 'Devil take it, Guy, you look like a cursed dandy!'

Chapter Two

'Sarah! You cannot return to Blanchland! I absolutely forbid it! Why, your reputation would be in shreds as soon as you crossed the threshold!'

Lady Amelia Fenton, her kittenish face creased into lines of deep distress, threw herself down onto the sofa beside her cousin. 'Besides,' she added plaintively, 'you know that you detest what Ralph Covell has done to the house, and have never wanted to set foot there again!'

Sarah sighed, reflecting that the only positive thing about the current situation was that it had successfully deflected Amelia from bewailing the loss of the red roses. She had been beside herself to discover that her artistic centrepiece was ruined—until Sarah had casually mentioned her plan to travel to Blanchland on the day following the ball.

Amelia got to her feet again and paced energetically up and down before the fireplace. She looked quite ridiculous, for she was far too small to flounce about. All Amelia's features were small but perfectly proportioned, in contrast to her fortune which was big enough to make her one of Bath's most sought-after matrimonial prizes.

Realising from Sarah's expression that she looked absurd, Amelia sat down again, frowning. 'I know you think I am making a cake of myself, Sarah, but I am truly concerned for your welfare!' She sounded small and hurt. 'Whatever you say, it will be the ruin of you to go there!'

Sarah sighed again. 'Forgive me, Milly! I must go. It is at Frank's request—'

'Your brother has been dead these three years!' Lady Amelia said incontrovertibly. 'It seems to me that it is asking a great deal to expect you to grant his requests from beyond the grave!'

Sarah, reflecting that her cousin had no notion quite how much Frank was indeed asking of her, tried to console her.

'It will not be for long, I promise, and it is no great matter. I am sure Sir Ralph cannot really be so bad—'

'Ralph has made Blanchland a byword for licentiousness and depravity!' Amelia said strongly. 'You may pretend that you are happy to accept this commission, but you *know* it will ruin you! What can be so important to force you back there? Oh, I could murder Frank were it not that he is dead already!'

Sarah burst out laughing. 'Oh Milly, I truly wish that I could confide in you, but I have been sworn to secrecy! It is a most delicate matter—'

'Fiddle!' Lady Amelia said crossly. She looked at her cousin and her anger melted into rueful irritation. She could never be cross with Sarah for long.

'Oh, I am sorry, my love! I know you were most sincerely attached to your brother and that you believe you are doing the right thing, but...' Her voice trailed away unhappily.

'I know.' Sarah patted her hand. At four and twenty she was Amelia's junior by five years, yet often felt the elder of the two. It was Amelia who rushed impetuously at life, Amelia whose reckless impulses could so often lead to trouble if not tempered by the wise counsel of her younger cousin. Amelia, widowed for five years, still seemed as heedless as a young debutante. Yet now it was she who was counselling caution and Sarah who was set on a foolhardy course.

'And to travel now!' Amelia said fretfully. 'Why, it is but two weeks to Christmas and I am sure we are in for some snow!'

'I am sorry, Milly, it is just something I feel I must do—'

'Excuse me, madam.' Sarah broke off as Chisholm, Amelia's butler, stepped softly into the room. 'There are two gentlemen here to see you—'

'I am not at home!' Amelia cried vexedly. 'Really, Chisholm, you know that I am not receiving!'

'Yes, ma'am, but you did give orders that Sir Greville—'

'Greville!' Amelia cried. 'Why did you not say so, Chisholm? What are you waiting for? Show him in at once!'

Not a muscle moved in the butler's impassive face. 'Very well, madam.'

Sarah, repressing a smile, wondered whether Amelia appreciated the long-suffering patience of her servants. They were all most sincerely attached to her, despite her grasshopper mind.

'Sir Greville! How do you do, sir? I had no notion you were returned from London!'

Amelia, her ill temper forgotten, smiled sunnily as her visitors were shown into the room. Indeed, Sarah felt that a less good-natured man than Sir Greville Baynham might have read far more into the warmth of his welcome than was intended. Greville had been Amelia's most constant admirer for the last few years and though she showed every evidence of enjoying his company, she had never accepted any of his proposals of marriage. Sarah privately thought that, should Sir Greville's attentions be permanently withdrawn, Amelia would miss him rather more than she anticipated. Unfortunately her cousin showed no sign of recognising that fact.

'Lady Amelia,' Greville was saying formally, 'please allow me to present Viscount Renshaw. Guy is staying with me at Chelwood for a few days. Guy, this is Lady Amelia Fenton and...' he turned to smile at Sarah '...her cousin, the Honourable Miss Sarah Sheridan, whom I believe you have already met.'

Sarah's heart had skipped a beat as she recognised the tall figure following Greville Baynham into Amelia's elegant drawing-room. Guy Renshaw. What dreadful bad luck that he should appear again just when she had succeeded in banishing from her mind that wicked smile and those disturbing dark eyes. And worse, it seemed she had been correct all along in recognising him, though there was little resemblance between the gangling youth who had once teased her mercilessly and this very personable man.

Guy Renshaw sketched an elegant bow. 'Lady Amelia, how do you do? I have heard much about you!' His voice was low-pitched and very agreeable, as melodious as Sarah remembered from that morning. She found that her heart was beating fast and had to take a deep breath to steady herself.

Amelia blushed and smiled as she gave the Viscount her hand. Sarah tried not to laugh. Judging by the rueful look on his face, Greville might be regretting introducing his friend to the lady he ardently wished to marry! Amelia was quite the most dreadful flirt and did not deserve his devotion whilst Guy Renshaw, as Sarah now knew, could scarcely be trusted.

'And, Miss Sheridan…' Lord Renshaw turned to her. There was a smile playing around the corners his mouth. He really was quite shockingly attractive and Sarah was sure that he knew it. The thought served to calm her. She would not provide the confirmation!

'Not only have you and I have met before, ma'am,' the Viscount was saying, 'but I would go so far as to say that we were childhood friends!'

'Were you indeed, Sarah?' Amelia's eyes were bright with curiosity as they moved from one to the other. 'How intriguing!'

Sarah looked at Guy Renshaw very deliberately and saw his smile deepen into challenge as he awaited her response.

'Lord Renshaw mistakes,' she said slowly. 'We were never childhood friends.'

It gave her a certain satisfaction to see the swift flash of surprise in his eyes. Guy Renshaw, Sarah thought, was all too sure of himself and his power to attract.

'How could we be,' she added sweetly, 'when Lord Renshaw spent the whole time tormenting me with spiders and toads? I do believe I thought him an odious boy!'

Amelia gave a peal of laughter. 'Dear me, Lord Renshaw, it seems my cousin has a long memory for childhood slights! You will have to try hard to win her good opinion!'

'I shall endeavour to do so, ma'am, if Miss Sheridan will give me a second chance!' There was speculation as well as amusement in the look Guy cast Sarah. She felt a shiver of awareness, as though he had just issued a challenge she was unsure she could meet. She looked away deliberately.

Amelia was patting the sofa beside her. 'How long do you plan to spend in Bath, Lord Renshaw? No doubt you will find our society sadly flat after London!'

'I doubt it, ma'am,' Guy murmured, casting another glance at Sarah. He took a seat beside his hostess. 'I fear, however, that I am only here for a few days. I am but recently returned from the Peninsula and am anxious to see my family again. I shall be returning to Woodallan the day after tomorrow.'

'Then you must come to my ball tomorrow night!' Amelia gave him a ravishing smile. 'It will be most apt for a returned hero, for I am celebrating the allied successes!'

They fell to discussing the Peninsular War and Sir Greville came across to Sarah and sat down next to her. She let herself be distracted by small talk. At least the arrival of the two men had had the effect of diverting Amelia's attention from her proposed visit to Blanchland, but Sarah suspected that it was only a temporary respite. Amelia was known for her tenacity and if Sarah was really unlucky the topic of the roses might be raised as well. Sarah had managed to skate adroitly over the cause of her accident but she would not put it past Guy Renshaw to mention the whole story just to put her out of countenance.

A footman and maid arrived with refreshments and

somehow, Sarah was not quite sure how, Sir Greville and Lord Renshaw exchanged places. It was done in the neatest and most unobtrusive manner, but Sarah did not miss the look of gratitude Sir Greville flashed his friend as he took his place by Amelia, and her opinion of Guy went up a little. She only hoped that the Viscount's motives towards herself were as irreproachable.

'May I join you?' Guy was smiling at her, the smile that made her heart do a little flip despite herself. 'I can assure you that it is quite safe—my preoccupation with arachnids and amphibians is a thing of the past!' He leaned forward to help Sarah to a Bath biscuit. 'I am most sincerely sorry for the spider on your chair—'

'It was a toad on my chair,' Sarah said severely, 'and a spider in the schoolroom! I beg you not to regard it, Lord Renshaw. I do not believe that I sustained any lasting hurt!'

'I am relieved to hear it,' Guy murmured, 'as I wish above all things to make a good impression upon you, Miss Sheridan!'

'A little late for that, my lord, when you were so destructive to my roses!' Sarah observed sweetly.

He lowered his voice. 'Was your cousin very displeased? If only you had vouchsafed your name and direction, Miss Sheridan, I could have escorted you back here and apologised to her!'

Sarah knew he was trying provoke her by reminding her of the set-down she had given him. A smile tugged at the corners of her mouth, but she repressed it ruthlessly.

'You know that that would scarcely have been appropriate, my lord! As for Amelia, she was a little dismayed. She is the dearest creature, but even she cannot concoct a red, white and blue flower arrangement without the red!'

'Ah, I see. The patriotic theme?'

'Precisely so!' Despite herself, Sarah found that they were smiling together. Guy was sitting forward, his entire attention focused on her in a most flattering manner. It was very disconcerting.

'I am so very sorry that I did not recognise you when we met earlier, Miss Sheridan,' he said softly, 'but how was I to know that the gawky schoolgirl I used to know had grown into such a beautiful woman? Such a transformation is enough to throw a fellow completely!'

Sarah felt a blush rising at the teasing note in his voice. There was admiration in the look he gave her; admiration and a more disturbing emotion. It seemed astonishing that she could be sitting here in Amelia's drawing-room with a gentleman she had just met again for the first time in thirteen years, and be feeling this intoxicating and entirely improper stirring of the senses.

'You are outrageous, sir!' she said, to cover her confusion. 'I believe you have not altered one whit!'

'Oh, you must allow me a little improvement!' Guy looked at her with mock-reproof. 'At the very least, I am taller than when you last saw me!'

'That was not at all what I meant! It seems to me that you were always given to the most excessive flattery! Why, I distinctly remember you practising your charms on my grandmother! She professed herself scandalised that one so young should be so adept at flirtation!'

'Well, I'll concede that I was ever inclined to practise on susceptible ladies!' Guy said lazily. 'You may find, however, that my scandalous behaviour has developed in other directions since then!'

Sarah was sure that he was correct and it seemed likely that the type of outrageous behaviour indulged in by a man of nine and twenty was infinitely more dangerous to her than that of a youth primarily obsessed with practical jokes.

'I do not doubt it, sir! Pray do not furnish me with the details, it would not be at all proper!'

'But then I am not at all proper,' Guy said ruefully. 'Though, to my regret, I believe you to be a very pattern-card of correctness, Miss Sheridan!'

'So I should hope! Pray do not pursue this line of conversation, sir!'

'Must I not?' There was a look of limpid innocence on Guy's face. 'I was presuming that our previous acquaintance would allow a certain informality—'

'Informality!' Sarah realised that she had raised her voice when she caught Amelia's look of curiosity. She hastily dropped her tone again. 'You presume too much, my lord!'

Guy shrugged, gracefully conceding defeat. Sarah had the distinct impression that it would only be a temporary reversal. She cast around for a safe change of subject. Genteel Bath society had scarcely prepared her for dealing with so flagrant a flirtation. She plumped for something she hoped would be innocuous.

'I understand that you had been abroad for some years, sir. Your family must be eager to see you after all this time.'

Guy took her lead courteously, though there was a flash of amusement in his eyes that told her he knew she was trying to deflect him.

'Yes, indeed,' he said agreeably. 'I was serving with Wellesley in the Peninsula for four years and only returned because my father's health has deteriorated and he needs my help at Woodallan.'

'I am sorry to hear of the Earl's ill health,' Sarah said, concerned. 'I hope that it is not too serious?'

For once the humour dropped away from Guy's expression and he looked sombre. 'I hope so, too, Miss Sheridan, but I fear the worst. It is very unlike him to admit that he needs my help, but he has intimated that he wishes me to take on more of the running of Woodallan and the other estates...' He made an effort to try for a lighter note. 'No doubt my mother will be glad to see me back—she has been cursing Bonaparte these four years past for prolonging the war!'

'It is several years since I saw your parents, although your mother and I still write,' Sarah said, with a smile. 'She told me in her last letter that she had high hopes of your swift return. She is kind—she sent me a very sympathetic letter when my father died.'

She looked up, to see Guy watching her. For all his levity, those dark eyes were disconcertingly perceptive. 'It must have been a difficult time for you,' he said gently. 'You must have been very young, no more than nineteen, I imagine? And then to lose your brother and your home in such quick succession...'

Sarah's mind immediately flew to Blanchland again. It seemed strange that she had so completely forgotten about Frank's letter during the past few minutes. She had lost a brother, but it appeared that she had gained a niece. What sort of a girl would Miss Olivia Meredith prove to be? Her letter had been very neat and proper, the writing of a young lady educated at one of Oxford's more select seminaries. But how to find her? She had to concoct a plan...

Sarah realised that Guy was still watching her, his

searching gaze intent on her face. It made her feel oddly breathless.

'I beg your pardon. I was thinking of home…' She tried to gather her thoughts and steer away from further confidences. 'Yes, I thank you… It was a difficult time.'

'And now you reside with Lady Amelia?' Guy smiled, looking across at where Amelia and Greville were engrossed in conversation, her chestnut curls brushing his shoulder as she bent forward confidingly. 'I imagine that must be quite amusing!'

Sarah laughed. 'Oh, I have been most fortunate! Amelia's society is always stimulating and she has been as generous as a sister to me!'

Guy lowered his voice. 'Do you think she will ever put Grev out of his misery and accept his suit, Miss Sheridan?'

It was a surprisingly personal question. Sarah raised her eyebrows a little haughtily and saw him grin in response.

'I beg your pardon, Miss Sheridan, if you think me impertinent. I am only concerned for my friend's future happiness, for I know he holds Lady Amelia in high esteem. But perhaps you think me presumptuous— again?'

Sarah unbent a little. 'There is nothing I would like more than to see them make a match of it, my lord. I have been promoting the alliance these two years past! Alas, Amelia is not susceptible to my arguments!'

'Nor to Greville's, it would seem,' Guy said, shifting a little in his chair. 'And you, Miss Sheridan? No doubt you have many suitors! I should be glad to have happy news of your own situation to take back to Woodallan with me!'

If the previous question had been bold, this one took

Sarah's breath away. Once again there was a teasing light in his eyes, daring her to give him the snub he deserved.

'I shall be happy for you to tell your family that I am in good health and spirits,' she said, with a very straight face, 'and to give them all my very best wishes!'

Guy did not seem discomposed. His smile broadened with appreciation. 'I shall take that as encouragement for my own hopes then, ma'am!'

'You should not do so, my lord,' Sarah said crushingly. 'I had not the least intention of encouraging you!'

'I was thinking that the gentlemen of Bath must all be slow-tops,' Guy said, apparently undaunted by her coldness, 'but now I perceive that you are very high in the instep, Miss Sheridan! Your good opinion is not easily gained!'

'Certainly not by an acknowledged rake who carelessly destroys my roses!' Sarah said coolly. 'Pray do not repine, however, my lord! There are any number of young ladies in Bath who would be delighted to flirt with you!'

'Minx!' his lordship said, with feeling. 'I have to tell you that I have no interest in them, Miss Sheridan!'

'Indeed?' Sarah hesitated over administering yet another set-down to him in a single day. She had the feeling that it would be inviting trouble.

'Naturally I do not include you in their company, ma'am! Will you dance with me at your cousin's ball tomorrow night?'

Sarah raised her eyebrows again. There was no doubt that Viscount Renshaw possessed a most persistent and provocative disposition, and that he was deliberately trying to incite a reaction.

'It is not certain that I shall attend, sir,' she said, still cool. 'I have other plans—'

His eyes danced with a secret amusement. 'Oh, surely you would not disappoint your cousin, ma'am? Shall I appeal to her to persuade you?' He glanced across at Amelia and Greville, still deep in conversation.

'Pray do not disturb them,' Sarah said hastily, aware that her colour had risen again. It was an understood thing that she would be present at Amelia's ball, for it would be the highlight of Bath's winter season. She suspected that Guy had guessed as much. His amused gaze rested on her face, moving over each feature with slow deliberation. Sarah felt inordinately uncomfortable under that observant scrutiny.

The clock chimed.

'Oh!' Amelia got hastily to her feet. 'I do beg your pardon, gentlemen! I am promised to Mrs Chartley's card party! Pray excuse me or I shall be very late!'

Greville and Guy stood up, Greville offering his escort to Amelia, who accepted prettily.

Guy took Sarah's hand and pressed a kiss on it. 'I am sure we shall see you this evening, Miss Sheridan. Do you go to the dance at the Pump Room?'

'Oh, yes, we shall be there!' Amelia said cheerfully, seeming blissfully unaware that her cousin was about to deny it. She gave Guy Renshaw a melting smile. 'It is the last public dance of the year, you know! But how charming to be able to see you again so soon, Lord Renshaw!'

Guy bowed. 'The pleasure will be all mine, Lady Amelia! Your servant, Miss Sheridan!'

They all went out together. Sarah watched from the window as the Viscount parted from Greville and Amelia with a casual word and a smile. She was aware of a certain conflict inside her and a faint disappointment. Guy Renshaw was a charming man and he had made his admiration for her very plain, but he was also a dangerous flirt who probably did not mean a word of it. It would be very foolish to read anything into his behaviour and even more imprudent to allow an unexpected physical attraction to disturb her.

Besides, he would be leaving Bath in a couple of days and so would she. Abruptly, Sarah remembered her commitment to visit Blanchland, and felt depression settle on her. She did not want to see what Ralph Covell had done to her beloved family home, nor to become embroiled in the problems of Frank's natural daughter, nor to ruin her own reputation in the process. Amelia was quite right—she must be mad. And Churchward had even offered her a way out by suggesting that an agent could represent her interests, yet for some reason she had chosen not to take it...

Sarah felt the beginnings of a headache stir. Since she had resolved on this rash course of action, she must at least plan how to accomplish it with a minimum of fuss. Blanchland was less than a day's journey from Bath, and if she were fortunate she would be able to find Miss Meredith quickly, discover the girl's difficulties and instruct Churchward on the best way to resolve them. The whole matter could be decided in a week— ten days at the outside. And no one need ever know.

The presence of Viscount Renshaw and Sir Greville Baynham caused quite a stir at the Pump Room that night. Sir Greville, whose family home was a few miles north of the city, had always been a universal favourite, with several young ladies expressing themselves willing to console him if Lady Amelia refused his suit. The

Viscount caused an even greater commotion, being fortunate enough to be rich, handsome and heir to an Earl
into the bargain.

It was a clear, starry night, and Sarah and Amelia had
walked the short distance from Brock Street to the
Pump Room, enjoying the fresh chill of the night air
that brought the colour to their cheeks and made their
eyes sparkle. As they handed over their cloaks and
Amelia cast a thoughtful look over her cousin, Sarah
saw her smile of approval.

'How pretty you look, Sarah! I would not have
dreamed of saying anything before, but I am so glad
you have cast off that hideous half-mourning!'

She saw Sarah's expression and added hastily, 'I
know you were a most devoted sister to Frank, my love,
but surely you are too young to wear black forever?'

Sarah could feel her lips twitching as she tried to
suppress a smile. Milly could be amazingly tactless at
times.

'I know the black was ageing,' she agreed mildly,
'but surely the lavender became me a little?'

Amelia looked contrite. 'Oh, sweetly pretty, my love,
but for a whole year? And even then you habitually
chose drab colours that are nothing to this delicious rose
tint you are wearing now!' She cast her cousin a sideways look. 'I did wonder whether the advent of Viscount Renshaw was the reason for your sudden—'

'Oh, look, Milly, it is Mr Tilbury and his sister!'
Sarah was aware that she had never shown much inclination for the Tilburys' company before now, but felt
she had to distract her cousin. Amelia, however, was
far too determined for that.

'Yes, I fear we will be in for much the same company
as ever tonight, especially with it being the end of the

season! As I was saying, it is fortunate that Greville has brought that charming man, Guy Renshaw, with him! I declare, Bath society seldom offers the opportunity to meet so prodigiously attractive a gentleman!'

Sarah knew that she was blushing and prayed that it could be put down to the heat of the room after the cold outside. She would never have admitted to Amelia that she had spent twice as long as usual at her toilette and agonised between the rose pink and the aquamarine silk. Sarah had been aware of a growing sense of anticipation all afternoon, and found that she was feeling quite nervous as she and Amelia entered the ballroom. She experienced an altogether unfamiliar sensation of breathlessness, her heart suddenly racing and butterflies fluttering frantically in her stomach. Her slender fingers tightened on her fan. This was ridiculous! Good gracious, she was very nearly in a fit of panic, and all because of Guy Renshaw, who had once put a toad on her dining-chair!

She could see Guy across the ballroom, deep in conversation with Greville and attracting considerable attention from the female guests. The reason was not hard to seek: the classical good looks of the Woodallan family, combined with the immaculate black and white of the evening dress, made him look extremely handsome and ever-so-slightly dangerous.

'Half my female acquaintance have already heard that the Viscount called on us earlier and have begged an introduction,' Amelia was saying, with a giggle. 'I declare, we have not seen so much excitement in an age!' She linked her arm through Sarah's and the cousins walked slowly down the edge of the ballroom.

'Greville looks very handsome tonight,' Sarah observed, giving Amelia a meaningful look. 'Not even Lord Renshaw can put him in the shade!'

'Oh, Grev looks very well,' Amelia said, so carelessly that Sarah wanted to shake her, 'and I am very fond of him, of course, but in a brotherly sort of way!'

'A favourite brother, perhaps,' Sarah said tartly.

Amelia cast her a look from under her lashes. 'Oh Sarah, do I treat him so badly? I do not mean to!'

'You know you do not value him as you ought! Greville would never lose all his money at cards, or drink himself into oblivion the way your late husband did—'

'No…' Amelia sighed soulfully '…Alan was such exciting company!'

Sarah sighed. In her opinion, Alan Fenton had been a wastrel with nothing to commend him, and she could never understand why Amelia appeared to value his dashing looks over Greville's integrity. They were almost upon Sir Greville now and she saw the glad light that sprang into his blue eyes as he looked at Amelia. It was too bad.

'Miss Sheridan.' Guy Renshaw took her hand, his touch evoking much the same shiver of awareness as it had done earlier in the day, and Sarah was instantly distracted. 'You look delightful. I would ask you to dance, but I fear that the excitement of the minuet might be too much for me!'

Sarah looked reproving. 'I know you find our entertainments dull, my lord, but there are country dances after eight, if that is your preference!'

'What, no waltzes?'

'Oh, the waltz is much too fast for Bath!'

'A pity! Perhaps I shall have to settle for a country dance after all, if you will so honour me. In the meantime, do you care for a little supper?'

'Thank you.' Sarah let him take her arm and steer her away from the others and into the refreshment room. He helped her to a seat in a secluded alcove, then crossed to the buffet table, where several young ladies immediately gravitated towards him and one of them artfully drew him into conversation over the merits of the strawberries.

Behind a pillar to Sarah's right, the young ladies' mamas were watching with gimlet eyes. Sarah tried not to listen, but at least half of her wanted to eavesdrop on their conversation. She was no cynic, but she knew that despite the pungent denunciation they would inevitably make of Guy's character, either would marry him off to their daughter with triumphant haste.

'A shocking reputation, Mrs Bunton, quite shocking!'

'Really, Mrs Clarke? Just how shocking would you say it is?'

'Oh, quite dreadful! Of course, that was before he went to the War—perhaps the rigors of campaign have instilled some respectability...but I doubt it!'

'Once a rake—' Mrs Bunton said meaningfully.

'Though marriage to a good woman may redeem him, of course!'

Both ladies paused, evidently dwelling on the benefits of a match with their particular daughter.

'They say that Lady Melville was his mistress for a whole year—'

'Oh, yes, I had heard that, too! A most impassioned liaison, by all accounts!'

'And then there was the business of Lady Paget—'

'Dreadful! They say her husband never recovered! But the family is rich, of course,' Mrs Clarke said, as if in mitigation, 'and rumour has it that Woodallan wishes him to settle down.'

'Emma could do worse...'

'Much worse... Or your own dear Agatha, though they say Lord Renshaw prefers blondes...'

It was perhaps fortunate that Guy chose that moment to extract himself from the bevy of debutantes and return to Sarah, whose ears were becoming quite pink from what she had been obliged to hear. His observant dark gaze did not miss her high colour; as he put the loaded plate before her, he gave her a wicked grin.

'Dear me, Miss Sheridan, whatever can have caused you such discomfort? You look positively overset!'

'I am very well,' Sarah snapped, trying to keep her voice discreetly low, 'just embarrassed at having been obliged to overhear a rehearsal of your amours, sir! It is well that you will be leaving Bath soon, you have caused such a flutter in the dovecotes!'

'Good gracious, I had no idea you could be so frank, Miss Sheridan!' Guy said admiringly, eyeing her outraged face with amusement. 'To bring yourself to mention such matters! I was fair and far out in thinking you a prim Bath miss!'

'I am prim! That is why I am so agitated!' Sarah took a steadying draught of champagne. 'I do not think it wise for you to distinguish me with your attentions, my lord!'

'Why not?' Guy looked genuinely hurt. 'Because you are so respectable and I am not? But you see, Miss Sheridan—' he lowered his voice '—I am very grateful for the condescension you are showing me! Your respectability cannot but help improve my shocking reputation, you see! If the good ladies of Bath see that you are prepared to bear me company, perhaps they will not think me so bad after all!'

'Nonsense! You speak a deal of nonsense, sir!'

Their eyes met and Guy smiled, the lightness of his tone belied by the intensity of his gaze.

'Very well, if you don't like my nonsense, perhaps the truth will serve instead! I have the oddest feeling, Miss Sheridan...' his fingers brushed the back of Sarah's wrist lightly but with a touch that seemed to burn her '...that we are kindred spirits, despite our differences...or perhaps because of them...'

Very deliberately Sarah freed herself and took a mouthful of food, glad that the hand that held the fork was so steady. Her heart was racing at his touch, so light, but so confusing. He was still watching her with that disconcerting mix of speculation and challenge.

'Tell me, Miss Sheridan, have you never wished for any excitement?'

Damn the man, would he never change the subject? Sarah felt acutely vulnerable. Just how far was he going to press this particular topic?

'My life is quite exciting enough, I thank you, my lord.' Her voice was quite calm. 'I have my books and my letters and my friends. There are concerts here at the Pump Room and if the weather is fine I may promenade in the park!'

'It sounds a positive orgy of entertainment,' Guy murmured, his eyes mocking her above the rim of his glass. 'Have you never been to London?'

'No, I have not.'

'You had no come-out, like other debutantes? No...' he looked at her thoughtfully '...I suppose your father died before you were old enough, and then your brother was too wrapped up in his travelling...'

'I liked living in the country,' Sarah said truthfully, 'and Bath is very pleasant.'

'That's certainly true. All joking aside, it seems a

delightful place. But have you no wish to recapture your youth?'

'I was not aware that I had yet lost my youth, sir,' Sarah said tartly. 'I am scarce in my dotage!'

'How refreshing to meet a young lady who does not think she is at her last prayers! So you consider that you still have plenty of time to throw your bonnet over the windmill!'

'What an extraordinary idea!' Sarah could not help smiling in return. 'I assure you I have no intention of doing so, my lord!'

'Ah, well, who can say?' Guy raised his dark eyebrows. 'Look at you this evening, Miss Sheridan, giving countenance to a rake!'

'I scarcely think that I am giving you countenance, my lord!'

'Maybe not, but I notice that you do not dispute the other half of my statement!' There was a teasing note in Guy's voice.

'As to that, I cannot say.' Sarah spoke with equanimity. 'Nor,' she added quickly, seeing the spark of devilment in his eyes, 'do I have any ambition to find out!'

'What a sensible lady you are, Miss Sheridan,' Guy murmured. 'So measured, so composed! Lady Amelia must find you a positive paragon of a companion!'

Remembering the concern she was currently causing her cousin, who had wasted another twenty minutes earlier that afternoon trying to persuade her against her trip to Blanchland, Sarah could not agree with him. She was almost glad to see the ponderous figure of Mr Tilbury approaching to request a dance. Guy did not demur when she excused herself and Sarah was annoyed that this should be so, then was even more irritated with herself for so out-of-character contrariness. She watched

Guy performing a succession of country dances with Bath's most eligible debutantes and told herself that she did not care in the least.

Guy presented himself a little late for his promised dance with her for he appeared to have had difficulty in tearing himself away from his previous partner, the extremely young and pretty Miss Bunton. Sarah discovered that this engendered in her a feeling of acute vexation akin to indigestion, the like of which she had never experienced before. She had to fight a hard battle with herself in order to greet him civilly, and was mortified to see the sardonic light in his eye that suggested he had seen and noted her reaction. Sarah was obliged to remind herself yet again that she had only met the man that very day and could have neither interest in nor opinion on his behaviour. Nevertheless, she kept her gaze averted from his, for she had the lowering suspicion that he could read her mind.

'You are very quiet, Miss Sheridan,' Guy observed softly, when the movement of the dance brought them together. 'I know it cannot be that you need to concentrate on your steps, for you dance too well for that. Have I then done something to displease you?'

Sarah saw the flash of mockery in his eyes and, in spite of all her good intentions, she felt her temper rise. He really did have the most regrettable effect on her composure!

'How could that be so, my lord?' she asked sweetly. 'I scarcely know you well enough to claim the privilege of being annoyed by your behaviour!'

She saw the look of amused speculation on Guy's face before the dance obliged him to move briefly away. Sarah tried to get a grip on her bad temper. She had no wish to betray the fact that he had the power to affect her, nor to be drawn into a conversation that could be dangerous, and she was afraid that she had already said too much. She received confirmation of this a moment later.

'I collect that you mean that one must care sufficiently for someone before their behaviour can influence one's feelings?' Guy said lazily, when they came back together again. 'In that case, I shall hope that time will see you quite exasperated with me!'

Sarah reflected ruefully that she had probably deserved that and would think twice before crossing swords with him again.

Guy seemed disinclined to let the matter drop, however, for when she did not reply he raised an eyebrow and said, 'What do you say, ma'am? Do you think you could find it in your heart to dislike me a little?'

Sarah smiled a little shamefacedly. 'I know you are trying to provoke me, sir—'

'Indeed? I thought the reverse was true for once!'

'Very well!' Sarah met his eyes squarely. 'I'll admit that I said something that I now deeply regret! Pray accept my apologies, my lord!'

The dance had ended, but Guy was still holding her hand. They were standing on the edge of the dance floor, surrounded by couples milling about as they either retired for refreshments or joined the set that was forming, yet it seemed to Sarah that they were entirely alone. Guy smiled and when Sarah looked up into his eyes she saw an expression there that was compounded of desire overlaid by wicked mischief. So strong was the conviction that he was about to kiss her that Sarah took an instinctive step backwards.

'Do not worry,' Guy spoke so softly that only she

could hear, 'I will not do it—at least, not here! But the temptation, Miss Sheridan, is acute.'

The colour flamed into Sarah's face as she realised that he had read her thoughts. 'Believe me, my lord,' she said, with as much composure as she could muster, 'so is the temptation to slap your face!'

Guy burst out laughing. 'So the honours are even, Miss Sheridan!' He pressed a kiss on her hand. 'Until our next meeting!' And he sauntered away to the card-room, leaving Sarah feeling breathless and outraged in equal measure.

Chapter Three

Sarah slept well that night, but awoke early with thoughts of Blanchland pressing on her mind once again. She was aware that she had as yet made no plans for her journey to her former home, other than a vague decision that she should set off the following day. This was all very fine, but she needed to be better prepared. She could not predict how Sir Ralph Covell would greet the unexpected arrival of his late cousin's daughter, nor had she decided whether she should take him into her confidence or not. If Churchward's information had been correct and Olivia had last been seen approaching Blanchland Court, this might prove a very bad idea indeed.

Sarah shivered and burrowed deeper under her blankets for both warmth and comfort. Not for the first time she reflected that she was involving herself in a situation that appeared to have Gothic overtones, but she was a most practical girl and could only believe that there was a perfectly simple explanation for Olivia's disappearance. No doubt the girl had gone to stay with a relative and forgotten to tell anyone. And the desperate matter on which she required advice would probably prove to be a romance, or, at worst, the need to go out into the world and earn a living as a governess. There was no need for worry.

Sarah threw back the bedcovers and crossed to the window. There had been a hard frost and the winter sun was rising in a pale blue sky. The house was astir with the peculiar excitement that characterised the day of a ball. Sarah had promised to help Amelia with her preparations, but she knew that her cousin would not be rising early and she needed some fresh air.

Amelia kept a small stable in the mews behind the buildings. There were her carriage horses, a gentle white mare that she occasionally rode in the park, and a decidedly more spirited one that Sarah enjoyed putting through its paces. The morning, with its crisp, fresh air, was perfect for a ride.

It seemed that Astra thought so, too, for her ears pricked up as soon as they left the quiet streets behind and reached the springy turf of Lansdown. Sarah enjoyed a fine gallop, leaving the toiling groom far behind, and only as she skirted Greville Baynham's land did she slow down and allow herself to think about the previous night.

There was no doubt that some kind of peculiar affinity existed between herself and Guy Renshaw, and she knew that if she had any sense she would leave it well alone. Sarah sighed, allowing the horse to pick its own way along the steep path. She could not deny that in some senses Guy was a very eligible *parti*, so eligible, in fact, that he would look to marry far higher than a penniless companion, no matter how well-connected. In other respects he was utterly ineligible, for his reputation and evident disinclination for settling down rendered him not just unsuitable but positively dangerous.

Sarah sighed again. She had had plenty of opportunities
to marry in the previous six years, but somehow none
of her suitors had quite matched her expectations and
she had been too fastidious to marry just for the sake
of it. She wondered now whether that had been a mistake. Living with Amelia was enjoyable, but how long
would it continue? Besides, she had had the running of
Blanchland and missed having her own establishment.
Yet it seemed typical that when her inclination had finally settled on a gentleman who more than met her
expectations, her choice should be totally inappropriate…

'Good morning, Miss Sheridan! It is a beautiful
morning, is it not?'

Sarah came out of her reverie in time to see the subject of her thoughts let himself through the gate that
separated the downs from Chelwood Park. He brought
his horse alongside Sarah's and gave her a smile, his
gaze openly appreciating her pink cheeks and bright
eyes.

'That's a very spirited creature you have there, Miss
Sheridan! It would be difficult to tell which of you looks
as though they have enjoyed the gallop more!'

He sat his own chestnut hunter with a skill that Sarah
did not find at all surprising and the casual elegance of
his attire would be enough, she thought, to have all last
night's impressionable debutantes swooning again. This
morning, with the breeze ruffling his thick, fair hair and
the sun lighting those expressive dark eyes, Lord Renshaw looked utterly devastating.

'Your cousin does not ride with you?' he asked, looking down the hill to where the groom was exhorting his
labouring horse up the slope. 'I see that you are alone,
to all intents and purposes.'

'I think not.' Sarah could not help wondering what intent or purpose he might have in seeking her out alone. She would have to be careful. 'Amelia does not care for riding, but I brought the groom.' She gestured down the hill, where Tom was still making heavy weather of getting the old cob to catch up. Guy laughed.

'So I see—and promptly left him behind again! I did not imagine you to be so keen a rider, Miss Sheridan! You did not mention it as one of your ruling passions last night!'

Sarah cast him a look under her lashes. 'I grew up in the country, so it can be no great surprise that I ride!'

'No, but you ride very well indeed, which is rare. I'll allow that it is commonplace enough to meet ladies who can prance about in the park and think that they look most accomplished!'

'You are very severe this morning, my lord!' Sarah could not help laughing. 'I am glad that my own small skill gains your approval rather than your censure!'

Guy smiled lazily. 'Oh, I am renowned as a hard critic, but I cannot find fault with you, Miss Sheridan!'

Sarah felt herself blushing under his scrutiny. For some perverse reason all she could think of was his threat—or was it a promise?—to kiss her on some future occasion. Would such a manoeuvre be possible on horseback? It was an intriguing thought. It would certainly require considerable skill, but— Sarah suddenly realised that Guy was still watching her, one dark eyebrow raised in teasing enquiry. Afraid that he would read her thoughts again, as he had the previous night, Sarah turned her horse's head abruptly away and was relieved to see the groom struggling up the last incline to join them on the level summit.

'There is an exceptional view from up here,' Guy

observed, looking out across the city to the Somerset hills beyond, 'and a keen breeze. It leaves me sharp set! Will you join us at Chelwood for breakfast, Miss Sheridan?'

Tom the groom, who had been encouraging his exhausted horse, cast Sarah a scandalised glance. She smiled.

'Thank you, my lord, but I do not think that would be very proper! I fear I must return to Brock Street for my breakfast!'

'My sensible Miss Sheridan! A bachelor household, even one so unimpeachable as Chelwood, is not an appropriate destination for a single lady!' Guy's dark eyes were full of mockery. 'A pity if you were to starve on your way home as a result!'

'I must be going, at any rate,' Sarah said, trying to crush her foolish excitement at his use of the phrase 'my sensible Miss Sheridan'. She turned Astra's head towards home. 'Amelia will need help with all the preparations for her ball tonight. Good day, my lord.'

'A moment, Miss Sheridan.' Guy put his hand over hers on the reins. 'Does Lady Amelia intend to be so fast as to have the waltz this evening?'

Sarah paused. 'I believe so, my lord.'

Guy let her go and raised his whip in a salute. 'Then save me a dance, Miss Sheridan!'

Amelia was in great good spirits. Silk drapes in red and blue swathed the walls and pillars of the ballroom, white candles filled the sconces and huge vases overflowing with red roses formed the centrepiece of her decorations.

The roses had arrived in the late afternoon and had caused much excited giggling and shrieking amongst the maids as they had tried to find sufficient receptacles in which to place them all. Several old, chipped vases had been pressed into service for the less prominent of arrangements and a chamber pot had even been proffered, though Sarah had seen Chisholm hastily hide it behind the umbrella stand before Amelia had noticed. There had been no card, which had led to much gossip and speculation, but when the pack of maids had gone and Amelia had swept off to see to the menus, Chisholm had stepped forward with a tiny, delicate posy of pale pink rosebuds with a card tucked inside. There were only two words, written in a strong black hand that Sarah had never seen before, yet instantly recognised: 'Penance? Renshaw.'

And now Sarah was wearing one of the rosebuds pinned to the bodice of her aquamarine gown and was full of a most heady excitement at the thought of seeing Guy again.

'Your decorations look very fine and patriotic,' Sarah said, catching her cousin at a quiet moment between the arrival of two parties of guests. 'I know you would not give away the secret before, but how have you managed the red, white and blue theme for the menus, Milly?'

'Oh,' Amelia laughed, 'the trout with garlic and tomatoes is red and there is woodcock in a white wine sauce—'

'And the blue?'

'Ice cream with bilberries! We call it *glace du Napoleon*! Cook has been swearing that this is his finest hour!' Amelia smiled as her gaze rested on the roses. 'They are magnificent, aren't they? Are you sure you have no idea of their provenance, Sarah?'

'Good evening, Lady Amelia. And Miss Sheridan! I am so glad that you decided to attend after all, ma'am!'

Sarah swung round to see Viscount Renshaw bowing punctiliously. She was not sure whether she was glad to see him or not. On the one hand, his arrival was timely in diverting Amelia from her question. On the other, there was a decidedly wicked twinkle in his eye.

Amelia opened her eyes wide. 'Lord Renshaw! Good evening, sir! But whatever can you mean? Why should Sarah not attend my ball? Sarah, you know you have been promised for tonight this month past!'

Sarah gave Guy Renshaw a fulminating look. 'I have no notion what his lordship can mean, Milly!'

'I beg your pardon.' Guy gave her a look of limpid innocence. 'I must have misunderstood you, ma'am. Lady Amelia, do I have your permission to take your cousin off and dance with her?'

Amelia looked speculatively from one to the other. 'You have my blessing, Lord Renshaw, but whether Sarah will agree is another matter!'

Guy took Sarah's arm. 'It is a waltz and you did promise me…'

He appeared to take her acquiescence for granted, steering her towards the dance floor and taking her in his arms in a manner that might be entirely appropriate for the waltz, but nevertheless deprived Sarah momentarily of speech. Their bodies touched for a brief second before he held her a little away from him with impeccable propriety.

Sarah was an accomplished dancer, but she found that waltzing in Guy's arms was a very different experience from attempting the boulanger with Mr Tilbury. Dancing with Guy was unnerving; the touch of his hands through the silk of her dress felt like a caress. His head was bent close to hers, and when their eyes met she could see the admiration in their depths, the flash of desire that he did not trouble to hide. It disturbed her and stirred something strange and sensual within her. Sarah closed her eyes momentarily, startled by her own feelings.

'You dance beautifully,' Guy said, after they had circled the floor a couple of times in silence. 'I remember that you were musical even as a child. You used to sing and play most prettily.'

'I do not recall that you were so eager to dance with me in our youth,' Sarah said, with a slight smile, glad of an innocuous topic of conversation when her thoughts had been anything but innocent. 'There was one children's ball at which you spurned me quite ruthlessly, my lord!'

Guy's arms tightened momentarily. Looking up, she saw a look of brilliant amusement in his eyes and her heart did a little somersault.

'I had no discernment in my youth,' he said regretfully, 'and our parents were forever trying to throw us together. I believe they wished us to make a match of it and naturally enough, I tried to rebel! What boy of sixteen wishes to contemplate matrimony—least of all with a young lady of eleven!'

'Perhaps they were a little misguided—'

'Just premature, I believe, Miss Sheridan!'

Sarah was vexed with herself for giving him the chance to flirt with her. Just when she had thought they could talk on uncontroversial subjects, he had turned the topic around! He richly deserved a set-down.

'More of your nonsense, sir!' she said crossly. 'I am no green girl to be taken in by your flattery!'

'No, indeed,' Guy agreed amiably, his smile teasing her. 'I forgot that you had so many years in your dish,

Miss Sheridan! My reputation is quite safe with you, is it not?'

Sarah was rendered momentarily speechless by his impudence. Before she could marshal her thoughts to deliver the cutting remark he deserved, the music whirled to a close.

Guy bowed. 'Perhaps you will spare me another dance later, Miss Sheridan?'

'I do not think that would be at all respectable, sir!' Sarah said pertly, unable to resist. 'As you have just pointed out, you must have a care for your reputation, and two dances could be considered fast!'

She saw him smile and knew he would have replied in kind had Amelia not arrived at that moment, bringing with her a very young man who had a hopeful look in his eye.

'Lord Renshaw, pray forgive my interruption,' Amelia began, 'but Mr Elliston believes that you may have been serving with his elder brother in Portugal, and is most anxious for any news...'

Guy bowed. 'Of course. You must be Richard Elliston's brother? I remember him well.' He gestured to the refreshment room. 'We could talk over a glass of wine if you wish...'

Young Mr Elliston looked quite overwhelmed at such condescension. Amelia smiled, taking Sarah's arm and drawing her away.

'He is very kind. Poor Jack Elliston has been quite worried—the family has had no news for nigh on six months!' She looked closely at Sarah. 'Are you quite well, my love? Your colour is very high! I do hope you have not taken a chill!'

'I do not believe so.' Sarah was astonished how calm she sounded when inside she felt quite shaken. For all that she had acquitted herself well enough, flirting with Guy Renshaw was an occupation requiring sterner nerves than hers. No doubt the society ladies who indulged in a little intrigue to relieve the boredom of their marriages were well versed in playing such sophisticated games. She was not, having little or no experience of the art of dalliance.

'Lord Renshaw seems to have been most charming to you,' Amelia was saying, her voice casual but her gaze alert as she took in Sarah's becomingly pink cheeks and sparkling eyes. 'I do believe he is trying to get up a flirtation with you, Sarah!'

Sarah took a glass of wine gratefully from a passing servant and drank half of it straight away before answering. Amelia's intent look deepened.

'Sarah! Whatever ails you? Are you sure you are quite well?'

Sarah laughed and pressed her cousin's hand. 'I am feeling very well, I thank you. I believe you must put my uncharacteristic behaviour down to Lord Renshaw's bad influence!'

Amelia's eyes widened to their furthest extent. 'Gracious, Sarah, how diverting! Surely you have not been encouraging him?'

'Not precisely, but...' Sarah hesitated '...I wonder if I have discouraged him sufficiently? He is, as you say, so very charming that it is difficult to resist...'

Amelia began to laugh. 'I should not worry, Sarah! You are scarcely a hardened flirt and Lord Renshaw is experienced enough to know the difference between a lady of easy virtue and a respectable spinster! I am more concerned that your own heart should remain whole!'

Sarah wrinkled up her nose and reached for her wine-glass again. 'Really, Amelia! Respectable spinster! You make me sound at least sixty and as dull as ditchwater into the bargain!'

'Better to be respectable than give in to Guy Renshaw's blandishments,' Amelia said drily. 'He has a truly terrible reputation, Sarah! Why, Mrs Bunton tells me—'

'Thank you,' Sarah said hastily. 'I have already heard her on the subject! I am in no real danger, I assure you, either from his lordship or from my own feelings! I know he can have no serious intentions and will not allow him to progress with any dishonourable ones!'

A little frown still marred Amelia's forehead. 'That is all very well, but it would not do to like him too much!'

'I know.' Sarah felt a little lurch of the heart as she spoke. Amelia had hit upon the very problem, for she was beginning to like Guy Renshaw very much indeed, and against her better judgement.

She let Mr Tilbury carry her off for the cotillion, noting that Amelia still looked concerned. She knew that her cousin had her own best interests at heart. Guy Renshaw could not be seen in the light of a suitable connection for a penniless companion. Her ineligibility could only mean that he could have no serious intentions, and designs of a less respectable nature would have to be ruthlessly crushed.

For a moment, Sarah felt an extraordinary disappointment. Guy's charm was very potent and Sarah knew that her own inexperience made it difficult for her to treat his admiration lightly. Then there was the peculiar physical attraction he held for her, the like of which she had never even dreamed of, let alone experienced before. For a moment, Sarah let herself imagine being in Guy Renshaw's embrace, recalling the hard strength of the arms that had held her in the waltz, the ripple of muscles beneath the smooth material of his jacket, the curl of that sensuous mouth...

Suddenly heated, Sarah felt her body diffuse with warmth and the colour flood into her face. It was fortunate that Mr Tilbury was rather unobservant, for it would have been impossible for him to believe that his own conversation could cause his companion to blush so vividly.

Sarah tried to concentrate on his observations on the price of coal, furiously castigating herself for allowing her thoughts to wander in so improper a direction. And this was hardly the first time!

The dance progressed in pedestrian fashion, with none of the zest of the previous waltz.

Guy was nowhere in sight, perhaps still talking with Mr Elliston, but Sarah noted a knot of people set a little back from the dance floor, with Mrs Bunton at its core. Several of the most influential hostesses in Bath had their heads bent close, their hairpieces waggling, their mouths forming shocked and horrified circles. One of them glanced in Sarah's direction and looked away again hastily. Sarah frowned. Surely her behaviour with Viscount Renshaw had not caused such scandalised debate? One waltz, even with a notorious rake, hardly constituted a social solecism. Besides, Mrs Bunton had been pushing her own daughter in Guy's direction only the night before.

Mr Tilbury addressed another of his remarks to her and Sarah temporarily forgot the group of gossiping matrons. However, she was reminded again swiftly as the dance drew to an end. As Mr Tilbury escorted her from the floor, Mrs Clarke drew her skirts aside and turned her back in the most pointed of snubs. Sarah stopped in surprise and Mr Tilbury's face flushed with outrage.

He was about to speak when Mrs Clarke said loudly, 'What can one expect with such low family connections? There's bad blood in the Covell family, which no doubt accounts for his cousin throwing her lot in with him! I wonder at Lady Amelia giving countenance to a woman who is clearly lost to all sense of decency!'

Shock rendered Sarah temporarily speechless. All around her she could see the looks of speculation and hear the chatter of rumour and gossip. She looked about desperately for Amelia, but her cousin was across the room, talking to Greville Baynham. There was no help closer at hand. Mr Tilbury was opening and closing his mouth like a stranded fish, his own expression one of painful embarrassment. Everyone else merely watched to see what would happen next.

Murmuring an incoherent apology to Mr Tilbury, Sarah hurried from the ballroom, almost ran up the stairs and instinctively sought shelter in her own room. Once there, she closed the door softly and leant back against it with her eyes closed. Mrs Clarke's sharply cruel words echoed in her mind: 'Lost to all sense of decency...'

There could be no mistake. Somehow, word of her intention to visit Blanchland had leaked out, been seized upon by eager gossips, and passed around the ballroom. Sarah felt outraged and humiliated. How dared they speak of her like that, make her the butt of their slander, rip her reputation to shreds in her very presence? She had seen them all, some condemning her already, others merely excited by scandal, but all watching her reactions for their own entertainment. Sarah had heard of times when the collective disapproval of Bath society had ruined someone's reputation, or left them a social outcast. It was just that she had never been on the receiving end before.

And why should she hide away here as though she had something to be ashamed of? Eyes flashing, Sarah flung open the door, ready to do battle in the ballroom. She would show Mrs Clarke and Mrs Bunton and all the other quizzes that she did not give a rush for their disapproval! She would not let them judge her and run away from them...

Sarah closed the door behind her and walked towards the stairs, still burning with outraged anger. She did not see the figure on the shadowed landing until it moved, and then she spun round with a gasp of alarm.

'Lord Renshaw! Good gracious, you gave me fright! Whatever are you doing up here, sir?'

'I wanted to speak to you, Miss Sheridan,' Guy said, coming forward into the circle of light cast by the single candelabra. 'I heard you come running up here and thought it best, perhaps, that we did not have an audience for our conversation.'

Sarah looked at him in puzzlement. There was something curious in his tone, some element that she could not define but that made her uncomfortable. It was impossible to decipher his expression in the flickering candlelight.

'I do not understand you, sir,' she said uncertainly. 'Surely it would be better to return to the ballroom—'

'Very well, if you are determined to face the extraordinary rumours that are circulating there,' Guy said coolly. 'Perhaps we could invite the whole of Bath society to join the conversation since they are taking such a close interest in your affairs!'

Sarah let out her breath in a long sigh. 'Oh, so you have heard—'

'I have! I could scarce believe it! Either you are seriously lacking in judgement, Miss Sheridan, or you are not the woman I thought you!'

Sarah stared at him, her temper soaring dangerously. She had been expecting him to sympathise with her in the face of the small-minded and malicious scandal-mongers, and to find herself condemned unheard was adding insult to injury.

'Oh really, my lord!' she burst out. 'It is the outside of enough to have to put up with the ill-informed gossip of spiteful matrons without such as yourself picking pieces in my good character as well!'

'Indeed?' Guy stepped closer to her, his physical presence completely overwhelming her. Now that he was so near, Sarah could sense the slow burn of his anger, though she still did not understand its cause. 'At the least you do not pretend ignorance! Are you telling me that the rumours are untrue, Miss Sheridan?'

Sarah hesitated for a fatal second, trapped by her own honesty. 'Yes! No! At least...I do intend to visit Blanchland, but it is not as you imagine...'

Guy brought his hand down on the banisters with a force that seemed to make the delicate ironwork shiver. 'Surely it can be no surprise that your apparent desire to spend the winter in a house of ill repute should set the town by the ears, Miss Sheridan! Good God, Blanchland is a place where no woman of respectability should dream of setting foot! You will not have a shred of reputation left to you!'

Sarah glared at him. 'I can scarce believe that you are giving credence to chance-heard rumours, my lord!

I should have thought better of you! You have not even paused to request an explanation!'

Guy had turned away, his face tight and angry, but now he swung back towards her.

'There can be no reasonable explanation! At least,' he corrected himself punctiliously, 'the best construction I can put on your conduct is that you lack any sense of proper behaviour and the worst—' his dark eyes narrowed murderously '—is that you are accustomed to the sort of society and pursuits that Blanchland has to offer! Neither is an adequate excuse!'

Sarah seldom lost her temper. The even tenor of life in Amelia's household was hardly ever ruffled by upset or disturbance, but now she found herself furiously angry. Guy's stubborn refusal to see anything but the worst in her was as distressing as it was infuriating. The situation was further exacerbated by the fact that she could not understand why he was so angry. Worst of all was a shaming desire to cry, as she realised that, despite the brevity of their acquaintance, his good opinion was something that she valued deeply. She swallowed hard and made a conscious effort to whip up her anger as a defence against the hurt she was feeling.

'That is enough, sir! I do not wish to hear you slander my reputation! And as for your playing of the moral arbiter, it is rich beyond belief! You are the greatest hypocrite I have ever come across!'

Sarah made to walk past Guy and seek the sanctuary of her room again, all thoughts of returning to the ballroom forgotten. She was shaking with anger and mortification. She had no clear idea of how such a confrontation could have occurred, nor did she wish to prolong it. For Guy to take her to task in such a way was not the conduct of a gentleman, but deeper than that, more hurtful, was his evident contempt and unjust condemnation.

Guy shifted slightly, but he did not move to let her past. There was something wholly unyielding about his stance, as though he had no intention of letting her go easily. For a long moment their eyes met in angry conflict, then Guy stepped forward and trapped Sarah between his body and the balcony rail.

He bent his head and brought his mouth down on hers in a kiss that was searching and utterly ruthless. Disbelief and fury welled up in Sarah. She pummelled his chest hard with her clenched fists, but he only tightened his grip on her, rendering her protests useless.

'I am living up to my reputation now, Miss Sheridan,' he said, raising his lips an inch from hers. 'I suggest that you start to do the same!'

His mouth returned to hers with a fierce demand. A shocking excitement swept through Sarah, setting her trembling in his arms. She could smell the faint, crisp scent of his lemon cologne, taste the sweetness of wine as his lips parted and moved over her own, lightly one moment, deepening again the next, but always in inexorable control. The merciless hands holding her hard against him did not relent for a moment.

Sarah gave up the struggle. She had no strength left to resist him, no will to do so. Despite the calculated nature of his embrace, to be kissed by him was such exquisite pleasure that she never wanted it to end. Her fingers uncurled against his chest and she slid her arms up about his neck. One of Guy's hands slipped down her back and over her hip, drawing her against the hardness of his body. He slid his other hand under the hair at the nape of her neck, his caress on the tender skin there causing Sarah to shiver. She made a small, inarticulate sound of surrender, pressing closer, completely abandoned to the kiss.

Something had changed, although Sarah was too adrift to realise what it was. Guy's cruel grip had eased and the touch of his lips, his hands, became gentle, exploring mutual pleasure rather than administering punishment. The aquamarine dress was slipping off Sarah's shoulders and the lace fichu tumbled to the floor. She felt the featherlight touch of Guy's fingers graze her collarbone before his lips left hers to trace a downward path from the line of her throat over the exposed curve of her breast. His breathing was as ragged as her own now. Sarah arched against him, weak with desire, stunned by her reaction to him.

His mouth returned to hers roughly, plundering its softness. He held her face still with one hand, upturned and open to his, his fingers tangled in her hair. His other hand gently brushed aside the silk of the dress and bared Sarah's heated skin to his touch. The deep, sweet invasion of her mouth went on and on. The pins tumbled from Sarah's hair and fell with a soft tinkle on to the marble floor of the hall below. She did not notice; did not notice as her hair fell from its carefully arranged curls to swirl about her bare shoulders, did not notice as her bodice slipped to her waist, leaving her half-naked in Guy's arms, did not notice as a door below opened abruptly and people spilled out into the hall.

'Oh!' There was a squeal from one of the women. 'I almost stepped on a pin!'

Sarah heard the voices, but could make no sense of them through the desire that clouded her mind. It seemed, however, that Guy retained just enough presence of mind to drag her back from the balcony and into the shadows before the assembled company turned as one to gaze up into the darkness of the upper hall.

'I say! Whatever is going on? Is there anybody up there?'

There was a giggle from one of the women, a guffaw, hastily repressed, from one of the men, and some murmured words and laughter before they all drifted off into the cardroom. Then there was silence.

Reality hit Sarah like a tidal wave. How could she be standing here in the candlelight, her clothing all awry, having allowed this man the most appalling liberties imaginable? Only seconds before he had questioned her virtue, and now she had comprehensively proved his point! She was trembling, her whole body shaking not with passion but with the enormity of what she had done. Where would it have ended? With her naked on the landing in full view of Amelia's guests? Her cheeks burned as she realised that she had been so lost in desire that she had not even thought of whom might see her. How could this have happened? She had always found Guy Renshaw attractive, but their verbal sparring had given her no clue to the shocking physical awareness that would flare between them. Why, when she had made to leave him on the landing she had not even liked him any more! And yet...

Sarah pulled her dress up over her shoulders and bent to pick up the discarded scrap of white lace. The point of a fichu, she remembered her mama telling her years before, was to preserve a lady's modesty. Well, she had no need of that! Her own behaviour had proved as much! And worse, memory stirred to remind her just how much she had enjoyed it, how she had ached for Guy's kisses, the touch of his hands on her body... How was it possible to dislike someone and want them at the same time? The thought made her despair.

More distressing still was the look of stony contempt on Guy's face. Whatever emotions had shaken her, they had evidently left him singularly unmoved. He still had hold of her wrist, but Sarah wrenched it from his grasp and walked past him to the door of her bedroom, her head held high and the effect ruined by the knowledge that his gaze had taken in the decadent effect of her plunging neckline. Her heart sank as Guy followed her into the room. All she wanted to do now was recover from her humiliation in private.

'You will oblige me by leaving me alone now, sir.' Sarah knew she had not achieved the icy tone she sought and could hardly bear to raise her eyes to his.

'A moment.' Guy's searing gaze swept over the dishevelled curls about Sarah's shoulders and lingered on the shadowy cleft between her breasts. 'You're good, I'll say that for you! Just enough untutored innocence mixed with passion!' He gave a cynical laugh. 'Good enough to leave me in some doubt! Anyway, I came to make you an offer—one that you may look kindly upon after your performance just now. I wish to spare you the trouble of looking for a protector at Blanchland. I am rich enough for any taste and I'm sure I can satisfy you! What do you say?'

The colour drained from Sarah's face. This was the final insult. She had refuted his accusations only to fall into his arms and apparently prove herself experienced. Was *carte blanche* the logical outcome? She supposed that might be so. Could she blame him for thinking of her as he did? Perhaps not, and yet she had hoped he would know her better than that. She had cherished secret dreams that had been far removed from this tawdry reality. She could scarcely believe that everything good and pure and sweet between them had been ground into the dust.

'Get out of my room!' It felt to Sarah that she must have shouted, but her words came out as a whisper. Guy's expression was blank for a moment, then he turned on his heel and the slam of the door echoed through the entire house.

'Sarah?' Amelia's tap on the door was almost silent and her cousin barely heard her whisper. 'Sarah, are you there?'

As Sarah struggled to sit up, Amelia turned the knob and stepped into the darkened bedroom. The lamp was turned down low, but there was enough light to see Sarah's stricken face and Amelia hurried forward in obvious alarm.

'Sarah! Whatever has happened?'

Sarah raised a face so blotchy and tear-stained that it was almost unrecognisable. A few minutes before she would have sworn she had no more tears left, but now she burst into tears all over again.

'Oh, Milly!'

Amelia sensibly did not press for an explanation, but gathered her cousin into her arms without a word. Eventually Sarah's sobs subsided a little again and she looked up.

'Has he gone?'

'He? Who?'

'Lord…Lord Renshaw…'

Several things became clear to Amelia at the same time. 'Yes, he left about an hour ago. I did not see him, but Grev said that he had gone. Was he with you before that, Sarah?'

A nod of the head was her only reply. Amelia's thoughtful gaze took in her cousin's tumbled hair and the blue dress that was lacking a piece of material it had certainly started off with. She raised her eyebrows. 'Here? He was with you here?'

Sarah nodded again.

Amelia glanced from her cousin to the bed. Try as she might, she could not keep the horror out of her voice. 'Oh, Sarah, surely he did not make love to you—?'

Sarah made a noise that was halfway between a sob and a laugh. 'No, it is not as bad as that!' She pushed the damp hair back from her face. 'Not quite, but nearly…' Slowly the story of the encounter came out, with Amelia sitting quite still and quiet as she listened.

'I felt so dreadful,' Sarah ended bitterly. 'I had told him that he had misjudged me, and then I behaved like the veriest trollop! Is it any wonder that he treated me like one? When he said—' She broke off on a sob, swallowed and started again, 'He made it all sound so sordid, Amelia, and that is exactly how it was!'

'You must not blame yourself,' Amelia said carefully, after a moment. 'I knew that you were more than a little in love with him, whatever you said before! Lord Renshaw had no right to speak to you as he did and, despite his reputation, I had not really thought that he would—' She broke off. 'Truly, the man is unforgivable!' She passed her cousin another handkerchief and patted her hand encouragingly.

Sarah blew her nose hard. 'Oh, dear, this is a terrible! To offer me *carte blanche*—'

'A poor reflection on Lord Renshaw rather than on yourself, my love!' Amelia said stringently. 'Pray put him from your mind. I doubt we shall see him again!'

Sarah thought that this was probably true. The idea gave her so much pain that she had to bite her lip to prevent herself from crying again. Yet if it was distressing to think of never seeing Guy again, it upset Sarah even more to think of the opinion of her that he would carry away.

'Will you still go to Blanchland, Sarah?' Amelia was asking carefully. 'Unfortunately, it is true that everyone is talking about it. I swear I told no one, but I wonder if the servants overheard—'

'Probably,' Sarah said tiredly. She got up and moved to turn up the lamp. 'Let people talk! I still intend to go tomorrow!'

'Sarah!' Amelia seemed uncertain whether to be glad or sorry that her cousin's familiar determination was reappearing. 'You cannot! Oh, surely you must see that it is impossible now! If you stay here and we put it about that it was all nothing but malicious gossip, the outcry will soon die down—'

'You mistake, Amelia.' Sarah was already pulling a couple of canvas bags from the cupboards, her actions showing a feverish energy. 'I intend to go, now more than ever! I will not have the likes of Guy Renshaw standing in judgement on me!'

Sarah rose early after a night with almost no sleep at all. Amelia had left her with a kiss after spending a fruitless half hour trying to persuade her cousin to change her mind. The more Sarah thought about it, the more her conviction grew. The misery she had felt at Guy Renshaw's stark contempt was hardening into anger now, humiliation turning into a burning fury. She was angry with herself for falling into his arms and confirming his opinion of her, but she was even more angry that he should ever have doubted her virtue. In the dark shadows of the night she had painfully admitted to herself just how much she had liked him. So much had been built upon so little: the roses, a couple of conversations, one waltz. And now she would have to learn to forget him.

With a heavy heart, Sarah dragged her bags to the bedroom door. If she was lucky, she could avoid Amelia, who always got up late on the morning after a ball. She could not bear another scene. She would take a hack down to the Angel and get the coach to the Old Down Inn and from there...

Sarah went out onto the landing, intending to tiptoe downstairs and find herself some breakfast before she left. She averted her gaze from the spot at the top of the stairs where she and Guy had had their encounter the previous night.

Far from being quiet, the house seemed very noisy. The shutters were flung back and servants were scurrying about in a frenzy. As she descended the stairs Sarah could see two large trunks, neatly bound with red rope, standing by the front door. Chisholm, looking as harassed as Sarah had ever seen him, was taking down what seemed like an endless list of instructions from his employer. Sarah stared in disbelief.

'...and cancel my attendance at Mrs Chartley's breakfast, if you please, and the card party at Colonel Waring's and any other invitations I have forgotten!'

'Yes, my lady.'

'And make sure that any invitations from Mrs Bunton and Mrs Clarke are returned unopened—'

'Yes, my lady.'

Amelia, looking fresh and radiant in a coffee-brown travelling dress and matching hat, turned to see her cousin watching her in amazement from the top of the stairs.

'There you are, Sarah! At last! Hurry and take some breakfast! Oh, and Chisholm—' her voice hardened '—if Sir Greville Baynham calls, pray tell him that I have left town and that his friends are not welcome in my house again—'

'Oh, Milly, you cannot do that! It is not Greville's fault!' Sarah recovered the use of her voice and hurried down to her cousin's side.

'No matter!' Amelia's chin was set defiantly. 'Sir Greville is to blame for having such poor taste in his friends! Now, are you almost ready, my love?'

Sarah watched bemusedly as two footmen threw open the main door and staggered out to the carriage under the huge weight of Amelia's baggages.

'Yes, but…what…?'

'I knew that I could not persuade you to change your mind,' Amelia said, seizing her arm and steering her towards the breakfast parlour, 'so I have changed mine! Dearest Sarah! I am coming with you!'

Chapter Four

'Seems to me you've made a dashed mess of things, Guy,' Greville Baynham said frankly, helping himself to a large plate of devilled kidneys. 'Didn't even give the poor girl a chance to explain!'

Guy stared gloomily out of the breakfast-room window. He had spent the best part of the night playing high and drinking deep, and this morning was left with a vicious headache and a feeling of sick disgust. At the back of his mind was the thought that Greville was very probably correct.

In his salad days he had tumbled into love several times with females who were either unsuitable or ineligible or both. It had not mattered then; his suffering was usually of short duration and there were plenty of ladies willing to help him recover and move on to the next conquest. As he had grown older he had seen that love rarely had much to do with these transactions and was quite content for this to be the case. The fact that his father wished him to settle down and provide an heir for Woodallan he viewed as a completely separate issue. Or, he *had* viewed it as such until he had met Miss Sarah Sheridan.

Guy shifted in his chair. He had told Greville about
the rumours that were circulating about Sarah and a
little of the scene between them, though, naturally
enough, he had not imparted the whole tale. Greville
had been frankly incredulous.

'Sounds all a hum to me,' he said judiciously. 'The
Bath tabbies usually prefer fiction to fact! They find it
so much more scandalous. Ten to one the whole thing
is nothing more than a Banbury tale!'

Guy pulled a face. 'I would like to agree with you,
Grev, but Miss Sheridan practically confirmed it! When
I asked her if it was true she was visiting Blanchland,
she did not give a convincing denial! What was I to
think?'

Greville waved his fork about descriptively. 'That she
was visiting her old nurse? That Ralph Covell wanted
to hand over some of her father's paintings? I don't
know—anything except what you clearly *did* think, old
chap!'

Guy did not deny it. Now he said, 'I suppose…I may
have been a little hasty—'

'Seems to me you should think about why you reacted as you did,' Greville said drily, demonstrating his
disconcerting habit of hitting the nail on the head. 'I
believe you must owe Miss Sheridan an apology, Guy.
Do you care to accompany me to Brock Street this
morning? I was intending to call on Lady Amelia anyway.'

Guy hesitated. He sincerely doubted that Sarah would
either offer an explanation or give him the chance to
apologise. It seemed most likely, in fact, that she would
never speak to him again. He thought again of the previous night, of how Sarah's initial resistance to him had
melted into response and how he had taken ruthless ad-

vantage of it. Much as he would have preferred to deny it, her willingness had raised an echo of genuine passion in him that had transcended the blind fury that had first prompted him to punish her. He had been as shaken as she was—or as she had appeared to be.

Guy paused. Supposing—just supposing—Sarah had been the innocent he had always thought her to be? How must she have felt to have her inexperienced reactions construed as calculated passion? How would she be feeling that morning, confronted with the discovery of her own desires and the memory of his contempt? There were no excuses. He had taken disgraceful advantage of her.

Guy gave a groan and buried his head in his hands. Looking at matters in the cold light of day, he was both stunned and disconcerted by his violent reaction to the gossip he had heard. As Greville had said, he needed to analyse why he had responded so furiously and the answer was not far to seek. Although he had not previously acknowledged it, his feelings for Sarah Sheridan ran very deep indeed. The knowledge was a shock on one level, but on another he was obliged to admit that he had known it from the first. The fact that he had known her such a short time was irrelevant to his feelings. And now he had made the most godforsaken mess of the whole business… He groaned again.

Greville was eyeing him with concern. 'I'll ring for an ice bag,' he said, getting up. 'And, Guy, have a shave before you go out. It won't help your cause to arrive in Brock Street looking half cut!'

The house in Brock Street was shuttered and it seemed to take an inordinate amount of time before Chisholm answered the bell. Nor was his demeanour particularly encouraging when he did so, for there was a look in his eye that seemed to imply that they should be using the tradesmen's entrance.

'Good day, Lord Renshaw. Good day, Sir Greville. May I be of service?'

Guy and Greville waited to be allowed over the threshold, but Chisholm remained obdurately in the way. Greville raised his eyebrows.

'Good day, Chisholm. Is Lady Amelia receiving visitors? Pray tell her that we have called!'

Chisholm folded his lips into a thin line. His stance seemed to suggest that such good humour was sorely misplaced.

'I regret to inform you, sir, that Lady Amelia has left town.'

There was a pause. Guy stepped forward. 'And Miss Sheridan? Is she at home?'

Chisholm's gaze seemed to turn even more glacial. 'I fear not, my lord. However, her ladyship asked me to give Sir Greville the following message.' He cleared his throat and avoided looking directly at either of them. 'Her ladyship wishes it to be known that she has gone to the country with her cousin. Further, whilst you are still welcome to visit here, Sir Greville, the same invitation does not extend to your friends. Good day, sir.'

Chisholm bowed neatly, stepped back and closed the door firmly.

Both Guy and Greville stared at the wooden panels in stupefaction, then Greville took a hasty step forward and reached for the bell again. Guy laid a hand on his arm.

'Grev! Wait!'

Guy did not think he had ever seen his friend so angry. Greville's grey eyes were burning with fury.

'How dare he say such things! The confounded impertinence of the man! Why, I'll—'

'He is only doing as he was instructed,' Guy pointed out quietly. 'Come away, Grev. There are people watching.'

It was true. Several curious passers-by, including the ubiquitous Mrs Clarke, were occupying the pavement at the bottom of the steps.

'Oh, Sir Greville!' that lady trilled, stepping forward to block their way. 'Lord Renshaw! Have you heard the news? Lady Amelia has gone to Blanchland with her cousin! I can scarce believe it, but it must be true for Mrs Bunton heard it from Lady Trippeny, who—'

Greville set his shoulders. He gave the gossip a look of comprehensive dislike. 'It is perfectly true, Mrs Clarke, but of no great import! Miss Sheridan has been called to Blanchland on an urgent family matter and her cousin has gone with her as chaperon! That is all! And I do beg you to remember that, before you indulge in idle speculation about the lady who is shortly to become my wife! Why, I shall be joining her at Blanchland shortly myself!'

Mrs Clarke's mouth rounded in astonishment. 'Oh, Sir Greville! And, Lord Renshaw—' she swung round on Guy accusingly '—were you aware of this?'

Guy tried not to laugh. 'Which part, Mrs Clarke? The bit about Lady Amelia chaperoning her cousin to Blanchland, or the part about Sir Greville being betrothed to Lady Amelia and joining her at Blanchland tomorrow? Or even...' his smile broadened '...the fact that I am shortly to announce my own engagement to Miss Sheridan? Yes, I am aware of all of it!'

Mrs Clarke backed away from them, almost tripping over the kerb in her haste to escape and acquaint Mrs

Bunton with her news. The two men nodded amiably to the rest of the crowd and strolled off down Brock Street with every appearance of nonchalance.

'I cannot believe we just did that,' Guy said under his breath, as they turned into The Circus and paused for a moment. 'The story will be all over Bath in less than a half hour! Did you mean what you said?'

'Of course!' Greville looked grim. 'You know I've been meaning to marry Amelia this past age! This ridiculous jaunt to Blanchland has simply precipitated matters!'

'Hope she sees it in the same light as you, old fellow,' Guy said feelingly. 'Do you mean to go there to offer her your protection?'

'Well, I hadn't thought of it until five minutes ago,' Greville admitted, 'but now I see I need to talk some sense into the foolish woman!'

Guy repressed a grin. 'Well, in that case you'd better travel with me! I'm for Woodallan, and you can break your journey there before travelling to Blanchland on the morrow.'

'Thank you!' Greville seemed to be recovering his good humour. The tense lines on his face eased a little. 'And what of your own plans, Guy? Thought you were touched in the attic when you said that about marrying Miss Sheridan!'

Guy shifted a little. 'Couldn't leave Miss Sheridan as the only one with a stain on her reputation, could I, Grev? That odious woman would rip her to shreds!'

'But will you keep your word?' Greville pressed. 'If not, Miss Sheridan will be thrown to the wolves anyway!'

'I suppose I'm honour bound to try to persuade her...' Guy gave his friend a lopsided grin. 'You may count this as your fault, for telling me to examine my feelings! Truth is, I'd offer for Sarah like a shot if I thought she'd have me, but I doubt she'll even consider it. Too much to forgive, I suppose! Devil take it, how have I managed to make such a confounded mess of things in such a short space of time?'

Greville laughed. 'Cupid's arrow, old chap! Strikes when and where, at will! And it seems to me that, of the two of us, you have the harder task!'

'Amelia, you know this will not serve! Instead of saving my reputation, you are only ruining your own! Why, both of us will be tarred with the same brush!'

Sarah and her cousin had been arguing all the way from Brock Street to Combe Hay. The beauty of the winter countryside had been ignored and the discomfort of the twisting road scarcely noticed as Sarah desperately tried to persuade Amelia to change her mind. The irony of the situation was not lost on her. Amelia had spent considerable time and effort in trying to persuade her to abandon the trip to Blanchland, yet here she was sitting in Amelia's carriage with Amelia's servants in attendance and Amelia herself beside her. And her cousin was adamant.

'I am a respectable widow whose good reputation can only help to protect you, dearest Sarah. Since it seems you are determined to go through with this mad plan, I feel it my duty to accompany you and save you from yourself!'

'You are very noble,' Sarah said, uncertain whether to laugh or cry, 'but pray do not make this sacrifice on my account! You have told me yourself that Blanchland is the most licentious house in the kingdom—you must know that even *your* good name will not be able to withstand the scandal! Oh, Amelia, pray do not go through with this!'

Amelia turned her dark gaze on her cousin. 'You have not told me why this visit is so important to you, Sarah, but I have to believe that it is of great consequence. If it matters so much to you that you are prepared to risk your reputation on it, I am prepared to do the same to help you. There! We shall have no more arguments!' She turned her shoulder and looked out of the window.

Sarah gave a sigh of exasperation. She could not deny that it was pleasant to have company on the journey and it was infinitely more comfortable to travel privately than on the public stage. But those were small benefits in comparison to the damage that this escapade would cause. No doubt the whole of Bath society would already have heard what had happened, and how could either of them ever show their faces there again? It was melancholy to think of Amelia being ostracised for an act of misplaced kindness.

Sarah looked at Amelia's determined profile. She felt a strong sense of guilt that she had not confided her quest in her cousin, but something made her hesitate. Time enough for that when Miss Meredith had been found and the mystery solved. At least arguing with Amelia had distracted her from melancholy thoughts about Guy.

They stopped for luncheon and to change the horses at the inn at Clandown, and Amelia confidently predicted that they would reach Blanchland by late afternoon, for the roads were good for the time of year. Sarah started to feel very nervous. How would she find her home after all these years? And how would Ralph react to their unexpected arrival? She barely knew her father's cousin; though she bore him no ill will for inheriting her home after Frank's death, she could hardly bear to think what he had done to it.

The journey progressed uneventfully until they neared the Old Down crossroads, where a sudden downpour took them by surprise and set the road awash. Within moments the horses had lost their footing and the carriage lurched off the road and into the ditch.

'No harm done, ma'am,' the coachman reported cheerfully as he helped Amelia and Sarah down on to the road, 'but it might be better if you took shelter in the inn whilst we haul it out. A nice dish of tea should help you over the shock!'

The Old Down Inn was accustomed to passing trade and soon put a private parlour at the disposal of its unexpected guests. Amelia regarded her dripping figure with deep displeasure, whilst outside the rain splattered against the window and emphasised the sudden decline in the good weather.

'Oh, I look hideous,' Amelia declared, wringing water from her cloak into a bucket helpfully provided by the landlady. 'This bonnet is quite ruined, and I have only worn it twice! A fine pair of figures we will cut, arriving at Blanchland in such a state!'

She glanced critically over Sarah, whose hair was drying in corkscrew curls about her face. 'Humph! Well, at least you look the part, Sarah, with your wild hair and soaking dress! Oh, this is too bad!'

'Thank you,' Sarah said drily. 'It is comforting to know that I already look like a demi-rep and I have not even set foot in the house yet! Do you care for tea and cakes, Milly? It might improve your temper!'

Amelia looked rueful. 'I'm sorry, Sarah, I know I am like a bear with a sore head! Truth to tell, I was feeling nervous before, but now I just feel downright unpresentable! Oh, to arrive in so undignified a state when we do not even know what we will find...' She took a cup of tea and moved over to the window. 'I had better not sit down or I shall cause a puddle! I wonder when this storm will cease—' She broke off with an exclamation and Sarah looked up from the fire, which she had been trying to coax into reluctant life with the poker.

'Whatever is the matter, Milly? You look as though you have seen a ghost!'

'It is Greville!' Amelia whispered, looking as though she was about to rush from the room. 'Greville and Lord Renshaw! Sarah, they are here!'

Sarah felt her heart leap into her throat. 'Oh, no, it cannot be! You must be mistaken, Milly!'

'I tell you, they were right outside the window—'

Amelia broke off at the sound of voices in the passageway outside. The parlour door opened.

'Good afternoon!' Greville Baynham said affably, as though he were meeting them in Milsom Street. 'An inclement day! I am glad to see that you appear to have suffered no injury when your coach left the road!'

Neither Sarah nor her cousin were up to answering him in kind. Sarah met Guy Renshaw's quizzical gaze, blushed crimson and looked hastily away. As he came towards her, she backed away from the fire, still holding the poker, and took refuge behind the parlour table. Amelia, obviously viewing attack as the best form of defence, burst into speech.

'You!' she said, in tones of ringing outrage. 'Whatever are you doing here, Sir Greville?'

'Came to find you,' Greville said imperturbably. He crossed to the fire and kicked it into a blaze, warming his hands. 'Heard you'd gone off on some mad start and thought that you might need some help—'

Amelia drew herself up to her full—tiny—height. 'Well, we do not, sir! Not from you, at any rate! We can manage perfectly well on our own!'

'I doubt that,' Greville said coolly. 'You have only been on the road for a few hours and already you are in a scrape! And as for your destination—well, that proves you have not the least notion of how to carry on! Good God, two gently bred ladies visiting a house of ill fame! Fit for Bedlam, both of you!'

Amelia's stormy gaze swept from Greville to Guy Renshaw and rested there for a moment. 'Do not preach to me, sir, when you keep such poor company!'

Sarah winced. Amelia seldom lost her temper properly, but when she did so the results could be spectacular. This promised to be one of those occasions. She caught Guy Renshaw's eye and saw that he was looking rather amused. A slow smile was curling the corners of his mouth and Sarah felt an answering gleam and stifled it at once. The last thing she wanted at that moment was to experience any kind of kindred feeling for Guy. He had humiliated her and insulted her, she reminded herself severely, and his charm was of the most superficial kind.

'It ill becomes you to speak of bad company when you are planning so rash an escapade, madam!' Greville said to Amelia, more coldly than Sarah had ever heard him. 'Do you forget that this will ruin your reputation forever? And yet you disparage those who seek to offer you their aid—'

'Offer their aid!' Two spots of colour were burning on Amelia's cheeks now. 'Forgive me, sir, but it seems to me that you came to censure rather than to support!

My cousin and I can do very well without such dubious assistance!'

'You may claim so, but you have as much idea of how to go on as a pair of schoolgirls! Less! At least a schoolroom miss knows her manners!'

Sarah caught her breath sharply as Amelia made a noise like an enraged kitten. The combatants faced each other fiercely across the table, Amelia with her fists clenched and Greville with a singularly unyielding look on his face.

Sarah could feel Guy watching her across the room and she found herself looking around for a means of escape. Guy was between her and the door, the window was too small and she could scarcely scramble up the chimney. A strange panic took hold of her as he came towards her.

As Amelia drew breath for another salvo, Guy reached Sarah's side and took her arm.

'I believe that we may safely leave these two to settle their differences, Miss Sheridan. May I beg a word in private?'

'Certainly not!' Amelia snapped, before Sarah could speak. She flashed Guy a look of contempt. 'Stand aside from my cousin, Lord Renshaw! You have done her enough harm!'

Guy looked from Amelia to Greville. 'My dear Lady Amelia, pray confine your quarrel to Sir Greville and leave Miss Sheridan to deal with me!' He removed the poker from Sarah's hand. 'I should feel safer if you were without this!'

Sarah had forgotten that she had been stirring the fire when they had arrived. She relinquished her weapon and edged away from Guy towards the door.

'A moment, Miss Sheridan.' Guy had turned back to

her with exquisite courtesy. 'Pray do not leave just yet!
It is still raining and your carriage is not fit for use!
Will you grant my request of a private interview?'

Sarah shook her head. 'My cousin is in the right of
it, sir. I do not care to have my business discussed in a
wayside inn!'

Guy inclined his head. 'Then come back with us to
Woodallan and discuss it there!'

'Impossible!' Amelia retorted, her colour still high.
'We must reach Blanchland before nightfall—'

'Must you?' Guy strolled into the middle of the room
and turned back to smile at Sarah. 'Had you thought
what might happen if you arrive at dinner time?' he
asked conversationally, looking from her to Amelia.
'Why, Sir Ralph may well be indulging in one of his
famous orgies and you would walk right into the middle
of it! Time enough for that once you have been there a
little while! But if you leave it to the morning, you will
find them all still abed. Not ideal, of course, but
less…active, perhaps, than the night before!'

'Outrageous!' Amelia declared.

'But true,' Greville said coolly.

'I fear Lord Renshaw may be right, Milly,' Sarah said
after a moment. 'Perhaps we should bespeak rooms here
for the night—'

'Out of the question,' Guy said briskly. 'You could
not so offend my parents' hospitality, Miss Sheridan, as
to take rooms within two miles of their house!'

Sarah flushed. 'If you were not to tell them we were
here—'

'Alas, I would find it quite impossible to keep the
truth from them! Their own goddaughter preferring the
dubious comforts of an alehouse to Woodallan! I am
sure my mother would be quite distraught!'

Sarah reached for her cloak. Somehow they had been outmanoeuvred. 'Very well, my lord. Since I do not trust you to spare your mother's feelings, we will come with you. However—' she glared at him '—do not think to dissuade us from our errand, nor to enlist the support of your parents in such an enterprise!'

Guy's dark gaze mocked her. 'Miss Sheridan! I could not possibly tell my parents that you intended to visit Blanchland! The shock might kill them!'

He held the door open for her. 'You look very pretty, Miss Sheridan,' he added, in tones low enough that only Sarah could hear. 'To see you with your hair like that gives me ideas—'

'I thank you,' Sarah snapped. 'I heard enough of your ideas last night, sir! I wonder that you dare to speak to me of them again!'

Guy detained her with a hand on her arm. 'In point of fact, Miss Sheridan, that is what I wished to discuss with you. I wished to apologise, but I will save it until we have gained the privacy of Woodallan!'

Sarah's lips tightened angrily. 'It may be that I do not wish to hear any of your excuses, Lord Renshaw!'

'You will hear me out, however,' Guy said, with what seemed to Sarah to be breathtaking arrogance. He offered her his arm, and laughed when she swept past him, ignoring it. Behind her, Sarah could hear Greville and Amelia starting to bicker again as they all went out into the yard.

'You realise that you will have to marry me now!' Greville was saying, in an exasperated undertone, to which Amelia retorted,

'I would rather walk across hot coals, sir!'

They journeyed to Woodallan in bad-tempered silence.

*   *   *

Woodallan lay two miles from the turnpike road, in a hollow beside a stream, sheltered by the hills behind and with a glorious vista of rolling country before it. The rain had cleared as quickly as it had come, and the house's golden Bath stone gleamed in the late afternoon sunlight. Next to Blanchland, it had always been one of Sarah's favourite places, and now she felt a lump in her throat as the years rolled back. She remembered walking up the long lime avenue as a child, clutching her father's hand, remembered playing hide-and-seek in the topiary garden, remembered tickling trout in the stream during the hot summers...

The Blanchland and Woodallan estates had marched together and the families been friends since the first Baron Woodallan and Sir Edmund Sheridan had sailed the seas together as privateers under Queen Elizabeth. It had always been a family joke that Frank Sheridan had inherited his wanderlust from his ancestors.

The carriage drew up in front of the main door and Guy jumped down to help her descend.

'Welcome back,' he said, and for a moment it seemed that he had invested the words with a greater significance.

Sarah shrugged the thought aside. It was too dangerous for her to start to feel at home in her childhood haunts, for in a week's time—two at the most—she would have to return to Bath and the life she was accustomed to. Time spent at Blanchland and Woodallan could only be a passing phase, but when she had planned her journey she had not spared a thought for the way in which old memories would be stirred up. She looked at Guy, who was looking up at the house with a half-smile on his lips.

'It must be a great pleasure for you to be home again,

my lord, after so long abroad,' she said spontaneously, and he smiled down at her, and for a split second Sarah was happy.

'Oh, it is, Miss Sheridan, for here I have all the things I most care for.'

Again, Sarah tried not to read too much significance into his words. She turned aside and followed Amelia and Greville up the steps, reminding herself that she was vulnerable to him and must be always on her guard.

The Countess of Woodallan was in the hall to welcome her son home, and, as word of Guy's arrival spread, it seemed that the house was full of beaming servants all wishing to greet him. Sarah and the others hung back until the crush had lessened a little, when the Countess turned and caught sight of her.

'Sarah! Good gracious, what a wonderful surprise! Forgive me for not welcoming you sooner, my dear!' She enveloped Sarah in a warm hug. 'And Greville! Guy…' she swung round accusingly on her son '…you should have told us you were bringing a party!'

Guy, who had been conversing quietly with his father's steward, came forward. 'I'm sorry for giving you no warning, Mama, but it was a spur-of-the-minute decision. Miss Sheridan and her cousin are travelling on in the morning, but I persuaded them to break their journey here tonight.'

The Countess swallowed her disappointment well. 'I am sorry to hear you will be leaving so soon. But perhaps—' she smiled at Sarah '—you will consider visiting us again on your journey back? You could stay for Christmas! That would be most pleasant, for we have so much news to catch up on!'

Sarah smiled a little stiffly. In the warmth of her welcome she had almost forgotten the reason for her visit, and the fact that she would be travelling on to Blanchland almost immediately. The Countess, suddenly aware of an air of constraint about her guests, turned her warm smile on Amelia. Greville stepped forward to make the introductions.

'Lady Woodallan, may I present my fiancée, Lady Amelia Fenton. Lady Amelia is Miss Sheridan's cousin.'

'I am not!' Amelia said hotly, then catching the look of amazement on her hostess' face, stammered, 'That is, I am Sarah's cousin, but I am *not* Sir Greville's fiancée!'

There was an awkward silence.

'I am afraid that Lady Amelia has not quite become accustomed to the idea yet, ma'am,' Greville said easily, ignoring Amelia's fearsome glare. 'I must apologise for imposing on your hospitality like this, particularly when you must be wishing to have Guy to yourselves!'

'You are very welcome for as long as you wish to stay,' the Countess murmured, trying not to stare at Amelia as though she had a lunatic in the house. 'But you look as though you were caught in the storm, my dears! I will show you to your rooms so that you may change, and send word to Cook to increase the covers for dinner. Guy, your father should have returned by then. He has driven over to Home Farm to talk to Benton about the milk yield, but I expect him back at any time!'

'Before you carry Miss Sheridan away, Mama, I should like to speak with her in private,' Guy said firmly. 'There is a matter to be settled between us that cannot wait.'

Sarah blushed scarlet and the Countess frowned. 'But, Guy, Miss Sheridan will be tired from her journey, and is drenched by the rain besides! Surely it can wait a little—'

'Oh, yes, indeed, ma'am,' Sarah added hurriedly, 'there is no urgency!'

'I am desolate to contradict you, Miss Sheridan,' Guy said smoothly, 'but it is imperative that we speak now. I do not wish there to be any further misunderstandings!'

'It seems to me that we have two ardent suitors here and two reluctant ladies!' a voice said, from behind them, and Sarah swung round to see her godfather in the doorway.

The Earl of Woodallan was leaning heavily on his stout ash stick and looked a lot older than Sarah remembered, but the expressive dark eyes, so like his son's, were as sharp as ever. 'Lady Amelia...' he gave as courtly a bow as ever his son could achieve '...and Sarah, my dear! What a delightful surprise! And Sir Greville, too! Well, Guy—' he turned to his son, the sardonic gleam in his eye belied by a smile '—good to see you back again, boy!'

'Sir!' Guy hurried forward to shake his father's hand, and Sarah took advantage of the moment to step back, throwing her godmother a pleading glance.

'If we could be permitted to change our clothes, ma'am—'

'Of course, my love.' The Countess swept up her goddaughter and Amelia, and shepherded them towards the stairs. 'Come along with me! The gentlemen are quite preoccupied and will not notice—'

The Earl's voice stayed them as they reached the half-landing.

'Charlotte, be sure to deliver Miss Sheridan to the

blue drawing-room just as soon as she is ready! Guy will be waiting for her!'

'Like father, like son,' the Countess murmured under her breath. 'I fear that an autocratic nature is in the Woodallan blood!'

It was three-quarters of an hour later that Sarah descended the stairs again. She was clean and dry, dressed in a becoming russet gown belonging to the younger of Lady Woodallan's daughters and with her hair neatly braided into a bun on the top of her head.

'Too austere, Miss Sheridan,' was Guy's comment as he ushered her into the blue drawing-room. 'You are too soft and sweet to pretend to such severity!'

He, too, had changed into clean buckskins, polished boots and an olive green jacket that fitted his broad shoulders to perfection. Sarah, experiencing a traitorous rush of feeling on seeing him, immediately went on the attack.

'By what right do you criticise my appearance, sir? Kindly refrain from becoming too personal!'

Guy grinned, unabashed, and gestured her to a chair before the fire. 'That was precisely the matter I wished to discuss with you, Miss Sheridan—Sarah. May I call you Sarah?'

'I am surprised you trouble to ask, sir!' Sarah said hotly. 'No, you may not!'

'Very well then, Miss Sheridan, I will not provoke you!' Guy sat down opposite her. Sarah, who was feeling quite on edge, resented his assumption of ease. 'I am grateful to you for granting me a hearing. I feared you would not. My behaviour in Bath—' He stopped, and started again. 'After the things I said, I could not blame you if you choose to deny me the chance to apologise.'

'I have promised to hear you out, my lord,' Sarah said coldly. 'Beyond that, I promise nothing.'

Guy grimaced. 'You are not making this easy for me, Miss Sheridan! I wished to apologise to you, both for my actions and my words last night—'

Sarah got to her feet, her face suffused with colour. Her instinct was to flee the room immediately out of sheer embarrassment. Despite herself, she could not prevent a scorching memory of the events of the previous night from invading her thoughts.

Anticipating her retreat, Guy moved swiftly to stand between her and the door.

'Please, Miss Sheridan—you promised me a hearing—'

'I have done so, sir,' Sarah said, as steadily as she could. 'You wished to apologise and I have heard you.'

'And?'

'And, sir?'

Guy gave a sigh of exasperation. 'And do you forgive me? I do not seek to justify myself in any way. What I did was inexcusable.'

Sarah paused. It did seem churlish to reject his apology when he seemed sincere, particularly as he had made no attempt to excuse his actions. She could feel a tiny corner of her heart unfreezing towards him and ruthlessly sought to conquer her weakness. It would never do to allow the spark of that earlier attraction to be rekindled into life. She had burned herself badly enough on that already.

'Very well, sir. I accept your apology.'

'That was not precisely what I asked.' Guy was frowning. 'I wished to know if you forgive me.'

'And the answer is no.' Sarah met his eyes very straight. 'I do not forgive you for speaking to me as you did, nor for believing me a...a woman of easy virtue. That I cannot pardon.'

Guy inclined his head. 'You are very frank and I accept what you say, Miss Sheridan. But there were mitigating factors—'

'Which you said you would not raise to justify yourself!'

Guy gave her a wry smile. 'That's true, but may we not sit down and talk a little more?'

Sarah looked at him for a moment, then reluctantly returned to her seat in front of the fire. Despite the uncomfortable situation, she had to admit that the atmosphere of Woodallan was very restful. The drawing-room, decorated in pale blue and gold, and with the small fire adding a heart of warmth, was most peaceful. The charm of Woodallan went beyond mere wealth or good taste—it was so tempting to relax into it, but Sarah knew she could not afford to do so. She did not belong here.

'You seem unaccountably determined to prolong my discomfiture, my lord,' she observed, knowing that the colour still burned in her cheeks. 'Generosity might prompt you to let the matter go now.'

'Forgive me, there is a reason that I shall come to shortly.' Guy sat forward, resting his chin on his hand. 'I am sorry for listening to groundless gossip and still more sorry for acting on it, as I have said, but I confess I am puzzled as to the truth, Miss Sheridan. What can have prompted you to decide to travel to Blanchland, when you knew that to do so would cause such speculation?'

Sarah hesitated. She was terribly tempted to tell him

the truth, but realised that this was only because she wanted him to think well of her again. Such a motive was hardly a good enough reason to give away the secret. If Guy could not trust her without proof, then she would not oblige him.

'It is a family matter,' she said evasively. 'I am fulfilling a request from my late brother.'

Guy frowned a little. 'Can you not be more specific, Miss Sheridan? I am trying to understand—'

Sarah shook her head. 'I appreciate your concern, my lord, but it is a private matter. I have told no one, not even Amelia.' She looked up and met his eyes. 'She does not know the reason for my quest, but she is prepared to trust my judgement and accompany me, even so.'

'Point taken, Miss Sheridan,' Guy murmured. He got to his feet again and strolled over to the window. 'But you must also take my point. Whilst your motives for travelling to Blanchland may be of the purest, the interpretation put on them will not be. It is inevitable that the world will make its own judgements. Miss Sheridan, if I could only prevail upon you to reconsider your visit? Could not your man of business undertake the commission to Blanchland? You could then stay here at Woodallan for a while and there would be no grounds for scandal…'

Sarah was tempted. The Blanchland visit had already caused so much trouble, and she had not even arrived. And to be able to stay at Woodallan would be blissful. She shook her head slowly. 'Do not press me, sir. There is much appeal in your suggestion, but I cannot. My brother has asked me to undertake this quest personally and I shall do as he wished.'

Guy looked at her for a moment, but she did not

retract her statement. He sighed. 'Then you must also take the consequences, Miss Sheridan. Greville may not have put it most delicately when he told Lady Amelia she would be ruined, but he is in the right of it. Without the protection of his name, she will be reviled. And the same must apply to you.'

Sarah frowned. 'I do not dispute the truth of your words, sir, but I am not surprised that Amelia quarrelled with Sir Greville over it! He was insufferably righteous, and to make an offer in such a manner is to beg a refusal! As for my own situation, I feel it is not as acute as Lady Amelia's. I have no position in society to support—as a poor relation I have no prospects to ruin!'

'You may choose to see yourself in that light, Miss Sheridan,' Guy said quietly, 'but others will think differently. I myself...' he hesitated '...I believe that you should consider... In short, it would give me the greatest pleasure if you would do me the honour of marrying me.'

Sarah stared at him in total disbelief. 'Are you mad, sir, or is this some ill-timed jest?'

Guy's lips tightened angrily, though he was clearly trying to keep control of his temper. 'Neither, madam! I saw it as a way out of your present difficulties—'

'Thank you!' Sarah was on her feet as well now, facing him across the room. 'Despite my lack of prospects, I had not viewed marriage as a solution to my problems!' She was astounded at the strength of her own anger. 'Yesterday you told me that my behaviour suggested that I was some sort of trollop and you treated me as such! Scarcely the conduct of a man prepared for matrimony! Then today you suggest I marry you to provide a way out of an unfortunate predicament! Forgive

me, my lord, if I do not fall into your arms with tears
of gratitude!'

Guy winced. 'I realise that this is not the way you
might have wished it—'

'Very true! I do not wish to hear this at all!'

'Yet you should know that I have already given people to understand that we are shortly to become betrothed in order to protect your good name!'

Sarah looked at him in infuriated silence for a moment before bursting out, 'You take too much upon
yourself, my lord! Upon my word, of all the high-
handed, arrogant, ill-conceived ideas—'

Guy closed the distance between them in two strides.
He seemed amused rather than angered by Sarah's outrage. 'I am aware of your opinion of me, Miss Sheridan,
but I believe you are being less than honest. Confess
that you like me a little!'

Sarah glared up at him. 'I shall not! Conceited, overbearing…'

She was incensed to see that Guy was actually grinning. He took her hands. 'Come, come, Miss Sheridan,
we could be here for some time at this rate! Say you
will consider my proposal, at the least!'

Sarah's treacherous heart did a little somersault. The
warm touch of his fingers was distracting. 'Certainly
not, my lord!'

'Then you force me to be less than chivalrous!' He
was drawing her closer. Sarah resisted, feeling her heart
start to race.

'It would be more surprising to find you behaving in
a gentlemanly fashion, sir!' The words came out more
huskily than she intended. His proximity was having a
disastrous effect. Sarah was suddenly aware of the in-

timate heat of the room, the sweet scent of lilies by the fireplace, the sensitivity of her skin beneath his touch...

'Unfair, Miss Sheridan!' Guy murmured in her ear. 'Have I not just behaved in the most gallant manner possible? Alas that you force me to a point of clarification on our discussion earlier.' His lips brushed her hair, causing Sarah to shiver. She desperately tried to step back but found that her limbs would not obey her.

'Clarification, sir?' Her words came out as a whisper.

'Indeed. I wish you to know,' Guy continued, 'that when I apologised for my behaviour that night it was in relation to our argument and the unfounded accusations I made against you.' He looked directly into her eyes. 'I do not intend to apologise for...what came after.'

He was very close now. Sarah's gaze moved involuntarily to the hard line of his jaw, his mouth... She felt herself turn hot all over and wrenched her gaze away, fixing it sternly on a potted palm in a corner of the room.

'And yet I believe, my lord, that you were acting under a misapprehension...'

'In a sense...I'll allow I thought myself deceived and believed you...experienced. Yet my behaviour was very much in accordance with what I had wanted ever since I first saw you, Miss Sheridan...'

Sarah felt smothered by the heated atmosphere and her own emotions. Her heart was beating light and fast in her throat and she knew she had to put some distance between them, but she could not seem to break away from him. She could not be so weak as to fall under his spell again so soon, not when he had traduced her character and shown his lack of faith in her, then compounded his sins by a high-handed proposal that she could only refuse…

Guy let go of her hand, but only to draw her closer still, until their bodies were almost touching.

'Deny that you felt the same way, too, Miss Sheridan. Deny it if you dare!'

'I do deny it!' Sarah wrenched herself free of him and backed away. She was utterly confused by the emotions he could stir up in her. 'Tomorrow I shall leave here for Blanchland and you need not concern yourself with my affairs any further, my lord. It will no longer be any of your business!'

Guy's expression was inscrutable. He made no move to touch her again, but his voice held her still when she would have run away. 'You have made your feelings plain, Miss Sheridan. I must disappoint you, however. I have made this my business and I do not intend to disengage now. You may have as much time as you wish to get used to the idea, but the fact remains—you *will* marry me!'

Chapter Five

Dinner was a surprisingly good-humoured meal, considering that Sarah was avoiding Guy and Amelia and Greville were evidently not speaking to each other. The Earl and Countess took charge effortlessly, the former charming Amelia and the latter regaling Sarah with tales of her married daughters and their families. Guy and Greville fell to discussing horses, the food was excellent, and the meal passed without incident. It was only later, when the gentlemen rejoined the ladies, that the Earl took a seat beside Sarah and broached the delicate subject. They had chatted for a while about Sarah's life in Bath, reminisced about earlier times and talked about developments in the Woodallan estate, before Sarah had unwisely remarked that the Earl must be glad to have his son and heir restored to him. Lord Woodallan smiled.

'I must admit there were times when I thought I'd never see Guy again! I suppose he had to get rid of his restlessness before he was prepared to settle down. In my youth it was the Grand Tour and these days it is the War, but either way...' He twinkled at her. 'And now

I find that he is all set for parson's mousetrap, but the lady of his choice is not willing!'

Sarah blushed. 'Sir—'

The Earl patted her clasped hands. 'I know I am an interfering old man, but I only wished to say that nothing would make me happier than to see Jack Sheridan's daughter take her place in due course as mistress of Woodallan.'

Sarah looked away. 'Thank you, sir. I am sorry... there are difficulties...'

'I guessed as much,' the Earl said drily, 'but perhaps they will resolve themselves more easily than you might think, Sarah! Just do not keep my scapegrace son waiting too long, I beg you. He may seem a rogue, but he has many sound qualities—I should know, for he inherits them all from me!'

The Earl of Woodallan's study faced southwest, looking across the bowling-green and the formal parterre to the deer park and the Mendip Hills beyond. On this particular evening, the heavy brocade curtains were closed against the night and two lamps burned on the tables each side of the fire. Guy, who had just finished a game of billiards with Greville, found his father sitting in one of the armchairs, perusing a well-worn leather bound book. He invited his son to pour them both a drink.

'Brandy for you, sir?' Guy asked, crossing to the decanter and pouring a generous measure into the two cut glasses that stood there. He took one across to his father, noting the effort it seemed to cost the Earl simply to stretch out a hand for the glass. The Earl managed to conceal his weakness most of the time, but his son could see the changes that illness had wrought in him.

The Earl fixed Guy with his piercing dark gaze and said gruffly, 'I meant it when I said I was glad to see you back in one piece, boy. I must admit there were times in the last four years when I wished you'd had a brother!'

Guy laughed. He sat down opposite his father, stretching his legs out towards the grate. A fire burned there and its warmth was comforting.

'I am here now, sir, and don't intend to go travelling again!'

The fierce black gaze looked him over. 'You look well enough on it, I suppose,' the Earl said. 'A bad business, though. Must have had its nasty moments.'

'Yes, sir, although there were none when I thought I would not see my home again!'

'You were lucky,' the Earl said unemotionally. 'The quacks tell me I shouldn't touch this stuff,' he added, tilting the brandy glass to his lips with evident enjoyment, 'but it makes no odds now.'

'I expect it helps sometimes.'

The Earl gave him a sharp look. 'No fool, are you, boy? You know I'm dying. No...' he made a gesture as Guy shifted uncomfortably '...denials are for the women and the medical men. I know the truth. It's one of the reasons I wanted you back here.'

'Of course. You know that I will do anything in my power—'

The Earl put his glass down with a hand that was not quite steady. 'There is something I have to ask of you, Guy, a particular commission before you can come home for good and settle down. Set up your nursery, perhaps.' There was a glint of a smile. 'It pains me to send you away no sooner than you arrive, but I have no choice.'

Guy made a slight gesture, at a loss. 'Name your commission, sir. I will undertake it.'

'In a moment.' The Earl turned aside, picking a letter from the table at his elbow. 'Tell me, what is the nature of the quarrel between you and Miss Sarah Sheridan?'

Guy met his father's quizzical gaze. 'Forgive me, sir, but I do not wish to discuss it. It is...a personal matter.'

'I see,' the Earl said slowly. 'Can it be anything to do with her intention to return to her home at Blanchland? I take it that that is her destination tomorrow?'

Guy jumped. Some brandy spilled. From early childhood his father had had an uncanny knack of reading his mind and the young Guy had sometimes wondered whether the Earl had supernatural powers. Their eyes met. Guy had always found it impossible to lie to his father.

'Devil take it, sir, how can you possibly know that? I cannot believe that Miss Sheridan would have mentioned it—'

'She did not,' the Earl confirmed with a smile. 'In point of fact, she refused to tell me the difficulties that afflict your relationship. I take it that I am correct in thinking that you wish to marry the lady?'

Guy grinned reluctantly at his father's perspicacity. 'Yes, sir. You mentioned earlier that you wished to see me settle down... Well, almost as soon as I met Miss Sheridan I had such thoughts, for all that I had known her so short a while.' He shifted in his seat. 'They were thoughts quite alien to the lifestyle of a rake!'

'It happens to us all sooner or later,' his father said drily. 'But you quarrelled—over Blanchland?'

Guy shifted slightly again. 'More or less. I thought that her decision to go there reflected ill on her character and judgement. I said some terrible things to her, for which I am truly ashamed. When I had had chance to reconsider, I realised that I might have misjudged her, and apologised. But still she refuses to tell me the reason for her decision—'

'I believe that I may throw some light on that,' the Earl said, surprisingly. 'You had better read this letter now.'

Guy took the proffered sheets with a certain curiosity. He had no notion what to expect, but now he saw that it was in a gentleman's hand and read the signature as that of Francis Sheridan. He remembered Sarah telling him that her quest to Blanchland was in connection with her brother and frowned.

'But Frank Sheridan...'

'Yes, he has been dead these three years,' the Earl agreed readily. 'Unusual, is it not! There was a covering note from the lawyer...' He passed it over.

Julius Churchward's note was brief and to the point. A situation had arisen that had prompted him to send the enclosed letter to the Earl. He was confident that the letter from Lord Sheridan would be self-explanatory, but he felt that he should add that Miss Sarah Sheridan had also been given a letter from her late brother. He remained his lordship's humble servant, etcetera. Guy raised his eyebrows.

'As clear as day!'

The Earl laughed. 'Read the letter, Guy.'

Guy settled back in his chair and scanned the sheets with close interest.

Dear Sir

I am conscious that you will find it most odd in me to be communicating with you from beyond the grave, but I find I must. I am compelled to

contact you to ask that you do me a service, not
for my own sake—I know your feelings on that
matter only too well!—but for the sake of my sister, and indeed to aid your own grandchild.

Guy looked up, his gaze suddenly startled, but the
Earl's expression was hooded. 'Finish the letter, boy.'

At the time of writing, Miss Meredith is fifteen
years old and attending a seminary in Oxford. She
is a pretty, behaved girl who has never caused either myself or her adoptive parents any concern. I
have no reason to suppose that she will not progress from her school to make a suitable and entirely respectable marriage in the fullness of time.
I only wish I had the means to ensure it. Unhappily
I cannot. I am dying and I am aware that that will
leave Miss Meredith and her parents without the
security that my family has been able to provide,
albeit at a distance, for all of her life.

I could think of only one plan. I have instructed
Dr Meredith and his wife that if ever their daughter
is in great need, they should contact Julius Churchward. They are good people and I am persuaded
would only resort to this if the need was genuine
and severe. Once Churchward receives any com-
munication from them, he is to contact Sarah and
acquaint her with the problem.

I have thought much about asking my sister to
go to the aid of my natural daughter. It is most
irregular. I should, of course, have made the request to you directly, sir, but the truth is that I did
not dare. You made your feelings for me quite
plain all those years ago and even now I know that

you cannot forgive me.

But now I am beseeching you, for the sake of the love you bear Sarah as her godfather, to stand her friend. Her innate goodness will prompt her to do what is right, but she may be in need of protection. And I commend Miss Meredith to you as an innocent child who does not deserve to suffer for her father's faults. Forgive me for my presumption. I can only add that if you see fit to answer my request I will be forever thanking you for your kindness.

Francis Sheridan.

Guy put down the pages of closely written words and reached for the brandy decanter again.

'I see,' he said slowly. 'Miss Sheridan goes to Blanchland at her brother's request to aid his natural daughter.' He met his father's sardonic gaze. 'What do you wish to tell me about the detail of this letter, sir?'

The Earl gave a rueful shrug. 'How do you read it?'

Guy's gaze narrowed. 'That you have a grandchild whom, for reasons of which I am unaware, you have chosen not to acknowledge. To say that I am astounded would be to understate the case. And if Frank Sheridan was her father, then who—?'

'You have—you had—three sisters, Guy.'

'Yes, but—' Guy was aware that he sounded incredulous '—you imply that *Catherine* had Frank Sheridan's child? But she was only sixteen when she died... She died of a fever—'

'Childbirth fever,' the Earl said heavily. Suddenly he looked old and tired. 'You had no idea, Guy?'

'Not the least in the world!' Guy put his glass down. His head was spinning. He had only been twelve when

his elder sister had died and had never questioned that
the family tragedy had hidden a catastrophe of even
greater proportions. It seemed incredible.

'I can scarce believe it,' he said slowly. 'But
surely...I mean...could they not have married? Sheridan was wild, but he was not an unsuitable match.
Surely he would not have abandoned her!'

The Earl shook his head slowly. 'That is at the root
of the whole tragedy, Guy. Catherine did not tell anyone
until near the end and none of us even guessed. Looking
back I cannot believe that we were so blind, but it was
so. Oh, we knew that she had a *tendre* for him—Frank
Sheridan could charm the birds from the trees—but we
had no notion that it had gone any further! Why, she
was only sixteen and the sweetest child—' He broke
off. 'And by the time we found out, Sheridan had set
off on one of his harebrained trips abroad. The babe
was born and Catherine died whilst he was away.'

Guy stared into the glowing heart of the fire. 'What
happened when Frank Sheridan returned?'

The Earl's face was in shadow. 'There was the most
appalling scene, as you might imagine. He stood over
there—' the Earl nodded towards the fireplace '—paper-
white and shaking, and swore that he had not known,
that he would have married her. But, of course, it was
all too late. I called him a blackguard and a cad, and
threatened to have him horsewhipped from the house. I
never spoke to him again, to the day he died.'

'And the child?'

The Earl looked away. 'I am ashamed to say that I
allowed Jack Sheridan to take her away and to make all
the arrangements. I could not forgive her, innocent as
she was, for robbing us of our daughter's life. I knew
she was well provided for—Jack made sure of it, but to

my shame I never wanted to know more.' He cleared his throat. 'I believe that your mother would have acted differently, had I permitted it, but I was bitter and sick with anger. Even now, when this arrived—' he tapped the letter '—I was in two minds about how to act. I was tempted to burn it and forget about it for another seventeen years!'

'What made you change your mind, sir?'

'Two things,' the Earl said bleakly. 'Firstly, your mother told me plain that it was my bounden duty to help my goddaughter. And then, of course, Sarah arrived here.' He met his son's eyes. 'When I realised that she was prepared to do what I was not, for the sake of her brother's child, I felt ashamed. And also...' a smile warmed his voice for the first time '...she is all the things that Frank Sheridan was not. She is good and true and brave, and I do not believe we should let her go to Blanchland alone!'

Guy got up to put another log on the fire. He stirred it to a blaze before he replied. 'How much of this story do you think Miss Sheridan knows, sir?'

'Very little, I imagine,' the Earl said. 'Jack Sheridan swore that neither he nor his son would ever burden Sarah with the tale, nor do I think they would bring shame on Catherine's name in such a way. And that is why—' he leaned forward, suddenly urgent '—you must find Miss Meredith before Sarah ever sets eyes on her!'

Guy frowned. 'I collect that you do not wish Sarah to be aware of my sister's part in this?'

'Absolutely not! No one must ever know! It must remain a secret!'

Guy shook his head slowly. 'I do not like the sound

of this, sir. You must be more plain. What is it that you wish me to do?'

The Earl brought his fist down hard. 'Find the girl! Buy her off! Persuade her to go away! The difficulties she finds herself in may well be pecuniary and she may be open to persuasion! Do whatever you have to, to keep the matter a secret!'

Guy looked at his father in bafflement. 'You set me a strange task, sir,' he said wryly. 'I have never seen you act in such a way before. Are you sure that this is what you truly want? And as for deceiving the woman I wish to marry before the knot is even tied—it does not augur well for my future happiness!'

'And yet I must ask it of you, Guy,' his father said, fixing him with his fierce, dark gaze. 'It must be done. Catherine's memory must not be despoiled.'

They talked long into the night but Guy was unable to persuade his father to change his mind.

It was impossible to travel on to Blanchland the following morning. The rain of the previous day had frozen in deep ruts overnight, making the roads impassable.

'Another day and the frost will be hard enough for you to travel,' the Countess said cheerfully as she came to Sarah's room to acquaint her with the news. 'Or else it will thaw again and you can be on your way! But for the meantime, Sarah dear, I am very happy for you to prolong your stay!'

Sarah herself had mixed feelings. Having got so close to her destination, the waiting was hard to bear. Then there was the prospect of another day in Guy's company when she would far rather put some distance between them. And then there was the fact, which she would admit only to herself, that although half of her wanted to run away from him, the other half found him all too attractive.

She was spared Guy's company in the morning, however, for the gentlemen had gone out for an early ride and were not expected back before luncheon. Lady Woodallan, recognising a kindred spirit in Amelia, bore her off to inspect the still room, so Sarah was left to her own devices. This did not trouble her. She spent a happy hour reacquainting herself with Lord Woodallan's extensive library collection, then turned her attention to the glass cases containing an assortment of semi-precious stones that he had collected on his travels abroad. Here was the brilliant deep blue of the lapis lazuli that had so fascinated her as a child, the pale green of the peridot and the deep amber of the tiger's eye, flecked with gold.

The walls of the library were furnished with family portraits and Sarah paused on her way out to consider the large family grouping over the fireplace. Here was a younger Earl and Countess of Woodallan, smiling proudly as their four children played about their feet. Guy looked stiff and self-conscious in his child's velvet suit and Sarah smiled a little. His younger sisters Emma and Clara, the latter barely more than a baby, sat on the floor at their feet, but the eldest girl stood shyly by her mother's chair. She must have been a couple of years older than Guy, Sarah thought, and she looked grave but with a smile breaking through. Sarah frowned, trying to remember her name. Catherine. She had died when Sarah was only seven and Sarah had no clear memory of her.

Sarah moved on to pictures of Lady Emma and Lady Clara as debutantes, both fair-haired, brown-eyed and heartbreakingly lovely. The Woodallan looks were very distinctive, Sarah thought. She remembered them both with fondness as having a great sense of fun and thought with regret that it would have been very pleasant to accept Lady Woodallan's invitation and return for Christmas, when both daughters and their respective families were expected.

That, of course, was not the only proposal that had been made to her. And there to remind her was a portrait of Guy in his early twenties. The artist had captured brilliantly the wicked twinkle in those brown eyes and the unconsciously arrogant tilt to his chin. He looked strikingly handsome and Sarah's heart contracted a little.

She went out into the hall, closing the library door quietly behind her. The sun had come out and Sarah decided that she would take a walk before luncheon. She picked up her cloak, donned her boots and went out into the morning air.

A quick tour of the gardens took her through the parterre and downhill towards the fields that bordered the trout stream. Sarah leant over and dabbled her fingers in the crystal clear water, finding it icy. There was no danger of lingering outdoors today, for an easterly wind made Lady Woodallan's predictions of a hard frost seem very likely.

'Good morning, Miss Sheridan.' Sarah turned to see Guy leaning on a five-bar gate a few yards away. He must have moved very quietly; she had not heard his approach. 'Did you fancy sledging down the hill as we did as children?'

Sarah laughed. 'I do not believe there is sufficient snow, my lord! The last time we tried that there were drifts five foot deep!'

'I remember!' Guy pushed the gate open and strode through to join her. 'I borrowed a tray from the kitchen and found it ran faster than the proper sledge!'

'And you finished head down in a drift and Clara screamed and screamed because she thought you were dead!'

They laughed together.

'Perhaps we might try again when you return to Woodallan for Christmas,' Guy said, as they turned back towards the house. 'There is bound to be further snowfall before then. Indeed, I believe we are in for quite a cold snap!'

'So your mother was saying.' Sarah pushed her hands into the fur muff and shivered a little. 'I would not wish you to forget, however, that I have made no commitment to return for Christmas!'

'Of course.' Guy's smile was rueful. 'I am sorry, Miss Sheridan! It was my own hopes that were speaking! I do most ardently wish that you will stay a little at Woodallan after your quest to Blanchland is completed.'

'I shall see,' Sarah said cautiously. 'Shall we walk back, sir? It is too cold to tarry here!'

'By all means.' Guy fell into step beside her as they turned back up the hill. 'What are your impressions of Woodallan after all these years, Miss Sheridan? Does it bring back happy memories for you?'

Sarah paused. They were skirting a huge oak that stood alone in the middle of the meadow. In the summers long ago she had scrambled up into its spreading branches and sat feeling the sway of the tree in the breeze. Clara and Emma had been too scared to climb so high and Lady Sheridan had scolded her daughter for being a tomboy.

'Sometimes it is a mistake to go back, my lord.'

Guy's hand was on her arm. 'But if the past could also be the future, Miss Sheridan…?'

Sarah felt terribly tempted. To regain so much, to return to a place that held such happy memories… But the one thing that she really wanted—Guy's love—was not part of the bargain. His charm and kindness to her were dangerous, drawing her in again, stirring up feelings she wanted to forget, making her vulnerable. Many, more practical than she, would settle for such an advantageous marriage of convenience. Perhaps, Sarah thought, she might have done so herself were her feelings not engaged. But the thought of Guy with another woman in his arms made her feel quite sick. If she bore his name, she could not bear to lose him.

Sarah turned away abruptly and walked on.

'There is something I need to tell you, Miss Sheridan,' Guy said, after a moment. 'It concerns your trip to Blanchland. Would you care to discuss it here, or wait until we are back in the house?'

'Perhaps it would be better to talk as we walk back, my lord.'

'To avoid another uncomfortable tête-à-tête?' Guy gave her an ironic smile. 'Have no fear, Miss Sheridan! Even I am not so lost to all sense of propriety as to try to seduce you in my parents' house! However, if you wish, we shall talk of it now. The cold air is death to strong passion, after all!'

Sarah blushed angrily. 'Did you have some material point to make, my lord?'

'Indeed!' Guy stretched lazily, then drove his hands into his coat pockets. Sarah hastily averted her eyes. Such blatant masculinity at such close quarters was decidedly unsettling.

'I have to tell you that I am to accompany you to Blanchland,' Guy continued. He smiled at Sarah's evident annoyance. 'I am sorry, Miss Sheridan, but my father wills it so and I am sure you would not wish to disappoint him!'

'I thought that you said you would not tell your parents of my destination,' Sarah said crossly. She regarded him with suspicion. 'There is something very strange about this, my lord! Do you care to explain?'

'Very well,' Guy said obligingly. 'I believe that you received a letter from your late brother asking you to offer your aid to a certain young lady. The request necessitated you travelling to Blanchland. My father received a similar letter asking that he offer you all support in your search. Unfortunately he is too ill to undertake the obligation, so he has asked me to do so in his place. So I will be journeying to Blanchland with you, Miss Sheridan!' He held the gate open for her to walk through into the gardens. 'I am sure you cannot be pleased—'

'No, indeed! It is most unfortunate!'

Guy's ironic smile deepened. 'Thank you, Miss Sheridan!'

'Oh!' Sarah caught herself. 'Indeed, I am very grateful to Lord Woodallan for offering me assistance, but truly there is no need—'

'You waste your breath if you seek to dissuade me, Miss Sheridan,' Guy said drily. 'My father is adamant and I must do as he wishes.'

They walked on a little in silence. The winter wind was chill with an edge of sleet to it now.

'If you were to consult your own inclination rather than your duty—' Sarah began.

'Then the answer would still be the same. I am at your disposal!'

Sarah gave an angry sigh. 'Frank should not have burdened Lord Woodallan with such a commission!'

'I agree with you,' Guy said readily. 'I also believe that your brother must have felt he had placed you in an invidious position, not to say an irregular one! He was appealing to Lord Woodallan as your godfather and the person who could offer you protection. Had he known that Blanchland had become a house of ill fame I am persuaded he would never have laid such a charge on you!' He shrugged. 'As it is, I am astonished you accepted the obligation!'

Sarah pulled the brim of her bonnet closer about her face to protect her from the sting of the wind. 'I know it must seem most singular,' she admitted, 'and, to own the truth, I did not wish to do so! But Frank has asked it and the girl is my niece whether I like it or not, so...' Her voice trailed away. She was not sure whether she was glad or otherwise of Guy's support in the matter. Had it been Lord Woodallan, as Frank had intended, she would have accepted his help unequivocally. But Guy was a different matter and now Frank's actions had made it impossible for her to keep him at a distance.

'How do you intend to present your case to Sir Ralph?' Guy asked, watching lazily as doubt and worry chased each other swiftly across Sarah's expressive face. They were approaching the door of the house now. 'Do you intend to reveal the whole to him?'

Sarah bit her lip. Guy seemed to have a talent for hitting on precisely the matters that concerned her. She still had not decided how to tackle that problem, uncertain whether to take Sir Ralph into her confidence or not. Sarah's heart sank as she realised how ill prepared

she was for the whole venture. What thoughts she had
had since leaving Bath had been all to do with Guy
himself and nothing to do with Olivia Meredith at all!

'I have not really decided...' She knew she sounded
vague. 'I confess I need more time to fashion a tale...
Oh, dear,' she finished, despairing, 'was there ever such
an ill-thought-out enterprise!'

Guy's lips twitched. 'My dear Miss Sheridan, can I
not persuade you to change your mind, even at this
eleventh hour? Despite my reluctance, I am willing to
stand your friend and go to Blanchland on your behalf!'

For a moment, Sarah was tempted. To wash her
hands of the whole matter was very appealing, but she
had not persisted this far in order to turn back now.

'Thank you, sir. It is a generous offer, but I feel I
must go myself.'

'You are very obstinate, Miss Sheridan!' Without
warning, Guy stopped and took her hands in his. 'Obstinate, difficult, determined to cause a scandal—'

'I will thank you to be quiet, my lord!' Sarah was
pink with indignation. She dropped the muff and could
not free herself to pick it up again. 'Let me go! Someone will see us!'

Guy shrugged. 'Very probably! I cannot say that the
thought disturbs me!'

'Oh!' Sarah tried disengage herself again. Guy refused to let go.

'You yourself,' Sarah said furiously, 'are arrogant
and high-handed—'

'I believe you have already told me, Miss Sheridan!'
Guy was smiling down at her with the wicked amusement that always made Sarah's pulse race.

'If you are to accompany me to Blanchland, I trust
that you will behave with decorum, my lord!'

'I think that that is very unlikely. You had best be prepared for the worst!' Guy turned her hand over and pressed a kiss on the palm. 'Do not forget,' he said caressingly, 'that I still have to persuade you to accept my hand in marriage. I shall be doing my utmost to convince you!'

Sarah wrenched her hands away, knowing she was trembling violently. It was intolerable that he should have such an effect on her!

'Pray do not persist in this ridiculous jest, my lord! We both know you cannot mean it!'

'Never more serious, I assure you, Miss Sheridan! As I said yesterday, you will have time to become accustomed to the idea.' Guy was laughing at her. 'What you will not have is the chance to refuse me!'

Sarah drew breath for a scathing retort but broke off as the door swung open to reveal the butler, his expression as wooden as the door panels. 'Luncheon is served, my lord. Miss Sheridan,' he bowed politely, bending to retrieve the muff, 'allow me, madam—'

But he was talking to thin air. With a fulminating glance, Sarah had stalked off, leaving Guy still grinning as he watched her indignant figure walk out of sight.

After lunch the sleet turned to light snow that lay like icing across the parkland.

'Oh, how pretty!' Amelia exclaimed, as she stood by Sarah in the library and looked out across the hills. 'If it continues like this, I fear we may have to stay some time!'

Sarah looked exasperated. 'It is only five miles to Blanchland, Milly! If the worst comes to the worst, I shall walk there tomorrow!'

Amelia's face fell. 'Would you not prefer to stay at Woodallan, Sarah? It is so pleasant—'

'Of course I would rather stay here!' Sarah said crossly. 'How could I possibly favour Blanchland over this? The fact is that I have lost a week already since the letter arrived and—'

She broke off, remembering that Amelia was not party to the letter's contents. Amelia gave her a curious look.

'Is time a material factor then? I had not realised.'

'No, I am sorry.' Sarah looked shamefaced. 'I did not say...'

Amelia pressed her hand. 'Time enough for you to tell me all about it when you are ready.' She gave Sarah a penetrating look. 'I understand, however, that Lord Renshaw accompanies us?'

Sarah felt the telltale blush creep into her cheeks. 'So I am told. It was not at my instigation!'

Amelia raised her eyebrows. 'On his own inclination, then—'

'No!' Sarah realised she sounded too vehement and tried to calm down. 'That is, he tells me that Frank wrote to Lord Woodallan, asking him to help me in my quest. Unfortunately, the Earl is too ill to accompany us, so...' She shrugged.

'So Lord Renshaw comes instead!' Amelia frowned. 'Are you sure about this, Sarah? It sounds all a hum to me!'

Now it was Sarah's turn to frown. 'Whatever can you mean? Of course I am sure!'

'Only that it seems a little odd. I am not sure why, but...'

'Yet it must be so. Guy—Lord Renshaw,' Sarah corrected herself meticulously, 'knew of the purpose of my visit, and that can only have come from Frank's letter.'

Amelia shrugged lightly. 'As you say, my love. I must surely be making a mystery out of nothing!' She moved across to the writing box. 'Now, since it is not really the weather to go out, I shall write some letters.'

'I'll sit with you and read a book,' Sarah said, selecting one from the shelves. She settled in an armchair beside the roaring fire, and for a time there was no sound but for the pages turning softly and the scratch of Amelia's nib on the paper. Sarah, however, was hardly concentrating. Amelia's words had raised some doubts in her mind, yet she was unsure what it was that disturbed her. Never mind—tomorrow she would reach Blanchland at last and unravel the mystery of Olivia Meredith.

Dinner was another very pleasant meal and was followed by charades and card-playing before bedtime. Lady Woodallan was chatting to Amelia as they ascended the stairs and it was completely by chance that Sarah, trailing a little behind, heard the conversation between father and son in the hall below.

'You have told her that you will go, then,' Lord Woodallan was saying as he lit the remaining candles to see them up to bed.

'I have, sir.' Guy sounded a little grim.

'But not the rest? Not about—?'

'No. It is as you wished.'

'Good.' Woodallan sounded relieved. 'Then you will see to it, Guy. Find Miss Meredith—and make sure that Miss Sheridan does not—'

Guy glanced up at that moment and Sarah shrank back into the darkness at the top of the stairs. Her mind was racing as she puzzled over what she had heard. So what Guy had told her was true, but only up to a point—his father did want him to accompany her to Blanchland, but not simply to give her his aid! Apparently he had his own reasons for wishing to find Olivia, and she was not to be made aware of them...

'Sarah!' Amelia called, a little impatiently. 'Where are you? I am waiting to say goodnight!'

She yawned widely as Sarah hurried up the remaining few steps, then gave her cousin an affectionate peck on the cheek. 'Sleep well, my love!'

But Sarah tossed and turned for over an hour as she tried to work out what connection the Woodallan family might have with Olivia Meredith and, more importantly, why she should not be privy to it. Her musings shed no light, however, and in the end she fell asleep, to dream that she was chasing a fair-haired girl across the park at Blanchland, but, just before she reached her, the girl disappeared.

Chapter Six

Blanchland stood on the top of a rise, surrounded on three sides by a woodland of tall pines. As the carriage drew nearer, all the occupants could see that it was a supremely elegant house of pinkish stone with a small gold cupola on the roof, where Lord Sheridan had once housed the telescope he had used for astronomical observations. In the morning sunlight, with the bright white fields as a backdrop, it looked very beautiful.

Just seeing the house again almost brought tears to Sarah's eyes. She blinked hard to keep them at bay and set her mouth in a determined line.

'I had almost forgot how pretty it is...'

They drove through Blanchland village, huddled at the bottom of the hill, and started the climb to the gates of the house. It was very quiet. The frost glittered in the sun but no one moved in the still landscape. Sarah repressed a shiver.

She knew that Guy was watching her and the sympathy she could see in his eyes made her feel dangerously close to breaking down. As Amelia leant forward to speak to Greville, forgetting for a moment her antipathy to him, Guy bent close to Sarah and touched her gloved hand. The fleeting contact gave her both comfort and confusion.

All had gone to plan that morning. They had left Woodallan early, sped on their way with the Earl and Countess's good wishes and pressing invitations to return for Christmas. The Earl had shaken Guy's hand and wished him luck, and Sarah had searched the face of both men for some clue to Guy's secret errand at Blanchland, but there was nothing. Her doubts gnawed at her and added to her disquiet, but there was nothing she could do until the time Guy chose to tell her—or she dared to ask him.

Now that she had almost arrived, Sarah was prey to mixed feelings. Just seeing her old home again was emotional enough, but she was apprehensive as to what she might find there. Would Sir Ralph have ruined it beyond repair? Would he throw them all out into the snow—or worse, would he be indulging in some loathsome orgy? There was only one way to find out...

The silence, as they drew up on the forecourt, was almost sinister. All the windows of the house were shuttered and nothing stirred.

'Perhaps no one is at home,' Amelia said hopefully. 'It seems deserted. Perhaps we should go back to Woodallan—'

'We only left there a half-hour ago!' Sarah said firmly. She stepped forward and rang the bell hard. They all heard it echo distantly before the silence settled again. The horses stamped impatiently on the gravel and Sarah jumped. Her nerves were on edge and she knew she was not the only one. Greville was looking grim and exchanged a quizzical look with Guy, and Amelia was shivering and peering around fearfully, as though she expected satyrs to jump out of the nearby bushes.

'Oh, good, there is no one here! Let us go at once! Sarah—'

Sarah turned the door knob. The door was not locked and opened with a creak of protesting hinges that sounded loud in the morning quiet. Amelia gave a little shriek.

'Oh, how Gothic! I declare, I will not set foot inside!'

'Then pray wait in the cold!' Sarah snapped, her nerves getting the better of her. 'Gentlemen? Will you accompany me?'

Greville and Guy followed her over the threshold and after a moment so did Amelia, who clearly preferred not to be left alone. Inside the house it was almost as cold as in the open air. Sarah could see her breath crystallise on the air before her.

All the windows were shuttered and the hall was deep in darkness. She could just see the cobwebs that festooned the ornate central chandelier and the thick dust on the tiled floor. There was a stale smell in the air, the scent of dirt and decay. Sarah shivered violently.

'It is scarce welcoming...'

'Most quelling,' Guy agreed. He strode forward and flung open a few doors. 'Hello! Is anybody there?'

His voice echoed strangely around the high ceilings, but there was no reply. Amelia gave a little shriek. 'Oh, my goodness! How disgusting!'

She was staring with fascination at a lewd statue of two entwined lovers raised on a plinth at the side of the hall. Their entangled limbs and suggestive expressions were grossly indecent. Sarah looked away hastily.

'You are fortunate if that is all you find to offend you here, Lady Amelia,' Greville said drily. 'Since you have chosen to come here of your own free will, I beg you not to give way to missish vapours!'

Amelia fired up at once. 'Pray do not be so ungentlemanly, sir—'

Sarah put her hands over her ears. She was not sure that she could stand their wrangling at that moment and evidently someone else felt the same.

'God's teeth!' a voice roared from the top of the stairs. They all spun round. A huge man in straining waistcoat and breeches, a monstrous bedcap still perched on his balding head, was standing staring down on them. He clutched his head and gave a groan.

'Madam, I must ask you to desist from that shrill cacophony! A termagant female is more than flesh and blood can stand!'

Sir Ralph Covell, for it could only be he, did not cut an attractive figure. His embroidered waistcoat strained over an ample stomach and his little blue eyes peered suspiciously from beneath heavy black eyebrows. His complexion was high, suggesting a choleric temperament and his voice loud enough to shake the windows. Sarah, feeling a sudden rush of apprehension, wondered if he was about to throw them all out of the house without another word.

Then, miraculously, Sir Ralph's face broke into a smile of startling sweetness. He hurried down the stairs towards her, arms outstretched.

'Well, if it isn't little cousin Sarah! My, my, child, how you've changed! And what a pleasure to see you again!'

He came forward, enfolding a stunned Sarah in a bear hug. 'I never thought to see you at Blanchland again, my dear, but you are very welcome in your old home!'

Sarah, released with all the breath crushed out of her, found herself struggling to form a suitable response. Only five minutes previously she had been racking her brains to think of a way to explain her presence at Blanchland. She had imagined Sir Ralph unwelcoming at best and most probably downright hostile. This bon-homie was as startling as it was unexpected. She caught Guy's amused gaze on her and realised that he was trying not to laugh. Seeing her lost for words, he stepped forward, holding out a hand.

'How do you do, Sir Ralph? I am Guy Renshaw— we have met in London, but several years back. I must apologise for our intrusion in your house—'

'No intrusion at all, sir!' Sir Ralph had seized Guy's hand and was pumping it energetically. 'My cousin is always welcome here and any friends of hers can only be my honoured guests!' He bustled over to the windows and started to throw the shutters back with gusto. 'That's better! Let the dog see the rabbit!'

His smiling gaze swept round to encompass Greville and Amelia, both of whom Sarah thought were looking as stunned as she felt.

'Greville Baynham!' Ralph beamed. 'Remember you from that club in Bath last year! Now, what was its name…?'

Greville cleared his throat, looking discomposed for the first time. 'Sir Ralph. May I make you known to my betrothed, Lady Amelia Fenton?'

This time, Amelia did not argue with him, but dropped a little curtsy. She was looking quite bewildered. Sir Ralph smiled sunnily. 'Delighted, my dear, delighted! Would be more delighted if you could speak in a slightly softer tone, though! My head this morning, don't you know…' He turned back to Sarah, a slight frown marring his brow.

'Sarah, my dear, you are most welcome to visit, as I hope I have made clear! However, there is one small problem...' Sir Ralph came to an unhappy stop and rubbed his hands together with undoubted embarrassment. A deeper shade of red came over his already puce countenance. He looked like a schoolboy caught out in some unfortunate escapade. He stumbled on. 'You see...you may not be aware... I hold small house parties here every so often...my revels, as I like to call them—'

'Indeed, sir, I am aware.' Sarah tried not to smile as she wondered how her cousin would broach this delicate subject. It was proving extremely difficult to dislike Ralph, for he seemed as eager to please as an overgrown puppy.

'Ah, good.' Sir Ralph looked gratified. 'Good! I rather thought that my parties were getting a name for themselves! How agreeable! But—' he suddenly seemed to recall the problem '—I am not at all certain, however, that they are the sort of affairs for a gently bred young lady! There are gentlemen, you know, and ladies of...ah...' He floundered to a halt.

'Dubious virtue?' Guy supplied, helpfully.

'Oh, you mean Cyprians!' Sarah said heartily. 'Why, yes, cousin Ralph, I have heard all about them!'

Ralph looked slightly winded. 'You have?' He recovered himself a little. 'But perhaps you did not realise—there are masques and plays, and a pagan ceremony to celebrate the winter solstice—'

'I will not regard it,' Sarah said blithely, ignoring Amelia's look of horror and Guy's amusement. 'If you are happy for me to be your guest, cousin Ralph, I will only thank you for your generosity!'

Ralph frowned again. It was obvious that his mind was currently too befuddled to unravel the puzzle before him. 'I find it most singular that you were aware of

Blanchland's reputation yet still chose to come here!' he said at last, clearly puzzled. 'I do not like to criticise, Sarah, my dear, but I do not feel it is at all the way for a young lady to go on! Why, like as not you will find yourself with your reputation in tatters! I do feel you should show a little more concern!'

Sarah dropped a meek curtsy. 'I am persuaded that you are correct, cousin Ralph! Mama always said that I had no decorum! I am so very sorry if I have shocked you!'

Now it was Sir Ralph's turn to appear lost for words. 'I do not expect that you will be staying long…' he said hopefully.

'Oh, no!' Sarah agreed with a blithe smile. 'It is simply that Frank asked me to conduct a little business in the neighbourhood, but I expect that I shall be gone directly! And do not worry that I will disturb you, cousin Ralph! I shall be so quiet you will scarce know I am here!'

She heard Guy laugh and smother it with a cough.

'Well, then…' Sir Ralph seemed a little at a loss, clearly uncertain how to deal with his unorthodox relative. 'Well, then,' he said again, lamely, 'you will need rooms, I suppose, and refreshment…' His shoulders slumped as though the thought of it was almost too much. 'I will call Marvell. Marvell is my general factotum…' he glanced at the clock '…if he is from his bed… Pray excuse me! No way to greet ladies… If you would care to wait in the drawing-room, I shall see you are served with coffee! Join you shortly…' And he hurried off, bellowing for the servants.

'What an odd man,' Amelia said, casting another doubtful glance at the statues as she followed Sarah into the drawing-room, 'but he seems quite harmless! Perhaps we shall find that the Blanchland revels have been quite overrated!'

Sarah would have liked to agree, but she had seen the wry look that had flashed between Guy and Greville, a look that said louder than any words that their troubles were only beginning.

'It's quite disgusting!' Amelia said indignantly later, throwing herself down on Sarah's bed and causing a huge dust cloud to rise into the air.

'I know, Milly—' Sarah sneezed and averted her eyes from the garish painting of naked nymphs cavorting in a stream that hung above the bed '—but you were aware of what it would be like here.'

Amelia looked blank. 'Oh, no, I did not mean the picture! No, the dust! Everywhere! These curtains are filthy and my room cannot have been cleaned for an age! I shall speak to the housekeeper immediately after luncheon!'

'I feel we may be fortunate to have any luncheon,' Sarah said drily. She thought about unpacking her trunk and decided against it. There really was nowhere clean to put all her clothes. 'I doubt that Sir Ralph's guests will arise before this afternoon and I am not even sure that there is a housekeeper here any more! Certainly Mrs Lambert left after my brother died and I do not imagine Sir Ralph finds it easy to keep servants...'

'He certainly does not keep any good ones!' Amelia opined, running her finger along the dust on the bed-head. 'Look at this, Sarah! I would have plenty to say to my servants if this was the state of my house! And as for that undrinkable coffee...'

'It is still a beautiful place, though,' Sarah said, a little wistfully. She was standing at the window, looking out across the rolling Somerset hills. Beyond the ring of woodland, the fields tumbled away towards the village and beyond. It gave one the impression of standing on top of the world.

'Yes,' Amelia said, her tone softening, 'it is indeed a lovely house and it is a crime that it should have been allowed to become so neglected.' She brightened. 'I was wondering what I should do with myself whilst you were about your mysterious quest, my love! Well, now I have my answer! I shall bring order and cleanliness to Blanchland!'

Sarah raised a mental eyebrow at the thought of Amelia sweeping through the house like a new broom. She rather thought that Sir Ralph would be terrified at the prospect.

'You will tell me what all this mystery is about once it is resolved, will you not?' Amelia asked, a little plaintively, tracing the pattern on the bedspread. 'I know it is a personal matter, but I do so dislike secrets!'

'Of course!' Sarah touched her cousin's hand. 'I am sorry to be so secretive, Milly—it is only the fact that the tale is not really mine to tell that holds me back!'

'Sir Ralph did not seem very curious,' Amelia observed thoughtfully. 'I am surprised he did not press you more on the reasons for your presence here!'

'I think he was too embarrassed,' Sarah said, with a giggle. 'Poor Ralph, I believe he thinks we will put a blight on his revels!'

'Well, we may try!' Amelia got to her feet. 'Sarah, I have been thinking about Lord Renshaw's purpose in accompanying us. I know that you said that the Earl decreed it, but are you sure that it is not also because Guy wishes to be near you? It seems to me that his lordship is intent on pursuit—of one description or another!'

Sarah knew that a telltale blush burned her cheek. She was not sure whether it would be worse to tell Amelia the truth about Guy's proposal or distract her by sharing what she had overheard the previous night. But that would involve too many explanations; besides, she knew that Amelia's real interest lay in the romantic aspect of the case.

'Well...Lord Renshaw has made me an offer, Milly, but it is not at all as you imagine!'

Amelia looked understandably bewildered. 'An offer? But not as I imagine? Pray, how do you think I am imagining it, Sarah?'

'No, I mean, it is not at all romantic—' Sarah struggled, aware that she was making a mull of things. 'That is, Lord Renshaw offered me the protection of his name in much the same way as Greville offered for you! Now you understand me?'

'Oh, I see!' Amelia's brow cleared. 'It seems to me that the gentlemen have been suffering an excess of chivalry,' she added, in an acerbic tone. 'What was your answer, Sarah?'

'I told him that he need not put himself to the trouble! I dare say I was not very gracious, but I thought his actions high-handed and arrogant—'

'He was not, then, proposing because of his behaviour to you the night of the ball?' Amelia asked delicately. 'If he realised that he had mistreated an innocent girl—'

Sarah blushed vividly. 'No! He did mention the... incident, but said...' she hesitated '...that he regretted all the things he had said, but he did not regret what he had done!'

'Well, that's honest at least!' Amelia laughed. 'Why did you not accept him, Sarah? You know you have a *tendre* for him—'

'I do not!' Sarah said hotly. She met her cousin's amused gaze and added, a little shamefacedly, 'I'll admit that he is a prodigiously attractive man and I might have had a small partiality for him before, but that is quite at an end! Why, there are a dozen reasons to refuse him! I think him altogether too presumptuous and sure of his own charm! And you of all people should understand, Amelia, for Greville's overbearing behaviour did not find favour with you!'

Amelia pursed her lips, distracted as Sarah had intended her to be. 'No, indeed! To announce to all and sundry that we were betrothed! It quite puts me out of patience! And it is very out of character!'

'Yes.' Sarah regarded her cousin thoughtfully. 'Yet it is odd, for you have been always blaming Greville for being too courteous! It seems he cannot do right in your eyes!'

Now it was Amelia's turn to look away in confusion. 'Well, you must allow that he is generally a very amiable gentleman! I thought him so amiable that he was almost dull!'

'Yet for all your protests I believe you find this display of autocratic behaviour rather attractive,' Sarah said shrewdly. 'You had best be quick if you wish to stake your claim, Amelia! I believe some of the ladies at this houseparty might find him attractive, too!'

Luncheon proved to be the disappointment that Sarah had suspected. There was only herself and Amelia present, for the gentlemen had apparently gone out for a ride and Sir Ralph's guests had still not put in an appearance.

'I dare say they have ridden over to Woodallan for a square meal!' Amelia said darkly. 'It is the outside of enough! First they force their company on us and then they promptly disappear!'

They rang the bell several times and finally a slatternly maid appeared who seemed amazed to be asked to provide some food. An inordinate amount of time later, she returned with a plate of stale bread and smelly cheese, slapped it down on the table and strode out again.

'Monstrous!' Amelia said, two bright spots of outrage burning in her cheeks. 'The sooner I take matters into my own hands, the better!'

Sarah nibbled a crust of bread, forced down a little of the cheese, then went to fetch her cloak. She had resolved to set off immediately on her quest to find Olivia and, as Guy was out of the way, it seemed a good opportunity. She did not want him dogging her footsteps, and if she was able to steal a march over him, so much the better. Perhaps, if she was really lucky, she would find Olivia at once and they could all escape from this awkward situation.

The path down to Blanchland village was muddy where the sun had melted the snow. Water dripped from the bare branches of the overhanging trees and Sarah picked her way with care, huddling in her cloak against the cold. She had walked that path many a time when she was a child and enjoyed passing all the sites she remembered from then: the hollow tree where she had played hide-and-seek, the stile over the hedge into Farmer Burton's field, where once she had been chased by a bull, the old tumbledown gatehouse… Sarah sighed

over her memories, picked up her skirts where the mud
was an inch deep, and entered the main street of the
village.

She noticed a change at once. Blanchland village was
only small, one main road with houses on either side,
but it had always been a bustling community. Now,
however, half of the cottages looked either empty or
neglected, the land overgrown with weeds and the re-
taining walls tumbling into the street. There was no sign
of life except for the smithy, from where the clang of
hammer on iron could be heard.

The doctor's house was the only residence of any size
in the village, set back a little from the road, with a
modest carriage sweep before it and neatly tended gardens all around. Sarah rang the bell, but there was no
answer. She had hardly expected to find Olivia Meredith
at home, but hoped that her mother or even a servant
might be present to give some information. However,
the house had a closed and shuttered air very similar to
Blanchland and there was something watchful about its
silence. Sarah tiptoed through the shrubbery and round
the back, and peered in at the scullery window, but there
was no sign of life. Then, something moved behind her.
She saw the reflection on the glass and spun round with
a gasp of alarm. An old man, clutching a garden hoe in
a vaguely threatening manner, was standing right behind her.

'B'aint no one 'ere, miss, so it would be best that
you go...'

'I am looking for Mrs Meredith,' Sarah said haughtily, feeling embarrassed at being caught prying. 'Pray
tell me, will she be home soon?'

'No,' the old man said. He offered no further information and waggled the hoe at her. 'Best to leave, ma'am!'

Sarah raised her eyebrows at the threatening tone and the fierce light in the man's blue eyes. Somehow his antagonism made her want to stand her ground. 'And Miss Meredith? Is she at home?'

'No,' the man said again. 'Powerful many folks looking for Miss Meredith these days!' He shifted slightly. 'Now then, ma'am, I'm sure you would not like me to call the constable—'

'I should like it above all things,' Sarah said crossly, 'so that I may tell him how unwelcoming you are to visitors here in Blanchland! Why, in my father's day no one would have spoken thus! What has happened to turn this place so unfriendly?'

The old man lowered his hoe slowly, peering at her from beneath his thatch of white hair. 'And who might you be then, ma'am?' He took a step forward. 'Never Miss Sarah come back to us!'

Recognition struck Sarah at the same time. 'Tom! I am so sorry! I did not recognise you! Why, it must be fifteen years—'

'Fourteen and a half,' the old man said, 'since I left Blanchland. And two since I came back. Aye, and a mistake that was good and all!'

Sarah sat down on the garden wall and gestured to him to join her. Tom Brookes had been the head groom at Blanchland when she had been a little girl, but had left when Sarah was nine years old to join his brother in running an inn down in Devon. Evidently the venture had not worked out.

'What happened to the inn, Tom?' Sarah asked sympathetically. She knew that he had sunk all his savings into it.

'Locals didn't like the competition,' Tom said morosely. 'Lot of trouble, Miss Sarah, so in the end I came home. Went to the big house, but Sir Ralph wasn't taking on staff, not even those who'd worked for the family before. No horses anymore, neither.' He spat on the path. 'Begging your pardon, Miss Sarah, but the house ain't the same as it used to be. No one takes care of it—no one wants to work there neither, with the things that go on! Shocking, it is. No...' he shook his head '...it was the worst of all times when the old lord died.'

'The village seems as bad,' Sarah said. 'Why, it is deserted! I would scarce have recognised it! What happened to the school, Tom?'

'Closed. I misremember when. But it's a bad business...'

'And Mrs Meredith—has she left, too? I know that the doctor died a few years back, but I thought that his wife and daughter continued to live here?'

Tom was watching her thoughtfully with his very blue eyes. Sarah had the suspicion that he was nowhere near as simple as he was pretending to be.

'Mrs Meredith's gone to stay with her sister near Glastonbury,' he said, in his thick Somerset burr. 'I don't know when she'll be back, Miss Sarah, and that's a fact.'

'And Miss Meredith?' Sarah persisted. She had a feeling that there was something he was not telling her. 'You said that lots of people were looking for her?'

'Aye.' Tom threw away the piece of grass he had been chewing and straightened up. 'Powerful few. And all of them gentlemen. Always gentlemen asking after Miss Olivia! First some young gentleman that's staying at the big house, then a lord that's a friend of Sir Ralph...' he looked as though he was about to spit

again, but thought better of it '...and today a mighty
fine gentleman with his London clothes and his gold...'

A small shiver went down Sarah's spine. 'A gentleman from London?'

'Oh, no, Miss Sarah! London clothes, London manners, but...' Tom hesitated. 'Mrs Anthrop said as he was
from Woodallan, and she should know, for her daughter's in service there now that there's no work at the
big house!'

Sarah frowned. So Guy had already been asking
questions in the village! In fact, he had deliberately mis-
led her by telling her he was going out riding when he
was actually looking for Olivia. Sarah's eyes narrowed.
She had been right to be suspicious last night. Lord
Woodallan and his son were pursuing some secret quest
of their own!

Sarah stood up and shook out her skirts. She could
not afford to lose any time in the hunt, or Guy would
get there first!

'Gave me some money,' Tom was saying, with a dis-
paraging sniff, 'and told me to tell no one he was asking. But as it's you, Miss Sarah...'

Sarah smiled. 'Thank you, Tom. Miss Meredith must
be very pretty, I suppose,' she added, 'to be so admired.
She was a lovely little girl—'

'Aye,' Tom said grudgingly, 'a proper lady is Miss
Meredith! And well to a pass, like you, Miss Sarah!
How comes it that you're not married?'

'I fear I am too particular,' Sarah said, and heard the
old man laugh for the first time. 'Well, I had best be
going if Miss Meredith is not at home. But, Tom—'
She stopped, suddenly struck by a thought. 'If you see
her, pray tell her that I was looking for her.' She gave
him a very straight look. 'And if she is in any need of

help, please let her know that I will stand her friend. Indeed, I am here for that very purpose!'

The old man touched his cap. 'I'll be sure and do that, Miss Sarah. If I see her.'

Sarah nodded. 'Thank you. Good day, Tom!'

The old man watched her walk away though the shrubbery, but when she was gone, he did not return to his hoeing.

Out in the main street Sarah hesitated, but could see no other purpose than to return to Blanchland. It was dispiriting, for she had hoped for some clue to Olivia's whereabouts, but it seemed that there was nothing further she could learn. And yet she had really learned quite a lot. She walked slowly along the village street, thinking. She now knew that Olivia was pretty and much sought after. Could that be the source of her problems? If one of the gentlemen from the house had taken a fancy to her, it could spell trouble for a provincial doctor's daughter, especially one with no male relatives to protect her. Sarah frowned. Tom had said that there was a young gentleman and a lord at the house who had both been asking after Olivia. No doubt they were both Ralph's guests and she would meet them later.

And she had also learnt that Guy had been asking questions—and paying for silence... As though in answer to her thoughts, she saw the familiar bay stallion tied up outside the smithy and, as she watched, Guy's tall figure emerged into the street. He turned for a parting word with the smith and some money changed hands, which the smith slid hastily into his apron. Sarah hesitated, in two minds as to whether to avoid him, but it was too late. He had seen her.

'Miss Sheridan! Taking an afternoon stroll?'

'Lord Renshaw.' Sarah knew she sounded cold. She

could not help it, harbouring the suspicions she did. Guy raised an amused eyebrow.

'Dear me, have I done something to offend you, Miss Sheridan? Something else?' He looped the reins over his arm and fell into step beside her. 'Have you had any success in your enquiries?'

'No,' Sarah said. She looked him straight in the eyes. 'Have you, my lord?'

'Ah.' A rueful smile curled Guy's mouth. 'It seems you have had *some* success, Miss Sheridan! You know, for instance, that I have been making enquiries of my own!'

'Indeed! Money buys much, my lord,' Sarah said sweetly, 'but old loyalties are worth more!'

'So it seems!' Guy still seemed rueful. He looked down at her and the expression in his eyes made her heart skip a beat. 'I can understand why you command such loyalty, Miss Sheridan! Do you not trust me, then?'

'No,' Sarah said, surprised and disturbed to find that it was true.

Guy laughed. 'You may do so. I swear that I would never do anything to hurt you, Sarah!'

'That is not the point, my lord,' Sarah objected, trying to ignore the fact that he had addressed her by her given name, and in so caressing a tone that she found it difficult to concentrate. 'You have not answered my question! Why have you been asking after Miss Meredith?'

Guy shrugged. He gaze was clear and untroubled. 'I thought to spare you some effort! If I were to find her first, you would have no need to make enquiries and we could all go home! That is all!'

There was a silence. Sarah did not believe him and

she felt hollow with hurt at his duplicity. She had given him the chance to confide and he had deliberately chosen not to do so...

'Penny for your thoughts, Miss Sheridan,' Guy said lightly.

'Oh—' Sarah looked away in confusion '—they are not worth half that, my lord! I was merely reflecting on the differences in the village since my father's time.'

Guy did not challenge her although she had the uncomfortable feeling that he did not believe her. Sarah knew that they both felt that the other was withholding something, but they fell to talking about Blanchland, a topic that lasted all the way back to the house and which both of them knew was assumed over more important preoccupations.

There was a different smell in the entrance hall at Blanchland when they got back, a mixture of beeswax and fresh flowers. Sarah stopped and stared. The terra-cotta-and-black-tiled floor was shining and the white marble pillars, no longer festooned with cobwebs, glowed softly in the light. Guy whistled.

'What a remarkable transformation! And so quickly! Your handiwork, Lady Amelia?'

Amelia was standing by the stairs, sleeves rolled up to her elbows, an old apron over her dress. Beside her was a small maid, clutching a polishing cloth and looking terrified. Amelia smiled.

'That's very good, Mary.' She turned to Guy and Sarah. 'I have only made a start on a few of the rooms, but Mary tells me she has two sisters who can come in to help tomorrow! And it does look much better, does it not?'

'The flowers?' Sarah questioned, wondering where

her cousin had found such luscious blooms in the winter.

Amelia beamed. 'Why, they are from your father's hothouses, Sarah! Of course, it is all going to rack and ruin, but Mary tells me an old man called Tom comes in to tend to them sometimes—'

From the staircase came the tread of someone descending. Amelia looked up, closed her lips in a straight, disapproving line, and whisked the small maid through the door to the servants' quarters without another word, rather in the manner of a fairy godmother. Sarah raised her eyebrows.

'Well, well! What have we here?'

The voice was oily. When Sarah looked up at the man standing on the half-landing, she thought there was something altogether too unwholesome and greasy about him. Tall and thin, he was dressed all in black, with a quizzing glass on a gold chain about his neck. She guessed that he was about forty years of age, but the look in his eyes, at once knowing and weary, suggested that he had seen enough for a lifetime. This, then, must be the first of Sir Ralph's guests, and perhaps even one of Olivia's suitors.

'The Honourable Miss Sheridan, I presume!' the man said, smiling in a somewhat predatory manner. His pointed chin jutted like the beak of a bird of prey. He reached the bottom of the stairs and bowed. 'We heard of your arrival. Delighted to meet you, my dear! Edward Allardyce, at your service.'

Lord Allardyce stepped forward and raised Sarah's hand to his lips. His mouth was wet against her skin. His black, knowing eyes appraised her thoroughly. 'Such a pleasure to meet unsullied innocence after a stay in this house!'

Sarah felt Guy stiffen beside her. His face looked as though it had been carved from stone. He gave the slightest of bows, so slight it was almost an insult.

'Allardyce.'

'Renshaw!' Lord Allardyce did not appear to have noticed Guy's frosty tone. 'A pleasure to see you again, old fellow!' He shot a look at Sarah. 'I believe you had that delicious opera singer in keeping when last we met in London! Good to see that your taste has improved!'

Guy's mouth tightened. 'Miss Sheridan is my father's goddaughter and I am here in his place to assist her in some family matters,' he said tightly. 'I do not anticipate that Miss Sheridan will wish to remain any longer than is absolutely necessary!'

'I should think not!' Allardyce gave an affected shudder. His black eyes gleamed. 'The place is filthy and the food atrocious! Assure you, I was about to leave myself when Miss Sheridan's arrival made everything so much more interesting!'

Guy took a step forward. Sarah could feel his tension, tight as a bow about to snap.

'I don't believe you heard me, Allardyce—'

For a moment the other man hesitated, then he laughed. 'I heard you, Renshaw. The irreproachable Miss Sheridan is out of bounds—to both you and I!' He turned and strolled away with deliberate provocation. 'Too bad! But there is plenty more sport in this house, when all is said and done!'

There was an expression of almost murderous fury on Guy's face. He took a step after the departing figure, but Sarah put her hand on his arm to restrain him.

'Do not! It is not worth it!'

For a second Guy looked so angry Sarah thought he

had not even heard her, then his expression softened and he covered her hand with his for a brief moment.

'I beg your pardon, Miss Sheridan. I wish you had not had to hear that.'

'It is nothing, my lord,' Sarah said a little shakily. 'I believe I shall have to hear worse if I remain at Blanchland!'

'Yes—' Guy's expression was brooding '—that may well be true! But I do beg you to be careful of Allardyce, Miss Sheridan. He is...' Guy hesitated '...a deeply offensive man and not one with whom you should ever associate!'

Sarah wondered whether that was why Amelia had hurried the little maid away so abruptly and, as she went up the stairs to prepare for dinner, she could not help but speculate again whether it had been Lord Allardyce who had been asking after Olivia. She shivered, remembering his unctuous voice and greasy manner. And Allardyce was only the first of Ralph's guests that they had met! She could not help but wonder what on earth the others would be like.

Amelia's influence had not yet reached the food and dinner was an unpalatable meal redeemed only by the quality of the wine. It had quickly become apparent to Sarah that Sir Ralph's guests could only visit for two reasons—the Blanchland wine cellar and, presumably, the entertainment Ralph provided with his revels. Neither was a good enough reason to draw her to Blanchland, but his guests were a different kettle of fish.

The houseparty were an oddly assorted mixture, a group who apparently had only their interest in the revels in common. Sir Ralph himself appeared to be directing his amorous attentions towards a Mrs Eliza Fisk, whose husband was also present but seemed to be asleep most of the time. Mrs Fisk was decidedly fat and past the first flush of youth, but Sir Ralph evidently liked plenty to get hold of.

There were two other ladies, of dubious age, status and virtue: Lady Tilney, who had transferred her attentions from Lord Allardyce to Greville Baynham with alacrity, and Lady Ann Walter, a statuesque blonde, who was eyeing Guy with feline speculation. Lord Allardyce did not seem unduly disappointed by Lady Tilney's defection, for he was seated next to Sarah at dinner and was making a great fuss of her. His attentions made Sarah feel faintly sick and very wary. Amelia, meanwhile, was busy charming a young man who looked barely out of leading reins and was quite obviously dazzled by her.

'Young Justin Lebeter,' Allardyce said, following Sarah's gaze. 'He has a doting mama, a lazy trustee and more money than sense, which accounts for his presence here! It is shocking to see the young fall into such bad company!' The malicious twist to his thin mouth suggested that he really found the corruption of innocence rather amusing. 'Perhaps Lady Amelia may save him—she is rather high in the instep, is she not?'

Sarah chose not to reply. She was already feeling decidedly vulnerable in this disreputable company. There was nothing openly licentious about their behaviour, but an unpleasant undertone to the conversation, an innuendo that could not be ignored, made the whole experience very uncomfortable. Added to this was an air of suppressed excitement, as though it was only a matter of time before the façade of civility cracked to reveal the lechery beneath.

Sarah applied herself to the mock turtle soup, but it

was stone cold and tasted of little but salt. It was impossible to force it down. Her eyes seemed drawn by some curious magnetism to the frieze of nude characters that cavorted around the room. Everywhere one turned there were images of lewdness in the worst possible taste, with some truly shocking cartoons framed on the wall. Sarah felt the colour rising to her cheeks and hastily looked away.

Lord Allardyce viewed her discomfort with amusement. He allowed his appreciative gaze to linger on Sarah's figure, taking in the demure high-necked evening gown, the neatly coiled hair and the modest shawl. His smile broadened.

'My dear Miss Sheridan, you could not be making more of a statement if you spoke it aloud! Whatever can have prompted a pattern-card of rectitude such as yourself to come to this nest of reprobates? Why, you will surely be ruined, if not in deed, at least in word!'

Sarah's eyes narrowed at the turn the conversation was taking. 'I have family business here at Blanchland, my lord.'

'Ah! The mysterious family business!' Allardyce sat back, his button-black eyes bright with speculation. 'It must be pressing indeed to bring you to this house! Have you not heard of Sir Ralph's revels? Naked orgies and cavorting in the snow—'

An obsequious footman dressed all in black removed Sarah's untouched bowl of soup and placed a plate of steaming mutton before her.

'Cavorting in the snow?' Sarah said, deliberately indifferent. 'It all sounds rather cold, my lord! One must be careful not to catch a chill, I should think!'

For a second Allardyce looked taken aback, then he smiled in appreciation of her tactics.

'Very sensible, Miss Sheridan! I can see you are a lady not easily shaken! But is your practicality proof against the black arts?'

Sarah looked up, startled. 'Against witchcraft? Surely not even Sir Ralph would indulge in such foolish practices!'

Lord Allardyce's smile was positively vulpine. 'There is a little temple in the woods where—'

'Oh!' Sarah smiled brightly, cutting him off before he should have the chance to go any further. 'You mean the grotto! I used to play there as a child! There is a spring in the rocks—it is indeed a charming place!'

Allardyce looked put out. He was not accustomed to both his compliments and his intriguing hints falling on such stony ground. He gave up temporarily and applied himself to his mutton. Mr Fisk appeared to have fallen forward into his. Further down the table, Sir Ralph was feeding mutton stew to Mrs Fisk in a coquettish manner that made Sarah feel faintly nauseous. Sir Ralph looked up, caught her eye, and put his fork down with an abashed expression.

Next to him, Lady Tilney was pouring Greville some more wine, leaning forward to display her rampant cleavage and running her fingers along the back of Greville's hand. Greville did not look as though he minded in the least. Sarah knew that Amelia had also seen and that the slightly brittle gaiety she was showing young Lord Lebeter was a direct result. Lebeter was at least enough of a gentleman to behave with propriety, and his youthful face showed some embarrassment at the increasingly uninhibited behaviour of the company.

Sarah reflected ruefully that Guy and Greville both seemed remarkably at home in such scandalous surroundings. She knew enough of Guy's reputation to be unsurprised, but a dull weight seemed to settle on her stomach that owed nothing to the greasy mutton. It did not matter how much she told herself to disregard it—it seemed his behaviour still had the power to disturb her.

There was a roaring log fire in the room and the heat was growing all the time. Sarah fanned herself surreptitiously and noted the reddening faces of the other diners. Guy was the only one who still looked cool, immaculately sophisticated in his evening clothes, as though he were in a London drawing-room rather than amidst a raffish houseparty. As Sarah watched, Lady Ann Walter rested one white hand on Guy's shoulder as though to emphasise a point she was making, then raised it to caress his tumbled fair hair in a gesture so intimate that Sarah almost caught her breath out loud.

'I believe that Lady Ann and Lord Renshaw were acquainted before,' Lord Allardyce said slyly in her ear. 'I fear you may have lost your beau, Miss Sheridan...'

Guy was laughing now at whatever Lady Ann was whispering in his ear. Sarah stared transfixed at the strong, brown column of his neck, the thick fair hair curling over his collar, the flashing white smile. Lady Ann was also watching him, with hunger in her gaze. Sarah felt an extraordinary jealousy twist inside her, so strong that she had to look away.

'You quite mistake the case, my lord,' she said coldly, aware that Allardyce was watching her avidly. 'Lord Renshaw accompanies me on behalf of his father, no more and no less. I have no claim on him.'

Allardyce looked unconvinced. 'Is that so? It would be interesting to see whether Lord Renshaw feels the same way, ma'am. Perhaps a taste of his own medicine would do the trick...'

For a moment Sarah was tempted, but she knew that she would be playing into Allardyce's hands. Besides, she had just claimed to be unconcerned by Guy's behaviour and was not about to show that the reverse was true. Still, the idea had held brief appeal. To make Guy jealous…if only she could! A small smile curved her mouth at the thought; at that moment, Guy looked up and straight at her. The amusement died from his dark eyes as he saw Sarah's smile and Allardyce bending close to her, one hand on her arm. Sarah felt as though she was pinned in her seat by the intensity of his stare and wondered if she imagined the anger she had read there. Then Allardyce laughed softly and the spell was broken. Sarah looked away, the colour mounting in her cheeks.

'That's the spirit, Miss Sheridan! That is all it takes!'

'I do not care for this conversation, sir!' Sarah snapped. 'Pray let us change the subject!'

'Very well,' Allardyce murmured, 'by all means let us discuss the weather if you wish it, Miss Sheridan!'

The mutton had congealed on Sarah's plate. The obsequious footman removed the covers and brought in a raspberry mousse. There were murmurs of appreciation, but not for the skill of the cuisine. The dessert wine, one of the late Lord Sheridan's finest, was circulating the table and the giggles and uninhibited behaviour was becoming more strident.

Sarah caught Amelia's horrified gaze as Lady Tilney dipped a finger into the dessert and held it out for Greville to lick, a lascivious glint in her eye. It seemed that Mrs Fisk was intending to use the mousse even more creatively, for she was encouraging Sir Ralph to dip his spoon into a bowl balanced on her magnificent bosom. Mr Fisk snored before the fire. Sarah felt as though she was getting hotter and hotter. Wherever she turned, it seemed there were images of wantonness.

'Excuse us, Sir Ralph—' Amelia's icy tones cut across the growing raucousness '—I believe it is time for the ladies to retire.'

Sir Ralph leaped up like a scalded cat, sending the bowl of mousse flying from Mrs Fisk's chest. 'Lady Amelia! Of course, ma'am! Pray retire! Ladies—' he looked hopelessly at Ann Walter and Lady Tilney '—perhaps you would be so good as to wait for us in the drawing-room.'

Lady Tilney giggled, trailing her fingers down Greville's cheek. 'Don't be so silly, Ralphie! We want some port...'

Lady Ann was feeding Guy grapes from the burgeoning fruit bowl. Sarah watched her pop them into his mouth and felt physically sick.

'As I said,' Amelia said pointedly, 'the *ladies* will retire...'

She got haughtily to her feet, raising her eyebrows when neither Guy nor Greville stood up. Lord Lebeter hurried to hold her chair, whilst Allardyce gave Sarah his arm to the door. Sarah's last image of the dining-room was of Greville with Lady Tilney sitting squarely on his knee and Guy twirling one of Lady Ann's blonde curls about his finger. Then the door was closed firmly in her face and almost immediately a burst of wild laughter could be heard on the other side of the panels.

Sarah could feel Amelia shaking like a leaf as they made their way up the stairs, but could not tell whether it was from anger or misery. She felt little better herself. Although she had told herself that life at Blanchland would contain some aspects she found distasteful, being confronted by the reality was both more shocking and more painful than she had imagined. In her heart of hearts she had expected that both Guy and Greville would act as gentlemen and defend her and Amelia from the harsher realities of Ralph's revels. The proof had shown them to be less than gentlemen and more than inclined to throw themselves into the spirit of the place. Never had Sarah felt so alone. When her father had died she had at least had Frank to provide some comfort and when he, too, had gone, Amelia's companionship had been solace. Here, both of them were in a completely unfamiliar situation and had nowhere to turn.

As soon as the door was closed, Amelia threw herself onto the bed and burst into angry tears.

'How dare he! How dare he profess to love me and then behave like that with that common little trollop! I hate him!'

Sarah sat beside her and stroked her shoulder tentatively. 'Milly! Please don't cry! Ten to one Greville is doing it to make you jealous—'

Amelia's pointed little face looked like an angry cat. 'Jealous! I would not have him now if he begged on bended knee! That vulgar strumpet was all over him— it was disgusting! I could not tell whether it was the food or the behaviour that revolted me more!'

'It was truly repellent,' Sarah agreed, with a shaky smile. 'That mutton—'

'Never mind the mutton! Did you see the way that that woman behaved with him? Licking her fingers, indeed! I dare swear—' Amelia broke off, gave an infuriated squeak and pummelled her pillow hard.

'Well,' Sarah said, struggling to be even-handed, 'Guy's behaviour was almost as bad. I know he is reputed a rake, but I did not wish to witness the evidence! Lord Allardyce told me that he and Lady Ann Walter—'

'Allardyce!' Amelia gave a disgusted snort. 'He is more unwholesome than the rest put together! I do beg you to be careful there, Sarah!'

'There is no need,' Sarah said, pressing her hands together. 'We shall not stay. I see now that it is impossible! We shall leave at first light!'

Amelia stopped punching her pillow and stared at her cousin. 'Leave? But you have yet to accomplish your quest!'

'It is of no consequence. Churchward may act as my agent here. When I think of what we have endured—'

'But we cannot go now!' Amelia, with a complete change of heart, stood up and started to pace about the room. 'Why, those wretched creatures downstairs would believe that they have chased us away! I could not bear them to triumph!'

As if in confirmation, there was the sound of running feet in the passage outside, followed by giggles and growling sounds. Sir Ralph—Sarah devoutly hoped that it was he—was becoming amorous.

'Let us play hunt the squirrel!' she heard one of the ladies shout. 'Greville darling, you may hide in here with me...'

A door closed along the passage. Sarah wrinkled up her nose with distaste. 'Good God, I thought we were rid of them—'

'Oh, Lord Renshaw,' a melting female cooed outside, 'I fear I shall be easily caught if you are doing the hunting...'

Sarah found that she was about to laugh hysterically. It was all so dreadfully like a bad melodrama and she had to stuff her hand into her mouth to stop the giggles erupting. Amelia's face was buried in the pillow again and her shoulders were shaking, but Sarah suspected that her affliction was laughter, not tears, this time. So it proved. When the growls, murmurs and titters outside the door had subsided, Amelia raised her head and said, 'Oh, Sarah, what are we to do?'

Sarah met her cousin's quizzical gaze. She was astonished to find that she was inclined to be angry, not afraid. 'We will not run away!' she said stoutly. 'I could not bear those odious creatures to win! They do say, Amelia, that revenge is very sweet. I have an idea…'

Chapter Seven

It was much later when Sarah left Amelia's bedroom and ventured across the darkened landing to her own room. She was feeling weary but still buoyed up by the plan that she had hatched with her cousin. The urge to laugh at the ridiculous antics of Sir Ralph's guests had fled now, but the flame of revenge that had taken hold of both herself and Amelia still burned very brightly. Sarah thought it unlikely that she would sleep, despite her tiredness.

Instead of retiring to her room, she tiptoed down the stairs to the library in search of a book to help her calm herself. The hall was in darkness now and it seemed that whatever revelling was still going on was probably taking place behind closed doors upstairs. Sarah refused to think about it. She opened the library door tentatively and was relieved to find it all in darkness.

Sir Ralph had sold many of Lord Sheridan's books upon inheriting Blanchland, but the old oak shelves still held a few volumes, steeped in dust and smelling strongly of damp. Sarah climbed the little wooden step-ladder and selected a couple of her old favourites. It did not seem as though anyone had touched them since she had last been at Blanchland. She curled up in an old armchair and turned the pages slowly, enjoying the re-discovery, and relaxing as silence took over the house.

The door opened suddenly and the candle flame scuttered in the draught. Sarah jumped violently and the books fell from her hands. For a moment the shadowed figure in the doorway was unrecognisable, and then Guy Renshaw stepped forward into the circle of candlelight and Sarah let her breath go on a long sigh. Not Lord Allardyce, then, but possibly just as dangerous. It had definitely been a mistake to go wandering after the lights were out.

'Good evening, my lord. Could you not sleep?' Sarah was proud of the steadiness of her voice and even prouder that she sounded so uninterested. She picked her books up and stood looking at him with polite in-difference.

At some point in the evening Guy had removed his jacket, and his linen shirt revealed rather than concealed the ripple of taut muscles beneath the fine material. His cravat was undone, giving him a slightly dishevelled air that Sarah could not deny was attractive. The important point, she reminded herself sternly, was that Guy's rumpled look was no doubt the result of some activity she did not really wish to dwell on. His fair hair was tou-sled, probably by feminine hands, and there was a glitter in his dark eyes that was deeply disturbing.

'I have not yet attempted to sleep,' Guy said smoothly, 'being too occupied with other activities. But you, Miss Sheridan—I had thought you retired hours ago.'

Sarah felt a rush of fury at the Guy's casual reference to his recent debauchery. She gave him a cool little smile.

'I wonder that you had time to notice, my lord! You were...somewhat occupied! '

A smile that was not reassuring curled Guy's mouth. The flickering candlelight made him look very tall and gilded his skin with a bronze sheen. 'Oh, I noticed, Miss Sheridan. I noticed that Lord Allardyce was most attentive and that his compliments were not unwelcome to you!'

Sarah shrugged indifferently. 'His lordship was amusing.'

'I see. You did not consider my warning worth heeding?'

'I considered your judgement faulty, my lord,' Sarah said coldly, 'as demonstrated by your own choice of company.'

'I see,' Guy said again. He took a step forward, until he was close enough to touch her. She could sense the tension in him. 'Do you then object to the company I keep?'

'I have no opinion,' Sarah said, neatly sidestepping the trap that had been laid for her, 'other than that of any gently bred lady who does not wish to see the amorous affairs of others displayed before her!'

Guy put his hand under her chin and tilted it up to force her to meet his eyes. 'You have no personal feelings on the matter? Even though I have given you the right to an opinion?'

It cost Sarah a huge effort to meet his gaze so calmly. 'You may remember that I declined your offer of marriage, my lord,' she said steadily, 'and with it the privilege to a hold an opinion on your behaviour.'

She saw the flash of some emotion in his eyes, vivid as lightning, before his expression was veiled once more.

'Indeed. I do recall that.' His fingers brushed Sarah's cheek, sending shock waves tingling through her. It was terribly difficult to concentrate and even harder to remain indifferent to him when her whole body was responding to his touch. 'Is it possible to make you change your mind, Miss Sheridan?'

'I doubt it. But I have observed that you do not repine too much, my lord!' Sarah stepped back, her books clutched to her chest like a shield. She wished this had never started. The mockery in that intent dark gaze suggested that Guy was not going to let it go easily. 'Excuse me. I am tired and must retire.'

'In a minute.' The challenge in Guy's tone was more apparent now. 'I thought you were down here reading because you were unable to sleep, Miss Sheridan?'

'That was a half-hour ago.' Sarah took a wary step sideways. He moved negligently to block her path to the door.

'And now you find you are conveniently tired? I was hoping that you would indulge my curiosity and tell me why my offer of marriage was repugnant to you.'

Sarah frowned, aware of the quicksand at her feet. She did not wish to get involved in this conversation when she was tired and her emotions were worn to a thread. She felt intensely vulnerable, all too aware of this man and the power he could exert over her senses.

'I believe that that discussion must await a better occasion, my lord,' she said, a little huskily. 'It is late—'

She broke off as Guy took the books out of her hands and placed them very deliberately on the table beside her. He held her gaze with his. Sarah knew what was about to happen and knew also that he was giving her plenty of time—time to run away, time to make an excuse, any excuse, to leave before it was too late. She

did not move. She felt breathless, incapable of anything
other than standing there and watching him as he
watched her. She could see a pulse beating in the hollow
of his throat and felt a shocking urge to press her lips
against the skin there... She tore her gaze away, but
only to trace with her eyes the hard line of his jaw, the
curve of his mouth...

Sarah was never sure which of them moved first.
Guy's arms closed around her and it felt confusingly
right to be there. This was a softer and sweeter kiss than
the one at Amelia's ball and for a moment she freed
herself a little.

'My lord, you mistake your companion—'

'Certainly not!' She felt Guy smile and it made her
weak with longing. 'I could never mistake you for anyone else, Sarah. And if you think that I would ever let
Allardyce touch you—'

His lips returned to hers before Sarah could reply.
The last vestiges of common sense were draining from
her mind, leaving her pliant in his arms. He was so
gentle, but there was a current that ran hot beneath the
tenderness. Sarah felt the tension uncoil within her. It
was easy to forget that she did not trust him, that only
an hour before he had probably held Lady Ann Walter
in his arms... Jealousy, sharp and shocking drove
through her like a knife. She stepped back and Guy
released her at once. In the shadowy library it was impossible to read his expression.

'I must go.' Sarah knew she sounded breathless.
'Good night, my lord.'

Guy did not try to stop her, but she knew he watched
her from the doorway as she made her way upstairs,
and for some reason the knowledge made her want to
cry.

*   *   *

The morning brought more snow, drifting white over ground that was already frozen hard. No one was stirring when Sarah donned her pelisse and boots, and went for a walk. She had not waited for breakfast, correctly assuming that there would be none. Later, when Amelia started to put her plans into practice, the food would definitely improve, but for now Sarah did not relish stale bread and cold coffee.

Close to the house lay the formal gardens, bare of colour now, the snow transforming the empty branches into ice sculptures. Sarah wandered beyond the rose garden and out into the park, her feet crunching on the frozen ground. At a little distance from the house, she turned to look back at the elegant façade of Blanchland, sitting serenely within its ring of trees. Sarah sighed. Was everything as deceptive as the view before her? Blanchland looked exactly as it had done ten years before, and yet the happy days of her childhood there were gone forever. Sir Ralph had turned the house into something unrecognisable, yet it looked just the same on the outside...

Sarah turned her back on the view before she became too melancholy. She did not want to think about the home she had lost, nor to think about Guy, to whom her thoughts inevitably turned. Her instincts told her to trust him, but at the same time a contradictory conviction suggested that he was hiding something from her. Perhaps he was as deceptive as the view.

The woodland closed about her and the dead leaves were crisp beneath her feet. Here, sheltered from the wintry breeze, was the little grotto that Lord Allardyce had referred to the night before. It had always been one of Sarah's favourite places.

She stooped to enter the mouth of the cave, then

straightened up and looked around. It was just as she remembered it. The faint light reflected off the shells that lined the interior, giving it a ghostly glow. In one corner, a natural spring bubbled softly over stones into a pool. It was very peaceful and made a nonsense of Allardyce's suggestions of black magic. Sarah sat down on the stone bench beside the pool and trailed her fingers in the icy cold water.

A shadow darkened the entrance and Sarah jumped, feeling relief as she recognised the newcomer. Perhaps Allardyce's stories had made her more nervous than she had realised.

'Tom! Good gracious, you startled me!'

'Sorry, Miss Sarah!' Tom Brookes touched his cap diffidently. 'Saw you walking this way and waited to catch you on your own.' He glanced over his shoulder and the very secrecy of the gesture made Sarah shiver a little. 'I've a message for you from Miss Meredith. She sent this for you.'

He fumbled in his pocket and took out a small package, wrapped in brown paper. Sarah looked at it curiously. 'But is there no letter, Tom?'

The gardener looked awkward. 'Don't know, ma'am. This was all I was given. From a friend of a friend, if you know what I mean…'

'And Olivia—where is she now?'

The gardener looked awkward. 'Can't say, ma'am, to be sure! At this very moment she could be in any number of places…'

Sarah smiled, understanding him. 'Very well. I shall not ask any more questions!' She put the little package in the pocket of her pelisse. 'Thank you, Tom. If I need to find you—'

'I'll be in the greenhouses, ma'am, trying to find flowers for Lady Amelia.'

Sarah smiled. 'A hard task in December! Amelia is a household tyrant, I fear! But I thank you, Tom.'

The gardener turned his cap around in his hands. 'Lovely job, ma'am,' he said, and the old West country phrase made Sarah smile again. She waited until she heard his footsteps crunch away from the grotto, then took the parcel out once more. Her fingers were a little clumsy with the cold, but eventually she managed to remove the brown paper and dropped the contents into the palm of her hand.

It was a locket.

Sarah gave an exclamation of surprise. The locket looked very old, for the pattern chased in the gold was worn and smooth beneath her fingers. The clasp opened with a tiny click to reveal the portraits inside. Sarah held it up to the light.

On the left was a lady with chestnut ringlets, sparkling brown eyes and a wide smile. She looked as though she would have been fun to know and Sarah's own smile widened in response to the obvious happiness that the painter had captured. She also looked a little familiar. The picture on the right... Sarah almost dropped the locket on to the stone floor. It was Guy's face that looked back at her from its setting in the golden frame: the thick fair hair, tied back here in an old-fashioned queue, the striking dark eyes, the high cheekbones and firm line of the mouth. The painted gaze seemed to mock Sarah's astonishment.

She looked back at the other portrait again. The lady was in a low-cut gown with one ringlet resting in the creamy hollow of her throat. Little of her dress was visible. But in Guy's picture the artist had at least included the bottle-green frieze coat that fitted those broad shoulders so well... Enlightenment came to Sarah in a blinding flash. The locket was old and the pictures were also antique, from at least fifty years before. The gentleman in the picture had to be Guy's grandfather.

Once Sarah had thought of this, the differences rather than the similarities seemed clear. The gentleman in the picture had the same unconsciously arrogant tilt to his head that Guy had, but none of Guy's easy humour was perceptible. The man's eyebrows were more heavily marked, adding to the air of aloofness, the dark gaze hooded. Sarah shivered a little. It was becoming cold in the grotto, and whilst the realisation that the man in the picture could not be Guy Renshaw brought some reassurance, it also raised questions she needed to consider. She got to her feet a little stiffly and turned towards the entrance.

Immediately, her foot scuffed a tiny scrap of paper that had fallen unnoticed from the locket when first she had opened it. Sarah bent to pick it up.

Miss S
Please meet me at the Folly Tower at twelve tonight.

Yours, O.

Sarah wrinkled up her nose. It seemed that Miss Meredith had a penchant for melodrama, for why else choose a midnight rendezvous at the ruined tower? In winter! Sarah shivered a third time at the thought and made for the pale sunshine she could see outside.

Once out in the daylight she carried on walking away from the house, all the while trying to make sense of the locket. Had Olivia Meredith sent it just to hide the note, or in an attempt to give her another, coded, message? More importantly, how had it fallen into Olivia's possession? It could hardly be a coincidence, so what was her connection with the Earls of Woodallan? Once again, Sarah remembered the mocking dark gaze of the portrait, the arrogant lift of the head. Finding such a trinket in Olivia's possession underlined the sinister role Guy seemed to be playing. Sarah remembered the conversation she had overheard between the Earl and his son. It had been important to find Olivia first, and Guy had been making enquiries, offering money... Sarah tried to make sense of the ever more complex pattern.

There was no reason to doubt that Olivia was Frank Sheridan's daughter, for her brother had told Sarah that himself. It seemed, however, that Olivia also had a connection with the Woodallan family that was not so clear. Sarah frowned as she remembered Guy assuring her that Frank had written to Lord Woodallan asking for his aid. That was probably true, although Frank's reason for asking now seemed more complicated than had first appeared. It could not be solely because Sarah was the Earl's goddaughter. Woodallan himself must also have some link with Olivia. Sarah shook her head over the questions with no answer. She could always ask Guy directly, but for some reason she hesitated over from such a course of action. His secretive behaviour had created a barrier between them.

'Miss Sheridan!'

Sarah jumped as the voice penetrated her thoughts. She had been walking almost aimlessly through the woods and now found herself back on the south side of Blanchland, where the frozen lake sparkled in the early sun. Coming towards her, a large brindled wolfhound at his heels, was Guy Renshaw himself.

Sarah blushed, aware of a feeling of guilty embarrassment. She was not sure whether it was her recollec-
tion of the previous night or her suspicions that were
making her feel so uncomfortable, but facing Guy in
the cold light of day was proving difficult. She said the
first thing that came into her head. 'Good gracious, my
lord, wherever did you find that dog?'

Guy laughed. He was looking as casually elegant as
ever, his resemblance to the gentleman in the locket
very pronounced. It made Sarah feel very self-
conscious.

'I believe he has adopted me! He is Sir Ralph's pet
and of a wholly gentle disposition!'

Sarah watched dubiously as the hound ran off to sniff
excitedly amongst the reeds. 'He seems very happy to
have some exercise! I doubt Sir Ralph is prone to taking
long walks!'

Guy fell into step beside her, glancing at her with a
look of such evident admiration that Sarah was once
again forcibly reminded of the scene in the library. A
deeper shade of colour crept into her cheeks that she
hoped could be attributed to the chill morning air. She
quickened her step towards the house. Some thirty yards
ahead of them stood the Folly, a small tower built by
Lord Sheridan in a position that gave a superb view of
the surrounding countryside. It immediately brought
Olivia to the forefront of Sarah's mind again.

'Perhaps we could all go skating this afternoon,' Guy
was saying thoughtfully. 'The ice looks thick enough to
be safe. Did you skate here as a child, Miss Sheridan?'

Sarah wrenched her mind away from the mystery of
Olivia and her locket and answered him slightly at ran-
dom. 'Skating? Oh, yes, it was great fun! I have not

tried for years, but I believe I would not have lost the skill.'

'You sound as though you were thinking of something else, Miss Sheridan,' Guy observed acutely, giving her a searching look from his very dark eyes. 'Perhaps it is Miss Meredith who occupies your thoughts? Do you have any plans to continue your search today?'

Sarah mentally damned him for his perception. 'I had not thought of it,' she lied, evading his eyes. 'Since I made little progress yesterday, I am at a loss to know what to do next. And you, my lord?' She recovered her poise sufficiently to look straight at him. 'Do you have any plans in that direction?'

Guy shrugged easily. 'I think not. I am, however, entirely at your disposal if you wish me to escort you—'

'Oh, no,' Sarah said, too quickly, 'I should not put you to that trouble, sir! That is, if I should decide to make further enquiries...'

'Of course.' Guy rescued her smoothly from her floundering. His perceptive gaze swept over her once more. 'If you should change your mind, Miss Sheridan—'

'Oh, I shall not!' Sarah said hastily. 'I feel too tired today to go venturing far!' The locket and the note seemed to be burning a hole in her pocket and she turned her face away to hide her confusion.

'The consequence of your late night excursion to the library, I expect!' The mockery was back in Guy's tone. 'I trust you found your way back to your bed safely, Miss Sheridan!'

Sarah could feel herself blushing. 'Of course! I am not afraid of Blanchland after dark, my lord! I grew up here! Now, if you will excuse me, it grows cold and I would wish to be indoors.'

Guy bowed slightly. 'I will see you later then, Miss Sheridan! If you are fortunate, you may find that your cousin has brewed some coffee and provided breakfast! I know she was working on it as I left the house!'

Sarah watched his tall figure stroll towards the lake again, the dog trotting eagerly at his heels. She did not believe him when he said that he had no interest in pursuing his search for Miss Meredith any further. There was a lump in her throat that felt like unshed tears and the hard outline of the locket scored her fingers. With a sigh, Sarah turned to ascend the steps to the terrace. She knew she was as bad as he, for she had lied, too. The sad fact was that she did not trust him, but now the deceit was becoming intolerable.

When Sarah got back to the house she found not only coffee and fresh bread in the breakfast room, but what appeared to be a whole army of maids cleaning the dining-room under Amelia's watchful eye.

'I simply could not bear to eat another meal in such disgustingly dirty surroundings,' her cousin greeted her. 'I have high hopes that this afternoon we may start to tackle the bedchambers, for I fear there may be fleas and worse—'

Here she broke off as the crashing of moving furniture became too loud to sustain a conversation. When matters quietened down again she added mischievously, 'Lady Tilney and Lady Ann are in the morning-room should you wish to avoid them, my dear! They were both much put out to be disturbed by all the noise!' Amelia gave a little giggle. 'I fear Lady Tilney looks quite raddled in the daylight and Lady Ann is much the worse for too little sleep! I offered them my rose petal cream to rejuvenate their skin, but they declined!'

Sarah tried not to laugh. 'Amelia—'

'Oh, I have only just begun,' her cousin said, understanding perfectly Sarah's unspoken question. Her eyes
sparkled. 'There is no end to the commotion I can cause
when I try!'

'And Greville? Have you seen him today?'

Amelia's smile became positively angelic. 'Poor Greville! I believe he has a headache this morning! I have
mixed him a concoction of raw eggs, tomato extract and
liquorice!'

'Oh, Amelia!' Sarah started to laugh. 'Almost I pity
him! And how does Sir Ralph take this transformation
of his house?'

'Oh, Sir Ralph is most impressed!' Amelia said
blithely. 'He told me I was a spirited little filly and that
I had a free hand to do whatever I wished! So...' She
picked up a duster and started to wield it industriously.

'Maybe he will not feel so happy when he discovers
the keys to his wine cellar are lost,' Sarah mused.

'Maybe not,' Amelia confirmed with a smile, 'but by
then it will be too late!'

It was a day of irritating inactivity. Sir Ralph's guests
all declared themselves too exhausted by their early rising to even think of skating that afternoon, and they
whiled away a few hours in the library with Sir Ralph's
prized collection of erotic French lithographs. When
Sarah went down to the lake she discovered that the ice
was too thin to risk going out and later it began to snow
in earnest, huge flakes falling from a pewter sky, so she
retired to her room with a book. She tried to ignore the
ribald laughter and conversation that floated up the
stairs.

Guy had disappeared at some point in the afternoon

and did not reappear until dinner and, despite her attempts to think on other matters, Sarah could not but
wonder where he had gone. The rendezvous with Olivia
weighed on her mind. It seemed a long time until midnight.

Dinner was a meal quite unlike the previous night. It
soon became apparent that Amelia had taught the cook
some simple but nutritious recipes, for the first course
was a delicious vegetable soup, followed by trout in a
white wine sauce. The eyes of all the guests lit up as
they took their first tentative mouthfuls, and even Mr
Fisk woke up with the words, 'Food! Excellent!'

Mrs Fisk looked somewhat discontented by the fact
that her spouse stayed awake for the entire meal, but
this was nothing to the emotions of the others on finding
that there was no wine. At first, when a large jug of ice-
cold water had been brought in, no one had commented,
but as the meal progressed and the famous Blanchland
wines were not forthcoming, Lady Tilney could not
contain herself.

'Turned puritan, Ralph?' she asked coyly, fluttering
her lashes at him. 'Or are you trying to reform us all?'

Sir Ralph looked discomfited.

'Lady Amelia—' he began, to break off at once,
clearly unable to criticise Amelia after she had magi-
cally produced such delicious food. Sarah, knowing that
the responsibility for the absence of wine lay firmly at
Amelia's door, waited with amusement to see what
would happen next.

Her cousin had been conversing with Justin Lebeter
and looked up at the expectant pause.

'The wine? Oh, dear, I was hoping that you would
not ask...' She cast her eyes down modestly. 'I fear the

key was lost when we did our cleaning today. The maids swear that they have scoured the house for it, but it cannot be found...'

There was an outcry, but it came mainly from the ladies.

'No wine? How dreadful! How shall we survive! Sir Ralph, pray do something!'

Guy caught Sarah's eye with a quizzical lift to his eyebrows, but she kept her expression to one of limpid innocence. She was not going to give Amelia away.

'Surely there is wine in this exquisite sauce?' Greville Baynham said, his gaze challenging Amelia's across the table.

Amelia sighed. 'Oh, yes, but that was the last of yesterday's bottles. And I do feel that too much wine can dull the palate. Do you not agree, Lord Lebeter?'

Justin Lebeter looked as though he was about to agree with anything Amelia would care to say. Lady Tilney gave a snort of disapproval.

'I am happy for my palate to suffer in a good cause!'

'Indeed!' Amelia said sweetly. 'I suspected that your taste was already jaded, Lady Tilney!'

Sarah thought she heard Greville smother a laugh.

'You promised me a bath in the vintage champagne, Ralphie,' Mrs Fisk grumbled petulantly from further down the table. 'You said it was one of the specialities!'

'Damned waste!' her husband grunted. Mrs Fisk glared malevolently.

'Did you know anything about this, Miss Sheridan?' Lord Allardyce asked with a sly smile. 'You are deep in your cousin's confidence, after all!'

Sarah returned the smile very pleasantly. 'I knew the keys were lost, of course,' she admitted, 'but then I realised that there was this refreshing spring water to replace it! Have you tried it, Lord Allardyce? It comes from the spring in the grotto and is so very bracing!'

Allardyce wrinkled up his nose with distaste. 'I thank you, but no, Miss Sheridan! Water is for the peasants!'

'You will become quite thirsty, then!' Sarah said, applying herself to her food.

There was an ill-tempered silence for a while.

'You must send to Bath for more wine tomorrow, Ralph!' Lady Tilney said stridently. 'This is really not to be borne!'

'The roads are so bad that I imagine it will take several days for the wine merchant to reach us,' Amelia said, smiling brightly.

'Perhaps Lord Renshaw will take pity on you and send to Woodallan for supplies!' Sarah put in, with a quick sideways look at his lordship. 'For myself, I could drink the spring water for days!'

'I cannot imagine that it could be good for us!' Lady Ann Walter shuddered. 'There may be so many noxious substances that have drained into it! Why, it could be quite poisonous!'

'But perhaps quite improving for the skin, Lady Ann,' Amelia suggested blandly.

Her ladyship flushed angrily.

Something seemed to have happened to the spirit of the house party, Sarah thought, as they all turned back to their food again and the silence became prolonged. It could not simply be the wine, but there was an atmosphere of near gloom in the dining-room. Amelia, eating heartily, seemed quite unaware of it. Even Lord Allardyce, so suggestive the previous evening, confined his conversation to platitudes about the weather. Once the meal was ended, no one lingered at the table and, as there was no port to circulate, the ladies and gentlemen all retired for a game of whist. It was, Sarah thought, one of the few vices still left to them.

At fifteen minutes to midnight that night, Sarah donned her cloak and boots and slipped out of her room. Since dinner, she had watched the clock and found herself unable to settle to doing anything to pass the time.

There was a light still showing under the drawing-room door as Sarah crept across the hall, and she tried to open the front door as silently as possible. The snow had stopped and the sky was clear with a bright white moon. It was an eerie but beautiful scene. Sarah hesitated. Her footsteps would be all too clear in the snow, visible to anyone who chose to look. She could only hope that no one would be abroad that night and that more snow would fall before morning.

She set off at a brisk pace, keeping in the moon shadows and taking as much cover as she could from the trees. The night was very quiet, though every so often some snow would tumble from the branches, making Sarah jump. Despite telling Guy earlier that nothing at Blanchland frightened her, she was distinctly nervous and wishing that Olivia had suggested a meeting in a nice warm parlour instead of a lonely tower. It seemed most sensible to keep the meeting as brief as possible, and suggest another appointment in the daylight—unless Olivia's situation was so extreme that she needed help at once. Sarah paused to consider the possibility. She had no idea what she would find at the Folly Tower and felt woefully unprepared.

She had just crossed a clearing deep in snow when a scuffling sound behind her made Sarah freeze and spin around. She could see no one lurking under the trees, but some sixth sense told her that she was not alone, and, whilst she hesitated over whether or not to call out, a dark figure detached itself from the shadows and hurried forward. Sarah's instinctive squeak of alarm died unheard and she let out her breath on an angry sigh.

'Amelia! What the—what on earth are you doing here?'

'I heard you leave the house and I followed you,' her cousin said, somewhat out of breath. 'What are you doing here, Sarah?'

'Never mind what I am doing!' Sarah gave Amelia's arm a shake. 'How could you be so foolish, Milly? Why, you could have got lost, or fallen into danger—'

'All the more reason why you should not be wandering around on your own, then!' her cousin replied with spirit. 'Where are you going, Sarah?'

'I am going to the Folly to meet Miss Meredith,' Sarah said crossly. In the distance she heard the faint chimes of the Blanchland church clock. 'There's no time to explain now, for I am late as it is! I suppose you had better come with me!'

'Who is Miss Meredith?' Amelia enquired, trotting along behind Sarah through the wood. 'And why are you arranging a meeting in the middle of the night?'

Sarah smiled despite herself. She was amazed at how much better she felt to have some company. 'Miss Meredith is my niece and the reason I came to Blanchland. As to why—'

'Your niece!' Sarah marvelled at Amelia's instinct for gossip even under such circumstances. 'You mean that she is Frank's daughter? But Frank never had a child—'

'This is no time for a rehearsal of the Sheridan genealogy,' Sarah hissed back. She almost stumbled over a tree root and put out a hand to steady herself. 'Oh, this is ridiculous! I wish the wretched girl did not have such a sense of the dramatic!'

They were reaching the crown of the hill and came out of the trees to see the dark bulk of the tower looming before them. Amelia clutched at Sarah's cloak.

'Sarah, are you sure about this? Why can you not meet up in daylight? I do not like this!'

'Nonsense!' Sarah knew that one of them had to be bracing or they would both run away in a fit of panic. 'We are going to meet a seventeen-year-old girl, not a monster! Pray go back if you do not wish to stay with me!'

Amelia shuddered. 'I will not walk on my own through the wood! Where is the girl, then? There is nobody here!'

Sarah pushed open the tower door and peered into the interior. It was pitch-black. The Folly Tower had been built by her great-grandfather and on a fine day one could see three counties and the sea from the top, but tonight Sarah could not even see in front of her nose.

'Olivia?' It came out as half-whisper, half-croak. Sarah cleared her throat and drew breath to call again. The words were never spoken. Something soft and smothering pressed down over her head and she was grasped in an iron grip. Beside her, she heard Amelia start to scream and then someone dropped her hard on the stone floor of the tower and all hell seemed to break out around her.

The confusion resolved itself so quickly that Sarah could almost have imagined it. Within seconds, Amelia's screams had died away and the suffocating cloth was removed from Sarah's face. She struggled to sit up and found herself cradled in gentle arms that held her firmly but surely. A lantern had been placed on the stone floor and cast a small pool of light about them. Sir Greville Baynham was standing behind the lantern and Amelia was kneeling and peering into Sarah's face with so fearful an expression that her cousin almost burst out laughing.

'Oh, Sarah, are you much hurt? He dropped you with such a jolt I was sure you had broken some bones!'

Sarah moved a little gingerly and the restraining arms that held her loosened their grip very slightly. She did not need to turn her head to know that it was Guy who held her; the feel of his arms was familiar and the warmth of his body against hers was reassuring, but she had to break the contact.

'I am very well,' she said a little shakily, gratefully accepting Greville's help to ease her to her feet, 'but whatever happened? Someone attacked me—I was certain they were about to carry me off!'

'Most probably they would have done had we not arrived in time!' Guy said drily. He was still holding her with a steadying hand under her elbow. Both he and Greville were dressed in dark cloaks and the snow was falling off their boots onto the floor. 'Somebody ran out of the tower as Lady Amelia started to scream, but they were lost in the darkness before we could see them. We did not pursue them, for our first thoughts were for the two of you. It is fortunate that we arrived when we did.'

Sarah thought it fortunate, perhaps, but also deeply suspicious. How had Guy and Greville come to be wandering about the wood at precisely the time she had arranged to meet Olivia? And where was Olivia now? Someone in addition to herself had obviously known of the rendezvous. It would be better to keep very quiet on the subject of her own activities. Aware that some difficult questions were about to be asked, Sarah avoided Guy's too-perceptive gaze and made a business of brushing the dirt from her cloak.

'Well, I am grateful to you both,' she said guardedly. 'Some poacher taken by surprise, I expect! There is no harm done!'

'The point in question is how the devil did you come to be taking a walk at this time of night, Miss Sheridan?' Guy said forcefully. 'Have you taken leave of your senses?'

Sarah glared at him. She only just managed to swallow the retort that sprang to her lips, aware that he could provoke her into a response all too easily and that she might give something away.

'Perhaps Lady Amelia would care to answer that question,' Greville said smoothly, stepping forward into the light. 'I have noticed that where your cousin leads, you are not far behind, ma'am! Or is it the other way about?'

Sarah and Amelia exchanged a quick glance. Amelia gave a careless little shrug.

'Why, it is no great matter, Sir Greville! Sarah could not sleep and, as I had not yet retired, we decided to take a short walk. The snow looks very pretty in the moonlight!'

'Not from inside a darkened tower!' Greville said grimly. 'Next you will be telling me that you thought to climb to the top to look at the view! What nonsense is this?'

Amelia's lips were set in a mutinous line. She picked up the lantern. 'Let us not stand about here in the cold! Poor Sarah will be wanting her bed!'

'At the least, it will have cured her insomnia,' Guy

said, with an ironic lift to his eyebrows. 'A persistent affliction, Miss Sheridan! Can you improve on Lady Amelia's version, ma'am? It lacks something in originality!'

Sarah did not meet his eyes. 'It is as Amelia says, my lord. We thought it would be pleasant to take the air!'

'Cut line, Miss Sheridan,' Guy countered derisively, 'and spare us the tales of moonlit views, fresh night air and the like! I never heard so thin a tale!'

Sarah looked at both of them. Guy was planted four-square before her, his expression unyielding. Greville was beside the door, giving the impression that they were unlikely to be allowed out until they came up with the truth. The flickering lantern cast huge shadows up into the vaulted roof and gave the whole scene an appearance of unreality. Sarah gave Guy a challenging glance.

'Very well, my lord! If you don't like my tale, perhaps you can offer an alternative!'

Their gazes locked, Sarah's defiant, Guy's thoughtful. He shifted slightly.

'A midnight rendezvous seems most likely, Miss Sheridan!'

Sarah's eyes narrowed. How far would he go to discover the truth? She knew that he had things to hide, just as she had, but she judged him eminently capable of calling her bluff. There was no doubt that this was very awkward.

'I am not in the habit of arranging night-time trysts, sir,' she snapped. 'No doubt the atmosphere of Blanchland is affecting your judgement!'

'I was not suggesting that you were creeping away secretly to meet Allardyce,' Guy said pleasantly, 'for you have your cousin with you! Although, perhaps, knowing his tastes—'

Sarah blushed bright red and it was Amelia who threw herself into the breach.

'I see that your observations are as offensive as ever, sir! If it comes to that, how do you explain your timely but somewhat questionable arrival?' She turned sharply on Greville. 'Perhaps Sir Greville would care to answer? Is Sir Ralph holding one of his bacchanals in the woods tonight?'

Greville started to laugh. Amelia looked so furious at this inappropriate response that Sarah was glad she was holding the lantern and unable to set about him with her bare hands. Now that her temper was up, there was no stopping her.

'By what right do you question us anyway, Sir Greville?' Amelia demanded hotly. 'Even if we choose to go *dancing* in the woods all night long, it would be none of your affair! Kindly mind your own business!'

Greville gave her a derisive little bow. 'My dear Amelia, I only question your behaviour as I fear you are setting your cousin a bad example! You, an older woman, should take it upon yourself to act responsibly—'

'Monstrous!' It sounded to Sarah as though Amelia was about to explode. The lantern wavered dangerously and she took it out of her cousin's wayward grip, then wondered if she should have done so when it appeared Amelia was about to slap Greville. He caught her arm in a negligent grip and turned towards the doorway.

'Fascinating as this encounter is, Lady Amelia, I feel we should be taking up your suggestion and returning to the house. Miss Sheridan, could you light the way?'

'Allow me,' Guy said, taking the lantern. 'I should

not like to be at the mercy of your somewhat dubious sense of direction, Miss Sheridan!'

Sarah was beginning to feel as annoyed as her cousin, who was arguing with Greville in a furious undertone. Before she could frame a blistering reply, however, another figure stumbled out of the trees and into the circle of light at the folly entrance.

'Renshaw?' a voice said incredulously. 'Baynham? What the deuce—'

It was Lord Lebeter who came towards them, blushing suddenly as he saw Sarah and Amelia. 'Ladies! I beg your pardon! I thought—'

It was evident to Sarah exactly what Lord Lebeter was thinking. In a place like Blanchland, where no activity was apparently too outlandish, he must have thought he had stumbled into some new entertainment.

'Evening, Lebeter,' Guy said laconically. 'Do you suffer from sleeplessness also?'

'Oh…' Justin Lebeter looked self-conscious. 'A short stroll before I turn in… Thought I saw a light up here…'

'We were just returning,' Sarah said helpfully, as his words ground to a halt. 'Would you care to walk back with us, sir?'

Nobody spoke as they trudged back through the snow and it seemed to Sarah that a distinctly awkward atmosphere had settled over the group. The presence of Justin Lebeter at least ensured that neither Guy nor Greville persisted in any awkward questions, but Sarah knew that they would scarcely give up so easily. Once they got back to the house, both Sarah and Amelia made sure that they divested themselves of boots and cloaks so quickly that the gentlemen had no further opportunity to interrogate them.

As she mounted the stairs, Sarah's mind was full of

all the unsolved issues. To the question of the locket was now added the reason for Guy and Greville's presence at the tower, the absence of Olivia, the mystery attacker... And what had Lord Lebeter been doing strolling about the woods at midnight? Matters were becoming all too complicated...

Sarah pushed open her bedroom door and set the candle down on the bedside stand. A movement in the corner of the room caught her eye and she spun round with a muffled gasp.

In a chair by the wall was a slender young lady, watching her with huge, apprehensive brown eyes. As Sarah recoiled, she said hastily, 'Miss Sheridan? I do beg your pardon for intruding in such a way, but it was my only chance! I am Olivia Meredith, and so very happy to make your acquaintance!'

Chapter Eight

Miss Olivia Meredith bore a startling resemblance to both the portraits in the locket and also to the current Viscount Renshaw. Sarah stared, and reflected that there could now be no question over her relationship to the Woodallan family. Here was the same thick blonde hair, tied in long braids in Miss Meredith's case, and the deep brown eyes that provided such a striking contrast to her fairness. Olivia's face was the oval shape of the lady in the locket, but her other features were discernibly from the Sheridan side of the family, and it gave Sarah a curious feeling to see the fusion. Here was an example of what a child might look like if it had herself and Guy for parents.

Sarah realised that she was staring and that Olivia, huddled deep in the armchair, was looking even more apprehensive than before.

'Forgive me, Miss Meredith,' she said hastily, 'it is just that you remind me—' Sarah broke off, suddenly remembering that Olivia might have no idea of her parentage.

'I am sorry if I startled you, ma'am,' the girl said quickly. 'I could think of no other way of meeting you in private! It was Tom's idea—Tom Brookes, you know—for he and his family have been hiding me.'

'I see,' Sarah said slowly, coming forward and taking off her cloak. 'Then the meeting at the Folly Tower—'

'Oh, it was all a ruse! Tom knew that if he let a few rumours drop that I would be at the Folly, Lord Allardyce would leave the house and the coast would be clear for me to seek you out here!'

'I see!' Sarah said again, grimly. 'I must remember to congratulate Tom on his strategy! Having us all tripping about in the snow must have afforded him considerable satisfaction!'

Olivia let out a peal of laughter, then clapped her hand hastily to her mouth. 'Oh, dear, how dreadful! I am so sorry, Miss Sheridan, but you see, we had to thwart Lord Allardyce at all costs!'

The fire had burned down and Olivia was shivering a little, though whether from cold or the thought of Allardyce, Sarah could not guess. She stirred it to a glow, then sat back on her heels to survey her niece.

'Is Lord Allardyce the reason you wrote to Mr Churchward? You must tell me how I can help you, Miss Meredith. But first—are you hungry or thirsty? I can always send to the kitchen for some food—'

But Olivia was shaking her head. 'Oh, no, thank you, Miss Sheridan. Mrs Tom feeds me very well! I will not keep you from your bed for long, but if I could just explain my difficulties...'

'Of course,' Sarah said. She sat down opposite. Olivia's head was bent, a shade of colour in her cheeks. She played nervously with a pleat of her skirt.

'Tom Brookes told me that you had come to help me,' Olivia said, in a rush. 'When I wrote to Mr Churchward, I scarce expected that he would ask you to come here yourself—' She broke off, looking confused, to start again, a deeper pink colour now in her pale face.

'I think you should know, Miss Sheridan, that my mother—my adoptive mother,' she corrected herself carefully, 'told me of my connection with your family a few years ago. Believe me, I have no wish to push myself on your notice, but I had nowhere else to turn!'

Sarah smiled at her niece's anxious face. 'There is no question of you putting yourself forward, or being unwelcome, or anything like that, Miss Meredith! You know now that I am your aunt, and I am very happy to have found you!'

Olivia smiled back a little tremulously. 'Thank you. I must own that it is strange to find I have another family and I am sorry—' her face fell '—that I never knew your brother, my...father.'

'Yes.' Sarah hesitated, trying to think of something both true and complimentary to tell Olivia about Frank Sheridan. 'I was very fond of Frank. He was...a most interesting and charming man and I am sure he would have liked you, Olivia. I may call you Olivia, may I not?'

'Oh, please!' Olivia had started to look a little happier.

'And you must call me Sarah, for I cannot bear to be called 'Aunt'! It makes me feel far too old!'

Olivia giggled. 'I cannot believe that you are many years older than I, Miss—Sarah! It will be like having a sister!'

'Excellent! We must talk much more, but perhaps the most pressing matter is for you to tell me how I can help you, Olivia. Your letter to Mr Churchward suggested that you were in either grave danger or dire need;

as I have already met Lord Allardyce, I can perhaps imagine—'

The light fled from Olivia's face, leaving it looking pinched and cold again. Sarah leant forward and instinctively touched her hand. 'Come! It cannot be so bad—'

'I am sorry,' Olivia said in a rush. 'It is such a silly matter, but I did not know where to turn. Oh, I am not explaining myself at all well—'

'Start at the beginning,' Sarah counselled, settling back in her chair. 'You were away at school in Oxford until recently, I believe?'

'Oh, yes! I came back to Blanchland only a few months ago. Mama was worrying about what I should do here, for I know she wishes to see me respectably settled and there is so little society hereabouts! Until recently I believed that she hoped I might go to Bath for a season, but there were insufficient funds. I believe Father had not invested wisely and when Mama became ill—' Olivia shrugged prettily '—all our remaining money had to go on medicines. I did not repine, for I was sure that matters would resolve! The family of one of my school friends offered to help me find a position—a governess or companion would have done, I should not have minded! But then...'

Olivia stopped and looked away into the fire. 'Then Lord Allardyce came here, to Blanchland.'

Sarah had been quite still during Sarah's rehearsal of the events that had led to this point. She could imagine Mrs Meredith's hopes and fears for her daughter, the unlucky investment of the money given by Lord Sheridan, the difficulties as Olivia's prospects shrank with the loss of fortune. She had seen it herself—without money it was always a struggle. Sarah knew that she had been lucky to have both a family name to ensure her position in society and a rich cousin willing to help her. Olivia had had neither, but had still determined not to call in the debt owed by her father's family. Not until Lord Allardyce had come to Blanchland...

'I first met him in the village and he was most attentive,' Olivia continued. 'He took to calling on us and Mama was most excited—I believe she thought I might catch an Earl! But I did not like him, nor did I believe that his intentions were at all honourable!'

Remembering Allardyce's penchant for the pure and innocent to refresh his jaded palate, Sarah could well imagine why Olivia would appeal to him. Not only was she young and beautiful, but she had an utterly unspoilt quality.

'Then, one day, he called when Mama was from home and although I refused at first to see him, he insisted. He asked me—' Olivia looked up, caught Sarah's eye, blushed and looked away. 'In short, he proposed that I should become his mistress. He promised me all manner of comforts to ease my life, but at such a price! Believe me, Miss—Sarah, I was not even tempted!'

'I believe you,' Sarah said truthfully. There was something so transparently innocent about Olivia that Allardyce's proposal could not help but be repugnant to her. 'But I do not suppose that Lord Allardyce took his dismissal lightly?'

'No, indeed! He pestered me for days until I scarce dared step outdoors! And then he came to us one day, all triumphant, to tell us that he had purchased the lease of the house from Sir Ralph and that he would throw us into the street unless I agreed to his demands!'

Sarah sighed. It was so simple when one had the means. Allardyce would barely have noticed the price of a lease and it was just the lever he needed. Mrs Meredith, whose health was not strong in the first place, would have been almost beside herself with worry.

'What did you do, Olivia?'

Miss Meredith sat up a little straighter. 'Why, I set off straight away to come here to see—'

'Sir Ralph?'

'No...' Olivia looked momentarily confused '...Lord Lebeter!'

For a moment Sarah wondered whether she had been listening properly. The sudden introduction of Justin Lebeter into the situation threw her briefly, until she reflected that, with a young lady as lovely as Miss Meredith, there would surely be a welcome suitor as well as a villainous one. It probably explained Lord Lebeter's surprising appearance at the Tower earlier that evening. He, too, must have heard the rumour that Miss Meredith would be there, and had gone to find her.

'Are you then already acquainted with Lord Lebeter?' Sarah asked carefully.

'Oh, yes!' Where Olivia had been cast down before, her eyes now sparkled very brightly indeed. 'Lord Lebeter is the brother of one of my school friends, you see, and I met him originally at her house. Then, when my circumstances changed, I did not believe that I should ever see him again. Imagine my feelings when I saw him riding through Blanchland village one day!'

Sarah raised her eyebrows. In the face of this dewy-eyed bliss she suddenly felt a very old aunt indeed.

'Of course,' Olivia added, blushing, 'I was a little cast down to think of him staying here, for Sir Ralph's parties have such a shocking reputation! But he is so truly the perfect gentleman that I cannot believe—' She stopped, overcome by natural delicacy.

'So when you were in trouble, you naturally turned to Lord Lebeter,' Sarah prompted.

'Oh, yes! But the terrible thing was that he had just that morning left Blanchland to visit in Devon, and when I approached the house I was met instead by Lord Allardyce! I was so afraid of what he might do that I ran away, which was how Tom found me, and the rest you know!'

Sarah felt slightly breathless at the dash through the events that had led to Olivia's disappearance. 'I am sorry to appear a slow-top,' she said, 'but if I could just clarify a few points—'

'Oh, of course!' Olivia said obligingly. 'What is it that you wish to know?'

'Well, firstly, how did you come to write to Mr Churchward?'

'Oh, Mama suggested that as soon as Lord Allardyce started importuning me! But I thought to turn to Lord Lebeter first!'

'Of course. And when you ran away from Lord Allardyce, Tom helped you—'

'Yes, for he found me hiding in his greenhouse!'

'I see. And he has been hiding you ever since?'

'We thought it was a good idea,' Olivia explained. 'Lord Allardyce has been looking everywhere, but of course he did not think of the servants! And, as Tom works here, he was able to watch Lord Allardyce and make sure that he did not get too close.'

'I see,' Sarah said again. 'Were you not tempted to seek Lord Lebeter's help once he returned here?'

Olivia's eyes sparkled again. 'I was, but Tom and Mrs Tom thought it a bad idea. They were afraid that Lord Lebeter might be as bad as Lord Allardyce, and though I knew that could not possibly be true, I could

see that such a course of action would not be at all
respectable! Besides, I had written to Mr Churchward
by then and Tom advised me to await his reply. When
he saw that you had come to help me, Sarah, he said
that everything would be all right and tight and that, if
Lord Allardyce kicked up a fuss, you would set your
cousin on him! Is she very fearsome, Sarah?'

'Very!' Sarah said, lips twitching at the thought of
Tom's description of Amelia. 'But I am sure that she
will like you, Olivia! She is your relative, too!'

Olivia looked very struck by this, but also rather apprehensive. 'Well, I hope she may like me, for I wish
to meet her above all things! So, what do we do now,
Sarah?'

Sarah sat back. 'I think, perhaps, that you should
come back to Bath with us, Olivia, and your mama, too,
of course. I shall speak to Amelia in the morning. Lord
Allardyce will not trouble you once he sees you have
friends to help you, and once we are in Bath we may
consult Mr Churchward over the lease of your house,
and speak to Amelia's man of business about the investments, and make lots of plans! How does that suit
you?'

Olivia's eyes had regained their sparkle. 'Oh, may
we indeed? You are so kind! Why, I think that would
be the most exciting thing in the whole world!'

'And, of course,' Sarah said with a twinkle, 'we shall
give Lord Lebeter your direction in case he wishes to
call! Now, can you be ready to travel tomorrow?'

Olivia's face fell a little. 'I fear that Mama is not
very strong at present and will not be well enough to
go for a day or two, although such good news will lift
her spirits! I am so sorry, Sarah!'

It was bad news, but Sarah swallowed her disappoint-

ment. Her instinct was to take Olivia away from Blanchland as soon as possible, but it was clearly unfeasible
to do so without Mrs Meredith's presence at her daughter's side. That left the dilemma of what to do with
Olivia in the meantime, for Sarah had no illusions as to
the lengths Allardyce might go to thwart her plans. It
was essential to prevent him from finding her niece and
every delay meant danger.

'Can Tom continue to hide you, Olivia?' she asked
cautiously. 'He seems to have been most adept at it so
far, and we must be careful until we have you well away
from here. I should not like Lord Allardyce to find
you—'

'No, indeed!' Olivia shuddered. 'I am sure that we
may stay with Tom a little longer. I am sorry for the
delay, Sarah, but I am sure Mama will be recovered
directly.'

The grandfather clock in the hall struck one. Olivia
was yawning and Sarah felt quite exhausted. She stood
up. 'I should not keep you any longer, Olivia, for you
look quite done up! Oh, but there is something I must
return to you!'

Sarah reached across for her cloak and dug deeply
into the pocket. Olivia's note and the locket were still
there. Sarah took it out and handed it to her niece.

'You will be wanting this back, for it is very pretty.
Do you know where it came from, Olivia?'

Olivia wrinkled her brow. 'I thought…that is, I have
had it since I can remember and I rather thought that it
was a present from my father, but—' She broke off,
uncertain, watching Sarah's face. 'Am I mistaken, then?
It is just that I look so very like him—like the man in
the picture!'

Sarah hesitated. It was understandable that Olivia

would think the locket a gift from the Sheridan side of
the family, but she knew that it had never been one of
their heirlooms. On the other hand, so strong a resemblance to the Woodallans could hardly be by chance.
Sarah took a deep breath.

'I wondered whether the locket was from your
mother,' she said carefully.

The colour flooded Olivia's face in a huge wave.
'Oh! I cannot believe so! I do not know who my mother
was, but I understood her to be a servant or—' she
stopped, and finished poignantly '—I hoped you might
be able to tell me, Sarah!'

Sarah did not think twice but went across and hugged
her. 'I do not know who told you that she was a servant,
Olivia, and even were it true it would not matter! We
know your father was my brother, and that makes you
a Sheridan, but now I have seen the locket, I may be
able to find out who your mother was as well. Be patient—I will do what I can!'

Olivia hugged her back hard. 'It is enough that I have
found you, Sarah! More than enough, for I cannot believe my good fortune!'

Sarah swallowed the huge lump in her throat and let
her go. 'It is nice for me to have family, too! Now, does
Tom have some cunning plan to spirit you out of the
house again?'

Her niece wrapped herself up in her cloak once more.
'I must go down to the servants' door and he will be
waiting!' The spark of excitement rekindled in her eyes.
'This is all very dramatic, is it not?'

'Very,' Sarah agreed, wondering if it was her age that
left her preferring a slightly more mundane existence.
'Surely Tom does not expect you to descend the main

stair, though? I am disappointed in the man! I had pictured a far more ingenious scheme!'

She moved towards the door. 'I will go first and check that the coast is clear. Keep well hidden over the next few days, Olivia, and if you have need of me, send word by Tom. As soon as your mama is well enough to travel, we shall be away to Bath!'

She kissed her niece on the cheek. 'Now, take care and I will see you soon, for we have much to discuss!'

She watched as her niece sped away down the stairs and was swallowed up in the shadows. The servants' door closed behind her with a soft click and Sarah turned back to her room. It seemed very quiet without Olivia's bright presence. Sarah sighed. She had a lot to think about, but she was too tired to make sense of it now. Wearily she prepared for bed, and was almost instantly asleep.

Sarah woke late, roused only by the tap on her door as Amelia came in bearing a breakfast tray.

'You are very wise to stay in your room, my dear!' she greeted her cousin cheerfully. 'Sir Greville has already been quizzing me about last night's escapade and I thought Lord Renshaw would dispense with the proprieties and march in here to demand an explanation!' She saw Sarah's look of alarm. 'Oh, I have told him nothing, but the tale of insomnia is wearing a little thin and anyway...' she put the tray down on the end of the bed '...I wish to know myself what is going on! Do try this fresh bread,' she added, pushing a plate towards her cousin. 'I have taught the cook bread-making and this is her first attempt! Not bad, I think!'

Sarah sat up and pulled the tray toward her. There

were rolls with butter and honey and the most delicious-smelling cup of chocolate.

'What do you wish to know, then?' she asked with her mouth full.

'Why, everything!' Amelia looked affronted. 'You have an unknown niece whom you were to meet at the Folly Tower last night! Tell me about that, for a beginning!'

Whilst she ate her breakfast, Sarah slowly recounted the whole of Olivia's story, from Churchward's visit to the surprise of finding her waiting in her room the previous night. The only part she left out was her suspicions of Guy's conduct and Olivia's speaking resemblance to the Woodallan family. That felt too personal to share, even with Amelia, but Sarah was beginning to realise that she would have to sort the matter out with Guy, and soon. When she had finished, Amelia gave a heavy sigh.

'That loathsome man, Allardyce! Can we not spirit Miss Meredith away from here at once, Sarah?'

Sarah shook her head slowly. 'I wish we could do so, Milly, but Mrs Meredith will scarcely entrust her daughter to strangers! I fear we must just wait patiently for a few days, difficult as it is!'

Amelia stood up and picked up the tray. 'Well, I have my tasks to complete to help me pass the time! We hope to finish cleaning the bedrooms today.' She looked around and wrinkled up her nose. 'I wonder that you can breathe in here for all this dust, Sarah!'

After her cousin had gone, Sarah got up and dressed slowly, thinking about what she should do next. Frustrating as it was, she felt inclined to say nothing to Guy about Olivia. The fewer people who knew that she had met Miss Meredith, the better. She did not like the concealment, but it was better than risking Allardyce hearing of Olivia's whereabouts. Eventually, of course, she would have to speak to Guy. As soon as anyone saw Olivia they would realise that she must be related to the Woodallan family, and Sarah needed to know the truth before that happened. Her heart was heavy when she thought of confronting him.

Sarah was determined that she would not spend the enforced wait in moping about the house. It was a bright morning with crisp snow and she walked down to the lake, finding Tom Brookes in the old tumbledown summerhouse that sat by the shore.

'Morning, Miss Sheridan!' he greeted her cheerfully. 'Is all well?' He was cleaning a pair of skates, evicting a family of spiders that had evidently taken up residence inside the boots, and polishing the steel runners to a shine.

'All's well with me,' Sarah said with a smile. 'And your own family, Tom? Your extended family?'

Tom gave her a shrewd look. 'Some improvement this morning, I'm glad to say, ma'am! I don't think it will be long—' He broke off as Guy Renshaw came through the door. 'Good morning, my lord! These will be ready for you directly!'

Sarah found herself blushing, and shrank back a little into the hut's shadowy interior. She was uncertain whether it was guilt or nerves that prompted the reaction, or simply the fact that Guy always seemed to have this regrettable effect on her. He noted her presence with a quick lift of the eyebrows.

'Miss Sheridan! Did you intend to go skating as well, ma'am?'

'That would be very pleasant,' Sarah said primly. 'It

is too fine a day to stay indoors!' She turned to Tom
Brookes. 'Perhaps you would be so good as to polish
my own skates when you have finished Lord Renshaw's, Tom? They are old, but I hope they will still
fit!'

'And in the meantime, you could come tobogganing
with me, Miss Sheridan!' Guy said persuasively. 'Tom
has already made the sledge shipshape and I am inclined
to try it on the long hill beyond the house!'

He picked the sledge up with a word of thanks to
Tom, and stood aside for Sarah to precede him out of
the hut. The sun was bright on the snow. Sarah blinked
a little.

'Tobogganing is all very well when one is a child of
ten, my lord—'

'But for a lady of your advanced years it is quite
beneath your dignity?' Guy grinned at her. 'For shame,
Miss Sheridan! I thought you had more spirit than that!'

'It is not that!' Sarah hesitated. In truth the thought
of the enforced intimacy of the small sledge and the
exhilaration of the flight downhill was quite exciting,
but she could hardly explain that to Guy.

'I should enjoy it, I am sure, but—'

'But it is scarce ladylike!' Guy was shaking his head
in mock dismay. 'It is a pity to see you so trammelled
about with rules and conventions! Take a risk, Miss
Sheridan!' He gave her a teasing look. 'You are willing
enough to do so under other circumstances!'

Sarah knew that he must mean her midnight rendezvous with Olivia and a rush of apprehension caused her
steps to falter. She had known it would only be a matter
of time before he challenged her on last night's activity
and she dreaded it. The necessity of lying—or at least
omitting certain facts—was quite alien to her nature.

However, it seemed that Guy did not intend to quiz her just yet. They had reached the top of the long field that tumbled down the hill towards Blanchland village and he put the toboggan down and gave it an experimental push. The polished runners slid across the snow with a smooth hiss.

'There! That seems to work well enough! And if you will not join me, Miss Sheridan...' Guy shrugged, folded his long body inside the little sleigh, and pushed himself off down the slope.

Sarah found that she was laughing spontaneously as she watched his progress down the hill. At the bottom he stood up, dusted some stray snow off his jacket and picked the sledge up as calmly as though he were walking into some drawing-room. Sarah was still laughing as he reached her side, barely out of breath from his climb.

'Oh, that looks prodigious good fun, my lord, if a little dangerous! If the London hostesses could see you now, your sophisticated reputation would be quite undone!'

'I trust you to tell no one!' Guy agreed. His fair hair was tousled by the breeze and his eyes were bright with laughter. 'You see how much I am in your power, Miss Sheridan! Come now, admit that you would like to try it, too!'

'Well...' Sarah hesitated. It was very tempting. She glanced round. Blanchland Court was all but hidden by a dip in the hill and the village looked very far away.

'No one would see you,' Guy continued, reading her mind. 'Besides, what do you care for the foolish rules of society? If one cannot enjoy oneself...'

'You are very persuasive, my lord!' Sarah's eyes were sparkling at the prospect. She felt reckless, as though she was behaving like a naughty child, and it was very stimulating.

'I will steer,' Guy went on, 'and you may sit before me and admire the view!'

Sarah drew back a little. 'But surely there cannot be room for both of us in that little toboggan! And it would be so—'

'So enjoyable!' Guy agreed, with a wicked smile. His dark eyes challenged her. 'Well, Miss Sheridan? Do you join me or not?'

He climbed into the sledge, holding out a hand to help Sarah sit in front of him. She was surprised to find that he was correct; the sledge was quite roomy and she could curl up, tucking her skirts about her in a way that was almost decorous and soothed her fears about preserving the proprieties. She had just started to feel better, when Guy put his arms about her.

'What on earth—'

'I cannot steer unless I reach about you, Miss Sheridan,' Guy said innocently. 'For shame, to suspect me of other motives!'

Sarah hesitated. She could hardly draw back now, but the small space that she had managed to preserve between their bodies was now to no avail. After a moment she tentatively allowed him to slide his arms about her waist, whilst still trying to lean forward and away from him. Guy laughed.

'Very modest, Miss Sheridan, but hardly effective! Move a little closer to me so that I may steer properly— I promise not to accuse you of compromising me!'

Sarah edged closer to him. The material of his coat brushed her hair and she was astounded at the urge she suddenly felt to snuggle closer still and press herself against him. She could smell the mingled scent of fresh air and Guy's lemon cologne and it was decidedly intoxicating. Alarmed by her body's peculiar reaction, Sarah was about to pull away when they set off down the hill.

It was breathtaking. The speed built up quickly and the wind burned her cheeks with an icy chill. Sarah almost cried out with the exhilaration of it, her excitement given an edge by the thought of how very badly she was behaving. Then, suddenly, the bottom of the hill rushed up towards them and they skidded into a snow drift and overturned. Winded, dazed for a moment, Sarah lay still and looked upwards through the bare lacy branches of a tree at the blue sky overhead.

'Sarah?' Guy's fingers were icy on her cheek, his expression concerned as he leaned over her. 'Are you much hurt?'

Sarah drew a shaky breath. 'I think not.' Her gaze took in the snow all over his coat and a smile started to curve her mouth. She raised a hand to brush the powdering of white out of his ruffled hair. Guy caught her hand in his. The concern had died from his eyes, leaving an intensity that was far more disturbing.

'Sarah, you have snow in your eyelashes...'

Sarah's eyes fluttered closed as he bent over and gently brushed the ice from her face. A second later, when he took her mouth with his, she felt as though she were melting in exactly the same way as the snow. A shaken sensation swept over her that had nothing to do with her abrupt descent into the snowdrift. Her fingers grazed the rough stubble of his cheek, then tangled in his hair.

Neither of them noticed the discomfort of their surroundings. Sarah knew enough now to realise that Guy was exercising considerable restraint in his kiss, and paradoxically, the knowledge made her want to provoke him into losing his control. She wriggled further beneath him, pulling him closer, pressing her body against his. A groan broke from his lips and he raised his head to look down into Sarah's eyes, his own glittering with a barely repressed desire.

'Sarah...'

Sarah knew that she had incited this ruthless passion and she revelled in the knowledge, giving him back kiss for kiss. It was only when a fall of snow tumbled from the branches above that Sarah was recalled to reality by the ice slipping down her neck.

'Oh!' She sat up and tried to brush down her coat. Guy had got to his feet and was viewing the scuffled snow with rueful amusement.

'I must choose somewhere more comfortable next time!'

Sarah blushed. 'Do not presume that there will be a next time, sir!'

Guy gave her a quizzical look. He picked her up easily and set her on her feet, keeping an imprisoning arm about her. Sarah struggled.

'Let me go!'

'You were not so eager to escape a moment ago!'

'Oh!' Sarah blushed even more with vexation. 'You are so—'

'I know.' Guy kissed her hard on the mouth and let her go. 'There! Let me help you rub that snow away. You look as though you have been rolling on the ground!'

Sarah gave him a fulminating look. 'I think it best if you escort me back to the house now, my lord!'

'Certainly, if you wish all Sir Ralph's guests to draw the same conclusions,' Guy said agreeably. 'I thought it unlikely I could persuade you to another descent of the hill!' He smiled at her. 'Admit that it was enjoyable, though!'

Sarah felt an answering gleam tug at her mouth. 'It was—quite exhilarating, my lord!'

Guy held the field gate open for her and they started to walk along the tree-lined path back towards the house.

'And yet you still refuse to marry me,' he mused. 'You have an unusually obstinate disposition, Miss Sheridan!'

Sarah looked at him. 'When I spoke of enjoyment I was referring to the tobogganing, my lord!'

'And the rest?'

There was a disquieting gleam in his eyes. Sarah looked away. 'A strong…physical attraction is hardly a good basis for marriage, my lord!'

Guy nodded. 'Well, surprisingly I would agree with you, at least in the sense that I believe it is only one important part of a good marriage! There are other qualities—a like-minded approach to life, perhaps, an enjoyment of similar interests—that may sound less exciting but are equally rewarding.'

Sarah sighed. Once again he had not mentioned love, which only served to prove to her how right she had been in refusing him. She felt hollow with disappointment.

'There are other things I would look for in a husband,' she said, more hotly than she had intended. 'Honesty and trust—'

Guy's glance was suddenly bright. 'Brave words! So, Miss Sheridan, what were you doing at the Folly Tower last night?'

Sarah stopped, neatly hoist by her own petard. She

had been thinking of Guy's secret quest to find Olivia first, and had given no thought to her own actions. She bit her lip.

'Well, Miss Sheridan?' Guy's tone was scrupulously polite. 'Surely you do not advocate qualities in others that you do not espouse yourself?'

Sarah realised how badly she had miscalculated. Guy's demeanour was generally so agreeable that it was easy to forget the core of steel that lay beneath the even-tempered exterior. Now, however, she was forcibly reminded. He was looking singularly intractable.

'I went to the Folly Tower to meet with Miss Meredith,' she said candidly.

'I see.' Guy pushed his hands into his coat pockets. His expression was inscrutable. 'So that farrago of nonsense you enacted last night was all for our benefit?'

Sarah did not allow that to provoke her. 'I had not explained the whole matter to Amelia and I assumed—' she shot him a quick look '—that Sir Greville was not party to the situation. I could not see the benefit in rehearsing the whole there and then!'

Guy let that pass. 'How did Miss Meredith contact you?'

'She sent me a note.'

'How was it delivered?'

Sarah cursed him. 'Tom Brookes delivered it,' she said reluctantly. 'Miss Meredith's message asked me to meet her at the Folly Tower at midnight, so I went to meet her.'

'But she was not there?' Guy's scrutiny was relentless. Sarah could only be grateful that he had not yet asked her anything that would require a direct lie.

'As you saw,' she said woodenly. 'Miss Meredith was not there, but someone else was.'

'Yes.' Guy turned away, to consider the view of Blanchland through the curtain of trees. The Folly Tower could just be seen in the distance.

'Strangely, I had heard a rumour that Miss Meredith would be at the Folly Tower—a rumour that proved to be false. I wonder if your mystery assailant was also aware of that rumour?'

'Very possibly,' Sarah said carefully.

'Yet you do not know who he was?'

'No, I do not know—'

'But perhaps you might hazard a guess...'

Sarah pulled a face. 'You question me hard, sir! To what purpose?'

'I am testing your veracity,' Guy admitted easily, 'for, despite your apparent openness, I believe you are hiding something, Miss Sheridan!'

Sarah flushed and hoped that it could be attributed to anger, not guilt. 'I have answered your questions quite truthfully, my lord!'

'Sins of omission, not commission,' Guy murmured. 'Tell me, Miss Sheridan, do you think that the note and the rumour were laying a deliberately false trail?'

Sarah chose her words with care. 'In the light of what happened, I believe it must be so, my lord.'

'And Lord Lebeter's part in all this? What can that be? These woods were damnably crowded last night, were they not?'

Sarah saw with relief that they were about to emerge onto the carriage sweep at the front of Blanchland.

'Lord Lebeter claimed to be suffering from insomnia,' she said.

Guy laughed. 'I heard him! A common complaint! So, do you intend to try to seek Miss Meredith out again?'

'No,' Sarah said truthfully, 'I shall wait for her to contact me. Excuse me, my lord, I must change out of these damp clothes.'

Guy bowed slightly. 'Very well, Miss Sheridan. You have managed not to tell me a word of a lie, but even so...'

He sauntered off towards the games room, leaving Sarah standing on the gravel and feeling a mixture of relief and guilt. Just how much he knew she could not tell, but it could only be a matter of time before he pressed her for the whole story. Yet if anyone could be accused of withholding information, it had to be he, for he had as yet breathed no word of his own purpose in searching for Olivia.

Sarah ran hastily upstairs to get changed before anyone saw her. Further down the corridor a veritable army of maids was dusting and scrubbing, and Sarah could hear Amelia's voice calling instructions and exhortations. She dived into her room before her cousin could remark on her dishevelled state, and did not emerge again until the bell rang for luncheon.

In the afternoon, Amelia was persuaded to abandon her cleaning efforts for a while and join Sarah, Greville and Justin Lebeter on an expedition to go skating on the lake. The other members of the house party declined with expressions of horror, except for Sir Ralph, who somewhat surprisingly chose to join them. The thickness of the ice was tested to the full when Sir Ralph lumbered onto it, but he proved surprising agile on his skates and even performed an elegant skaters' waltz with Amelia.

This time, Sarah kept well away from Guy and gave him no opportunity to speak with her alone. The look of amusement he cast her showed that he perfectly understood her attempts to avoid him and left her with the unsettling impression that he was only biding his time.

A small bonfire was burning by the greenhouses as they made their way back to the house, and Amelia stepped aside for a quick word with Tom Brookes, who was industriously feeding the flames with what appeared to be old books and papers. Sir Ralph, deep in conversation with Greville Baynham, did not appear to notice the conflagration until a stray breath of wind whirled a fragment of paper into his path. He bent absentmindedly to pick it up, cast it a vague glance, then stopped abruptly in the middle of his sentence.

'My lithographs! My books!'

Everyone stared at the bonfire, where one of the books was shrivelling, its pages curling and turning dark brown. Nearby ashes gave mute testimony to the demise of other volumes. One last edition fell open as it succumbed to the flames, revealing the saucy cartoons inside. Sir Ralph was wailing and appeared to be about to rake through the ashes with his bare hands.

Amelia put a consoling hand on his arm.

'I am so sorry, Sir Ralph. They had the woodworm and smelled quite unpleasant besides! It is the library, you know—I suspect you may have a problem with the drains...'

Sarah looked at Sir Ralph's stricken face and privately wondered whether Amelia had gone too far this time. There would be no more cosy evenings in the library for Sir Ralph and his guests, tickling their appetite with erotic prints.

'Did you sort through the volumes yourself, Lady Amelia?' Greville was asking, with a speculative look. 'What a selfless act!'

Sir Ralph's shoulders slumped and he trudged off alone towards the house. Sarah was about to follow her cousin indoors, but at that moment Justin Lebeter caught up with her.

'Miss Sheridan—may I have a moment of your time? In private?'

Sarah stood back to allow the rest of the party to pass them, and waited for him to speak. Olivia's beau was tall and fair, with a rather earnest expression and bright blue eyes. He fixed these pleadingly on Sarah's face.

'I am sorry to approach you like this, ma'am,' he stammered, a little red in the face. 'Indeed, it is only my concern for…that is, I am anxious to find a certain young lady, and I had heard—' He broke off self-consciously.

Sarah raised her eyebrows. 'Yes, sir? You had heard…'

'That you came to Blanchland to see Miss Olivia Meredith!' Lord Lebeter said in a rush. 'I would not listen to gossip, but I am anxious to see the young lady myself—'

'I see,' Sarah said drily.

Justin Lebeter flushed an even brighter red. 'Oh, no, I would not wish you to misunderstand me, ma'am! Miss Meredith is an old school friend of one of my sisters and I had an invitation for her to visit—' Here he broke off again at the somewhat sceptical look in Sarah's eye. He squared his shoulders. 'The point of the matter is that Miss Meredith seems to have disappeared and I am worried about her! I wondered whether you had seen her, ma'am?'

Sarah relented of her teasing. It seemed that Lord Lebeter was made of sterner stuff than first appeared and he did seem sincerely concerned about Olivia. She wished that she could reassure him, but that was impossible whilst Olivia was still in danger.

'It is true that I came here to meet with Miss Meredith,' she said, wishing that she did not always need to choose her words with such care, 'but I have found that she is from home at present. I am sorry, Lord Lebeter—I really cannot help you.'

Lebeter's eyes narrowed thoughtfully, and for a moment, Sarah had the feeling that he knew far more than he had said.

'Forgive me, ma'am,' he said again, 'but I was under the impression that you had actually met with Miss Meredith.'

Now it was Sarah's turn to feel uncomfortable at being forced into a direct denial. 'No, indeed,' she said, a little too quickly, 'you are mistaken, sir.'

'I see,' Lebeter said. He looked both embarrassed and awkward, as though he wished to accuse her of something but could not quite find the words. After a moment, he bowed abruptly and walked on ahead of her into the house. Sarah, aware that Guy had seen the exchange from the doorway, followed with her face averted. The whole incident had been disconcerting because she hated the deceit and knew that Lord Lebeter was genuinely worried about Olivia. She also had the distinct impression that Lebeter had not believed her, and wondered why. And if Lebeter should express his doubts to Guy—what then?

Chapter Nine

Sir Ralph was still sunk deep in gloom at dinner. The loss of his beloved lithographs and his prized collection of erotic books was a blow that he could hardly bear and he ate his way through the first course in a stolid silence. The food was excellent once again, and it appeared that Sir Ralph's guests were beginning to resign themselves to the lack of wine, some of them even grudgingly complementing the spring water on its purity. The fish course, a fine salmon in anchovy sauce, was followed by a syllabub brought in by the black-clad footman whom Sarah now knew to be the obsequious Marvell. Amelia had made no secret of the fact that she disliked him, but her clean sweep of the servants had so far failed to dislodge him.

Marvell delivered the syllabub with an ingratiating smile, whispering something in Lord Allardyce's ear as he did so that brought an arrested look to the peer's eyes. Allardyce's pensive gaze travelled from Amelia to Sarah, where it lingered in blatant appraisal before he applied himself to the dish before him. Sarah turned her shoulder, uncomfortable as always with his scrutiny.

Amelia and Greville, having spent an afternoon without bickering, were actually sitting next to each other at the table, which meant that Sarah had Greville on one side of her and Justin Lebeter on the other. Despite their difficult encounter that afternoon, Lebeter proved pleasantly attentive and was far more comfortable company than Allardyce. For once, Sarah began to relax and actually to enjoy the meal.

The syllabub tasted of lemon, but with a curious aftertaste that was so sweet as to be almost cloying. Sarah paused to consider the flavour and noticed that Guy was the only one not eating, having waved away the food that Marvell had offered him. She took another thoughtful spoonful, almost certain that she did not like it and wondering what Amelia would think. This would certainly not be one of her recipes. Her cousin, however, seemed oblivious to the food, for she was leaning close to Greville and seemed utterly absorbed in what he had to say. Sarah smiled, thinking how pleasant it was to see them in accord for once. Almost without thinking, she took another mouthful of syllabub, then pushed the bowl away, repelled by the taste.

A huge haunch of beef followed the syllabub and everyone applied themselves with enthusiasm. After a while, Sarah observed that a curious change of mood appeared to have come over Sir Ralph's guests. They were chatting and laughing as freely as though the wine had been circulating for hours, rediscovering the uninhibited enjoyment that had characterised the first dinner Sarah had experienced at Blanchland. Mrs Fisk leant forward and playfully stuck her tongue in Sir Ralph's ear. Lord Allardyce was trailing kisses along Lady Tilney's bare shoulder, but his eyes met Sarah's across the table, wide with mockery and lust. Sarah looked away hastily, suddenly anxious to escape. This was much worse than the first night. Sir Ralph's guests seemed totally unrestrained, their expressions glazed as they neglected their food for more exciting pleasures.

Sarah was about to get to her feet when something even more strange occurred. Lord Lebeter leaped up and rushed from the room without a word, the door slamming violently behind him. No one except Sarah appeared to notice. She turned to look at Amelia, about to suggest that they retire, and experienced a dreadful shock. Amelia's hand was resting on Greville's thigh and, as Sarah watched in utter amazement, she leant forward and pressed a lingering kiss on his mouth.

Sarah gave a little squeak, part-dismay and part-disbelief. How could Amelia, so proper, so much a high stickler for convention and good behaviour, have succumbed to the gross conduct of Sir Ralph's party? It was impossible and yet, before her very eyes, Greville and Amelia rose from the table and went out of the room, entwined in each other arms. They paused frequently to embrace each other, playfully and lovingly kissing and stroking until Sarah thought her eyes would fall out with shock.

There was a movement beside her as Guy slid into the seat vacated by Justin Lebeter. Unlike the rest of the company, his gaze was steady and his voice held a note of emphasis that immediately caught Sarah's attention, despite her agitation.

'Listen to me, Miss Sheridan. We do not have much time. How much of that syllabub did you eat?'

Sarah gazed at him in bewilderment. 'Only a few spoonfuls. I did not care for the taste. What—?'

'The syllabub contained an aphrodisiac, Miss Sheridan.' Guy's gaze was urgent. 'Do you understand me? It held some kind of drug that increases the sexual appetite.' He gestured at the others. 'That is the explanation for what you see before you. And if you ate any at all, you will soon feel the same.'

Sarah could feel the blood draining from her face. 'But I only ate a few mouthfuls! And I feel perfectly well—'

'No matter.' Guy leant towards her, his face set. 'It takes longer to work on some than others, and it may be that the lesser dose will have less severe an effect, but we cannot stay here discussing it! You must come with me—'

'No!' Sarah got to her feet, suddenly terrified. Everywhere were scenes of the most shocking debauchery as Sir Ralph's guests threw themselves wholeheartedly into the orgy. The lurid pictures on the wall, the statues, the romping nymphs on the frieze, all seemed to mock her with their knowing eyes. She gave a little moan of terror.

Guy's hand closed about her wrist so hard that the pain cut through her hysteria. He was already on his feet and pulling her towards the door.

'Listen to me, Sarah,' he said again. 'You *must* stay with me. It is the only way that you will be safe. I promise—'

And then it happened. They were out in the hall, in the flickering candlelight. Sarah felt a curious feeling steal over her, a weakness that left her warm but trembling. An irresistible urge to touch Guy came over her, and she raised her hand to stroke his cheek. The skin felt smooth beneath her fingers, deliciously cool. She brushed her fingers across the curve of his mouth, wishing she could pull it down to meet hers. Her heightened senses were full of him—the smell and the touch, the need for more...

She saw him smile as he gently took her hand and restrained her caresses.

'This is where matters become rather difficult,' he said, and even through the fever in her blood, Sarah thought she heard a note of regret. It did not matter, however, for he had already swept her up into his arms and was carrying her up to her room. Sarah turned her face against his neck and pressed little kisses into the warmth of his throat, and felt very happy. In the heat of her desire, alone with Guy was precisely where she wanted to be.

Sarah woke to pale darkness. Her mind felt as shadowy as the room, floating, insubstantial. She blinked, and the light came into focus. The candle beside the bed was burned so low it was almost out, but beyond it the grey shade of dawn was creeping into the room. Sarah turned her head very slowly.

Guy was lying beside her, and very deeply asleep. The cold morning light cast shadows across his face, highlighting the tension there, the hollows and lines of exhaustion. Sarah jumped as though stung, and immediately his eyes flew open and he reached across and grabbed her.

'Oh! Let me go! What are you doing here?' Sarah's words came out in a muffled scream.

She lay quite still, staring up into his face in horrified incomprehension.

Guy's dark eyes searched her face for a moment, then he let her go and sat up. 'You do not remember anything?'

'Remember what? I...' Sarah's voice trailed away and she frowned. Vague memories flickered through her mind, vivid dreams... She could see the dining-room and images of debauchery wherever she looked; she could remember a feeling of confusion when Amelia disappeared; she saw Guy, speaking to her urgently; recalled a feeling of intense frustration and thwarted desire… And always his voice, speaking to her soothingly, his arms holding her gently but with none of the passion that she desperately wanted and had begged for…

'Oh, no!' Sarah's eyes were wild. 'It was not a dream?'

'It was not a dream.' Guy took her hands in a steadying clasp. 'Sweetheart, listen. It is all over and you are quite safe. Nothing happened, I promise you—'

'But I remember!' Sarah said desperately. 'The things I said—what I did! Oh!'

She tried to free herself, but Guy refused to let go. His voice was very calm and quiet.

'You were not responsible for your actions. I swear you came to no harm, Sarah!'

Sarah burst into tears. She could not have stopped herself even had she wanted to. As it was, the flood of tears was a welcome relief from the horrors of night, the shock and the shame. She cried, and Guy held her trembling body in his arms, murmuring endearments and holding her gently until she calmed at last and fell quiet.

'I dare say that you will be wanting to change your clothes, and have some food and drink,' Guy said, very practically, when at last he let her go. 'I will go to fetch something from the kitchens. Do not open the door whilst I am gone.'

His matter-of-fact tone had the desired effect. Sarah moved almost mechanically to strip off her dress, wash her tearstained face and find some fresh clothes. All the

time, her words and actions from the previous night
flashed through her mind like some terrible play. She
had repeatedly tried to entice Guy, rubbing herself
against him in an utterly shameless way and begging
for his kisses. She had tried to pull off her own clothing,
never mind his! It seemed impossible, unbelievable, and
yet… One thing she did remember with utter clarity was
that Guy had repeatedly refused her, and the worst thing
was that she was so confused that she did not know
whether to be glad or sorry…

A knock at the door recalled her from the dreadful
nightmare, and she went to let Guy in. Whilst she pulled
back the curtains and tidied the room, he coaxed the
fire into life, then drew Sarah over to sit beside it. She
noticed that he had had a chance to change, but not to
shave, and that there were shadows as well as stubble
darkening his face.

'How are you feeling now?' he asked, his tone still
carefully neutral.

Sarah hesitated. 'A little better.' She met his eyes
directly. 'I would not like you to think that I am without
proper feeling, my lord, for the experiences of last night
were hideous. Nevertheless, I do believe that I owe you
my thanks. Matters…must have been very difficult for
you.'

There was a pause, then Guy's expression lightened
considerably. 'It relieves me that you have not fallen
into a fit of the vapours or an irreversible decline, Miss
Sheridan, despite so shocking an experience!' He
smiled ruefully. 'And, yes, it was very difficult for me.
To have you begging me to do all the things that I have
wanted to do for some time—and then to resist!' He
shook his head slowly. 'I surprised even myself!'

Sarah blushed rosily and poured a cup of tea to try

to distract herself. 'How could such a thing happen? I had grossly underestimated the dangers that might befall us here at Blanchland....'

Guy grimaced. 'I can only suppose that Sir Ralph habitually resorts to such stimulants to arouse the jaded appetites of his guests. It is not to be expected that you would even imagine such a thing, Miss Sheridan. How could you? But that was one of the reasons I was so concerned to think of you coming here alone! An innocent abroad, with no idea of the perils that awaited you!'

Sarah shuddered. 'How dared that man Marvell do such a thing? I saw him whispering to Lord Allardyce as he served the syllabub, but I had no idea—' She broke off. 'It is truly disgusting!'

'I saw it, too,' Guy said heavily, 'and cursed myself that I made no connection until it was too late! As it was, I only refused the dish myself because I do not care for cream!' His gaze swept over her with repressed amusement. 'Had I eaten it, Miss Sheridan, the outcome would have been much different, I assure you!'

Sarah sighed, wondering how she would have felt if she had woken that morning under other circumstances. What had happened was dreadfully shocking and a true lesson against wandering unprepared into unfamiliar circumstances. Blanchland had plumbed the depths of depravity and nothing in her past experience could have helped her begin to understand such things. She was not a green girl, being well aware that a seamier side to life had always existed—but for one who had grown up and lived in relatively sheltered circumstances, such knowledge as she now had was deeply distressing. Had Guy and she both succumbed to the lure of the aphrodisiac...

Sarah took a comforting mouthful of tea and viewed

Guy across the rim of her cup. She was sensible enough
to realise that that would have been far preferable to
some of the things that might have happened, and despite the fact that the aphrodisiac effect had now worn
off, she was forced to admit that it might have been
rather exciting...

Sarah replenished her cup, turning her thoughts aside
from such matters. She had learned a great deal about
herself, as well as others, in the past twelve hours.

'I must commend your quick thinking, my lord!' she
said ruefully. 'Once you had realised what was happening you acted very swiftly. I realise how much I owe
you—'

Guy sat back in his chair, relaxing a little. 'I hope
you understand, Miss Sheridan, that what I did was
solely for your protection. I had to get you away from
the others as quickly as possible, but I could not have
risked leaving you alone. You might have become ill,
or wandered off and fallen into some trouble...I am
deeply sorry for all the distress this must have caused
you. It is truly appalling.'

Sarah made a slight gesture. 'Please, let us not speak
of it any more. I have learned a great deal that in my
foolish naïvety I did not know...'

'There is nothing foolish about your innocence, Miss
Sheridan,' Guy said, a little roughly, 'and I am glad that
not all of it has been dispelled this night...'

'Is anyone else awake yet?' Sarah asked hastily, anxious to change the subject. She had not really given
much thought to anybody's situation, but suddenly wondered what other disasters the aphrodisiac had wrought.

Guy shook his head. 'The house is quite still. I believe they all took far more syllabub than you, so will

be feeling the effects both more strongly and for longer—'

'Amelia!' Sarah suddenly put her teacup down with a clatter that sent the remaining liquid cascading onto the hearth. 'Oh, no.' Her wide-eyed gaze turned back to Guy, imploring his reassurance. 'Did I imagine... surely she did not...?'

A shadow touched Guy's face. 'Miss Sheridan...you force me to be frank with you. You did *not* imagine that your cousin and Sir Greville...' he hesitated '...they did indeed leave together.'

Sarah pressed her hand to her mouth. 'Then they... Oh, no...'

Guy fixed her with a very straight look. 'There is nothing you can do, Miss Sheridan. There would have been nothing I could have done either. Both of them were under the influence of the drug.' His gaze was watchful. 'Forgive me, but it will be less of a shock for Lady Amelia than it would have been for you...'

Sarah looked away. She knew what he meant. Amelia was a widow and therefore more knowledgeable of the ways of the world, but even so...

'I believe,' Guy continued in the same measured tone he had used earlier to reassure her, 'that Lady Amelia and Sir Greville sincerely love each other, for all their wrangling. I am certain that all will be well. It may not be very conventional, but there are times when matters might be so very much worse.'

'I know.' Sarah groped for her handkerchief, finding that the realisation of Amelia's situation had made her cry again. How foolish and naïve they had both been, to think that they could come to Blanchland and escape unscathed! Yet how right Guy was to point out that both of them could have woken in far more terrible circum-

stances that day. If it had been Allardyce, or Ralph Covell... Sarah shuddered. She had to look beyond the hy-
pocritical rules of society and realise that both she and
Amelia were, if not fortunate, at least safe...

Sarah dried her tears and stood up, walking across to
the window and looking out over the cold white landscape. She rested one hand on the thick velvet curtain.
They would have to leave Blanchland now. There was
no other way. That, of course, meant changing her plans
with regard to Olivia, for whom she had not spared a
single thought in the last few hours, and for the moment
she was too tired to make any plans.

Guy had also stood up and now came to stand behind
her at the window. 'It is a beautiful place but blighted,
Miss Sheridan,' he said softly. 'You have to let it go.'

'I know,' Sarah said. She turned back to him. He was
watching her with great gentleness in his eyes.

'Forgive me for pressing you at such a time,' he said
with constraint, 'but you must also know that you have
to marry me now. Whatever your previous doubts...'

Sarah swallowed hard. She wanted to tell him that
she loved him, but the words seemed to stick in her
throat. Her previous attraction to him, so sudden and
violent, had grown swiftly into love as she had observed
how fine a man he was, and she was sure that even the
difficulties over Olivia could be overcome if only they
could speak of it. She just needed a little time to prepare...

When she did not reply, a slight shadow seemed to
touch Guy's face and he turned away.

'There is still the issue of Miss Meredith to be resolved, of course,' he continued. 'Before all last night's
events began, Justin Lebeter asked me to speak to you
about her.' Guy looked at Sarah thoughtfully. 'He is

certain that she is in grave danger and is almost as certain that you know her whereabouts! What do you say, Miss Sheridan?'

Sarah caught her breath. This was sudden, if not unexpected, and she felt woefully unready. To give herself time, she walked over to the bed stand and poured herself a glass of spring water. It was exactly as she had feared the day before—she did not know how Lebeter had guessed her complicity; whether it was simply an instinct, or whether he had seen or heard something, she could not tell. It was the worst piece of luck that he had not believed her denials and had chosen to go to Guy with his suspicions, for now she would have to discuss the subject of Olivia with Guy, and she did not really know how to approach it.

She sat down again in one of the armchairs before the fire, but Guy remained on his feet, evidently preferring to stand. It was extraordinary, but the intimacy of their previous exchange appeared to have completely vanished. Sarah felt her heart sink. She knew that Guy could reasonably expect her to trust him after all he had done to help her, and here she was, apparently demonstrating her lack of confidence in him. Her silence was going to cost her dear.

Guy was waiting for her reply with perfect courtesy, but the expression in his eyes was cold.

'Lord Lebeter is mistaken in thinking that I know Miss Meredith's whereabouts,' Sarah said truthfully. 'I did not lie to him, precisely—'

'Indeed? In the same way, perhaps, that you did not lie to me when we spoke of it?' The sudden contempt in Guy's voice cut across Sarah like a whiplash and she flinched. 'What a talent you have for being sparing with the truth, Miss Sheridan! I should tell you that Lord

Lebeter saw Miss Meredith leaving this very room! He even suggested to me that you may have been involved in procuring your niece's services as mistress to Lord Allardyce!'

The deliberate insult touched Sarah on the raw. She jumped to her feet, her eyes blazing. All the tension and distress of the previous night caught up with her. She did not even stop to think how they could have moved from intimacy to opposition so quickly.

'How *dare* you suggest such a thing, Lord Renshaw? I have never heard anything so immoral! Why, Olivia is my niece! And leaving that aside, I am hardly likely—'

Guy shrugged laconically. He seemed untouched by her fury. '*I* did not suggest it, it is simply what others are saying! And they have grounds for suspicion. Perhaps you view Miss Meredith as an unwelcome addition to the family? Relatives have been known to connive at such solutions!'

'If I thought that you had insulted me once before,' Sarah said, her voice shaking, 'that was as nothing to this! You will leave at once—'

Guy's only reply was to stroll over to the bed, toss the key onto the table beside it, and lie down with his hands behind his head. Sarah stared in speechless outrage.

'What do you think you are doing? You cannot stay there!'

Guy gave her an unrepentant smile. He sounded completely unconcerned. 'Can I not? But you see I am doing so! I have been here all night, after all, so what difference can a few more hours make? This is a comfortable way of waiting until you decide to tell me what I want to know.'

'But…' Sarah was not sure if it was bewilderment or rage that would win out inside her. 'This is quite preposterous! Surely it need not come to this! If we could only speak sensibly…'

Guy turned his head on the pillow and gave her a derisive look. 'I am perfectly willing to do so, Miss Sheridan—but on my terms! It seems to me that I did you a great service last night, but now, for reasons that only you understand, you are refusing repay me with your trust! Well, I cannot force you to tell me about Olivia, but I may stay here until you do!'

Sarah saw red. 'The reason that I do not trust you is because I know you are hiding something from me!' she said furiously. 'I heard you speaking to your father at Woodallan—I know you have some reason to find Olivia first! Oh, I cannot bear this! If you will not leave, then I will be the one to go!'

She snatched at the key, but Guy was too quick for her. His hand closed around her wrist and he pulled hard. Caught off balance, Sarah tumbled down beside him on the huge bed.

Before she could say a word, she found herself pinioned beneath him, with Guy's face a heart-stopping few inches from her own. Sarah's heart began to race.

'Now,' Guy said softly, 'what do you think that you owe me for my forbearance last night? Your provocations were enough to try the patience of a saint, yet I did not succumb!'

'Then pray do not undo all your good work now!' Sarah gasped. She knew that matters had slipped far beyond her control. There was a furious glitter in Guy's eyes and it was only now, when it was too late, that she realised just how far she must have pushed him the previous night. It must have cost him a great deal to

keep himself from touching her when she had begged
him to make love, and all that frustrated energy and
desire had still to be defused. His anger and his passion
sprang from the same source.

For an agonising second their eyes locked, then his
mouth came down on hers in an emphatic demonstra-
tion of his mastery. The desire flared instantly between
them and a searing warmth leapt through Sarah's blood,
leaving her weak and trembling, yet alive to every sensation.

She opened her eyes and met his gaze, heavy with
heat, before his mouth returned to hers with a feverish
compulsion that left her gasping. Anger was banished,
replaced by an urgent need. Of their own volition,
Sarah's hands slid under his jacket to feel the hard
warmth of his body beneath the linen shirt. Guy raised
himself on one elbow, leaning over to place a kiss on
the corner of her mouth, then another in the hollow of
her throat. Despite his gentleness there was an insis-
tence in his touch that made Sarah give a soft moan of
pleasure.

'Guy, please…'

'Please…what?' His voice was husky and she could
hear the smile in it. His fingers were easing her dress
from her shoulder, so that he could move his mouth to
where it had rested, pressing soft kisses against her skin.

'Are you conscious this time, Sarah?' Guy whispered.
He slid a finger under the curve of Sarah's gown and
she felt it slip down, revealing the flimsy chemise beneath. Just the brush of his hand against the soft swell
of her breasts set her trembling afresh, a feeling of exquisite need in the pit of her stomach. She felt Guy slide
the material down with deliberate slowness, exposing
her breasts as the chemise slipped lower. She waited in

an agony of anticipation to feel his touch against her naked skin, and her lashes flickered open to see him looking at her with such intense, concentrated desire that she could not move or speak. Their eyes held for a long moment of tension, then Guy lowered his head to take one taut nipple in his mouth and such slow, sweet pleasure shot through her that Sarah thought she would scream out loud.

'Do you surrender?' Guy's voice was ragged with emotion. He slid a hand across her bare stomach and Sarah arched against him.

'Yes...' She would have agreed to tell him anything. Olivia, Lord Lebeter, Allardyce, were all forgotten, irrelevant. 'Please...'

Guy bent his head to her breast again, teasing and tormenting her with his lips and tongue until Sarah writhed with need.

'So you will marry me?'

Through the desire that clouded her mind, Sarah dimly realised that this was the wrong question. Surely he was supposed to be asking her about Olivia... Her mind sheered away as Guy bit gently at her satin skin.

'Yes, yes, I will. Of course.'

For some reason she expected him to stop now that he had achieved his aim and when she felt his hand on the silken softness of her inner thigh, her eyes opened wide. 'But I thought...'

Whatever she had thought was never expressed, for Guy was caressing her with a tender urgency that made her cry out and just when she thought she could bear it no more, her whole body exploded in the most intense rapture.

It took Sarah some time to recover herself, but when she did so, she found that Guy had discarded her some-

what superfluous clothing and wrapped her in the bedclothes. She was curled in the crook of his arm, with
her head resting against his shoulder and, as it seemed
a little too late for embarrassment, Sarah chose instead
to snuggle a little closer. Her body felt drugged with
pleasure and she was very sleepy, but at the back of her
mind was the nagging doubt that something was wrong.
She raised herself a little and placed one hand on his
chest.

'Guy...'

'Sarah...' She felt his breath stir the tendrils of hair
about her face as he leaned over to kiss her. 'Are you
well?'

'Yes, very...' Sarah smiled. 'But you...I may not
know a great deal about love, but it is not fair—'

She felt him laugh against her hair. 'Much as I appreciate your sense of fair play, sweetheart, I fear that
that must wait!'

'But—'

'Don't tempt me,' Guy said, a little roughly. 'It is by
the nature of a miracle that I was able to stop at all!'
His voice warmed. 'After all, that is the second time I
have resisted you—'

Sarah moved slightly and the sheet slipped. Seeing
Guy's downward gaze and the sudden heat that leapt to
his eyes, she felt her own body suffuse with fire once
more.

'Get dressed,' Guy said abruptly. 'Please get dressed,
Sarah! I want to talk to you and I will never achieve it
at this rate!'

He turned his back as Sarah scrambled for her
clothes, and when she had rather haphazardly dressed
herself again, gestured to her to join him in the arm-

chairs by the fire. The daylight was stronger now, but still the house had not stirred.

'You accused me earlier of withholding information from you,' Guy began, 'and it is true that I did keep something back. I wish to God that I had told you sooner, Sarah, but—' He broke off. 'There are complications. However, I wanted you to know that Olivia Meredith—'

'Is your niece as well as mine?' Sarah suggested.

Guy stared. 'How the devil did you know that?'

Sarah burst out laughing. 'Because I have seen her! And as soon as I saw her…' Sarah shook her head, a rueful smile on her lips '…well, if you had told me that she was *not* related to you, I would not have believed you! I would even have believed that she was your daughter, were it that I could not think you steeped in debauchery quite so young!'

Guy gave her a look that brought the blood up into her face. 'Thank you! The resemblance is then so strong?'

'A speaking likeness! She also has in her possession a locket that depicts your grandparents, or so I believe. But she has no notion of her mother's identity, knowing only that Frank was her father. I must own myself surprised…that Catherine was her mother.'

Guy gave her a searching look. 'You have deduced that yourself?'

'It seemed the only explanation.' Sarah hesitated. 'Unless I have read it wrongly—'

'You have not. Were you shocked?'

Sarah met his gaze very candidly. 'How could I be, after what almost happened just now? I have learned a lot…I cannot judge or blame. Only…I am surprised at

Frank. He was a scoundrel, but he would not have abandoned an innocent girl…'

Guy sighed heavily. He leant forward, resting his
chin on his hand. 'He did not know. Catherine never
told anyone until it was too late and your brother
abroad. She died in childbirth and my father was so
racked with anger and grief that he refused to have anything to do with the child, leaving it all to your family
to dispose.'

'Poor little girl,' Sarah said softly, 'and poor Catherine. She can have been no more than sixteen.'

'Yes, the whole thing has been the most appalling
tragedy. My father—' Guy stopped, his face sombre.
'He cannot bear for Catherine's disgrace to be known,
Sarah. That is the reason he asked me to find Olivia
first, and to tell no one, not even you, that I sought her.
I am sorry.' He ran his hand through his hair, further
disordering the already dishevelled locks. 'It must appear that I did not trust you, but it was only that I had
given him my word…'

Sarah was frowning. 'But I do not understand, Guy.
Supposing you had found Olivia first—what were you
to do? What did your father ask of you?'

For a moment, she thought that Guy was not going
to answer her. He got up and threw another log onto
the fire. The shower of sparks that shot upwards illuminated his grim expression.

'He asked me to pay Miss Meredith off. His plan was
to make it worth her while to disappear. You were never
to know.'

Sarah was shocked into silence for a moment. She
stared at Guy's averted face whilst anger and outrage
warred within her.

'I suppose he is ashamed of Olivia's existence—' she began, in a voice that shook.

Guy looked at her. There was grief and pity in his face. 'My father wished to protect Catherine's memory. He acted from the best of motives. You must remember that Miss Meredith is nothing to him, whilst his daughter's honour and reputation is everything—he could not bear for her memory to be disgraced. I told him that I thought him misguided, but he is a proud old man...'

Sarah was struggling with her feelings. 'Olivia is my niece, too! He had no concern for my opinion! Why, I thought that he had asked you to accompany me to Blanchland to give me support and protection, not to undermine and deceive!'

She jumped to her feet, unable to sit calmly discussing so great a betrayal. 'I cannot believe that, all the time, you were planning to trick me! And then to have the audacity to accuse me of being sparing with the truth—'

Guy came swiftly to her side. He caught her hands in his. 'Sarah, listen to me!' His tone was forceful. 'I had no intention of falling in with my father's plan—'

'Olivia would never have agreed to it!' Sarah said wildly, bursting into tears. 'She has the integrity that other members of her family seem to lack!'

'I am sure you are right.' Guy had gathered her into his arms and was stroking her hair gently. 'It was an ill-conceived plan! We will go to my father and find another solution, I promise you!'

He said no more as Sarah wept uncontrollably into his jacket. After a little while, as her sobs abated, he drew her down to sit next to him on the bed.

'Oh, why can I not stop crying?' Sarah wailed. 'This

is of all things the most intolerable! I am truly sick of
it!'

Guy pressed a kiss against her hair. 'It is scarce surprising. You have had a shock, one way and another.
Sarah, I wish to say that I am sorry for the things I said
earlier. I knew you were concealing matters from me
and it made me angry that you did not trust me. Fine
words, I know, from one who has just confessed to the
same fault! May we start afresh, sweetheart?'

He got no further, for there was a sudden loud shout
from the bottom of the stairs. They looked at one another. Even this, it seemed, had failed to rouse the
household, for no one stirred.

'I must go and see what is the matter,' Guy said reluctantly, retrieving the keys and unlocking the door.
'There may be some emergency.'

Sarah followed him out onto the darkened landing
and down the stairs. Tom Brookes was standing in the
entrance hall, his strained face breaking into relief as he
saw Guy.

'My lord! Thank God it's you! There has been a messenger from Woodallan. Your father—'

Sarah clutched Guy's arm. 'Oh, no, Tom! Is it—he
is not...?'

'No, ma'am,' the gardener said reassuringly, 'but I
believe he is taken quite poorly.' He turned to Guy. 'He
asks that you return at once, sir. I've your horse already
saddled—'

'Thank you.' Guy pressed Sarah's hand, where it still
rested on his arm. 'I must go, Sarah. Listen, this is what
you must do. Pack your bags, and I shall either return
or send a message later. Do not do anything until you
hear from me, but keep safe and tend to your cousin.'
He kissed her briefly. 'Tom—' the gardener was waiting

patiently '—pray keep Miss Sheridan—and Miss Meredith—safe until I return.'

'Olivia!' Sarah said suddenly. 'I never told you—'

'It will have to wait.' Guy kissed her again and ran for the door. Sarah stood on the steps beside Tom Brookes and watched as he rode off into the snow. She felt miserable and bereft, worried about the Earl's illness and wanting to be with his son. But deeper than that, some instinct told her that something was very wrong, and she was afraid.

'The most dreadful aspect,' Amelia said later, plucking at her bedcovers, 'is that I cannot remember a single moment of the whole experience! To be ravished by Greville, and yet to forget it all—it is most extraordinary.'

A delicate shade of colour came into her face. 'I knew at once this morning, of course. Forgive me, Sarah, for speaking to you of such things! I am just so very grateful that you are unharmed...'

'Oh, do not worry about me!' Sarah placed a comforting hand on her cousin's arm. She had managed to reassure Amelia of her own safety very successfully, mainly because her cousin was still so wrapped up in what had happened. 'Milly, what will happen?'

'Oh, do not fear,' Amelia said hastily, breaking into a radiant smile. 'It is no doubt very improper of me to say so, but all will be well. Greville and I have talked...' her colour deepened '...and we are to marry as soon as he may procure a special licence! I have been so foolish, Sarah, for I love him very much, and...' Her voice faded away and she lay back on the pillows, closing her eyes. Sarah realised that the effects of the drug must have been very strong indeed and blessed once again the chance that had led her to eat only a few spoonfuls.

Outside the window the snow was falling from a leaden sky. Sarah thought of her plans for them all to remove to Woodallan, and felt a pang of concern. The weather was poor and it now seemed that Amelia would not be fit to travel. She had not heard a word from Tom, whom she had sent to relay a message to Olivia. With all her heart, Sarah wished that Guy had not had to leave them.

'Apparently all Sir Ralph's guests have awoken with the wrong person,' Amelia said dolefully. 'I changed all the rooms about when I was arranging the cleaning—I thought it might be amusing! And now look what has happened!'

'The important thing to remember,' Sarah said staunchly, 'is that you and I woke up with the *right* person. Sir Ralph and his guests can take care of themselves!' She paused to consider how extraordinary it was that she could be speaking so openly on such delicate topics, but a short space of time had wrought a great change. She sought to inject a lighter note. 'Mr and Mrs Fisk are very happy, at any rate! Apparently they awoke to find themselves together and are so taken by their rapprochement that they plan a second honeymoon!'

The cousins caught each other's eye and started to laugh. 'Oh, dear,' Amelia said, between giggles, 'this is dreadful! At least I have been married and could be expected not to be too missish, but you, Sarah! I was supposed to be looking after you!'

'Lord Renshaw did that very successfully, I thank you! He was the perfect gentleman!'

Amelia gave her cousin a speaking glance and they

both collapsed into fresh laughter. 'I can well imagine!' Amelia said. 'Or rather, I cannot imagine it at all!'

Sarah stood up abruptly and went to the window, watching the dizzy swirl of snowflakes falling.

'Alan was never faithful to me, you know,' Amelia said quietly after a moment, clearly following some train of thought of her own. 'Oh, he was handsome and charming and such fun to be with, but he did not see the need to confine his attentions to one woman—especially the one he had married! It hurt me so deeply I could not bear to think on it! Which is why—when Greville first asked me to marry him...'

Sarah turned back to look at her. She had never seen Amelia's pretty face so creased with distress.

'I thought that you refused Greville because you claimed to find him dull...'

'I know. I appeared not to value his excellent qualities, but in fact I was just afraid, I suppose. Now I shall have to trust him.'

'And you could not commit yourself to a better man,' Sarah said warmly, coming back to the bedside. 'Greville loves you and has done so for a long time now.'

'I know,' Amelia said, a contented smile curving her lips. 'I am indeed truly fortunate! Oh, if only I could remember—'

'Yes—' Sarah gave her a naughty smile '—I can see that it must be very annoying for you. But never mind, you will have plenty of opportunity to find out!'

'Sarah!' Amelia's eyes flew wide open. 'Blanchland has wrought quite a change in you, and not one that is at all proper!'

'I know.' Sarah continued to smile. Her eye fell on yet another painting of cavorting nymphs. 'I suspect it is the influence of these dreadful pictures!'

'It is to be hoped that Guy will make a respectable woman of you, Sarah,' Amelia murmured. A slight frown touched her brow. 'You will marry him, won't you?'

Sarah turned her face away. 'Of course I will—now. Even I can see that some sort of conventionality must be observed after all that has happened!'

'Not because of that!' Amelia's hand pressed hers urgently. 'Because you love him! I know it, Sarah! Oh, if only I were not so tired I would soon make you admit it!'

Amelia slept for most of the day and Sarah stayed beside her. Greville Baynham, recovering from the effects of the drug more rapidly than his fiancée, had checked that Sarah was prepared to be left alone to await Guy's return, then had ridden off at once to purchase a special licence. Sarah suspected that part of his alacrity was to reassure Amelia, but thought that this at least was unnecessary. At last her cousin seemed utterly content and certain of Greville's love.

Sarah felt even more lonely without Greville's comforting presence, but consoled herself with the thought that Guy had said he would return shortly. In the meantime, there was still Justin Lebeter to protect them. The young peer, who had rushed from the dining-room the previous night, had apparently locked himself in his chamber and thrown away the key whilst the aphrodisiac took effect, not wishing to compromise his love for Olivia. When he had regained consciousness that morning he had had to beat on the door until Sarah, with the help of Tom Brookes, had let him out.

The Fisks had departed in a honeymoon glow early in the day, and Sarah had no wish to see either Sir Ralph or the remainder of his guests. She sat at Amelia's bed-side, fretting over the difficulties of returning to Wood-allan with the Earl very likely on his deathbed and his unwanted granddaughter in their party. Feeling restless, Sarah paced across to the window and sat for a time watching the snow, but its hypnotic swirling gave her no peace.

It was late afternoon and growing dark when Sarah left her cousin sleeping soundly and went downstairs for a breath of fresh air. She watched the daylight fade over the gardens and reflected that Guy would probably not be returning that night after all. Sarah let herself back into the house via the conservatory. The snow fall-ing on the glass overhead made a brushing sound, soothing and soft. It was strangely light and the scent of fruit and summer flowers contrasted oddly with drifts of snow outside. Sarah walked through both hothouses, then sat for a while beside the pond, wondering why her troubled mind would give her no rest. Whatever problems she was facing would surely be resolved once Guy was back by her side. Even so, she felt alone and uneasy. Suddenly the Gothic horrors she had dismissed previously did not seem so foolish after all.

Chapter Ten

Sir Ralph was lurking in the entrance hall when Sarah went back in from the conservatory. He looked nervous and distressed, and cast her the sort of wary glance one reserved for a dangerous animal.

'Cousin! Are you well?' He peered into her face, clearly trying to discern any signs of ravage.

'I am very well, thank you,' Sarah snapped, 'but infinitely regretting the quest that brought me back to my home! I wish I had never set foot here!'

'It was Marvell's fault,' Sir Ralph said pitifully, wringing his hands. 'Marvell and Edward Allardyce! I have turned the man off, and Allardyce is to leave at first light! It was never my intention that you should suffer, Sarah! There will be no more revels now, or ever! Oh, this is a tragedy!'

He wandered off, still mourning. Sarah watched him go, half-exasperated, half-pitying. Sir Ralph had never been accepted by the *ton*, who had considered him beneath their notice even before he had established his repellent revels. Now, it seemed that even the purpose he had found for himself was ruined.

Sarah went slowly upstairs to check that Amelia was

feeling better, then moved softly to close all the curtains and shut out the night. The house was very quiet and of Justin Lebeter there was no sign. Sarah shivered a little, resolving to lock herself in with Amelia until Guy returned.

The snow was still falling, but gently now. Sarah was about to pull the long landing curtains, when she saw torches flaring through the trees as they illuminated the way to the grotto.

So Sir Ralph had decided to hold his solstice revels after all, and only a half-hour after he had told her otherwise! Sarah frowned crossly. Perhaps it was too much to expect a leopard to change its spots, but she was surprised that Ralph's guests had any energy left to join in. She closed the curtains with an angry swish.

The door from the servants' quarters opened with something of a crash.

'Miss Sarah!' It was Tom Brookes who was staggering into the hall and even in the dim light, Sarah could see the livid bruise to his temple. She hurried down the stair and grasped his arm as he almost lost his balance.

'Tom! What on earth—?'

'Hit on the head,' Tom was saying, and Sarah could hear his disgust even through the chatter of his teeth, 'lying in the snow I dunno how long, and Miss Olivia gone—'

'Olivia?' Sudden fear sharpened Sarah's tone, but when Tom looked at her blankly, she guided him over to the stairs and helped him to sit down. 'There, Tom. You stay there and I'll call one of the maids to bathe your head. Steady... Now, you say that Olivia has gone—'

She broke off as Mrs Brookes came dashing through the door with what looked like half a dozen maids in tow, their faces registering everything from fright to excitement.

'Oh, Miss Sarah! There he is! As soon as he heard Miss Meredith had gone, what did he do but go rushing off to find you! I couldn't stop him! I said there was no difficulty because it was you as sent the message and...' She ran out of breath and stopped as she saw the look on Sarah's face. 'Lordy me, never tell me it wasn't you as sent the message to Miss Olivia—'

'It wasn't me,' Sarah said.

Amelia was emerging from her room now, evidently curious about the uproar, and Justin Lebeter appeared from the direction of the games room. It was clear that Amelia was feeling better for it took her only a moment to take charge.

'Susan, please fetch a bowl of warm water and some bandages. Lord Lebeter, could you help Tom upstairs? He needs to lie down and have absolute quiet. Keep back everyone! Give him some air!'

'My!' Mrs Brookes said, impressed, as Tom allowed Lebeter to haul him to his feet and support him slowly up the stairs. 'That cousin of yours, Miss Sarah! Proper cowed, my Tom is! I've never seen anything like it!' She looked more sharply as she saw Sarah pulling outdoor boots and a cloak from the cupboard.

'Where are you going, Miss Sarah? On a night like this with the snow...' she wrinkled up her nose '...and those pagan revels! Wait 'til Lord Lebeter is done, then he can go looking for Miss Olivia—'

'I fear there isn't time for that, Mrs Brookes,' Sarah was pulling on her boots as she spoke. 'At what time did the message come for Olivia?'

'We found it near on an hour ago.' Mrs Brookes was starting to look worried. 'There was a note pushed under the door. I assumed...Miss Olivia said that it was from you—that you wanted to meet. Oh, lordy!'

'Never mind,' Sarah said, feeling as though she was within an inch of throwing up her hands in despair herself. 'You had best get upstairs and make sure that Lady Amelia is not terrifying your Tom!' She paused. 'I don't suppose you know where Olivia was going for our assignation?'

'No.' Mrs Brookes bit her lip. 'I tried to persuade her against it—told her it was a dirty night to be out, but she said she was not going far! Oh, Miss—'

'Pray explain to Lady Amelia and Lord Lebeter when you may,' Sarah said rapidly, her hand on the door, 'and do not worry. All will be well!'

'Her poor mother—' Mrs Brookes began, but Sarah stayed to hear no more. Pulling the door wide, she slipped out into the snow.

The sky was clear and the moon rode high on ragged clouds. From the depths of the wood came the sound of chanting, most unearthly in the black-and-white landscape. Sarah shivered and furiously told herself to stay calm—it could only be Sir Ralph's foolish antics. She had once thought that they could harm no one, but after the previous night she was not so sure. Sarah remembered that, some sixty years previously, Sir Francis Dashwood had supposedly founded a club based on devil worship, where members dressed as monks and nuns and held licentious orgies. No doubt Sir Ralph modelled himself on that example. She took a deep breath. She knew she could not allow herself to become frightened.

Sarah tried to think clearly as she ran through the wood. Olivia had been lured from hiding by someone

using her name, and she was certain that it had to be
Lord Allardyce. Ralph had said that Allardyce and Marvell were in league, so possibly the servant had discovered Olivia's hiding place. One or other of them must
have dealt Tom a blow to keep him out of the way, and
now Allardyce meant to use the revels as a cover to
carry Olivia off...

Dodging between the trees, Sarah drew nearer to the
grotto and tried to keep in the shadows. Torches flared
about the entrance and the chanting was much louder
now, eerie in the quiet night. Sarah's skin crawled. She
could see a brazier burning in the centre of the grotto
and a curious smell, sweet and woody, was floating towards her. It made her head spin but it was too late to
go back now.

Sarah crept around the outside of the grotto and approached the entrance with extreme caution. She was
about to peer in at the door when several figures in long
flowing robes came running from the entrance and began to scatter throughout the wood, shrieking and
screaming in evident enjoyment. It was impossible to
identify the masked revellers, but Sarah recognised a
slender wraith that could only be Lady Ann Walter,
being hotly pursued by a man in black robes. Catching
her about the waist, he tumbled her into the snow and
the two of them rolled about in evident and amorous
excitement. Sarah drew back in disgust.

A sudden sharp sound from inside the grotto made
her jump. She edged forward and tried to see around
the corner of the entrance without giving herself away,
but the curve of the walls blocked her view. The smell
of the brazier was much stronger now, making her eyes
water and her head feel dizzy. If it was another of
Ralph's noxious aphrodisiacs... There was a scraping

sound, followed by silence. Sarah hesitated, barely breathing. She knew that someone must still be inside the grotto. Perhaps Sir Ralph, as high priest of whatever ceremony had just taken place, had stayed after the others to prepare the next stage of the revels... Sarah paused. She had to find out if Lord Allardyce had brought Olivia here.

Sarah drew herself up. Even if Sir Ralph were still in the grotto, he would hardly hurt her. And if it was Allardyce, or Marvell, or both... She shut her mind to that. Once he knew that everyone was alerted to his plan, Allardyce would surely not persist in his abduction of Olivia.

Sarah stepped forward, suddenly resolute, and as she did so a cloaked figure crossed her view, walking directly towards the entrance of the grotto. He put his hood back as he approached and the torchlight gleamed on his fair hair. Sarah caught her breath in shock and disbelief as the flaring light illuminated his face, and revealed not the expected features of Lord Allardyce...but those of Guy Renshaw.

Sarah felt as though all the breath had been knocked from her body. She was breathing hard and shivering violently. What was Guy doing at Blanchland when he had been summoned home to Woodallan? Why had he not told her of his return? What was his purpose at the revels? And why had she ever trusted him at all, when it seemed clear that he was utterly untrustworthy?

All those thoughts raced through Sarah's mind in an instant, followed by a wave of anguish so painful she could hardly bear it. She clung to the outside wall of the grotto to steady herself, calming slightly at the physical sensation of the cold snow and rough earth beneath her fingers. She would confront Guy. Now.

The shadows shifted and he walked past her, so close that Sarah almost imagined she had felt the brush of the monk's robes against her own cloak. He was moving purposefully, unlike the others who could still be heard shrieking and tumbling in the snow. Another worse suspicion grasped Sarah. She had assumed that it was Allardyce who had discovered Olivia, but supposing that it was Guy? He had claimed that he did not agree with his father's plan to spirit Olivia away, but was that true? Perhaps he had lulled her suspicions in order to remove Olivia before Sarah could prevent it...

Half of Sarah's mind argued that this could not possibly be true, whilst the other half grappled with all her doubts and suspicions. She was tired and alone, worn out with her concerns for Olivia and the accumulated tensions of the day. She loved Guy, but her tired mind was telling her that she might have made a mistake.

There suddenly seemed to be so many reasons to mistrust him; he had lulled her suspicions with soft words and kindness, had made her fall in love with him, and yet, what did she really know of him at all? Her instincts might tell her to trust him, but those instincts could be very wrong, and Olivia's life was at stake...

Sarah slid from her hiding place and began to follow Guy between the trees. She went slowly, keeping in the shadows, careful not to make a sound. Other figures in loose-flowing robes flitted across her line of vision. Her head swam with the lingering smell of the brazier. It was like another horrible dream. At one point a hooded figure with Sir Ralph's girth loomed out of the trees in front of her, but before he could utter a word, she pushed him hard into a snowdrift and he collapsed without a sound.

They were heading for the Folly Tower. Sarah could

see its dark shape against the lighter sky, and watched as Guy slipped inside. Now was the time to follow him in and confront him, but still she hesitated. She knew that it was the only way to learn the truth, to be reassured, to let Guy explain...

The blackness of the doorway yawned before her. Tip-toeing as softly as she was able, Sarah trod up to the door and peered in. The moon was bright through the tumbledown walls; it lit up the whole of the interior, including what looked like a bundle of rags on the earthen floor.

Sarah forgot her fear. With an exclamation, she hurried forward and turned the bundle over to reveal the white, unconscious face of Olivia Meredith. Her niece was as limp as rag doll and made neither sound nor movement. There was a bruise very similar to the one administered to Tom Brookes marring the perfection of her pale forehead, and a small cut that was sticky with blood.

Abruptly the moon went behind a cloud and plunged the whole tower into darkness. Sarah heard a step on the earthen floor beside her and felt the brush of cloth against her face. Someone caught hold of her arm in a punishing grip, dragged her to her feet and thrust her hard against the tower wall.

As abruptly as it had gone in, the moon re-emerged, flooding the tower with light again. It shone on Guy's furious face as he roughly thrust the hood of Sarah's cloak aside and stared down into her face.

'You! What the hell are you doing here, Sarah?'

Sarah struggled, but he held her tightly. He shook her hard. 'Well? What are you doing out here on the night of the revels? Answer me!'

Sarah's mouth tightened into an angry line. 'What do

you think I am doing, sir, joining in? Surely the question is to you rather than me—what are *you* doing here? You are supposed to be at Woodallan, or so you let me believe! You are the one skulking around in those ridiculous robes! And what have *you* done to my niece?'

Guy let her go so suddenly that she almost stumbled. His voice was drained of all expression. 'You think that I did that?'

'Why not?' Sarah gave him a look full of flashing anger. 'You told me yourself that the plan was to remove Olivia before anyone could know of her existence! Pay her off—bundle her out of the way... What does it matter how the thing is done? The honour of the Woodallans is paramount!'

She saw the glitter of rage in Guy's own face now and was perversely determined to provoke him further.

'You lulled my suspicions, made me believe you in earnest! I thought that it was Allardyce who was the danger, but I have made a mistake, have I not?'

Guy swore. He took a step closer, and suddenly Sarah was afraid. Her own pain had made her want to lash out at him, but now, belatedly, her instincts were telling her that she had made a terrible mistake.

'Allardyce is in the grotto, tied up to prevent him from carrying off your niece,' Guy ground out. 'That is the extent of the danger he poses! As for me, I told you the truth this morning, though you obviously did not believe me! And to think you believe me capable of hitting a defenceless woman—my own flesh and blood! Your opinion of me is truly flattering, Miss Sheridan!'

The sarcasm flicked Sarah on the raw. She recoiled from the disgust she saw in his face. 'If you had told me the truth from the start—'

'We shall leave the recriminations until later, if you

please, Miss Sheridan!' Guy said coldly. 'Just now it is *your niece*—' he stressed the phrase '—who needs your help.' The tension had left him now, replaced by something that chilled Sarah more—a cold indifference. The tone of his voice, the way he addressed her as 'Miss Sheridan' rather than by her name, suggested that he was unlikely to forgive her quickly, if at all.

Suddenly Sarah was overcome by an enormous lassitude. The light-headedness induced by the brazier's fumes and the accumulated shocks of the night had left her feeling tired and faint. She slumped against the wall of the tower. Guy's voice seemed to come from a great distance.

'If this is intended to gain my sympathy, I fear it will not work...'

'I'm sorry...' Sarah's words came out as a whisper. 'The smoke...the brazier—'

She heard Guy give an exclamation of exasperation, then his angry features swam briefly into view. 'Damnation! Sarah—' He shook her hard and her head swam all the more.

Beyond his shoulder, another face appeared and then another. Sarah closed her eyes. She knew she must be dreaming now. It sounded like Justin Lebeter's voice. 'Guy? What in God's name—?'

And then, to her immense gratitude, Sarah felt herself slide from Guy's grip into a dead faint.

Sarah opened her eyes. She was in her bedroom at Blanchland, a room that was becoming almost familiar to her. The bright light that crept around the closed curtains suggested that it was daylight outside, but the bedroom was gloomy and Amelia, sitting beside the bed, was holding a magazine up to the meagre light.

'Open the curtains if it would help you to read better,' Sarah suggested.

Her cousin jumped. 'Oh! You are awake! How do you feel, Sarah?'

'I am very well.' Sarah sat up and attempted to push back the covers and swing her legs out of bed, but her head started to spin and she lay back with a groan. Amelia tutted with annoyance.

'You see! You are not well at all! Pray keep still, Sarah!'

Sarah obeyed whilst her cousin moved across to the window and pulled back the curtains. She winced as her eyes adjusted to the flood of daylight.

'Oo-oof! What time is it, Milly?'

'About midday, I think. You have slept the clock around!'

'Olivia!' Sarah said, memory suddenly flooding back. 'What has happened? Is she safe?'

Amelia put a soothing hand on her arm and sat down beside her. 'Olivia is quite safe. In fact, she awoke before you!'

'And Tom?' Sarah struggled upright again, fighting sheets and blankets that seemed to have a mind of their own. 'What happened, Milly?'

'I shall not tell you if you do not keep still,' her cousin reproached. 'Tom is much better, although his wife is insisting he rest, which goes against the grain! All of Sir Ralph's guests have left, except Lord Lebeter, who seems barely able to leave Olivia's side! Guy has packed that poisonous Lord Allardyce off—a night tied up in the grotto soon cooled his ardour and I do not think he will approach Olivia again! Oh...' she smiled '...and Sir Ralph himself is a little sickly, I fear—we found him asleep in a snowdrift and he has taken an ague!'

'Oh, dear!' Sarah pressed a hand to her mouth, assailed by guilt at the memory of the portly figure she had pushed over in the snow. 'I seem to remember... It was all so extraordinary, Milly! Robed figures running everywhere, and that dreadful smell from the brazier—'

'Yes, Guy tells me that it was some kind of opiate used by Allardyce to induce hallucinations,' Amelia said with disgust, then stifled a giggle. 'You would have thought that there had been quite enough of that sort of thing! No wonder they were all rolling around in the snow regardless of cold! The doctor believes that you suffered an adverse reaction to it, Sarah, and that, coupled with the natural anxiety of the situation, led you to swoon! It is lucky it was not worse! That is twice that you have been fortunate!'

Sarah was beginning to remember just how bad it had been. She wondered briefly whether she could claim that it was a hallucination that had affected the balance of her mind and made her level those accusations at Guy, but concluded sadly that he was unlikely to believe her. Amelia was laughing again.

'Poor Sir Ralph, I would not wish you to misjudge him! Apparently he had not intended to hold the revels, but Allardyce needed them as a cover for his own actions, so he and Marvell conspired to arrange it all. Apparently Marvell let Allardyce down by running off with Lady Ann Walter! Meanwhile Ralph came rushing out to see what was happening and caught a chill for his pains!'

Sarah tried to smile, but the thought of Guy's anger made her feel stiff and cold. Amelia had not yet noticed.

'When we first saw you with Guy in the tower, it

looked as though he was trying to strangle you, Sarah—'

'I expect he would have liked to do precisely that,' Sarah said, so bleakly that her cousin stopped laughing and frowned.

'Why, what can have happened?'

'Only that I accused him of having attacked Olivia!' Sarah's hand smoothed the bedspread nervously. 'It is a little difficult to explain, Milly, but I knew that Guy had been asked by his father to find Olivia and spirit her away before her relationship to the Woodallans became public—so I thought that he—'

'Oh, dear!' Amelia looked stricken. 'Oh, Sarah, surely you could not think that Guy would do such a thing—?'

Sarah's face crumpled and two huge tears rolled down her cheeks. 'I know it was the height of folly— no, it was worse than that, it was a lack of trust that he will never forgive! I could have cut my tongue out when I realised the truth, but by then it was too late!'

She dabbed ineffectually at her tears, eventually giving up and crying wholeheartedly into the handkerchief that Amelia pressed into her hand.

'Well, this is very bad,' Amelia said at length, with an understatement that made Sarah laugh a little bitterly, 'but perhaps Guy will understand that you were distraught. After all, you had been through an unpleasant experience the night before, and with the tensions of the day...'

'Pray do not make excuses for me,' Sarah said with desolation. 'Guy has behaved to me as a gentleman should, and I have repaid his trust with base suspicions. Oh, I wish I had never been born!'

'I will send a tray up to you,' Amelia said, getting

up. 'You will feel better once you have eaten, and when you are well enough I will let you get up! It seems we are forever ministering to one another—it is enough to induce a fit of the megrims! '

'The Earl!' Sarah said suddenly, when her cousin was almost at the door. 'I thought he was ill? What has happened—?'

'The Earl is quite well. The message summoning Guy to Woodallan was as false as the one from yourself to Olivia!'

'But—'

'Later,' Amelia said inexorably, closing the door behind her with an emphatic click.

Sarah got out of bed and wandered listlessly over to the window. The short winter day was already closing in, and Sarah shivered at the cold view. Despite Amelia's optimism, she knew that Guy would not forgive her. She should have been running to him for help, after all, not hurling accusations at him.

Sarah dressed slowly, ate a little of the food Amelia sent up, drank a glass of spring water and went down the corridor to visit Olivia. It was easy to work out which room her niece was occupying, for Justin Lebeter was sitting outside the door in the attitude of a man who is prepared to wait all day just for a glimpse of the object of his devotion. He leapt to his feet as Sarah approached.

'Miss Sheridan! Are you feeling better, ma'am?'

'Yes, I thank you, sir.' Sarah smiled at him. 'I am come to see how Olivia is going on.'

Lord Lebeter's face glowed. 'Oh, she is much recovered! I am sure she will be glad to see you! Lord Renshaw is with her, with Mrs Brookes acting as chaperon, although as he is her uncle—' He broke off. 'Indeed, it seems odd to consider Renshaw as anyone's uncle, but I suppose...'

Sarah laughed. 'I see that he has told you the whole!'

'Well, a little.' Lebeter looked diffident. 'I understand that I have you to thank also, Miss Sheridan, for your efforts to protect Miss Meredith. Indeed, she has been speaking most highly of you. I had no idea...'

Sarah felt a swift rush of guilt. 'It was my fault. When you spoke to me of Olivia's whereabouts I was anxious only to protect her from Lord Allardyce. I had no wish to mislead you, but I thought it safer to tell no one what I knew. I am sorry.'

Lebeter shook his head. 'No apology necessary, ma'am, I assure you. I understand why you acted as you did. You will know now that I am hopeful of securing Miss Meredith's affections and I swear that my intentions are honourable.' He flushed endearingly. 'The discovery of her...erm...her antecedents is of no consequence to me.'

Sarah wondered fleetingly whether the Dowager Lady Lebeter would be so sanguine about a daughter-in-law with so dubious a family history. Justin Lebeter's mother was known equally as a demanding mama and a rampant snob, but young Lord Lebeter seemed quite determined; perhaps it would only strengthen his love for Olivia if he had to overcome adversity for her sake. The thought of adversity led Sarah to wonder about the Earl of Woodallan. If his granddaughter were to become Lady Lebeter, and take her place in society, he would have to come to terms with the fact that he could not sweep Catherine's shame aside. Those were issues for Guy to discuss with his father, but she acknowledged with a sinking heart that she could not avoid her part in the debate. As Olivia's closest relation on her father's side, she would have to be consulted.

Lebeter opened the bedroom door for her and she went in. Olivia was sitting up in bed, a clean white bandage around her head. She was chatting animatedly to Guy, who was leaning forward and smiling. Mrs Brookes knitted placidly beside the window. It was a charming family scene.

Guy looked up and saw Sarah, and the smile died from his eyes. He got to his feet and gave her a formal bow.

'Miss Sheridan. You are recovered, I see. I will leave you to talk for a little with Miss Meredith.'

'Oh, do not hurry away!' Olivia spoke impulsively. 'It is quite delightful to have both my new-found relatives here together!' She turned glowing eyes on Sarah. 'Lord Renshaw has been telling me all about my mother's family! I must own that it is almost too much excitement to take in at once!'

Sarah mentally raised her eyebrows. Guy must have done an exceptionally good job to have presented the story to Olivia in a manner that caused no unhappiness or embarrassment. She only hoped that his father would be so positive. She could feel Guy's sardonic gaze resting on her, reading her mind, almost challenging her to spoil Olivia's happiness with caution.

'I am glad to find you so much better, my dear,' Sarah said, avoiding comment. 'I was so very worried about you! When I heard you were missing——'

'Oh, it was all most horrid and quite like a Gothic romance!' Olivia shivered enjoyably, secure in the knowledge that she was now safe. 'When I received your note—or rather, the note purporting to come from you—I hurried off without a second thought! Mrs Tom did counsel me to wait, but I am too impulsive, I suppose! Anyway, I remember reaching the tower and calling for you, and then I remember nothing more until I woke up here!'

'Just as well,' Guy said laconically. 'I shall trust Lebeter to keep you from danger in future!'

Olivia giggled and blushed. 'I believe he was most disappointed that you had already dealt with Lord Allardyce! He told me he wished most strongly to plant him a facer!'

'Quite understandable,' Guy observed. 'I will see you later, Miss Meredith! Do not tire yourself!'

'Oh, no, I shall chat to Sarah for a little and then sleep,' Olivia confided artlessly. 'It has been so kind of you to spare me so much time, sir!'

'If you call your aunt by her given name, I suppose you should address me by mine also,' Guy said, making Sarah feel about a hundred years old. 'That is, if you would feel comfortable doing so!'

Olivia looked as though she had been given a present. 'Oh, may I do so, Guy? That would be most agreeable!' She looked from Guy to Sarah and back again. 'And I can now congratulate you together on your happy news! I was never more delighted than when I heard!'

Sarah knew that she was looking blank.

'Miss Meredith is congratulating us on our betrothal, my love,' Guy said, with gentle sarcasm. 'Perhaps you could try to emulate her enthusiasm!'

Sarah flushed. She had assumed that the last thing Guy would wish to do was marry her after her outburst the previous night, and certainly his cold behaviour to her had borne out such an opinion. The look he gave her was caustic, once more daring her to destroy Olivia's illusions. Sarah bit her lip and held her peace. Now was not the time to attempt to explain to Olivia that the engagement was broken.

'Before you go, you must tell us how you came to be here in time to rescue me,' Olivia was saying, blissfully unaware of Sarah's discomfiture. 'You did not finish the story! You had gone to Woodallan...'

'I am sure that Miss Sheridan does not wish to hear this,' Guy said, with a smile for his niece that pointedly excluded Sarah. 'I will finish the tale later, perhaps—'

'On the contrary, sir,' Sarah said coldly, 'I am very interested. You may remember that I asked you the same question myself—last night!'

'I remember!' Guy's dark eyes narrowed with comprehensive dislike. He resumed his seat. 'Very well, the tale goes thus. I hastened back to Woodallan and was glad to find my father better than expected—surprised even, that I had received a message summoning me back home! It did not take Dr Johnson to see that someone had tricked me in order to get me out of the way!'

Olivia giggled.

'I turned around to come back to Blanchland immediately,' Guy continued, 'but my horse threw a shoe at Old Down, and whilst I waited for him to be shod, I heard an extraordinary tale. There was a closed carriage in the yard there, and two fellows passing the time drinking in the bar. It made them loquacious. Apparently they had come down from London at the behest of a noble lord...' Guy paused. 'They were joking about what a man would be doing with a closed carriage in the middle of the night in winter, but I could think of a very good reason.'

Sarah noticed that Olivia had stopped smiling and her eyes were as huge as saucers. She looked like a small

child who was being told a fairy tale. 'Oh! What did
you do, Guy?' she whispered.

'The landlord of the inn was most helpful in persuading the men to enjoy his hospitality a little longer,'
Guy said with a grin. 'As far as I know, they are there
still! I hastened back here as soon as my horse was
ready. After that, it was a simple matter to don one of
those ridiculous robes, wait until the...ah...service in
the grotto was over, and force Lord Allardyce to tell
me what he had done!'

Olivia shuddered enjoyably. 'And that horrible man,
Marvell? What happened to him?'

Guy's gaze met Sarah's. 'He was...otherwise engaged, which was fortunate, since it meant that I did
not need to deal with both of them at once!'

'If you had only come to tell us of your return, my
lord, I am sure Lord Lebeter would have helped you,'
Sarah said sweetly, unable to resist provoking him.
'There was no need to play the hero all alone!'

'I had no time,' Guy said smoothly, only his gaze
betraying his antagonism to her, 'and I did not wish to
alert Allardyce to my presence when he had gone to
such trouble to remove me. Even you must understand
that, Miss Sheridan, for do you not justify your own
secrecy in this affair with the comfortable notion that
you were protecting Olivia from Allardyce?'

They glared at one another. It seemed that both had
forgotten Olivia, over whose sickbed they now fought.
Sarah's gaze dropped to her niece's startled face and
read the apprehension there. Olivia was no fool and had
already realised that she had in some way caused a rift
between her new-found uncle and aunt.

The look on her face gave Sarah pause. 'Pray forgive
us, Olivia,' she said hastily. 'Lord Renshaw and I have

matters to discuss, but not here.' She glanced towards the door and was relieved to see Justin Lebeter hovering on the threshold. 'We will leave you now, for I see that Lord Lebeter is hoping for a little time with you.'

She bent and kissed Olivia's cheek, noticing that her niece's eyes had lit up at the prospect of another visit from her beau. The squabble was already forgotten, but Sarah was ashamed of herself. She trod swiftly from the room, not waiting to see if Guy followed, and it was not until she had reached the door of her own room that she heard his quick steps behind her.

'Miss Sheridan! A moment of your time, if you please!'

Sarah swung round haughtily. 'You wish to speak to me, Lord Renshaw?'

Guy gave an ironic bow. 'You said just now that we had matters to discuss. Let us discuss them!'

'Downstairs—' Sarah began, but Guy shook his head.

'I would prefer some privacy,' he said silkily, 'and I have been in your room before, have I not?'

Sarah blushed. He hardly needed to remind her, and she was sure he had done so simply to embarrass her.

'Very well.' She turned her back as though it was of no consequence to her whether or not Guy followed her into the room, but knew with a tingling sense of awareness that he had come in and closed the door behind them. When she turned back, he was standing with his arm resting on the mantelpiece and was watching her with a cool indifference that made Sarah feel oddly at a loss.

'Well...' he made a slight gesture '...what did you wish to say to me?'

Sarah knew he was making matters deliberately difficult for her. She looked into his closed face and her composure broke.

'I am sorry! I know you are angry with me, but you must also know that I bitterly regret speaking as I did last night! But what was I to think? You had already told me of your father's plans—plans you had concealed from me when we came to Blanchland—and then to find you skulking about the grounds...and Olivia injured... I acknowledge that I reacted strongly, but—'

She knew that her appeal had failed even before Guy spoke. The look of cold withdrawal in his eyes did not fade. He looked at her with contempt.

'You simply showed what was in your heart, Miss Sheridan! We had already stumbled through a comedy of errors, had we not—the misunderstandings over your reasons for coming here, the facts I concealed from you, the secrets you refused to tell me... I suppose it is as well to know that we do not trust each other—at least that way we have no illusions!'

There was a frozen silence. Sarah felt as though her heart was breaking. She spoke hesitantly.

'Then surely it is better to forget that our foolish betrothal ever existed? Since you feel we cannot trust one another, it would be an appalling error to compound the situation by our marriage.'

They stood staring at one another for what seemed an age. Sarah was not sure what showed on her face; she almost broke down completely and pleaded for his forgiveness, begged for him to tell her that all would be well. Only the conviction that he would reject her held her silent. She remembered Guy's kindness and his gentleness, and the fierce heat of his passion for her, and looked into his cold face and felt her heart wither.

'You are mistaken, madam,' Guy said, after what seemed like centuries. His face was taut with anger and dislike. 'Not to go through with our marriage would be a greater error than that which has already occurred! I will not release you from the engagement, no matter how ill-starred it may be! When we were at Woodallan before, I made arrangements for the wedding to be held in the week after Christmas. The banns will have been read three times—and the marriage will take place!'

Sarah paled. 'You cannot mean to persist in this! It would be the most senseless act! I shall never agree!'

Guy gave her a mirthless smile. 'Unless you are prepared to stand up in church before my family and yours and refuse to marry me, you have no choice!' He took her arm and forcibly propelled her into a chair. 'Think about it, Sarah! In order to convince my father to accept Olivia, we shall need to act together. We cannot allow ourselves a show of disunity now! Worse, there is Allardyce to consider!' He paced restlessly across to the window, then turned to look down into Sarah's puzzled face.

'But Allardyce can pose no threat now!'

'No physical threat, perhaps, but think of the poisonous malice he can and will spread against both the Sheridan and Woodallan families! I know he has no proof positive of Olivia's parentage, but he has seen her—he will draw his own conclusions! And I would wager a fortune that he is already spreading scandal about you and your cousin, and your presence here at Blanchland! Remember what happened only two nights ago! Were you to break our engagement, the damage would be appalling!'

Sarah was silent. She could see the logic of his words, but equally inescapable was the misery of tying together two people who had so hurt each other that they could not be happy together. A lifetime was a very long time to be confronted by recrimination and broken dreams.

'It will not be so bad,' Guy said, and somehow his indifference was more painful for Sarah than ever his anger could have been. 'You will have regained you place in society, after all, and I am sure you will make a gracious mistress of Woodallan.'

It sounded quite chilling to Sarah. She wondered with despair how she could bear half a marriage when she still loved Guy, and knew beyond a shadow of a doubt that she had already lost him before the knot was even tied.

Chapter Eleven

They left for Woodallan the following morning. Olivia
was well enough to travel and her mother was also sufficiently recovered to contemplate the short journey
with equanimity. It was slow going, for the roads were
icy and pitted with holes, but eventually they rolled
through the gates and disembarked with gratitude.

Sarah felt both relief and discomfort in almost equal
measure. Her apprehension about the imminent wedding
was quite overshadowed by nervousness for Olivia, who
was staring up at the house with awe and trepidation.
Sarah also felt for Mrs Meredith, whose own concerns
must include the worry of losing her daughter to relatives far grander than she could have anticipated.

This time there was no welcoming party, just the
Countess of Woodallan awaiting them in the panelled
hall and looking almost as nervous as her guests. The
generosity of her welcome could not be faulted, however, and she hugged Olivia with tears in her eyes and
offered a very warm greeting to Mrs Meredith. A moment later, Guy's two sisters and their families came
flooding out into the hall, and in the general round of
kisses and exclamations, the tension eased considerably.

No one commented that the Earl was nowhere to be seen, but Sarah saw Guy draw his mother aside for a brief word, before he disappeared down the passage to the Earl's study.

The day dragged for Sarah, who had not expected Guy to spare any time for her but was nevertheless disappointed to be neglected. She thought of their bitter words the previous day and reflected that it was probably a state to which she would, through necessity, become accustomed. The Countess had given her the rose bedroom, in deference to her new position as Guy's future bride, and Sarah felt a complete fraud as she sat in splendid isolation watching the short day fade to winter dusk. Greville Baynham rode in at nightfall, but, apart from a flurry of activity to greet his arrival, the house sat in a brooding silence, waiting for the Earl to make his decision.

Guy and his father were the only members of the party missing when everyone assembled in the drawing-room for dinner that evening. The same tension was present as had been apparent earlier, as the family chatted amongst themselves and waited, with one eye on the door. The Countess checked the clock surreptitiously, well aware that dinner was spoiling. Olivia was almost white with anxiety and Sarah's heart went out to her. Such a public meeting with her grandfather would be enough to daunt all but the strongest spirit and, if he chose to not acknowledge her, the humiliation would be crushing.

Then the butler opened the door with a flourish and the Earl came in, leaning heavily on his son's arm, a gold-topped cane grasped in his other hand.

'Good evening,' he said, the same sardonic glint in

his eye that Sarah had often seen in Guy. 'My apologies for keeping you all waiting. I wished to be seen at my best when greeting my new relative. Miss Meredith—' the fierce glare softened as it rested on Olivia's pale face '—pray come here.'

Everyone seemed to be holding their breath. Mrs Meredith gave Olivia a little push, and she stepped forward to confront her grandfather, dropping a deep curtsy and allowing him to take her hand to raise her. The Earl's dark gaze travelled over her face.

'You are the image of your mother,' he said gruffly, at length. 'You are very welcome here, my dear.'

Everybody sighed in unison and a brilliant smile lit Olivia's eyes. The Earl offered her his arm and led her through into the dining-room, and Greville went up to Guy and clapped him on the back.

'Well done, Guy! I knew you'd pull it off!'

Justin Lebeter was shaking Guy's hand and Mrs Meredith was wiping away a tear, whilst the Countess was smiling and talking to her in an undertone. Amelia came up to Sarah and put an arm around her. 'Oh, Sarah, was that not wonderful! I can scarce believe that we are all one extended family now! Is it not extraordinary!'

Sarah was conscious of Guy watching her across the room. She ignored her own heavy heart and smiled brilliantly.

'Oh, it is delightful! I am so very happy for Olivia! Things have turned out so much better than I had hoped!'

'For all of us!' Amelia said, giving Greville a ravishing smile as he came over to her to lead her into dinner. She gave Sarah a swift hug. 'I am sure Olivia will always remember what you have done for her, Sarah! She has turned out to be most fortunate in all her relations!'

There was a lump in Sarah's throat. Self-pity, she told herself sternly, was the least attractive of emotions. Besides, it would achieve nothing. Guy had made his feelings for her plain, but she had no intention of making the rest of his family privy to the shaming truth.

With a sinking heart, Sarah saw the Countess instructing Guy to take her in to dinner. Lord Lebeter was busy charming to Mrs Meredith, who looked utterly bowled over, and there was a feeling of amity amongst the guests that made Sarah feel like the spectre at the feast. Guy reached her side and sketched a careless bow.

'Miss Sheridan, my mother suggests that I lead you into dinner.'

Sarah did not know whether he was deliberately trying to annoy her with his perfunctory attitude, or whether he cared so little to please her that he could afford to be offhand. Either way, she did not intend to let her irritation show. She gave him a cool smile.

'That would be quite appropriate, since we are betrothed, my lord!' She took his arm lightly. 'Come, let us not keep everyone waiting!'

Guy paid her very little attention during the meal, confining his conversation to his sister Emma, who sat on his left. Sarah ignored this manfully, for her part maintaining an animated discussion with Justin Lebeter on her other side and with Guy's sister Clara and her husband across the table. She was aware of more than one speculative glance as both Amelia and the Countess noted Guy's neglect of her, but this just served to bring more colour to her cheeks and an angry but becoming sparkle to her eyes.

It was inevitable that, at some point, the conversation would turn to the forthcoming marriage.

'We were so excited when Guy told us of the wedding!' Clara said, smiling across the table at her future sister-in-law. 'A whirlwind romance, and to your childhood sweetheart, too! Oh, Sarah, it is entirely delightful!'

Sarah could sense that Guy had paused in his conversation with Emma and was listening. She did not even glance at him.

'Yes, is it not a charming story!' Remembering how she had once denied that they had even been childhood friends, Sarah still managed to hit exactly the right, easy note. 'As soon as we met in Bath, Guy reminded me of how close we had been as children!'

'It is a tale to tell our own grandchildren, in fact,' Guy interposed, an edge to his voice. 'Just like a fairy tale!'

Sarah smiled at him blithely. 'What an enchanting thought, my lord,' she said sweetly. 'We must make sure to do so!'

'You must have been pleased to discover that the marriage could take place so soon,' Clara said, beaming. 'What with Olivia's arrival and the twelve days of Christmas and two weddings in the family, we shall be as merry as grigs!'

'It will be utterly thrilling!' Sarah gushed.

Guy shot her a speaking glance. His dark eyebrows snapped together. Sarah felt a strange exhilaration, like taking too much wine. She might not be able to make her husband love her, but she could surely irritate him. She knew that the frown on his brow, the ceaseless drumming of his fingers on the table, indicated that she had managed to break through the barrier of indifference that he had erected about himself.

The gentlemen rejoined the ladies swiftly after the meal, but Guy again showed little interest in talking to his fiancée. Instead he chatted to Amelia and Greville, affording Sarah the opportunity to study him covertly whilst she sat talking with Clara. The soft lamplight burnished his fair hair and cast a shadow across the planes of his face, accentuating the strong lines of cheekbone and jaw. He was smiling as he talked and Sarah felt her heart twist with longing and despair. She wanted him to love her, but she knew it was too late. She had had his love for the asking—and had twisted it out of recognition. As though sensing her regard, Guy looked up and his eyes, darkly shadowed, met Sarah's. Then he looked away with apparent boredom, and such misery choked Sarah's throat that for a moment she could not breathe. Was this, then, how her life was to be in future? In the middle of the warmth and love of this family, she alone would feel cold and alone.

She excused herself to the Countess and made her way unhurriedly to the door, intending to slip away to an early bed. To her surprise, Guy stood up and came across to her just as she was leaving.

'I will escort you to your room, Sarah.'

Sarah did not demur, though she felt awkward in his company. She knew that he was only offering to accompany her in order to show his family that all was well between them. They went slowly up the stairs and along the gallery, where more haughty pictures of Woodallan ancestors looked down. It was Sarah who broke the silence.

'Thank you for everything that you have done to help Olivia, my lord. I am very grateful that you were able to persuade your father to accept her into the family.'

Guy stopped walking. In the shadowy gallery it was too dark to see his face clearly.

'I have not forgotten,' he said slowly, 'that you were

the one who was brave enough to answer Olivia's plea for help in the first place.'

The compliment was unexpected. He took her hand, his fingers, long and strong, interlocking with hers. Sarah felt a shiver go through her.

'Brave?' She knew her voice sounded shaky. 'Surely you mean obstinate—or damnably foolish!'

'Maybe.' She heard the implication of a smile in his voice and felt her hand tremble in his. She tried to withdraw it. 'It was still courageous.'

For what seemed like hours, Sarah stood staring at him, captured by the expression in his eyes. One tiny tug of the hand would have brought her into his arms, but he did not move. It was Sarah who pulled away first, and her feet tapped on the wooden floor of the gallery as she fled from him.

It was Christmas Eve. Sarah, acting the part of the future mistress of Woodallan, accompanied the Countess on visits to tenants and villagers to distribute Christmas presents and good wishes. The carriage was laden down with everything from coal to oranges, tea to plum cake. Sarah was sure that she even saw the Countess slip some tobacco into the gnarled hands of various old gentlemen and a bottle of gin to one ancient lady. It was great fun and they were greeted warmly wherever they went, Sarah especially so as the young lord's future bride.

Naturally, Guy did not accompany them. His excuse had been that his father's illness made it essential that he act as host and entertain his male guests, but as these were all either family or close friends, this rang a little hollow. It rankled especially with Sarah, who could not avoid the assumption that he did not wish to be with her. The Countess noted her goddaughter's frozen expression but wisely held her own counsel, knowing that there were some times when even friendly advice was unwelcome.

Dinner that evening was very different from the family affair of the night before. The Woodallans were hosting a dinner and informal dance for the whole neighbourhood and numerous coaches drew up at the door decorated with holly and mistletoe. The great hall of the old house had been cleared for the banquet, a huge fire blazed in the medieval hearth and torches flared on the walls. It looked dramatic and festive.

Amelia had chosen a dress in Christmas scarlet for the occasion. 'I hope it does not seem too daring for the country,' she said doubtfully, turning before the mirror in Sarah's bedroom. She gave a little giggle. 'I am indeed a scarlet woman, so it is most apt!'

'You look wonderful,' Sarah said truthfully, for the deep red was most striking against Amelia's white skin and black hair. 'I wish I could wear something as bright as that to give me confidence! And you are no scarlet woman, Milly, but a Christmas bride!'

Greville, taking advantage of the special licence, had pressed Amelia to marry him the day after Christmas, and she had been happy to agree.

Amelia smiled. 'You look charming.' She considered Sarah's green silk with its overdress of gold gauze. ' I am sure Guy will have no complaints!'

'I am sure Guy will not even notice,' his fiancée said glumly.

The evening did nothing to disprove her opinion. This time Guy did not even lead her into dinner, and he spent the entire evening away from her side. They did not exchange a single word. Sarah chatted and smiled until she thought her face would ache, and anticipated how mortified she would be when her fiancé neglected to dance with her. Dinner seemed to last forever, but eventually the tables were cleared away and the hall prepared for the carollers.

The press of people was becoming greater by the minute, and Sarah felt very vulnerable as she stood alone on the edge of the throng. She reflected wryly that it was lucky she was dressed in green. At least some people might mistake her for the Christmas decorations.

A lot of wine had been consumed during dinner and the hall seemed to be becoming very hot. Sarah fanned herself and looked around surreptitiously for Guy. She could see Amelia and Greville, amorously entwined beneath some mistletoe and gazing into each other's eyes. Olivia and Justin Lebeter were standing together, heads bent close. Sarah stifled a sigh. Only she, it seemed, was on her own...

'Miss Sheridan?'

Sarah spun around. A tall young man with dark hair and an easy smile was looking at her hopefully. He gave a slight bow.

'Daniel Ferrier, at your service, ma'am! You may remember that we were neighbours once—'

'Daniel Ferrier!' Sarah gave him her hand. 'I remember you well! How are you, sir? Why, it must be all of six years since we met—'

'Seven, I believe, ma'am.' Mr Ferrier smiled warmly. He seemed quite dazzled that she should have remembered him at all.

Further conversation was cut short by the arrival of the bell ringers and the village carollers, who gave a hearty rendition of several traditional tunes before turn-

ing with gratitude to the pork pie and elderberry wine
that Lady Woodallan had laid out for refreshment. More
villagers were arriving for the dance, and the throng of
guests was quite overwhelming now. Sarah found herself pressed against Mr Ferrier rather more closely than
propriety demanded. Mr Ferrier did not appear to object.

'Would you care to dance, ma'am?' he asked her, as
the music struck up for the first set of country dances.

Sarah could not see Guy anywhere in the mêlée. With
a mental shrug, she accepted Daniel Ferrier's invitation,
and allowed him to swing her around to the music with
as much abandon as all the other guests. Sarah found it
pleasant not to be overlooked, even if she was dancing
with the wrong man. Bright-eyed and breathless, they
sat down as the music ended, to catch up on all the
years that had passed since they had last met.

Mr Ferrier's uncle, it transpired, had purchased him
a cornetcy in the 10th Foot and he had progressed to
the rank of Captain before selling out six months previously. He gave Sarah a very lively account of his time
serving in the Peninsula. In turn, Sarah told him of her
life in Bath, and they were so engrossed that at first she
did not notice that Guy had actually come across to ask
her for a dance.

He greeted Ferrier with a pleasant nod of the head,
but the expression in his eyes was watchful, his voice
cold.

'Please excuse me for stealing my fiancée away from
you, Ferrier. I fear I shall not have the opportunity to
dance with her otherwise!'

Daniel Ferrier could not miss the warning implicit in
the words. His gaze met Guy's for a long moment and
Sarah felt the sudden tension between them. This was
ridiculous, for Daniel Ferrier had never been any more

than a family friend, and besides, Guy had shown no interest in asserting his claim to her hand before. The silence threatened to become embarrassing, then Ferrier gave a nod of acknowledgement even slighter than Guy's.

'You are most fortunate, Renshaw.'

'So I think,' Guy agreed smoothly.

Sarah was beginning to find this male arrogance very irritating. She got to her feet slowly, making her regret rather more evident than was strictly necessary.

'Excuse me, Mr Ferrier. No doubt we may continue our conversation at a future date.'

'I should like that, ma'am,' Daniel Ferrier said, with a ghost of a smile. He bowed and sauntered away, and Guy put a firm arm about Sarah's waist and guided her into the set. It was clear that he was furious, for his mouth was set in a straight line and his eyes glittered with suppressed anger.

'Miss Sheridan,' he said, under his breath, 'you will do me the courtesy of forbearing to flirt with my parents' neighbours!'

The injustice of the remark took Sarah's breath away and prompted her good resolutions to fly out of the window. Suddenly a wholesale argument seemed a most attractive way of clearing the air. She could see that the other couples in the dance were watching them with curiosity, and she gave Guy a ravishing smile.

'You are speaking nonsense, my lord! Mr Ferrier is simply an old friend!'

'So I believe,' Guy said tightly. 'He will not become a new one, however!'

The steps of the dance forced them to part at that moment, but both of them knew the topic was not closed. When they came back together again, Sarah said, with a melting smile, 'It shows a certain arrogance, my lord, to ignore your future wife for the best part of three days and then to take exception when another pays her a little attention!'

Guy glanced around to make sure they were not overheard. His face was set.

'I do not care for other men paying attention to my wife!'

'Pshaw! You are just a dog in a manger!' Sarah twirled merrily to the music. 'You do not care for me yourself—you have made that clear!'

'It is scarcely appropriate for you to console yourself before the knot is even tied! I saw the two of you earlier—pressed so close a sixpence could not have come between you!'

The steps separated them again, giving Sarah the chance to prepare her next salvo.

'I had not realised that it would be more appropriate for me to wait until *after* the wedding!' she said, as they were reunited. She was well aware that she was starting to behave very badly and she was enjoying it, particularly as Guy did not appear to see the amusing side.

He spoke through gritted teeth. 'It would not be. As well you know!'

'Then I am condemned to a most lonely existence, am I not?' Sarah flourished an exaggerated curtsy at the end of the dance, and clapped enthusiastically. 'You are the most dreadful puritan, my lord! Since we are to make a marriage of convenience I am simply making the best of it!'

Guy kept hold of her arm. His grip was tight. He made no move to steer them back into conversation with any of their friends, but started to lead Sarah purposefully towards the door. Sarah could see everybody watching them whilst pretending that they were not doing so. She hung back, prevaricating.

'I am in need of a drink, my lord—'

'You may have one in the drawing-room. Whilst I speak to you.'

Sarah frowned. 'I do not wish to speak with you any further. You are being quite absurd!'

She might as well have saved her breath. Guy's arm was hard about her waist and he half-carried her across the hall and through the door of the drawing-room, kicking it shut behind them.

'Why do you not lock the door?' Sarah suggested helpfully. 'It was so effective last time!'

Guy looked almost murderous. 'Listen, Sarah—'

'I think not. I have heard enough.'

Guy continued as though she had not spoken. 'If you think that ours will be a marriage of convenience, you are sorely mistaken!'

Sarah paused. She had not expected this. She frowned a little. 'But that was the agreement! Since we are obliged to marry, it should be in name only!'

Guy smiled. 'I see! Not just a marriage of convenience, but one in name only! I do not think so! Certainly, *I* never agreed to such a thing!'

'But—' Sarah's mind skittered across the conversation they had had at Blanchland when Guy had pointed out that she would have to marry him for the sake of Olivia and of her own reputation. Perhaps the phrase had not been used, but the implication had surely been the same thing. The marriage would be for form's sake only. She looked at him accusingly.

'Surely you cannot pretend to have any feelings for me! Not when you condemned me outright for believing you capable of hurting Olivia!'

Guy drove his hands into his jacket pockets. 'Very direct, Miss Sheridan! Are you sure that you are prepared for an equally direct response?'

Sarah stared at him. She was half-wondering whether she did, in fact, want to know his feelings for her, or whether some things were better left unspoken. However, it was too late. Guy strolled across to the window, looking out into the snowy dark.

'Since there is to be truth between us, Miss Sheridan, I confess that I find you very attractive. I have always done so.' He turned back to look at her. 'So there is no possibility of a marriage in name only. Even were I to promise it, I know I would break the promise at the first opportunity.'

Sarah's throat was dry. 'But that is iniquitous! Why, you do not even *like* me! How can you expect—?' She stopped as he came across to her. He picked up one amber ringlet and let it slide through his fingers. Sarah turned her face away. She was trembling and she could not bear him to see the effect he had on her.

'I know you understand me.' Guy spoke a little huskily. He let go of the ringlet reluctantly and his fingers drifted across the soft skin of her neck. 'For you feel it, too. It is the one thing that unites us.'

Sarah clenched her fists. 'But I will not give in to it!'

Guy laughed. 'Ah! That must be the difference between us!'

Sarah was afraid that she would cry with frustration and hurt. 'It is not right! How can this be, when we have hurt each other and dislike each other and can never love each other—?'

Guy's only reply was to bend his head and brush his lips against the hollow at the base of her throat.

Sarah was really struggling now, against him, against

her treacherous feelings and, most of all, against the sensual excitement that was prickling along her nerve-endings, reminding her of how it had been between them. The touch of his lips was light, brushing first one corner of her mouth then the other in a teasing caress. Sarah's eyes drifted closed as he captured her lips, tenderly, seductively...

She wrenched herself away. 'No! I will not give in to this!'

Guy stepped back in an exaggerated gesture of deference. 'Very well, Miss Sheridan. But have you thought how it will be living with me, day in, day out, yet denying the craving of your body, refusing the comfort of my arms?' His dark gaze held her still. 'We shall see who wins in the end!'

It was late afternoon on the day before the wedding when Amelia found her cousin sitting quietly in the old chapel. The winter sun was slanting through the stained glass windows, making pools of colour on the stone floor. Amelia shivered, for the air was cold. It was three days since she had married Greville in a quiet family ceremony in this very place, but now the wedding decorations had gone and the dusty chill had settled again, and it seemed it had settled on Sarah as well. She had seldom seen her cousin look so pinched and drawn. Sarah was sitting quite still, her head tilted back as she apparently contemplated the faded gold stars on the white-painted ceiling. Her cloak was wrapped tightly around her and she seemed to have shrunk within it, drawn in on herself. Amelia frowned.

'Sarah? Have you been here all afternoon?' Amelia slid into the pew beside her cousin, noting that Sarah jumped as though she had not even heard her approach.

'Oh! Amelia! I am sorry, I was woolgathering! It is very peaceful here. No, I have been here but ten minutes. We have spent the afternoon on the final fitting of my wedding gown...'

Her voice trailed away. To her cousin, she looked very unlike a young lady excited at the prospect of imminent marriage.

'Have I missed much entertainment?' Sarah asked listlessly.

'No, not really. The children have been on an owl hunt!' Amelia said, laughing. 'Do you remember that from when you were young, Sarah? As though one could possibly catch an owl with those little broomsticks! Anyway, Clara's little boy got stuck up a tree and had to be rescued by Guy! The owl flew off, of course!'

Sarah smiled a little. 'He is very kind, is he not, Amelia? I remember you saying how kind Guy was when he spoke to Jack Elliston at your ball...' Her voice trailed off again.

Amelia frowned again. 'You sound very low, Sarah. Are you suffering from last-minute nerves?'

Sarah shrugged tiredly. She drew her cloak more closely around her, as though to keep out the cold. 'Surely you must have noticed how Guy has been avoiding me over the past week?'

Amelia looked uncomfortable. 'Well, I'll allow there seems a certain distance... But he is very busy—there is much to do here.'

Sarah shot her a withering glance. 'You know full well that not a host of duties could keep a man from his fiancée's side if he wished to be with her! Consider yourself and Greville! No, Guy chooses to shun me because he is trapped in a marriage he does not desire!

Having undertaken to marry me to avoid scandal, he knows it will cause a greater one to break the engagement now!'

There was a sudden scrape of stone on stone behind them. Both girls jumped and spun around, but there was nothing to be seen amongst the cold shadows of the church. The carved faces of the Woodallan tombs stared back at them.

'A mouse...' Amelia said doubtfully, drawing her skirts away from the floor. 'You speak of a marriage of convenience, Sarah, which is strange when you remember how ardently Guy courted you! What can have changed that?'

A shade of colour tinged Sarah's cheeks. 'Matters went awry from the start, Milly. It just took a little time for the whole to unravel!' She sighed. 'We neither of us trusted the other. I fell in love with Guy so swiftly, yet I barely knew him!' Sarah shook her head. 'Before we even reached Blanchland, I had overheard a conversation between Guy and his father that suggested that he was withholding information from me. So in return I did not confide when I had found Olivia...' She gave a despairing shrug. 'So you see, we had already sowed the seeds of distrust between us.'

'I suppose it only made matters worse when you found out that he had been searching for Olivia,' Amelia prompted gently.

'Yes...' Sarah fixed her gaze on the bright lozenges of colour on the stone floor. 'Guy told me that his father had asked him to find Olivia and persuade her to vanish without any trouble. I was appalled. It sounded so callous—as though Guy would do anything to prevent his sister's reputation being harmed! Oh, Guy swore that he would not have carried it through, that it would not serve…and I believed him, but I was shocked, and once again the doubt was there.'

'So when you came upon him in the Folly Tower, when he was supposed to be here at Woodallan—'

Sarah nodded dolefully. 'I told you that I rashly accused him of attacking her! To tell the truth, I was in turmoil, Milly! I had just convinced myself that I trusted him, and then I saw him acting so suspiciously! When I found Olivia unconscious…' her shoulders slumped '…well, I was tired and distraught, but it is no excuse. I showed that I did not trust him, and he cannot forgive me, and that was the end, as far as we were concerned! Whatever love was starting to grow between us has been crushed by this!'

Neither of them spoke for a little, then Sarah shivered convulsively. 'How can I marry Guy when this is between us? I would run away if I had anywhere to go, and damn Blanchland and damn the danger to my reputation! This is breaking my heart!'

Amelia put her arm around her. 'Come away from here. You are frozen, Sarah!'

They went out of the chapel slowly, still talking in low voices. Amelia latched the heavy door behind them and their footsteps died away along the gravel path to the house. It was only when they had gone and the silence settled once more that there was a flicker of movement behind the leper squint, the soft footfall as someone descended the stone steps. The figure paused by a window, waited until the two girls had disappeared from view, then quietly let himself out of the chapel.

It was late that night when Guy received a summons to his father's study. The room was set up much as it had been on the occasion when the Earl had broken the momentous news about his secret grandchild: there was a warm fire, a good book and two glasses for brandy.

'Sit down, Guy,' the Earl said, gesturing to the chair his son had occupied on the previous occasion.

'Another brandy, sir?' Guy raised his eyebrows. He poured for himself and brought the decanter across to his father.

'Thank you.' The Earl put his book down and considered his son thoughtfully. 'In point of fact, I asked you here so that I *could* thank you—for persuading me not to be such a stiff-necked old fool as to turn away my own grandchild because of the misdemeanours of her parents! It has been a pleasure to meet her.'

Guy smiled. His gaze was on the amber liquid swirling in his glass. 'I am glad that you like Miss Meredith. She is a credit to her adoptive parents, I think.'

'They did a good job,' the Earl concurred. His thick dark eyebrows drew together. 'Young Lebeter seems to know what he's about. I dare say I may trust Olivia to him. A fine thing to find and lose one's granddaughter in the space of a few weeks!'

'It is not as bad as that, sir,' Guy pointed out. 'The engagement is likely to be a long one. There is the Dowager Lady Lebeter to bring around, after all!'

'Difficult woman!' the Earl said feelingly.

'I understand that Mama is trying to persuade Mrs Meredith to take a house on the estate here, at least until Olivia's future is settled,' Guy added. 'A sound idea. Yours, I take it?'

'You do your mother too little justice,' the Earl said gruffly. 'It was her idea, and I was happy to endorse it. I should like to see more of the child.'

'Of course. I believe that Greville and Lady Amelia have also invited the Merediths to stay with them in

Bath, though I should imagine that with their own wedding…'

'They may wish for some time alone together first,' the Earl observed. 'We must give some thought to Olivia's presentation to society in a little, when matters quieten down.'

Guy moved to build up the fire, then resumed his seat across from his father.

'We spoke before of the danger of Allardyce spreading scandal,' he said, a little hesitantly. 'Do you think—?'

The Earl made a dismissive gesture. 'There will be speculation over Olivia's birth—it is inevitable. We need not regard it, however. With powerful friends…' He let the sentence hang.

Guy knew what he meant. The Earl of Woodallan had immense influence, for all that he had lived retired for the previous few years. Allardyce's malicious stirring could do little damage, particularly with Olivia safely betrothed and Catherine Renshaw long dead. Society would always gossip, but equally a new scandal would always come along to distract attention. Guy drained his glass and stood up.

'Well, I am happy that all has turned out for the best. You must excuse me, sir, if you will. There is much to be done before tomorrow—'

'There is another matter on which I wished to speak with you.' The Earl's tone had hardened slightly. 'I have been thinking that it would be better to postpone your marriage to Miss Sheridan.'

Guy's gaze narrowed. 'I beg your pardon, sir?'

'I believe you heard me. You had better sit down again.'

His son obeyed without demur. 'What is this all about, sir?'

The Earl sighed, fixing his son with his steely dark gaze. 'We have all observed that there is an estrangement between yourself and Miss Sheridan. It is hardly the best way to approach a marriage!'

Guy looked away. He spoke a little stiffly. 'It is true that there are some difficulties—'

'All the more reason to delay, then, assuming that you are able to untangle these difficulties at all! Perhaps it would be wiser to cancel—'

'No!' Guy put his glass down so abruptly that the liquid spilled. 'That cannot be, sir. We spoke just now of scandal—if my marriage to Miss Sheridan does not take place, the rumour and gossip will rip her to shreds!'

The Earl shifted slightly. 'So this is solely an altruistic act, Guy?' His voice was dry. 'Very noble of you, my boy, but another poor reason for marriage! No wonder you resent the girl so much that you can barely bring yourself to speak to her!'

Guy flushed. 'It is not like that, sir—'

His father continued as though he had not spoken. 'No, your motives do you credit, Guy, but it will not serve.' He lowered his voice confidentially. 'To tell the truth, it quite relieves me that you do not care for the girl. You are my only son, and heir to an Earldom. Why throw yourself away on a match that brings us no material benefits? Oh, the Sheridan name was once respected in this county, but she has no fortune or connections to recommend her—'

'You mistake me, sir,' Guy said, a note of barely concealed anger in his voice. 'I still wish the marriage to take place and I am surprised to hear you speak thus of your goddaughter!'

The Earl avoided his gaze. 'Well, I say that it shall not happen. The more I think about it, the more I am convinced that it would be a mistake! And do not trouble yourself over Miss Sheridan's situation. I will help her!'

'Help her, sir?' Guy's tone was dangerous. 'In what way will you...help her?'

'Why, to find a position, of course!' The Earl gestured largely. 'It would be best for her to travel at first, until the scandal of her trip to Blanchland dies down. There must be someone—a respectable lady travelling abroad—who would appreciate a companion. I can easily persuade Miss Sheridan that it would be in her best interests—'

'I do beg you, sir, not to interfere!' Guy's tone was clipped. 'I have said that I still wish to marry Miss Sheridan—'

The Earl brought his fist down hard on the arm of his chair. 'And I say you shall not! I will find some solution, deal with the girl—'

'As you would have had me deal with Miss Meredith?' Guy's body was rigid with anger now. He stood glaring at his father. 'I know how you like to arrange such matters, sir! Miss Sheridan is to disappear conveniently—'

'Is that so?' his father said, in an entirely different tone. 'You think that I will just sweep her aside, pay her off? You have known me for twenty-nine years, Guy—in all that time, how often have you seen me act thus?'

'Never! But I—'

'But you remembered that I had threatened to do so with Miss Meredith, so when I spoke of helping Miss Sheridan, you assumed I planned to treat her in the same way. No!' The Earl held up a hand as his son attempted to speak. 'Hear me out. There is something I wish you to consider. Imagine for just a moment that you have known someone not thirty years but a week…ten days, say.' His gaze took on a sardonic light. 'Think of Miss Sheridan, for example, as you knew her ten days ago.' He paused and took a draught of the brandy.

'She was alone in a difficult situation. She had always been alone, when one considers it! Her cousin gave her support, but Lady Amelia did not know the matter that took them to Blanchland! And you and I—who should have supported her, who had *promised* our aid—' he stressed the word '—we were the worst of all, for we deceived her! I never told her my secret desire to find Olivia first, and neither did you!'

'I told her later—'

'Too late! Miss Sheridan had started to trust you. You were someone on whom she thought she could rely, but slowly she began to feel that you were not being open with her. She did not know what to do. She had known you for less than two weeks and…' the Earl's voice was dry '…an instant and mutual attraction is not necessarily a basis for trust! She kept her own counsel, waiting for you to reveal the truth. Eventually you did—you admitted to something that appalled her! I had asked you to spirit away her niece, to pay her off, to help her to disappear!'

Guy was watching his father very gravely now. He did not interrupt.

'Imagine,' the Earl said, shifting in his chair as though he were in pain, 'how lonely it must have been for Miss Sheridan! She was the one who was brave enough to originally respond to Olivia's plea for help, she was alone in the world with only Lady Amelia to help her, she thought she could trust you and then she finds she knows not what to believe. Is it so surprising that, when Miss Sheridan finds her niece unconscious and apparently in your power, she jumps to the obvious conclusion?' The Earl smiled faintly. 'You yourself have demonstrated how easily that is done but five minutes ago!'

There was dead silence. A rueful smile began to curl the corners of Guy's mouth. 'Forgive me, sir, but you have the most damnable way—' He broke off, shaking his head.

'Of making you see the truth?' the Earl said drily.

Guy sat back in his chair with a sigh. 'How did you know what had happened between Miss Sheridan and myself?'

The Earl spoke with some considerable satisfaction. 'I heard it from Miss Sheridan. Those parts I did not hear, I worked out for myself. I was right, was I not?'

'Perfectly, but...' Guy frowned '...surely Sarah did not tell you this herself?'

'No.' The Earl smiled. 'I overheard. Miss Sheridan was speaking to her cousin and unaware that I was there. She said plenty more, Guy, but that is not for me to pass on. By the way...' a smile warmed his voice '...my real opinion of Miss Sheridan has been expressed once before. She is good and brave and true—so do not lose her, I beg!' His shoulders shook with laughter. 'I thought you were about to plant me a facer when I spoke so slightingly of her earlier!'

'If it had been anyone else, sir,' Guy said feelingly, 'I would have done so!'

'Well,' the Earl said gruffly, 'it was damnably hard to deceive you, but you needed a lesson! I could see you were about to throw away all that you held dear!'

Guy drained his glass. 'I had better go and find my bride...'

'And be quick about it!' his father advised.

Guy took the stairs in double time, but he was too late. A scandalised Lady Woodallan answered the door of Sarah's room and told him in no uncertain terms that it was bad luck for a groom to see his bride on the night before the wedding. Guy was left to kick his heels and hope against hope that he had not secured his own bad luck through his foolish pride.

Chapter Twelve

The church was brilliantly lit. Hundreds of white candles threw their light down from the sconces and illuminated the passages from the scriptures that were framed in red panels on the wall. Everywhere was Christmas greenery: branches of holly and laurel, pine cones and berries, red and gold streamers... Sarah, escorted up the aisle on her godfather's arm, caught her breath at the bright beauty of it all.

In the end there had been no escape. Lady Woodallan had come to her the night before and had spoken to her gently and sincerely about the family's happiness that she was marrying Guy and the conviction his parents held that she was exactly the right bride for him. The Countess had touched delicately on the short acquaintance between them, encouraging Sarah not to be afraid, and suggesting that she already knew and understood Guy so well that they might have known each other far longer. In the end, Sarah had burst into overwrought tears and her godmother had hugged her gently and told her that all would be well. Then Sarah had slept, and now it was her wedding day...

She was very aware of Guy beside her, so handsome

in green and white to complement her gown and the colours of the season. When she stole a look at his face, she thought he seemed grave, a little withdrawn, until he gave her a smile of such sudden brilliance that her heart leapt and she allowed herself to think that now, even if only for a little, his remoteness had vanished.

The service seemed to be over in minutes, both of them making their vows in clear and resolute tones. Sarah walked up the aisle on her husband's arm, aware of smiling faces all around them.

'Sarah, you look so beautiful,' Guy whispered to her. 'I *must* speak with you—'

He broke off as they reached the church porch and were inundated by a crowd of villagers all wanting to wish them well.

'A kiss for the bride!' someone shouted, holding up a sprig of mistletoe.

Guy bent his head and touched his lips to Sarah's. The kiss was light and cold, like the brush of a snowflake. Sarah shivered. The sky was darkening ominously with the next fall of snow and the air was chill, but she felt as though a tide of heat had swept through her. Aware of her blush, she turned closer into Guy's arms.

'Make way there!' The crowd parted good-humouredly to allow them through to the carriage just as the first flakes of snow started to fall.

Guy helped his bride up into the coach and took the seat opposite her. He leant forward urgently.

'Sarah, I know we have not much time alone, but I *must* tell you—'

The door swung open.

'Guy! I am so sorry—' The Countess of Woodallan was in the doorway, looking apologetic as her gaze moved from her son to Sarah. 'Would you object to taking up Olivia and Lady Amelia? They walked over to the church, of course, but now that it has started to snow…'

Guy gave Sarah a rueful smile. 'Not at all, Mama! Let them come up at once! This is no weather to be standing about…'

Olivia was very excited and chattered about the wedding for all of the short journey back to the house.

'Was it not fine? You look so lovely, Sarah… And the candles and the greenery—such a beautiful alternative to flowers…'

Sarah listened, and smiled and answered, and all the time she was aware of Guy's gaze resting on her. She felt his glance like a physical touch brushing her skin and making it seem curiously sensitive. The faint smile was still on his lips; when Guy's eyes met hers, she saw a flash of heat in his that completely flustered her. She lost the thread of what she had been saying to Olivia and fell silent. Guy's smile broadened slightly.

It was extraordinary. She could not understand it. Sarah frowned as she tried to make sense of this latest mystery. The last time she had seen Guy had been across the room at dinner the previous evening. He had ignored her, as had become his wont. Then, later, he had sought her out to speak with her—too late, for his mother had turned him away and they had not met again until they were in church… And now, mysteriously, his coldness had been banished by a warmth that threatened to be her undoing. He was treating her with an ardent attention that reminded Sarah of when they had first met. It was entirely appropriate for a bridegroom, but it was also deeply disturbing.

The carriage had completed the short journey from the church to the house, and Sarah gathered up her skirts

in one hand as she prepared to step down. Guy was too
quick for her. He swept her up in his arms, carried her
over the threshold and put her down in the hall to a
round of applause from the assembled guests. He was
laughing as he took the congratulations of his friends.
Sarah caught Amelia's arm.

'Milly, pray step aside with me for a moment—'
Amelia turned questioning eyes on her cousin.
'Sarah? Are you quite well?'

'Yes.' Sarah's grip tightened urgently. 'Quickly, before Guy sees—'

They slipped away to the ladies' withdrawing-room.

'What has happened?' Sarah lamented, viewing her
fearful face in the pier glass whilst Amelia helped her
adjust her gown and pinned the silver coronet more se-
curely on her curls. 'Yesterday he would not even speak
to me, yet now—'

'The little coronet was a good idea,' Amelia murmured, tweaking a curl into place. Sarah pulled her head
away.

'Are you listening to me, Milly?'

'Yes, of course,' her cousin spoke soothingly. 'I only
wished to compliment Lady Woodallan on recommend-
ing the coronet instead of a wreath of flowers, for in
winter—'

'Yes, yes!' Sarah said impatiently. 'But what about
Guy's behaviour—?'

The door opened and Sarah turned, expecting to see
her mother-in-law come to summon them to the wedding breakfast. It was her husband who stood in the
doorway. Their eyes met, Sarah's apprehensive, Guy's
glittering with an emotion that set her pulse awry.

'Lady Amelia,' he drawled, 'I would be obliged...'

Amelia, accurately reading the instruction implicit in

the tilt of Guy's head, smiled and started to walk towards the door. Sarah grabbed her arm, wondering if there was some sort of conspiracy going on.

'Milly, don't go!'

'Don't be foolish, Sarah!' Amelia gave Guy a conspiratorial smile and edged out, closing the door very deliberately.

Sarah, suddenly overcome with panic, turned away. She could see Guy's reflection in the mirror as he came across the room towards her.

'I imagine the others are waiting for us—'

'They can wait a little longer. Sarah—' Guy pulled her round to face him. 'I do need most urgently to speak with you...'

Sarah's eyes widened. 'On what matter, my lord?'

'Don't look like that,' Guy said raggedly. 'Damnation, this is enough to try the patience of a saint!'

He took hold of Sarah's upper arms and pulled her to him, his mouth hard on hers. Sarah's lips parted instinctively and she drew closer to him, sliding her arms around his neck. The kiss deepened, desire spinning up to engulf them.

The door opened.

'Guy,' the Countess's voice said, a little plaintively, 'your guests are hungry! There will be plenty of time for that later—'

Guy let Sarah go and she heard him swear under his breath. 'Very well, Mama. We will be with you directly.'

'Now!' the Countess said inexorably. She bustled forward to rearrange the lace dress that had once more become disarranged. Sarah knew that she looked ruffled and rosy as they rejoined the wedding guests, and knew also exactly what they were thinking. Her mind was in complete confusion. All she seemed able to concentrate on was the fact that Guy had something to say to her and that she was as devastatingly aware of him as she had been that morning at Blanchland.

The wedding feast was long and complicated. There was a warming soup to help the guests thaw out, followed by turbot in a herb sauce, dressed capon and a haunch of venison. Sarah barely noticed the dishes come and go. She picked at her food, too nervous to eat properly, and responded to the chatter of the family and friends around her, whilst watching Guy out of the corner of her eye. They had little chance to speak, but every so often Sarah would feel his gaze on her and her skin burned.

'Sarah.' Guy touched her hand lightly and she dropped her knife. She looked up to meet his gaze and blushed at the expression in his eyes. 'I wanted to tell you—'

'May I press you to a slice of Christmas pudding?' the Earl enquired genially, from Sarah's other side.

Guy made a slight gesture and turned away. Sarah could have wept with frustration.

The wassail bowl was brought in, a highly spiced mixture of wine, apple, nutmeg and ginger that smelled absolutely delicious. The Earl toasted the bride and groom and took the first drink, passing the bowl to Sarah. She drank deep, her head swimming a little. The other speeches followed, then the dancing was announced.

It was only when Sarah stood up that she realised how intoxicated she felt. The sauces had been liberally laced with wine, and the wassail bowl was particularly strong. She felt Guy's arm go around her waist and leant against him gratefully.

'Sarah?' His breath stirred her hair. 'Are you well? We may retire soon, but perhaps one dance first—'

'That would be very pl…pleasant.' Sarah tried to pull herself together. She swayed a little, and Guy looked at her closely. 'Why, I do believe that you are foxed—'

'Nonsense!' Sarah said with aplomb. 'I will dance with you, my lord!'

It was fortunate that Guy had requested a slow waltz as the first dance, rather than the more boisterous country dances that were customary. He held her gently and decorously as they circled the floor, but as the dance ended they were pulled apart and whirled off by the other guests, passed from partner to partner as the music speeded up and spun them into a progressive country dance. Finally, laughing and breathless, Sarah collapsed onto one of the benches and requested a lemonade.

After that, the dancing was fast and furious. Sarah saw Guy a few times across the room, but it was impossible to fight her way to his side. Whenever a dance ended there was someone else waiting to claim her, and Guy was similarly besieged by ladies taking advantage of the informality of the celebration to beg a dance. At one point, their eyes met and Sarah felt as though the whole noisy crowd had simply melted away. There was an intent look on Guy's face, a determination in his whole bearing that suggested it was only a matter of time before they would be quite alone.

Eventually Sarah extracted herself from the crowd and slipped unseen out of the ballroom. It was very quiet in the hall, the sound of the ball muted behind closed doors. Sarah peeped out of the window. The snow was falling fast now, swirling amongst the trees, smothering the landscape. It looked cool and tempting.

Taking a cloak from the closet, Sarah wrapped herself about and went outside.

The Woodallan gardens were like a magical white wonderland. Sarah tiptoed along the paths, her footsteps leaving indentations in the snow. She peered in at the ballroom window, feeling like a small child playing truant, then ran down the yew avenue to the spreading oak tree at the end. A wild excitement filled her, impossible to explain. The cold air stung her cheeks. She spread her arms wide and twirled around in the snow, the cloak swinging out around her.

'Sarah! What in God's name—?'

Strong arms captured her and held her still. Guy pushed the hood back from her face. There was snow in his hair and eyelashes, and he smelled of the cold air and, more faintly, of sandalwood cologne. Sarah felt her knees weaken.

'I'm sorry,' she said, raising a hand to brush the snow from his hair. 'I just needed to get away for a little.'

Guy gave her a little shake. 'Whilst you have been here carousing in the snow, I have been looking everywhere for you! You weren't in the ballroom, you weren't in your room—I thought you'd gone!'

Sarah frowned. The raw emotion in his tone cut through her wild spirits and brought her back down to earth. 'Gone? Gone where?'

'I don't know!' Guy let her go and took several paces away. 'Just gone—because you didn't want to be married to me!'

Sarah blinked. The cold air had sobered her considerably and she was quite composed enough to realise that this did not make much sense.

'Guy—'

'No, hear me out!' Guy swung round on her, full of tension. 'All day I have been trying to tell you—'

'Renshaw!' A voice roared out of the gloom. 'How d'ye do! I've come to toast the nuptials!'

'It is Sir Ralph,' Sarah whispered, trying not to laugh at the look of frustrated fury on Guy's face. 'He must have found the keys to his wine cellar!'

'Devil a bit!' the indignant baronet exclaimed, over-hearing her. He came up and enveloped her in a bear hug, snow and all. 'This is spring water, my lady, and every bit as refreshing as I used to find brandy to be! I'll have you know that this water cured me of my ague—had to do, for it was all I had in the house!'

'You should not stand about in the cold when you are only just recovered!' Sarah said, slipping her hand through his arm. 'Pray come inside, Sir Ralph, and join in the celebrations!'

They retraced their steps to the house, where Sir Ralph divested himself of his cloak and gave the bride another hearty kiss.

'You will excuse us, sir,' Guy said, with barely re-pressed impatience, 'if we do not accompany you back into the ballroom. I have something very urgent to dis-cuss with my wife—'

Sir Ralph winked. 'Know what you mean, my lad! Go to it! I'll find my own way to the party!'

He headed off towards the music, cannoning into the Countess of Woodallan in the doorway.

'Beg pardon, my lady!' they heard him say warmly. 'May I interest you in a glass of this delicious water, drawn from my own spring—'

Lady Woodallan excused herself, turning to Guy and Sarah with an enquiring frown as Sir Ralph wended his unsteady way across the ballroom. 'Who is that odd man? I positively do not remember inviting him and he seems quite inebriated!'

'Only on water, ma'am,' Sarah said, laughing. 'I fear that is my disreputable cousin, Sir Ralph Covell! I believe he has just discovered his potential as a merchant of fine spring waters!'

Lady Woodallan raised her eyebrows. 'Well, never mind him! You must both rejoin us—'

'No, Mama,' Guy said, very definitely. 'The entertainment is going very well without us! Besides, you will see that Sarah is in urgent need of a change of clothes, and more importantly, I wish to speak with her—uninterrupted!'

Lady Woodallan looked scandalised. 'But you cannot retire now! Everyone will know where you have gone! Besides, Sarah must be attended to her room and helped to undress—'

Guy raised an eyebrow.

His mother paused. 'Outrageous!' she murmured faintly. 'Not even your father would—'

'Pray return to the festivities, Mama,' Guy said, grinning, 'and leave me to attend to my wife!'

He took Sarah's hand and pulled her up the stairs, so fast that she was almost running by the time they reached the bridal suite.

'Oh, dear!' Sarah was laughing and out of breath at the same time. 'This is not at all the way in which the Countess would wish her new daughter-in-law to behave! I am sure she thought me quite lost to propriety!'

Guy closed the door behind them and leant against it as though he could not quite believe that they were alone at last.

'Sarah. I need to talk to you—'

'Yes, you have been telling me that all day—'

'Please!' Guy held up a hand. 'I cannot bear any more interruption!' He looked at her thoughtfully. 'However, before I start, you really must change out of your wet clothes, and so must I. I will be back directly.'

He started to walk towards the connecting door, but Sarah's voice stayed him. 'Guy…your mother was right, you know. I do need help with this dress. It buttons down the back, you see…' Her voice trailed away at the look in his eyes.

'Very well.' Guy's voice was brisk and impersonal. He took Sarah's cloak and draped it over the chair by the fire. 'Turn around…'

Sarah was desperately conscious of his deft fingers unfastening the dress. She could feel his tension communicating itself to her, making her tremble. The fastenings fell apart and she felt Guy's hand brush the transparent chemise beneath, heard him catch his breath. He cleared his throat.

'That will do, I think. You should be able to step out of it now. I will leave you to change.'

He went through to the dressing-room and closed the door with a decided snap.

Sarah raised her eyebrows. She understood just how much self-control he had been exercising and how difficult it had been for him. Whatever he had to say must be very important indeed.

She stepped out of the dress and removed her soaking satin slippers. They would never be the same again. Whatever had possessed her to run out into the snow without dressing properly? She went over to the window and looked out. It was dark and the snowflakes were still falling, and suddenly the firelit room seemed a far better place to be.

A noise from the next room recalled Sarah to the fact

that Guy would soon be rejoining her. She hurried to slip out of the chemise and into the only clothing that seemed to be available, a nightdress of fine lawn and a matching peignoir in a beautiful shade of eau-de-nil. She was standing before the mirror and brushing her hair when Guy reappeared, wearing a dressing gown in a dark shade of blue. For a moment they just looked at each other. Guy's face was shadowed and Sarah could not see his expression.

'If you would just sit down...' Guy looked around, but there was only one chair. After a moment's hesitation, he took her hand and led her across to the bed. Sarah's heart started to race, but then he sat down at the foot, as far away from her as he could get.

There was a silence.

'Guy,' Sarah said beseechingly, 'if you do not tell me what is going on, I will become very anxious...'

Guy's sombre expression lightened. 'I am sorry. It is simply that I have been wanting to have you to myself for the whole day and now that I have, I do not know where to begin!' He ran a hand through his hair. 'You know that I came to see you last night?'

Sarah nodded. 'Your mother was with me. She turned you away because it is bad luck to see your bride the night before the wedding!'

'It was bad luck for me *not* to see you!' Guy said drily. 'I had just been speaking with my father and he made me realise...' he looked up and met her eyes '—that I have treated you very badly from the start, Sarah. The way I behaved in Bath, slandering you and then practically coercing you to marry me... I was not truthful with you at Blanchland, and then I blamed everything on you and was too proud to see that I must bear some censure as well! I know I have made you very unhappy these last few days, deliberately avoiding you—'

'Oh, stop!' Sarah cried, unable to bear a rehearsal of all the things that had gone wrong over the past few weeks. 'I was equally to blame for making such a shocking mull of everything! Let us forget all about it—'

'I am happy to do so if you will forgive me,' Guy said sombrely. He shifted slightly. 'The truth is that I started to fall in love with you very quickly, before I really had the opportunity to know you. My feelings were so sudden and so violent that they took me by surprise—'

'You do not know me very well now,' Sarah said quietly. She traced a pattern on the bedcover, suddenly unable to meet his eyes.

'I think I do.' Guy's voice was insistent. 'I know enough to realise that I should have trusted my instincts all along. I know that you are brave and kind and good, and that I love you... Why are you crying?'

Sarah knew that her eyes were full of unshed tears. 'I did not know...I thought...I did not know that you love me.'

'It is true. What is the matter? Do you not love me? You have never told me that you do!'

There was a vulnerability in his face that Sarah had never seen before. She smiled brilliantly through her tears. 'Of course I love you. How can you be so foolish? I have loved you for *at least* as long as you have loved me—'

Somehow, she was not sure how, Guy was beside her and holding her very gently in his arms. She could feel the heat of his body through the silk of the dressing gown and she instinctively pressed closer to the comforting warmth. His lips moved against her hair.

'We have made a fine muddle of everything between us, but the important thing is that we care for each other and that we are married now...'

Guy's fingers were stroking the nape of her neck. Sarah found the gentle circular motion most distracting. The faint fragrance of sandalwood mixed with the scent of his skin made her want to touch him and she turned her head and pressed her lips to the hollow above his collar bone.

The effect of her tentative caress was dramatic. Guy bent his head swiftly and captured her lips with his, kissing her with all the fierce sweetness she remembered from before. All the frustrations of the day, the doubts and difficulties, were washed away as the simmering awareness between them finally flared into outright passion.

Sarah fell back against the pillows, drawing Guy with her and sliding her hands inside the robe. She realised with a sudden shock that he was wearing nothing at all beneath it; her hands slid over his bare chest and met with taut, smooth muscle. Her shocked gasp was lost as his mouth claimed hers again, drinking from its sweetness as she gave unstintingly, opening her lips to his, pliant with need.

Guy pulled back a little to shrug himself out of the robe and Sarah watched in fascination as the firelight enhanced the golden nakedness of his skin.

'This time,' he said breathlessly, 'you have the advantage over me, Sarah...'

Sarah's mind finally let go of the last shade of inhibition as she reached out to pull him tightly against her. She dug her fingers into the hard smoothness of his shoulders, smiling a little smile of satisfaction as she heard his sharp intake of breath, the groan of pleasure he could not hide.

'Sarah...'

He raised himself a little above her and undid the ribbon of the peignoir with fingers that shook slightly. The night gown beneath was of very fine lawn, almost transparent, and as Guy's hand skimmed over it, Sarah was achingly aware that it revealed as much as it concealed. Nevertheless, Guy was clearly not content to leave it where it was. Sarah felt him slide the slippery material down from her shoulders and closed her eyes as he bent to caress her breasts. Her body arched and writhed under the onslaught of such pleasure; his lips returned to hers to kiss her with a savage tenderness that was utterly sensuous and made Sarah squirm with wanting.

The nightgown soon joined the peignoir and Guy's robe in a tumbled heap on the floor. Sarah's lips felt swollen with kissing, her whole body suffused with desire, a painful longing in the pit of her stomach that demanded satisfaction.

'You said,' she whispered, 'that you would remember I owed you something...'

Guy paused. He propped himself up on one elbow and pushed the tangled hair away from her face. 'So I did...' He smiled a little. 'Are you ready to pay your debt, Sarah, because I must tell you that this time I will not stop...?'

For answer, Sarah pulled him back to her, a delicious smile curving her lips. 'You had better not,' she said.

The room was cold but Sarah was delightfully warm, the bedclothes wrapped around her and her new husband wrapped closer still, one arm lying possessively across her. She stirred and turned to look at him, her heart full of love as she considered his face, softened in sleep. Guy stirred and curled an arm about her, pulling her back down to his side.

'Sarah...'

'My love?'

Guy opened his eyes and smiled sleepily with re-membered pleasure.

'I did not hurt you, did I, sweetheart?'

'I do not remember,' Sarah said honestly. She blushed. 'It was...most enjoyable...'

'Then you might be prepared to repeat the experi-ence?'

'I do not know,' Sarah said, sounding prim. 'Is it morning yet?'

'I doubt it. It is still dark and no one is stirring. We did retire rather early.' Guy yawned and stretched, reaching over to light a candle. Sarah watched, fasci-nated, as the bedclothes slid from his powerful frame to reveal the taut line of shoulder and thigh, the slim waist, the muscular torso.

He caught her gaze on him, smiled and picked up one of her curls, tickling her neck. Sarah put up one hand to fend him off, realised that the sheet had slipped from her, too, and made a grab for it. Guy was too quick for her, snatching it away.

'Such modesty, after all we have done!'

The rosy colour flooded Sarah's face again. 'Oh, please...'

Guy pulled her down beneath him. 'I should like to please you, Sarah. Like this...and this...'

This time he made love to her with concentrated passion, lingering with infinite slowness over each caress until Sarah thought she would melt with pleasure.

'Did I tell you I love you?' Guy asked afterwards, cradling her to him.

'Yes...' Sarah's mind was cloudy with happiness '...but you may tell me again, as much as you wish, just as I shall tell you!'

They were awoken much later by a discreet knock at the door. Guy knotted the robe about his waist and went to answer, whilst Sarah hid behind the bed curtains and wriggled back into her nightgown and wrap. Guy reappeared, carrying a tray and put it down on the table by the bed.

'Mama thought that we might be hungry—I cannot imagine why! There are rolls and butter, ham, eggs, and this...' He gestured towards the large jug.

'What is it?' Sarah asked curiously.

'Blanchland spring water!' Guy poured it into a glass and toasted her with it. 'Mama tells me that all the guests are taking it with their breakfast and swearing that it is sovereign against the evils of too much drink!' He took a sip. 'Mmm, not bad. I do believe your cousin Ralph may at last have struck success with the *ton*!'

Sarah smiled. 'So Blanchland has at last given up the last of its secrets,' she said softly.

Guy leant over and kissed her. 'And in the process it has made everyone very happy. Olivia has been restored to her family and has found Justin Lebeter into the bargain! Amelia and Greville are united at last, and Sir Ralph has his spring water!' He kissed her again, his hands beginning to stray across the seductively smooth material of the peignoir, undoing the ribbon that Sarah had so carefully done up only minutes before.

'As for me,' Guy murmured, as his lips returned to hers, 'Blanchland gave you to me, Sarah, so I am the most fortunate of all.'

* * * * *

The Mistress
of Hanover Square

Anne Herries

Anne Herries lives in Cambridgeshire, where she is fond of watching wildlife and spoils the birds and squirrels that are frequent visitors to her garden. Anne loves to write about the beauty of nature and sometimes puts a little into her books, although they are mostly about love and romance. She writes for her own enjoyment and to give pleasure to her readers. Anne is a winner of the Romantic Novelists' Association Romance Prize. She invites readers to contact her on her website: www.lindasole.co.uk.

Chapter One

Amelia stood for a moment on the steps of her house in Hanover Square, gazing across to the Earl of Ravenshead's London home, which was at the far side. She knew that he was not in residence and supposed that he was at his estate in the country. It was only because she had wanted to do some shopping for Christmas and deliver some gifts that she and her companion had themselves come to town for a few days. She had hoped that she might perhaps meet the earl, at the theatre or at some other affair, but it had not happened.

'Is something wrong?' Emily Barton asked.

Amelia looked at her in surprise and then realised that she had sighed. Her companion was a sensitive girl and always seemed to know when Amelia was out of sorts.

'No, I was merely wondering if I had forgotten anything. I should not wish to arrive at Pendleton and then remember something I had left behind.'

'I am sure you will not.' Emily smiled at her. 'I helped Martha pack your trunks and I am certain nothing was left out.'

'Thank you, my love. I know I can always rely on your good sense.'

'You are not upset by your brother's visit, I hope?'

For a moment Amelia's eyes clouded. Her brother, Sir Michael Royston, had paid her a brief but intensely unpleasant visit to complain. He always seemed to be in a temper these days and Amelia had come to dread his visits.

'No, dearest. As you know, my brother is…difficult. However, I am not upset.' She took Emily's arm. 'Come, we must not keep the horses standing. I want to make good time, for the sky has all the appearance of bad weather and I would like to get to Pendleton before it turns to snow.'

'I am looking forward to spending Christmas with our friends,' Emily said and smiled as she glanced across the carriage. They had been travelling for some time now and the streets of London had given way to pleasant countryside. 'Before I came to you, Amelia, Christmas was always a time of regret.'

'Was it, my love?' Amelia Royston looked at Emily in concern. She was aware of her companion's secret sorrow, but it was something Emily hardly ever spoke of. 'Are you happier now that you have been living with me for more than a year?'

'Oh yes, much. If only—' Emily broke off and

shook her head. 'No, we shall not think of things that make us sad. Do you think that the Earl of Ravenshead will be at Pendleton this year?'

'Susannah said nothing of it when she wrote to invite us,' Amelia said, and a faint colour stained her cheeks. It almost seemed that Emily was reading her thoughts. 'Why do you ask, Emily?'

'Forgive me, perhaps I ought not to have spoken, but I thought…in the Season and at Helene's wedding earlier this year…I did think that perhaps there might be something—' Emily broke off and shook her head. 'It was not my place to ask…'

'Have I not told you that you may say anything to me, Emily? We are friends and have no secrets from each other. Since you ask, I shall tell you that I did think Gerard might speak some eighteen months ago, but he was called to France on family business. When we met him in London this year he paid me some attention, but…' Amelia sighed. 'I think now it was merely friendship he had in mind for us. There was a time when we might have married, but my brother sent him away. He married another woman some months later, which must mean that he did not suffer from our parting as I did.'

'You cannot be sure of that, Amelia. The earl may have married for various reasons. Perhaps it was on the rebound?' Emily frowned. 'I think you told me his wife has since died?'

'Gerard told me she was ill after the birth of their daughter and never recovered. I think that perhaps he is still grieving for her.'

'He will surely wish to marry again, if only for the sake of his daughter.'

'Yes, perhaps—though I am not sure I should wish to be married for such a reason.'

'I did not mean…please do not think I meant that he would marry you for the sake of his child,' Emily apologised and looked upset. 'I believe he likes you very well, Amelia.'

'Yes, I believe we are good friends,' Amelia agreed.

She leaned her head back against the squabs, closing her eyes. It would be very foolish of her to give way to emotion. She had cried too many tears when Gerard went away the first time. He had vowed that he loved her with all his heart, asked her to be his wife and then simply disappeared. When she was told he had joined the army, she had suffered a broken heart. She had not understood then that her brother had forced him to walk away from her—and threatened him and used violence. His desertion had left her feeling abandoned and distraught. When she first saw him again in company some four years later, she had been overwhelmed, and it had taken all her self-control not to show her feelings.

Gerard had been polite and friendly, but then, when someone had attempted to abduct Amelia when she was staying at Pendleton the summer before last, Gerard had been so concerned for her. She had believed then that he still cared, had begun to hope that he might speak, but he had been called away to France.

They had met again this summer. Gerard had been as generous, polite and kind as ever, but still he had not spoken of marriage. Of course there was no reason why he should. Too much time had passed, more than five years. If he had ever felt anything for her it had gone, or at least faded to a gentle affection. It was foolish of her to hope that he might feel more than mere friendship.

She opened her eyes and saw that Emily was looking upset.

'You have not distressed me, dearest.' Amelia smiled at her. 'We are almost there. I am so looking forward to seeing Susannah and Harry again.'

'I should never wish to distress you, Amelia. You have done so much for me, taking me in when many would have turned me from their door, because of my shame…'

'Do not look like that, Emily. You have more than repaid me for any kindness I have shown you. As for your shame—I will not have you speak of yourself in such a way. Come, smile and look forward to spending Christmas at Pendleton.'

'Amelia dearest,' Susannah exclaimed and kissed her on both cheeks. 'You look wonderful. That colour green always becomes you so well—and Emily, how pretty you look!'

'Oh, no…' Emily shook her head and blushed. 'It is this bonnet. I admired it in a milliner's window and Amelia bought it for me without my knowing. She said it was the very thing to brighten my winter wardrobe and of course she was right. She has such excellent taste.'

'Yes, she does.' Susannah looked fondly at Amelia. 'I may be biased, but I think Amelia is everything that is perfect and good.'

'Between the two of you, you will turn my head. I shall become impossible and start expecting to be treated like a duchess.'

Susannah trilled with laughter. 'You deserve to be a duchess,' she said. 'You must both come up to the nursery and see my little Harry. He is such a darling. His father thinks he is the most wonderful child ever born. I cannot begin to tell you all the plans he is making for when he can walk and go to school.'

'I always knew Harry Pendleton would be a doting father,' Amelia said, much amused.

'He spoils me dreadfully,' Susanna confessed as she led her friends up to their chambers. 'I've given you the apartments we had when I first stayed here, Amelia. I was so terrified of Harry's relatives and this vast house. I could not imagine how I should cope with it, but everything runs like clockwork. I hardly have to do a thing—just as Harry's mama told me it would be. And we always have guests so it is never too big or lonely, because people love to stay here. We shall have some twenty or thirty invited guests this Christmas, but it is quite possible that as many more will simply arrive on our doorstep. I tell Harry it is because he is such a generous host, but he thinks it is because they are all in love with me.'

'I dare say it is a mixture of both,' Amelia told her and smiled. She was delighted that her friend had not changed one bit since she became Lady Pendleton.

She might not be quite as impulsive as when she had first visited town as Amelia's guest, but if anything her confidence had grown.

Susannah took them to the nursery, where the young heir was being prepared for bed by his nurse. After some twenty minutes or so admiring the admittedly beautiful child, Amelia and Emily were taken to the apartment they were to share during the Christmas period. It had three bedrooms and a sitting room, which was pleasant if one wished to escape from the rest of the company at times, and was quite a privilege.

Amelia allowed Emily to choose the bedchamber she liked best, and was pleased when her friend chose the one Susannah had used during that first visit. It meant she could take the room she preferred, and felt perfectly at home in.

After Susannah left them to settle in, Amelia walked to the window and looked out. Her view was of the lake and park, and, as she watched for a moment, she saw three horsemen canter to a halt and dismount. They had obviously been out riding together for pleasure and were in high good humour. Her breath caught in her throat as she heard laughter and caught sight of one familiar face. So Gerard *was* to be one of the guests this Christmas!

Amelia realised that she had been hoping for it, her heart beginning to thump with excitement. Oh, how foolish she was! Just because Gerard was here did not mean that he would speak of marriage. Why should he indeed? Had he wished to, he had had ample opportunity to do so before this.

She turned away to glance in the mirror. She was still attractive, but she was no longer a young girl. It was quite ridiculous to fancy herself in love; the time for such things had passed her by. The most she could hope for now would be a marriage of convenience, as Emily had suggested on the way to Pendleton. If perhaps Gerard were looking for a mother for his daughter, he might consider Amelia a suitable choice.

Amelia shook her head, dismissing her thoughts as a flight of fancy. There were a dozen young and beautiful girls Gerard might think of taking as his wife. Why should he look at a woman of her age? She had just turned eight and twenty. Besides, he was probably still grieving for the wife he had lost. Why had he married only a few months after their parting? Her brother Michael had behaved disgracefully to Gerard, of course, but why had he not told Amelia at the time the real reason behind his sudden departure? She would have run away with him had he asked her then.

No, if he had ever loved her, his love had faded and died.

She must not spend her time dreaming of something that would never happen!

Her thoughts turned to her companion. She knew that this time of year was often sad for Emily, because of her secret sorrow. None of their friends knew of Emily's secret, but she had told Amelia the truth when they first met. In doing so she had risked losing the chance of a good position, for many would have turned her away. Amelia had admired her honesty. She had done everything she could to make Emily forget the past, but nothing could take away the ache Emily carried inside.

Amelia was thoughtful as she prepared to go downstairs. She was almost sure that Mr Toby Sinclair would be a guest at Pendleton that Christmas. He had paid Emily some attention earlier in the year, but nothing had come of it. If he were to offer for her…but nothing was certain. Amelia would not put the idea into her companion's mind, but if it happened she would be delighted.

If it did not, perhaps there was something she might be able to do to help the girl she had come to love almost as a sister.

Amelia was glad that she had seen Gerard from her window; the knowledge that he was here at Pendleton made it possible for her to meet him without that element of surprise she might otherwise have felt. She was able to greet him in the drawing room later that evening with perfect serenity.

'How nice to see you here, sir,' she said, offering her hand and giving no sign that her heart was beating rather too fast. 'People are arriving all the time. I think Susannah will have a great many guests this Christmas.'

'Yes, I imagine she will,' Gerard agreed. He held her hand briefly. 'How are you, Miss Royston? I trust you have had no further trouble since I last saw you?'

'None at all, sir—except for a raid by some foxes

on our hen houses. But I know you did not mean that.' Amelia laughed softly. 'You are referring to the abduction attempt made the summer before last when we were all here together, I imagine?'

'Yes, I was. I am glad nothing more has happened to disturb your peace.' He looked at her thoughtfully. 'I am glad that you are here this Christmas. I was hoping that I might have a private conversation with you concerning my daughter? I would rather like your advice.'

'I should be delighted to help you if I am able.' As he smiled, Amelia's heart stopped for one moment, and then raced on madly. 'Of course, my experience with children is limited to my orphans and the children of friends—but I am fond of them.'

'It is your feeling as a woman of compassion that I need,' Gerard assured her. One of the other guests was headed towards them; from her manner and gestures she was clearly intent on speaking with Amelia. 'This is not the time, however—perhaps tomorrow we might take a walk in the gardens?'

'Yes, certainly,' Amelia agreed. Her smile and quiet manner continued undisturbed. Gerard had asked for help with his daughter and she was quite willing to give it if she could, even if she could not help wishing that his request to walk with her had stemmed from a very different desire. Seeing him, being close to him, had aroused feelings that were not appropriate for a woman who was unlikely to marry. She closed her mind to the tantalising visions of herself in his arms...his bed. That way lay disaster and heartbreak! She must remember her dignity at all times. As a young woman she had not hesitated to confess her love, but things were different now. 'I am available to you at any time, my lord.'

'Do you not think we could be Gerard and Amelia?' he asked. 'We are friends of some long standing, I think?'

'Yes, indeed we are,' Amelia agreed. For a moment the look in his eyes was so intense that she could not breathe. He should not look at her so if he wanted nothing more than friendship.

Their conversation was ended as they were drawn into the company. Susannah's guests were of all ages and included some young people, who had been allowed to come down to dinner because it was nearly Christmas. The eclectic mix of young and old, Harry's relatives and friends of the couple, made for a lively evening. The younger members were sent to bed after their meal, but the older guests continued in their merry way until long past midnight.

It was not until the moment that she had decided to retire that Gerard approached Amelia once more.

'Shall we say ten o'clock for our walk?' he asked. 'If that is not too early for you?'

'I am always an early riser.'

'You must wrap up well, for I think it may be a cold morning.'

'I enjoy walking in any kind of weather, except a downpour,' Amelia assured him.

Their arrangements made, Amelia went upstairs

to the apartment she shared with Emily. She saw that Emily was looking thoughtful and asked her if she had enjoyed the evening.

'You did not find the young company too much, dearest?'

'It was a delightful evening,' Emily assured her. 'Mr Sinclair and I joined in a guessing game with some of the young people at the dinner table. I do not know when I have had such fun.' A wistful expression came to her eyes. 'I was an only child and I doubt I shall have…' She blinked hard, as if to stop herself crying. 'I am certain Mr Sinclair means to make me an offer, Amelia. What shall I do?'

'I believe you should tell him the truth. He will keep your confidence—Toby Sinclair is a true gentleman. If he still wishes for the marriage, he will make it clear to you.'

'And if he does not?' Emily lifted her head as if to seek guidance and then nodded as she answered her own question. 'I must bear it. You are quite right, Amelia. I cannot be less than truthful, though it may make things awkward for the rest of our stay here.'

'Perhaps if you could prevent him speaking for a few days, and then tell him just before we leave. If he needs time to consider his feelings, he would have his chance before following us to Coleridge.'

'You are so wise and sensible,' Emily said and looked relieved. 'I shall do my best to avoid being alone with him until the day before we leave.'

'Try not to brood on the outcome.' Amelia kissed

her cheek. 'I believe it may all turn out better than you imagine, dearest.'

Having done her best to reassure her friend, Amelia went to her own room. She dismissed her maid as soon as the girl had undone the little hooks at the back of her gown, preferring to be alone with her thoughts. It was easier to settle Emily's doubts than her own, for she had no doubt that Toby Sinclair was deeply in love. It was more difficult to understand Gerard Ravenshead's feelings.

Sometimes his look seemed to indicate that he felt a strong emotion for her, but at others his expression was brooding and remote. They were friends, but *was* that all? These days it seemed that Gerard thought of her as a mature lady in whom he might confide his worries concerning his daughter. He could have no idea of the passionate and improper thoughts his nearness aroused in her. She must be careful to conceal her feelings, otherwise there might be some embarrassment.

'No! No, Lisette…I beg you…do not do it…forgive me…' Gerard Ravenshead's arm twitched, his head moving from side to side as he sat in the deep wing chair in the library at Pendleton. He was dreaming…a dream he had had too many times before. *'No, I say! Stop…the blood…the blood…'* He screamed out and woke to find himself in a room where the fire had gone cold and the candles burned out.

Unable to sleep, he had dressed and come down

to read for a while and fallen into a fitful sleep. He hoped that his nightmare had woken no one. Having gone for some months without one, he had thought they were finished, but something had brought it all back to him.

Gerard rose from the chair and walked over to the window, gazing out as the light strengthened. It was dawn and another night had gone.

The library was an impressive, long room with glass-fronted bookcases on three walls, a magnificent desk, occasional tables and comfortable chairs, and three sets of French windows to let in maximum light. Gerard was an avid reader and, when at home in his house in Hanover Square, often sat late into the night reading rather than retiring to his bedchamber, where he found it impossible to sleep. Indeed, he could hardly remember a night when he had slept through until morning.

Gerard was a handsome man, tall, broad in the shoulder with strong legs that looked particularly well in the riding breeches he most often wore. His coats had never needed excessive padding at the shoulder. His hair was very dark but not black, his eyes grey and sometimes flinty. His expression was often brooding, stern, perhaps because his thoughts caused him regret. At this moment he wore a pair of buff-coloured breeches and topboots and his fine linen shirt was opened to the waist. A glass of wine was to hand, but he had scarcely touched it. Gerard had long ago discovered that there was no forgetfulness in a wine bottle.

Before falling into a restless sleep, he had spent the night wrestling with his problem. His daughter was in need of feminine company, and not just that of nursemaids or a governess. He too was in need of a female companion: a woman with whom he could share his hopes and dreams, a woman he could admire and respect. In short, he needed a wife. Having made one mistake with the young French girl he had married out of pity, he did not wish to make another. Easy enough to find a mistress or even a young woman willing to become Countess Ravenshead, but there was only one woman Gerard wanted as his wife—the woman he had been denied when he was a young man and head over heels in love.

He touched the scar at his right temple, the only blemish on a strong and handsome face, his eyes darkening at the memory it aroused. Amelia's brother had instructed his servants to beat him when he dared to ask for her hand as a young man; he had not been wealthy enough to please the proud Sir Michael Royston! However, it was not fear of Sir Michael's displeasure that made Gerard hesitate to ask Amelia Royston if she would be his wife now. Guilt weighed heavily on his conscience, because he had not told anyone the whole truth concerning his wife's death. It was the reason for his nightmares.

'Damn you, Lisette. Let me be...' His eyes were dark with memories as he relived the dream. *'So much blood...so much blood...'*

She *had* been ill for a long time after the birth of

her child, but it was not that illness that had caused her death. Lisette had died by her own hand.

He found her with her wrists cut in a bath of warm water. She was still alive when he dragged her from the bath, but barely breathing. He had tried frantically to save her, sending his servant for the doctor, but his efforts were in vain and she was dead when the doctor arrived. Lisette had been buried and Gerard mourned the loss of a young life.

He had not loved her, but she haunted his dreams because he blamed himself for her death. He had married her out of pity, because she was young, alone and with child, abandoned by her lover in a country that was not her own. He knew that the father of her child was an English officer, but Lisette had never named him. His own dreams turned to dust, Gerard had done what he believed was the right thing—a good thing—but he had been unable to love her; when Lisette finally understood that, she had taken her own life.

'I am so sorry...so very sorry...'

Gerard had never been able to confess the truth to another living soul. He carried it inside, where it continued to fester. If he allowed his guilt to haunt him, it would ruin his life. Gerard had no idea whether or not Amelia would marry him if he asked her. What would she think if she knew the truth concerning his wife's death?

He had been on the point of asking her to be his wife once, but an urgent message had sent him hurrying to his daughter's side in France. Little Lisa was a demanding child and she did not like her papa to leave her for long periods. Realising she needed more than her nurses, Gerard had brought her to England and placed her in the charge of an English nanny, but neither Lisa nor her papa was truly content.

Gerard had reached the conclusion that he would never know true happiness unless he asked Amelia Royston to be his wife. He could not marry her without confessing his secret, which was one of the reasons why he had hesitated so long, for he feared that she would turn from him in disgust. He had wanted to die on the battlefield the first time he lost Amelia; to let himself hope and then lose her a second time would destroy him.

This was ridiculous! He was a man of six and thirty and should be able to face up to the truth without fear of rejection. It might be better if he forgot about marriage altogether. He had broken Lisette's heart, causing her to commit suicide. Perhaps he would do better to remain unwed.

Amelia saw Gerard waiting for her the next morning as she went down to the hall. He was wearing a long coat with several capes, a warm muffler bound about his throat and a fur hat in the Russian style. He smiled his approval as he saw that she too was wearing a thick cloak and muffler, her gloved hands tucked inside a fur muff that hung suspended from a chain about her neck.

'I see you are prepared for the weather, Amelia. There is a fine frost this morning.'

'As there should be for Christmas Eve,' she replied. 'I think it will be just right for a brisk walk about the gardens, sir.'

'My daughter would not agree with you.' Gerard looked rueful. 'I believe I was wrong to leave her so long in France. She finds our English weather cold and damp and asks constantly when do we return to Paris.'

'Do you think of leaving England permanently?' Amelia asked, doing her best to conceal her feeling of acute disappointment.

'I considered it for a while,' Gerard confessed. 'However, I have decided that I should prefer to live in England where I have friends rather than mere acquaintances. Lisa must come to terms with the situation. I believe she will be happier once the summer comes.'

'I think you may have been in the habit of giving her her own way?' Amelia tipped her head to one side, her eyebrows slightly raised.

'Yes, I have spoiled her,' Gerard admitted and laughed. 'She is a little charmer and I fear that I may have given in too often to her whims—which may be why she is giving poor Nanny such a difficult time. I hear complaints that she is sometimes sulky and unresponsive, though with me she is very different.'

Amelia was thoughtful. 'Is the nanny well recommended?'

'Her references were good. She came from a family with whom she had served for more than six years.

However, I have wondered if she is a little too strict with the child. I may have been too lenient, but I would not have Lisa's life made a misery. It is not easy for a man alone...' Gerard glanced at Amelia, a rueful look in his eyes. 'I feel in need of a lady's advice. Some ladies take little interest in their children. They feel their duty is done once the heir is produced, but you make it your business to care for unfortunate children. You might be able to tell me what to do for the best as far as my daughter is concerned.'

Amelia kept her smile in place despite her disappointment. It was as she had feared—he wanted only to discuss his daughter. 'I would need to see Lisa and her nanny together. It would be best if it happened casually. If Nanny knows she is being observed, I should learn nothing.'

'You understand at once, as I knew you would,' Gerard said, looking pleased. 'I brought Lisa to Pendleton with me, though I did not allow her to come down to dinner last evening for she is not ready yet. However, she will be present at the children's party this afternoon. Susannah has lots of small presents and prizes for the young ones. I shall be there. Perhaps...if it is not too much trouble?' He arched his brows at her.

'I had intended to be there anyway. I enjoy these things and Susannah will need a little help to organise the games and present giving. It will be no trouble to observe your daughter and her nanny.'

'How generous you are...' He paused as Amelia gave an impatient shake of her head. 'It will be good to have a lady's opinion in this matter. I have no female relations that I may call upon.'

'Does your late wife not have a family?'

'I have no idea. I met Lisette after a bloody battle between the French and the Spanish troops. She had been ill used and I took pity on her. I married her to protect her and to give her unborn child my name. She never spoke of her family. I imagine they were killed during the conflict…' Gerard was looking straight ahead, a nerve flicking at his temple. 'I knew nothing about her, except that she was French and clearly of gentle birth.'

'You love the child very much, do you not?'

'I fell in love with her when she was born. I was present and helped bring her into the world for there were few doctors available to us—and so she became mine.' Gerard glanced towards her. 'After I left England, I was a disappointed man, Amelia. At one time I had nothing to live for. Indeed, I might have welcomed death on the battlefield. I married Lisette because it seemed the best way to protect her and I had abandoned all hope of happiness…but when her child was born I loved the child from the first moment of seeing her.'

'Yes, you mentioned something of this once before.' Amelia looked thoughtful. 'You said that your wife was ill for a long time after the child's birth?'

'She took no interest in the babe at all. I was able to secure the services of a wet-nurse. Often I cared for the child myself, changing her and feeding her as she began to take solid foods. Lisette had no interest in anything for a long time. When she recovered a little...' He shook his head, as she would have questioned him. 'After she died, I engaged the services of a nurse, and when the war was over I made the decision to keep Lisa in France with me. At that time I was not sure what to do for the best.'

'You thought you might live there because your child's mother was French?'

'I must confess that for a while I considered leaving the child in France with a nurse,' he admitted. 'I was a soldier, a single man—and my estate was in some trouble. I have rectified that now, though I am not as rich as Pendleton or Coleridge.' He gave Amelia a rueful look. 'When we first met I had hardly any fortune at all. I dare say that was the reason Sir Michael did not consider me a worthy husband for his sister.'

'He had no right to send you away.' Amelia hesitated, then lifted her gaze to meet his because she needed to ask. 'Why did you not send me word of what happened? Surely you knew that I would have gone with you had you asked? I would not have allowed Michael to prevent our marriage if I had known. I suspected that he had had a hand in it, but when you told me what he did to you—' She broke off and sighed. 'It was a wicked thing that Michael did to you—to us...'

'I ought to have known you would elope with me, despite what your brother said when he had me beaten,' Gerard admitted. 'I suppose I was humiliated and angry—even bitter. I was not certain that you loved me enough to defy him. At that time I did not expect to be my uncle's heir. He had a son who should have inherited. Had my cousin not died of a putrid chill, I must have made my living as a soldier. Perhaps your brother had some right on his side, Amelia.'

'No, he did not,' she contradicted at once. 'Your lack of fortune meant nothing to me, Gerard.'

'I am no longer a pauper. I have worked hard and my business ventures prosper. However, your own fortune surpasses mine these days. I well remember that you had nothing when I asked you to be my wife.'

'I did not expect that to change. It was a surprise when my great-aunt asked me to live with her—and when she left everything to me. She had told me that I would have something when she died, but I had no idea that she was so wealthy.'

'It was a stroke of luck for you, I suppose.'

'Yes…though it has its drawbacks. My brother and sister-in-law are resentful of the fact that I inherited a fortune they believe should have gone to them. Michael has been unpleasant to me on more than one occasion since my aunt died.'

'They had no right to expect it. Lady Agatha might have left her money anywhere.'

'Indeed, she might,' Amelia said. 'I believe her deceased husband also had relatives who might have hoped for something—but they at least have not approached me on the matter.'

'And your brother has?' His brows arched, eyes narrowed and intent.

'Several times,' Amelia said. 'It has been the

subject of endless arguments between us. Michael thinks I should make most of the money over to him. I have no intention of doing what he demands, but it has made for bad blood between us.' She hesitated, then, 'I have not spoken of this to anyone but Emily—but his last visit was almost threatening. I was a little disturbed by it, I admit.'

'Sir Michael is of a violent temperament…'

Amelia was silent for a moment, then, 'You are thinking it might have been he who tried to have me abducted at Pendleton the summer before last? I believe you thought it then?'

'It is possible, but I may have been mistaken. My own encounter with him may have coloured my thinking. If it was him, why has he not carried the threat further? Why stop at one attempt?'

'I do not know. For a long time I thought that there might be another attempt, but nothing happened.'

'It is puzzling. The likely explanation seems that it was actually Susannah who was the intended victim and you were mistaken for her. As you know, there was some awkwardness between the Marquis of Northaven and Harry Pendleton at that time.'

'That is one possibility, and yet I cannot think that we are alike. Emily is convinced that my brother means me harm. She overheard something he said to me some months ago and she suggested that he would benefit if I died.'

'Would he?'

'At the moment he is the largest, though not the only, beneficiary.'

Gerard nodded. 'It might be wise to change that and let it be known that you have done so, Amelia.'

Amelia's expression was thoughtful. 'I cannot think that Michael would wish to see me dead—even for a fortune. My brother is bad tempered and arrogant, but I would not have thought him a murderer.'

'It would not hurt to take some precautions. I could arrange for you to be watched over—as I did once before. And changes to your will might help if you would consider making them.'

'Yes, I may do so after the New Year. We are to attend Helene and Max's ball at Coleridge. Shall you be there?'

'Yes, I believe so,' Gerard said. 'As you know, both Harry and Max are particular friends of mine.'

'And their wives are good friends of mine,' Amelia said. 'I should be grateful if you could arrange some kind of protection, for Emily as well as me. I have no idea how it may be done and it may not truly be necessary. I shall, of course, pay the men myself.'

'As you wish,' Gerard said. 'The breeze is very cold. I think we may have some snow. Should we return to the house before we freeze to death?'

'Yes, perhaps we should,' Amelia replied.

She had the oddest feeling that he had been on the verge of saying something very different, but at the last he had changed his mind. Nothing more of note was said between them, and they parted after returning to the house. She pondered on what might have been in Gerard's mind as she went in search of her hostess.

It was good of him to say that he would find suitable men to protect her if he thought her in danger from her brother's spite. If, of course, it was her brother she needed protecting from…but who else could it be?

'What made you think I would be interested in such an outrageous proposition?' The Marquis of Northaven looked at the person sitting opposite him in the private parlour of the posting inn to which he had been summoned that evening. He had considered ignoring the note sent to his lodgings in town, but curiosity and a certain intuition had brought him here. However, to the best of his knowledge he had never met the gentleman before. 'Kidnapping is a hanging offence…'

'I had heard that you have a score to settle with a certain gentleman.'

'Where did you hear that?' Northaven was alert, suspicious. The other man's features were barely visible in the shadows, his face half-covered by the muffler he wore to keep out the cold.

'One hears these things…of course there would be money once the ransom was paid.'

'Money…' Northaven's mouth curved in a sneer, a flash of hauteur in his manner. 'I have not yet run through the inheritance my uncle left me.'

'Then forget I asked you. I had thought you might care to see Ravenshead brought down, but if you do not have the stomach for it there are others willing, nay, eager to do my bidding.'

'How would this bring Ravenshead down?' Northaven asked, eyes narrowed, menacing.

'He imagines he will marry Amelia Royston. I do not wish to see that happen. Once I have finished with her, she will marry no one!'

The Marquis of Northaven shivered, feeling icy cold. He had done much in his life that he was not proud of, but something in the tone of the person who was asking him to arrange Amelia Royston's downfall was disturbing. Northaven had seduced more than one young woman, but contrary to what was said and thought of him, he had taken none against their will. Indeed, they usually threw themselves into his arms— and why should he say no? Handsome beyond what many thought decent, he had an air of unavailability that made him irresistible to many ladies. He was by no means a white knight, but neither was he the traitor some thought him. He might cheat at cards when desperate; he might lie if it suited him and would not deny that he had sailed close to the edge a few times, but a cold-blooded murderer he was not.

Northaven had been angry with the men who had once been his friends. He had hated the holy trilogy, as he was wont to call Harry Pendleton, Max Coleridge and Gerard Ravenshead. He hated them because they despised him, believed him worse than he truly was, but with the turn in his fortunes of late much of his resentment had cooled. He would have dismissed the proposition being made to him out of hand, but he was curious to hear more.

'Supposing I were interested in bringing down

Ravenshead,' he said. 'What would you be willing
to pay—and what do you plan for Miss Royston?'

'I was thinking of ten thousand guineas. Her fate
is not your affair. All you need to do is to deliver her
to me.'

The words were delivered with such malice that
Northaven's stomach turned. He imagined that Miss
Royston's fate might be worse than death and it
sickened him. He was well aware that Amelia
Royston had once thought him guilty of the callous
seduction and desertion of her friend; he had
allowed her to believe it, but it was not true. A few
months previously he might have left her to her
fate. He had then been a bitter, angry man, but
something had happened to him the day he watched
a young girl marry the man she loved—the man she
had risked everything to save when she thought he
was about to die.

No woman had ever loved Northaven enough to
take a ball in the shoulder for him. Susannah
Hampton had been reckless and could easily have
died had his aim been slightly to the left. The
moment his ball had struck her shoulder, Northaven
had felt remorse. He had been relieved when
Susannah made a full recovery. Something drove
him to mingle with the crowd on her wedding day.
When her eyes met his as she left the church on her
husband's arm, they had seemed to ask a question.
He had answered it with a nod of his head and he
believed she understood. His feud with her husband
was over.

He had not fallen in love with her. Yet she had touched him in a way he had never expected. He had suddenly realised where he was headed if he contin- ued on his reckless path: he would end a lonely, bitter man. For a while the resentment against his one-time friends had continued to burn inside him, but of late he had felt more at peace with himself.

Perhaps at last he had found the way to redeem himself.

'Let me think about it,' he said. 'Ten thousand guineas is a fair sum—and I have no love for Ravens- head. Give me a few days and I shall decide.'

'Meet me here again in two days and I will tell you more. We can do nothing over Christmas. Miss Royston goes to Coleridge in the New Year—and that will be our chance…'

Chapter Two

Gerard cursed himself for a fool as he parted from Amelia. He had let yet another chance slip, but after discussing his daughter and her brother the time had not seemed right. If he had asked Amelia to marry him in the same breath as telling her that she ought to think of changing her will, she might have thought he was asking her for reasons of convenience to himself. He had made his circumstances clear so that when he did speak there would be no misunderstanding. He was not in need of a rich wife, though Amelia was extremely wealthy. Her fortune was yet another reason why he hesitated—but the burning problem besetting him was whether her opinion of him would suffer when he told her the truth of Lisette's death.

To conceal the details from her would not be honest. If they were to come out at some time in the future, she might feel that he had deceived her and there would be a loss of trust. All in all, Gerard considered that he had done what he could to prepare the ground for a future proposal. He felt they were good friends, but he could not be sure that anything of their former love was left on Amelia's part, though every time he saw her he was more convinced that she was the only woman for him. She was beautiful, charming and the scent of her always seemed to linger, making him aware of a deep hunger within. He wanted her more than he had ever wanted anything in his life. Without her…

'My lord…' The footman's voice broke through Gerard's reverie. He turned as the man approached him. 'This was delivered for you early this morning, sir.'

'For me?' Gerard stared at the parcel wrapped in strong brown paper and tied with string. 'Was there a card? Do you know who delivered it?'

'It was a gentleman's man, sir. I do not know his name, but he said his gentleman had bid him deliver this to you here.'

'I see…thank you.' Gerard frowned as he took the parcel. He had left gifts at the homes of some friends in London; however, he had told no one but Toby Sinclair that he was coming here for Christmas. The gift might have come from one of the other guests, but it was more normal to exchange them after dinner on Christmas Eve. He shook the parcel gently and discovered that it rattled. Intrigued, he took it into a small parlour to the right of the hall and untied the strings, folding back the paper.

There was no card, but inside the paper was a wooden box. He lifted the lid and stared at the contents. At first he thought that the doll must be a present for Lisa. However, the head was lying at an odd angle, and, as he lifted it out, he saw that the porcelain head had been wrenched from the stuffed body. It was broken across the face and the body had been slit down the middle with a knife or something similar.

Gerard felt cold all over. There was something disturbing about the wanton destruction to what had been a pretty fashion doll, the kind that was often used to show off the wares of expensive couturiers rather than a child's toy.

It could hardly have been broken accidentally. No, this had been done deliberately. He could not imagine who had sent such a thing to him or why. However, he felt that the broken doll was a symbol of something—a threat. The implication was sinister for it must be a warning, though he could not think what he was being warned about or why it had been sent to him at such a time.

Gerard realised that he must have an enemy. His first thought was that he had only one enemy of any note that he knew of and that was the Marquis of Northaven. Northaven had been bitter because Gerard, along with Harry and Max, had ostracised him after that débâcle in Spain, blaming him for the fact that the French troop had been expecting an attack. Northaven had engineered a duel with Harry, which had almost ended in tragedy, but since then none of them had heard much from him. It was as if he had dropped out of sight.

Somehow, it seemed unlikely that the doll had come from Northaven. The man had always denied betraying his friends to the Spanish; he had been prepared to fight any of them in a duel to clear his name—but this doll was something very different. It was meant to disturb, to sow confusion and anxiety—though its message was obscure. Was the sender threatening his daughter?

Gerard felt sick inside as he pictured his daughter being mutilated as the doll had been. Surely the sender could not be threatening Lisa? She was an innocent child who had harmed no one. Besides, what had he done that would cause anyone to hate him to this extent?

'Gerard…' Harry entered the room behind him. 'I thought I saw you come in here.'

'Yes. I wanted to open this…' Gerard held the box out to him. 'One of your footmen gave it to me a moment ago. Apparently, it was delivered earlier this morning.'

Harry looked at the doll, his eyes narrowing as he saw what had been done to it. 'Good grief! What on earth is that about?'

'I have no idea. I wish I did.'

'A threat, do you think?' Harry's mouth was a grim white line. 'To your daughter—or a warning?'

'Perhaps both…'

'There was no message?'

'None that I could find.'

Harry picked up the box and looked inside. Then he saw a small card lying in the discarded paper and string and held it out to Gerard.

'If you value her, stay away from her. This is your one and only warning and sent in good faith. Ignore it and the one you love may end like this.' Gerard frowned as he read the words aloud. 'What can that mean—how can I stay away from my own daughter?'

'Are you sure the doll is meant to represent your daughter?' Harry asked. 'Only a few of us even know she exists, Gerard. Perhaps the person who sent this does not know you have a child.'

Gerard stared at him and then nodded. 'You are right. Only a handful of my friends know about Lisa. So if the doll isn't her...' His gaze narrowed. 'You don't think—Amelia...?'

'It makes more sense,' Harry said. 'Whoever sent this used a fashion doll, not a child's toy. Amelia is an extremely elegant woman and it is more likely that the doll represents her. We suspect an attempt to kidnap her was made that summer at Pendleton. Max had an idea that the reason no further attempts were made to kidnap her was because you were no longer around.'

'Yes, he mentioned something of the kind some months ago, but I did not think it possible. Good grief!' Gerard was horrified. 'You think they tried to abduct Amelia because they thought I might be about to ask her to marry me—and then I returned to France. Nothing happened while I was away, but now I am back...'

'And you receive this warning.' Harry looked concerned. 'If that is the case, Amelia could be in grave danger.'

Gerard frowned. 'She told me this morning that Miss Barton had asked her if her brother would benefit from her death. Apparently, he has been demanding that she hand over most of the fortune her great-aunt left her.'

'Is Royston such a brute?' Harry pondered the question. 'I do not know him well, but I would not have thought it. He might bully her into giving him money, but murder?'

'Northaven?'

'I am not sure that the murder of a woman is his style. He would be more likely to force a duel on you if he wished to pursue a quarrel.'

'My thoughts entirely. It must be Royston—I can think of no one else who would be affected if she were to marry me.'

'You cannot think of anyone who has cause to hate you?'

'None that I know of,' Gerard replied, but looked thoughtful. 'Everyone makes enemies, but I cannot think of anyone who would wish to harm me or mine. Royston does not like me. He had me beaten when I asked for Amelia's hand as a young man— but surely he has not harboured a grudge all this time? Besides, why harm his sister? If his quarrel is with me, why not have me shot? There are assassins enough to put a ball between my shoulders on a dark street.'

'Royston had you beaten when you asked for Amelia?' Harry's brows shot up as Gerard nodded. 'The scar at your temple! I knew something had happened but you never spoke of it... You have never sought retribution?'

'How could I? Whatever happened, Royston is Amelia's brother. I love her, Harry. I would do nothing to harm her. He has no reason to hate me that I know of—I swear it.'

'Then this threat must have been made in order to gain control of her fortune,' Harry said grimly. 'If you marry her, he loses all chance of inheriting if she dies.'

'Good grief! If I ask her to marry me, I could be signing her death warrant.'

'And if you do not, she remains vulnerable,' Harry pointed out. 'You cannot allow this threat to alter your plans.'

'I am damned whichever way I go!' Gerard cursed. 'I must arrange protection for her. She must be watched around the clock.'

'And for yourself,' Harry warned. 'Do not shake your head, Gerard. You need someone to watch your back, my friend. I am not certain that we have reached the heart of this business. You need to investigate this affair immediately. I shall question my servants. Perhaps one of them may know something of the man who delivered that thing.'

Gerard had replaced the broken doll and closed the box. 'The footman knew nothing, but someone else may have seen the messenger who delivered this thing. Any clue would be welcome, for at the moment I have little to go on.'

'You know you may call on me for assistance?'

'Yes, of course. Please say nothing of this to your wife or Amelia for the moment. I do not wish to throw a cloud over the celebrations this Christmas. Besides, I believe Amelia must be safe enough here for we are aware of the danger…' He frowned. 'Does it not strike you as odd that I was warned? If the rogue wants Amelia dead—why warn me of the possibility?'

'Perhaps he simply wants to prevent you speaking to her?'

'Perhaps…' Gerard looked thoughtful. 'Or someone else sent it to alert me to danger. Something puzzles me, Harry. I think there is more to this than we yet know, but I confess I have no idea what it may be.'

Amelia was thoughtful as she went upstairs to change. Speaking to Gerard confidentially had made her think about her situation. It was hard to think that her brother could mean her harm, but she could not deny that he had several times spoken to her in a manner that might be thought threatening.

Perhaps it would be sensible to take some precautions, though she would hate to think her life might be in danger. Of course, if she were married, her brother would have no hope of her fortune—which might be why he had several times made it plain that he would never agree to her marrying Gerard. She was her own mistress, of course. Michael must know that he could not stop her marrying whomsoever she wished.

Amelia looked out of her bedchamber and watched her companion walking towards the house. Emily Barton's head was down and her manner one of thoughtfulness. She was quite alone.

Emily had a gentle beauty with her dark honey-blonde hair and blue eyes that were startling in a pale face. However, because of her modest manner and way of dressing, she was often thought unremarkable until she smiled, when she could look stunning. Amelia frowned, because of late Emily had seemed quieter than usual. She was clearly brooding.

Amelia suspected she knew what was troubling her. Emily had been scrupulous in confessing her shame when she applied for the position as Amelia's companion.

'I must tell you that I have a secret, Miss Royston.' Emily had looked at her steadily. 'Only my parents and a few servants knew, for my father did his best to hide my shame.'

'Your shame—are you telling me that you have borne a child out of wedlock?' Amelia had sensed it instinctively.

'I…was forced,' Emily told her, cheeks pale, eyes dark with remembered horror. 'He was not my lover—but he held me down as he raped me, and, later, I knew that I would bear his child.'

'My dear,' Amelia cried. 'It is shocking that men can be so vile. Please tell me what happened then.'

'My father never believed that it was not my fault, but I swear to you that I am innocent of duplicity in this.' Emily's eyes brimmed with tears, though she did not weep. 'If this makes me unacceptable as your companion…'

'No, do not think it.' Amelia smiled at her. 'What you have told me makes me more determined to give you a home. You will live with me, meet my friends and learn to be happy again, my dear.'

'You are so very kind…'

'I know what it is to have a broken heart, Emily.' She shook her head as the young woman raised her brows. 'Put your shame behind you, my dear. I absolve you of blame.'

If only Emily had been able to put her shame and unhappiness behind her! Amelia knew that she still had days when she was deeply unhappy.

She must do something to help her companion. For some time now Amelia had been considering the idea of trying to find Emily's child. The babe had been taken from her at birth and she did not even know where her daughter was. If she could be told that the little girl was well and healthy, living happily with her foster parents, perhaps this deep ache inside her might ease.

Amelia had hesitated because she did not wish to cause her companion more pain, but to see Emily unhappy even when she was in company was hard to bear.

Instead of brooding on her own problems, she would think about Emily. Surely there must be a way of finding the child?

Having changed into a fresh gown, Amelia prepared to go down and join Emily. She would say nothing to her for the moment, but after Christmas she would see what could be done.

Alone in his bedchamber, Gerard paced the floor. It seemed he was caught between a rock and a hard place—if he spoke to Amelia and she accepted his offer of marriage, it might place her in danger. Yet if her brother did plan her death in order to inherit her fortune, she needed protection. If she married, she would no longer be at the mercy of her grasping relatives.

He was aware of a burning need to protect her. Amelia was his, the love of his life. He could not give her up because of an obscure threat. He would make every effort to keep her safe. It would probably be best to let her know he believed she might be in some danger, but he was sure that she was safe enough for the moment. Harry would alert his servants to be on the lookout for strangers, and by the time she was ready to leave Pendleton he would have measures in place for her protection. He would summon the men he had used once before.

He could at least do this for the woman he loved, though he was still undecided whether to speak to her of marriage. Did he have the right? Amelia was still beautiful, a woman of fortune and charm and she must be much sought after. He had heard whispers, her name linked with various gentlemen, but nothing seemed to come of the rumours. Gerard had no idea whether she had received offers. If she had, she had turned them down—why? Was she sus-

picious of the motives behind every proposal that
came her way? Did she imagine that no one could
love her for herself? Surely not! And yet if her
brother had been browbeating her because of her
fortune, it would not be surprising if she thought
others interested only in her wealth.

Gerard decided that he would tell no one else of
his suspicions until Christmas was over, because he
wanted it to be a happy time for Amelia and his
daughter. He certainly did not wish to cast a shadow
over the festivities for Susannah and her guests.

'Susannah asked me to help with the younger
children,' Emily said to Amelia as they went downstairs together that afternoon. 'She thinks that they
will need help to unwrap their presents and Nanny
has been given time off.'

Amelia saw the happy smile on her face. Emily
loved children and the knowledge that her own
daughter was living with another family must be
torture for her. She wondered if Emily had ever tried
to discover the whereabouts of her child, but
supposed it was unlikely. She had devoted her life to
her ailing mother until that lady died and had then
been forced to look for work. Perhaps Amelia might
mention the possibility to Emily another day, but
now was not the time.

'I think Susannah is very brave to have the
children's party without her nanny, for I am certain
that some of the ladies have no idea of looking after
their own children.'

'I think it will be great fun. I always wished that I had brothers and sisters, and envied those who did.' The wistful expression had come back to Emily's face.

Amelia saw it and made up her mind that she would ask someone to make enquiries concerning the lost child for her. However, it would be better to say nothing to Emily for the moment in case the child could not be found.

'I am certain that we shall enjoy ourselves this afternoon,' Amelia said. 'I am eager to meet Gerard's daughter. She has been brought up in France until the past few months, and I dare say she may not understand English as well as she needs to if she is to communicate with the other children. I know that Gerard's nanny will be present, so we shall have help.'

The two ladies smiled at each other as they approached the large salon where the celebrations for the younger guests were taking place. Entering, they saw that the room had been decorated with silver and gold stars; there was also a crib with wooden animals and a doll representing the Baby Jesus and two of the servants were dressed as Joseph and Mary. Some of the other servants were dressed as the three kings, and they had big sacks of gifts. These would be distributed to the children at the end of the entertainment.

All kinds of delicious foods that might appeal to children had been set out on a table: sweet jellies, bottled fruits, cakes and tiny biscuits, also fingers of bread and butter with the crusts cut off and spread with honey.

'Amelia…Miss Barton.' Gerard approached them with a smile. 'May I have the pleasure of introducing my daughter, Lisa, to you? Lisa—this is Miss Amelia Royston—and Miss Emily Barton. Greet them nicely, my love.'

'*Bonjour*, Mademoiselle Royston, *bonjour*, Mademoiselle Barton,' Lisa said and dipped a curtsy. 'I am pleased to meet you.' She tipped her head and looked at Gerard. 'Was that correct, Papa?'

Her manner was that of a little coquette. She was pretty, an enchanting little doll dressed in satin and frills, her dark eyes bright and mischievous; ringlets the colour of hazelnuts covered her head and were tied with a pink ribbon. Amelia adored her at once, completely understanding why Gerard had fallen in love with his daughter. For although Lisa did not carry his blood, she was undoubtedly his in every other way and the affection between them was a joy to see.

'It was charming, Mademoiselle Ravenshead.' Amelia smiled at her and held out her hand. 'Your English is very good. I see that you have been attending your lessons. Shall we go and see what Lady Pendleton has given us for tea?'

'Papa always speaks to me in English.' Lisa hesitated, then placed her tiny hand in Amelia's. She looked at her in a confiding manner. 'I am hungry, but Nanny said that I was not to eat anything. She says that the food is not suitable for me.'

'Oh, I think it would be a shame if you were not to have any of it,' Amelia replied. 'Perhaps not too much chocolate cake, but I think a small piece and some bread and honey could not hurt anyone.'

'We always had honey for tea in France,' Lisa told her with a happy smile. 'Nanny says a boiled egg is better, but I like honey for tea.'

'Well, do you know, so do I. Shall we have some?'

'Yes, please. Can I have a piece of cake? Nanny doesn't allow me cake.' Lisa looked sorrowful and then a smile peeped out. 'I have cake sometimes with Papa.'

'I think Christmas is an exception, don't you? Besides, Lady Pendleton would be very upset if all this lovely food went to waste—do you not think so?'

'Yes, I should think so,' Lisa said, giving her a naughty look. 'Could I have some of that red jelly, please?'

'I think perhaps that would be acceptable,' Amelia said. 'We shall have bread and honey and a jelly each—and then a piece of cake. How does that sound?'

'I beg your pardon, Miss Royston, but I do not allow my charge to eat such rich food as a rule.'

Amelia turned her head to look at the woman who had spoken. The child's nanny was a severe-looking woman with iron-grey hair and a thin mouth. She was perhaps fifty years of age and had doubtless ruled more than one nursery with a rod of iron. Amelia took an instant dislike to her, but hid it behind a polite smile.

'I believe we should relax the rules a little, Nanny,' she said pleasantly. 'This is Christmas, after all, and the earl asked me especially to make sure that his daughter enjoys herself. Lisa will not eat too much.'

'It is just that I do not wish her to be sick all night, ma'am.'

'I do not think it likely,' Amelia said. 'Please do what you can to help with the other children, Nanny. Lisa will be quite safe with me.'

The woman nodded and moved away. From the set of her shoulders, Amelia guessed that she was angry. She hoped that her refusal to accept Nanny's authority would not lead to some form of punishment for Lisa later.

'Do you like to play games?' she asked Lisa, making up her mind that she would speak to Gerard on the subject of his daughter's nanny later.

'I do not know, mademoiselle. I have never played any—except that Papa takes me up on his horse with him sometime. We run and chase each other in the garden when Nanny cannot see us. Is that a game?'

'Yes, one kind of a game but there are many others. Do you not have puzzles or a hoop to play with?'

'Papa gave me things when we came to England, but Nanny says I should study my books. She says playing with toys is a waste of time.'

'Does she indeed?' Amelia kept her voice light and without criticism. 'Lady Pendleton has several games for us to play today—musical chairs and pass the parcel, and I have seen some spilikins. I think that you and I might play these games together. It is Christmas, after all—and there are prizes to be won.'

Amelia smiled as she saw the little girl's face light up. Gerard was right to be concerned about his daughter's nanny. Lisa was clearly a high-spirited child and needed discipline, but not to the extent that she was forbidden time to play or the food that she enjoyed.

Two hours later, Amelia had fallen totally in love with her new friend. Lisa had blossomed, becoming a natural, happy little girl, as they joined in noisy games of pass the parcel and musical chairs. Susannah had been in charge of the music and saw to it that every child managed to win a small gift, which was most often sweetmeats or a trinket of some kind. Lisa won a little silver cross on a pink ribbon, and as a gift she was given a doll with a porcelain head and a stuffed body. It was wearing a pink satin dress that matched hers and, when the party ended, she ran to show it to her father.

'Beautiful,' he said and kissed her, gazing at Amelia over the child's head. 'Has this scamp of mine been good, Amelia?'

'Oh, I think so,' Amelia said. 'We have enjoyed ourselves, have we not, Lisa?'

'Oui, merci, mademoiselle,' Lisa said and curtsied to her. 'Will you come and see me again, please? I would like you to be my friend.' There was something a little desperate in the child's look as she saw her nurse coming to claim her. 'Please…'

'Yes, certainly. I shall come in the morning,' Amelia said. 'I have a gift for you, Lisa—and I think we could go for a walk together in the park or even a ride in the carriage since it is cold. You, your papa and me—how would that be?'

'I should like it above all things, *mademoiselle*.' Lisa threw herself at Amelia and hugged her.

'Come along, Miss Ravenshead,' Nanny said. 'You are over-excited. You will never sleep and I shall be up all night with you.' The woman shot a look of dislike at Amelia.

Mindful that it would take time to replace her, Amelia made no reply. However, she turned urgently to Gerard as Nanny led the child away.

'I must speak to you privately. I have made certain observations and I think you should consider replacing that woman.'

'You do not like her either?' Gerard looked relieved. 'I am so glad that I asked you to take note, Amelia. She was recommended to me, but I have thought her too sour. I was not sure if I was being unfair—and I know that children need discipline…'

'Not to the extent that all the joy of life is squeezed out of them,' Amelia said as they walked from the room into a smaller parlour where they were alone. 'Lisa is high-spirited, but she is a delightful child and has good manners. I think Nanny is too strict with her. She is not allowed to play or to have honey for tea—and that I must tell you is a terrible deprivation.'

'And entirely unnecessary,' Gerard said and laughed. 'I knew I might rely on you, my very dear Amelia. I was afraid that my partiality for Lisa made me too lenient. I have a nursemaid. I shall put her in charge and dismiss Nanny. Oh, I will give her a year's wages and a reference, but she shall not have charge of my daughter again.'

'Oh dear, the poor woman. I feel terrible now for she has lost her employment, and at Christmas— but I confess that I did not like her. I once employed a woman of that sort at the orphanage and had to dismiss her soon after, because she ill treated her charges. I do not understand why some people feel it is necessary to treat children as if they were criminals.'

'Some can be little monsters. I remember that I used to put frogs in the bed of my nanny.'

'Did you? I did that once and she went to my father. He sent me to bed and I was given nothing but bread and water for two days—and I had to apologise.'

'My father thrashed me. It did me the world of good, for as he said—think what a shock it was for the poor frog.'

'The frog…' Amelia went into a peal of delighted laughter. 'Oh, no! That is a great deal too bad of you, sir. You have a wicked sense of humour.'

'Yes, I have at times,' Gerard admitted. 'Though I have not laughed so very much of late. Amelia…may I tell you something?'

'Yes, of course.'

He led her towards a little sofa. 'Please sit down. This is not easy for me. I have wished to tell you something that almost no one else knows, but I fear it may give you a bad opinion of me.'

'Have you done something wicked?' she asked with a smile.

'I have not told you the whole truth about something.'

Amelia's smile faded. This was clearly serious. 'Please explain. I do not understand.'

'I told you that my wife died after a long illness?' Amelia nodded. 'It was not quite the truth. She had been ill, but she had recovered in her physical health at least, though I know now that she must still have been suffering in her mind.'

'Gerard! Please explain. I do not understand.'

'Lisette seemed happy enough while she was carrying the child, but afterwards…she complained that I did not love her—that I thought more of the child…'

'Surely any father would love their child? Perhaps she was pulled down by the birth? I have heard that some women are deeply affected by childbirth.'

'Yes, it may have been that…' Gerard hesitated. Now was his chance to tell her the whole truth, but he was reluctant. 'I may have neglected her. I tried to be good to her, to give her my protection and all that she needed, but perhaps it was not enough for her. I am not the man I was when we first met, Amelia. I have become harder, I think, less caring of others.'

'Oh, Gerard! I cannot think that you deliberately mistreated your wife?'

He stroked the little scar at his temple. 'No, not deliberately, but I may have been careless perhaps.

Lisette was vulnerable, easily hurt. I should have been kinder.' He paused, then, 'It may not be possible for me to love anyone completely. Something died in me the night your brother had me thrashed. At first I believed that you knew—that you felt insulted by my love. I suppose that I became afraid to show love, and Lisette suffered because of my lack.'

Gerard hesitated. He wanted to tell her that Lisette's death was his fault, to tell her of the night when Lisette had crept into his bed and offered herself to him—of the way he had turned from his wife, because she was not the woman he had loved so deeply. It would be right and fair to make Amelia aware of what he had done, but he could not bear to see her turn from him in disgust. He knew that Lisette had been terribly hurt—that it had driven her to a desperate act.

'What happened—how did she die?'

'One day when I was out she ordered a bath and then…' He paused, almost choking on the words. 'When I returned I found her. She had slashed her wrists and bled to death. I pulled her from the water and did what I could for her. She died in my arms…' His face twisted with pain. 'I did not mean to hurt her. She must have been desperately unhappy and I was not there for her. Something in me must be lacking. How could I not know that my own wife was so desperate that she would take her own life? I have blamed myself for her death ever since.'

He had told her the truth, leaving out only a few details that he felt unable to communicate.

'Gerard…' Amelia was on her feet. She held out her hands to him, her expression understanding and sympathetic. 'My dear—how terrible for you! It was a tragedy for a life was lost—but it was not your fault. Lisette could not have recovered completely from the birth. How could you have known she was unhappy if she did not tell you?'

'She may have been unwell, but I was not aware of it. I should have known.'

'You rescued her when she was alone. You married her, were kind to her so she turned to you, gave you her heart. If she felt unsure of your love, it may have made her desperately unhappy, but the blame is not all yours.'

'You see things so clearly…' Gerard moved closer, his eyes searching her face. 'So you do not hate me? You will not turn away in disgust? You understand that I am not as I once was?'

'I could never hate you. Surely you know…'

'I know that you are a wonderful, wise and lovely woman,' Gerard said passionately. 'I would be honoured if you would become my wife, Amelia. You were prepared to marry me all those years ago. Dare I hope that you still find the idea agreeable?'

'Gerard…' Amelia gasped. 'Yes…'

She meant to say more, but he lowered his head to kiss her on the lips. Amelia responded with all the love that was in her, her arms going about his neck as her body melded with his. This was what she had longed for, dreamed of so many lonely nights! She had never expected to be so fortunate.

'My beautiful Amelia,' Gerard said. 'I am a fool! You are such a sensible woman. You understand everything. You would not do something stupid because of a foolish quarrel. I should have asked long ago. You are exactly the woman I need in my life. You will not expect more than I am able to give.'

Amelia withdrew a little. She waited for him to say the words she needed to hear, but he did not speak of love and she was conscious of a slight disappointment.

She looked at him uncertainly. 'I had thought you meant to ask me before, but then you seemed to withdraw and I was not sure you cared for me.'

'I have always admired and cared for you,' Gerard replied. 'We should have married years ago had your brother not had me beaten for having the temerity to approach you.' He paused, then, 'I fear Sir Michael will not take the news kindly, Amelia.'

'Michael may be pleased for me or stay away from my home. I am not obliged to him and he may not deny me this time. However, *you* should take care, for I know he can be a spiteful man, Gerard.'

'I shall take care for myself and for you. I do not forget that someone made an attempt to abduct you, Amelia. It will be my first duty to protect you, my dearest.'

'Thank you. I feel it unlikely that Michael would do more than vent his displeasure on me verbally— but it is always best to be careful.' She looked at him, her doubt writ plain on her face. 'Do you wish to announce our engagement at once?'

'That is entirely up to you, Amelia. If you wish for more time to consider…'

'No, I think not,' Amelia told him. 'I have given you my answer and I shall not change my mind.'

'Then you have made me the happiest man alive,' Gerard said. 'I have a Christmas gift for you, Amelia—but it is not a ring. I was afraid to tempt fate. However, I did commission a ring. I shall send to my jeweller and have it delivered at Coleridge.'

'Perhaps we should announce our engagement at the ball there,' Amelia suggested. 'We shall consider ourselves pledged, Gerard—but tell only our best friends until the ball.'

'As usual you have solved the thing,' he said and leaned forwards to kiss her softly on the lips. 'I look forward to our wedding, Amelia. You are a good friend and you will be a wonderful wife. Lisa already adores you and this is the best thing I can do for her. You will have the comfort and security of marriage and I shall have a beautiful gracious wife…we shall all get on famously.'

Amelia allowed him to kiss her, but she did not cling to him as she had the first time. At the back of her mind a tiny doubt had formed. She did not want to think it, but she was afraid that Gerard had proposed to her because he needed a suitable wife and a mother for his delightful daughter! Much as she knew she would love Lisa, she could not help thinking that if things had been different she might have been the child's mother. She would be a good mother to Lisa, but her heart ached when she thought of what might have been.

* * *

Did Gerard imagine that she had remained single because she had not received another offer? Amelia frowned as she went up to change for the evening. She might have been married soon after Gerard disappeared, but she had refused every man her brother brought for her to meet. Michael had tried to push her into marrying a marquis, but she had not allowed him to bully her.

Since she came into her fortune, she had received six offers of marriage. Not one of the gentlemen had made her feel that she wished to be married, even though she believed that at least one had been in love with her. Despite the hurt Gerard's apparent desertion had inflicted, she had never ceased to love him. No other man could ever replace him in her heart.

Amelia's feelings now were mixed. Gerard had proposed and she had accepted, but the doubts had begun to creep in. Was he truly in love with her—or did he simply wish for a convenient arrangement? He needed a mother for Lisa, and he wanted a wife who would not make too many demands.

She tried to remember his exact words, but had only a vague memory for his proposal had swept all else from her mind. She thought he had told her that he cared for his wife, but he could never love with all his heart, because something had died in him the night Michael sent him away. Lisette had wanted more and because of that she had become desperately unhappy. Amelia imagined that she had still been low after the birth of her child, for more than one young one woman had been known to suffer a deep melancholy after giving birth.

Amelia frowned. Gerard's words as he proposed seemed to indicate that he was looking for a comfortable marriage that would not make too many demands on his emotions. Was he saying that *she* must not expect too much—that he simply needed a complaisant woman to care for his child and his home?

Did he care for her at all?

What nonsense was this? She was such a fool! Amelia's thoughts were confused as she changed for dinner that evening. For years she had regretted the love she had lost. She had felt the years slipping away, her youth lost. There were times when she believed she would die an old maid, unfulfilled and unloved.

Recently, after meeting Gerard again, she had begun to long for him to speak. Now he had proposed and she had accepted, and yet she was beset by doubts. A tiny voice in her head was telling her she should not hope for a love match. Gerard was older and he had undoubtedly changed from the young man who had declared his love so passionately. He had spoken of caring for Amelia and of looking forward to her becoming his wife—not the words of a man desperately in love. Not the passionate declaration she had hoped to hear!

Gerard *had* asked her to marry him because it was a convenient arrangement. He wanted a wife— a mother for his beautiful daughter. Had he not asked her to give him her opinion of Lisa's nanny? She had done so and her thoughts coincided with his, which had made him feel she would make an ideal wife and mother. In her first rush of delight that he had spoken, Amelia had imagined that he was proposing because he loved her as she loved him. However, she was certain that he respected and liked her—and was that not a perfectly sound basis for marriage?

She took a turn about the room, her thoughts tumbling in confusion as she came to terms with her situation. Was a marriage of convenience acceptable? Could she be happy as Gerard's wife, knowing that he cared for her but was not in love with her?

Of course she could! Amelia scolded herself for the feeling of disappointment she had been experiencing since leaving Gerard. She was no longer a green girl. She ought not to expect romance at her age. Her heart told her that Gerard was the only man she would ever love. If she behaved foolishly and changed her mind, because his proposal was not the declaration of love she desired, she would be cutting off her nose to spite her face—and that would be ridiculous.

Amelia was faced with the choice of remaining unwed for the rest of her life or marrying the man she loved, understanding that he did not feel romantic love for her. Had she been that young girl of so many years ago, she would have demanded an equal partnership where both partners loved, but the years had taught her some hard lessons and she was a woman of sense. The prospect of remaining single all her life was one she had faced, because there seemed no alternative. However, she now had a chance of some happiness. She would have a husband who cared for her in his own way and she would have a family; she was still young enough to give Gerard an heir. In her mind she saw pictures of their sons growing through childhood to manhood, hearing their laughter as an echo in her head and seeing their smiling faces. If she did not marry, she would never have a child of her own to love. She might not have the passionate love she had longed for, but she would have a family, children and companionship.

It was enough, she decided. She would make it enough, and perhaps Gerard would recapture some of the feeling he'd once had for her. His kiss had told her that he was not indifferent in a physical sense. He found her desirable. Perhaps in time true love would blossom once more.

A marriage where the feeling was stronger on one side than the other was not unusual. People married for many reasons, quite often for money or position. She acquitted Gerard of wanting her fortune—he had made it plain to her at an earlier time that he had enough for his needs. He wanted a companion, a sensible woman who would love his daughter and not make too many demands. Could she be that woman? Amelia decided that she could. She had had years of learning to hide her emotions; it should not be too difficult to give Gerard the kind of wife he desired. It would be a convenient arrangement for them both.

Amelia picked up her long evening gloves and pulled them on, smoothing the fingers in place. She glanced in the mirror and smiled at the picture she presented. She looked serene, untroubled. No one would ever guess at the ache in her heart.

She was about to open her door when someone knocked and Emily walked in. It was obvious that she was distressed and Amelia forgot her own problems instantly.

'Something is wrong! I can see it in your face, Emily.'

'Mr Sinclair…I could not prevent him from speaking,' Emily said, her voice catching. 'I told him that I must have time to consider…and I think he was angry with me for his face went white. He inclined his head and walked away from me without another word. I should have called him back, but I could not speak.'

'Oh, my poor Emily,' Amelia said. 'Could you not find the words to tell him the truth?'

'I was afraid of what I might see in his eyes,' Emily confessed. 'We must somehow manage to speak to each other while we are both guests here…' She gave a little sob. 'I am in such distress for I would not hurt him for the world and I am sure he was hurt by my hesitation. Yet how could I tell him the truth?'

'Do not distress yourself, my love,' Amelia said. 'You have done nothing wrong. Many other ladies ask for time when first asked that question. When next it happens, you will be ready to make your confession.'

'Yes, I shall. I intend to seek Mr Sinclair out tomorrow evening after the celebrations. One of us may leave the following day—I could go home if he did not wish to leave.'

'Do not be so pessimistic, Emily.' Amelia was encouraging. 'I still believe that Mr Sinclair will be more understanding than you imagine—and now, my love, you must wish me happy. The Earl of Ravenshead has asked me to be his wife and I have accepted him. We shall not announce our engagement until the ball at Coleridge, but I wanted you to know.'

'Amelia!' Emily's face reflected surprise and then pleasure. 'I am so very happy for you, dearest. I have thought that perhaps you liked him and he liked you, but I was not sure what your intentions were regarding marriage.'

'It will be…a convenient arrangement for us both, for my brother will have to accept that he is no longer my heir. Especially if I should have a child, which I hope will be the case.'

'A convenient arrangement?' Emily looked puzzled. 'It is not my business to pry, but are you sure that is all it is? I am sure the earl has a deep regard for you, Amelia.'

'Ah, yes, we are comfortable together—good friends,' Amelia said, avoiding Emily's probing gaze. She was doing her best to appear dispassionate, but Emily knew her too well. 'Shall we go down, my love? We do not wish to keep Susannah and her guests waiting.' She saw a doubtful look in her companion's eyes. 'You must not think that I would wish to dispense with your company, Emily. While I should be happy to see you marry a gentleman of your choice, I should be sad to lose you. Be assured that your home is with me until you decide to leave.'

'You are always so generous,' Emily replied. 'Thank you for making that plain to me. Like you, I have met only one man I would care to marry, but you know my thoughts and I shall say no more, for this is Christmas Eve.'

Amelia noticed how thoughtful her companion was as they went downstairs and joined the other guests. She smiled and nodded to the company, but was quiet and merely nodded her head when Toby offered her his arm to take her into dinner. Obviously, he had controlled his hurt feelings and was determined to remain Emily's friend. Amelia had always thought him a likeable young man and now found she approved of his manners—he was everything he ought to be as a gentleman.

Gerard took Amelia in to dinner. He told her in a whisper that he had confided their secret to Harry and Susannah, also to Toby Sinclair.

'For the moment I have asked that they keep the news to themselves,' he said. 'We shall make our announcement at Coleridge, as we planned.'

'I have told Emily, for it would have seemed secretive and unkind had I excluded her. She would have been worried that her position might not be secure had she heard something from another person.'

'I doubt that Miss Barton will need to work as a companion for long,' Gerard said. 'You must have observed that a certain gentleman has a distinct partiality for her company?'

'Yes, I know that Mr Sinclair has made Emily an

offer, but she is a little nervous of her situation in life and asked for more time.'

Gerard raised his brows. 'She feels that she may not suit the ambitions of his family, because she is employed as a companion?'

'I believe she does feel something of the kind, but I hope the matter will be resolved satisfactorily.'

'Toby will inherit a decent estate when his father dies, but I am certain he will make his own fortune. Although he is close to his family, I do not think he would allow them to dictate to him in such a matter— and I see no reason why Emily should not be acceptable to them. Toby is of good family, but he is not the heir to an illustrious title, merely his father's baronetcy. I see no cause for anyone to object to his choice.'

Amelia nodded. She had wondered if she might ask for Gerard for help in trying to find Emily's child, but she had hoped to find a way of concealing the mother's identity. Even if that was impracticable, now was not the time or place to reveal it.

'Well, we must hope for a happy outcome,' she said. 'I was wondering when you thought would be a suitable moment for us to marry? Do you wish for some time to make your arrangements or would you prefer the wedding to be held quite soon?'

'Personally, I believe the sooner we marry the better for all concerned,' Gerard said. 'I know that my daughter would be happy to have a new mama— and I am certainly looking forward to our wedding. Do you wish for a longer engagement or shall we settle it for a month after the ball?'

'I think a month after the ball should be adequate time,' Amelia replied. 'It will give me a chance to make necessary changes. Will you wish to live at Ravenshead on a permanent basis?'

'Are you thinking that you would like to spend a part of the year at your estate, Amelia?'

'I like to spend some part of the summer in Bath and I must visit London several times a year to oversee my children's home, but I dare say I shall like Ravenshead very well.'

'There will be time enough to decide once you have visited,' Gerard told her. 'We must have the lawyers draw up the settlements, Amelia. I should not wish to control your fortune, though I will help you to manage it if you so wish. It might be a sensible idea to put a part at least in trust for your children.'

'That is an excellent notion,' Amelia agreed, a faint blush in her cheeks. 'I have a great deal of property—mostly houses. Great-Aunt Agatha acquired a considerable portfolio during her lifetime. I have wondered whether it might be better to sell most of them and re-invest the money. I should greatly appreciate your opinion, Gerard. I have my man of business, naturally, and my lawyers—but there has been no one I could turn to with my problems. No one I could truly trust. I have good friends, of course, but one does not like to ask advice in these matters.'

'I am sure Harry would have been happy to help you, Amelia. He has an excellent head for business. However, you have me now, my dearest. Any concern—the slightest worry—you may address to me, and I will do my best to take it from you.'

'Thank you, Gerard. You are most kind…' Amelia spoke carefully. He seemed so considerate, but was it merely the kindness he would offer to any friend?

Gerard looked at her oddly. She thought he was about to speak once more, but they had reached the dining room and Amelia found that she was sitting between Gerard on her left side and an elderly gentleman she knew slightly on the other. The time for confidences had passed, and though she made polite conversation with both gentlemen throughout dinner there was no chance of talking privately to Gerard.

Amelia glanced round the dinner table. Everyone was smiling and looking pleased. Susannah was a generous hostess and her cooks had excelled themselves. Course after course of delicious food was served to the guests and it was late before Susannah rose to take the ladies through to the drawing room. The gentlemen remained to drink port and smoke their cigars, while the ladies took tea in the drawing room.

It was nearly eleven o'clock when the gentlemen joined them at last, and then the present-giving ceremony took place. Susannah and Harry had bought gifts for all their guests. The footmen took these round on silver trays and there was a great deal of exclaiming and cries of pleasure as the small gifts were unwrapped to reveal things like Bristol-blue scent bottles for the ladies and enamelled snuffboxes for the gentlemen.

Amelia had already exchanged personal gifts with Susannah and Harry and would open those she had received in privacy. She had purchased a silver-gilt card case for Gerard, which she planned to give him the next morning after breakfast.

Chapter Three

It was five and twenty minutes to twelve when the guests separated. The older members of the family said goodnight and went up to their rooms, whilst the younger guests donned cloaks and greatcoats and went out to the waiting carriages. They were driven to Pendleton church, where they joined villagers for the midnight mass. This was a special part of Christmas as far as Amelia was concerned. She felt that this year it was even more so, because she was sharing it with her fiancé. Now that she had made up her mind, the thought warmed her and she felt a little thrill of happiness. How much better life would be in the future, even if her husband were not desperately in love with her.

Amelia left the church on Gerard's arm, feeling happy. The bells had begun to ring and it was almost a forerunner of their wedding day. As they paused for a moment for the carriages to come forwards to pick them up, their breath made patterns on the frosty air.

'Gerard…' Amelia began, but was shocked when he suddenly pushed her to one side so that she stumbled and fell against a prickly holly bush. 'What…?' Before she could finish her sentence, a shot rang out, passing so close to her that she felt a puff of air. She was struggling to recover her balance, as Gerard took out a pistol and fired at something in the shadows.

Almost at once, Amelia found that Harry and Susannah were at her side, assisting her. Everything else was confusion as people shouted and rushed about, some of the men setting off in pursuit of the would-be assassin.

'Amelia dearest,' Susannah cried, looking at her anxiously. 'Are you hurt? I do not know what happened…'

'The earl saw him just in time,' Emily said, for she too had rushed to Amelia's side. 'I noticed someone lurking over there in those trees. However, I did not realise what he meant to do until I saw him lift his arm.'

'Did you see his face, Miss Barton?' Harry asked. 'I'm dashed if I noticed anything until I heard the shot.'

'He was wearing a dark hat and a muffler,' Emily told him. 'I am sorry. I know that is of little use to you, but it was all I saw.'

Harry nodded and looked grim. 'Forgive us, Amelia. We expected something might happen, but not like this…on such a night. What kind of a man would attempt murder on Christmas Eve?'

'What do you mean?' Amelia stared at him. Her wrist stung where a thorn had penetrated her glove and she was feeling a little sick inside. 'Why did you expect something to happen?'

'Come, get inside the carriage, ladies,' Harry said. 'We must take you home. Gerard will explain later. He is coming now…' He glanced at the earl, who had gone after the assassin. 'Any luck?' Gerard shook his head and Harry swore.

'Amelia, forgive me for pushing you into the holly,' Gerard apologised. 'I knew I must act quickly—but have you been hurt?'

'A mere scratch,' Amelia told him. 'Had that ball found its mark, I might be dead.'

'I think it was meant more as a warning to me,' Gerard said. He climbed into the carriage with her and Emily. Susannah had gone with some of the other ladies and Harry. 'I received a threat this morning, when I returned from our walk, Amelia. It was somewhat obscure and I was not truly certain of its meaning, though I had an idea that I was being warned to stay away from you.'

'To stay away from me?' Amelia stared at him in dismay. 'What can you mean?'

'I think someone had guessed that I meant to ask you to marry me—and whoever that person is he has decided that he does not wish for the marriage to go ahead.'

'He would rather see me dead than as your wife?'

Amelia's hand shook and she felt cold all over. 'Who could be so evil? I do not understand who would do such a thing.'

'Your brother threatened you,' Emily reminded her. 'He warned you against renewing your acquaintance with the earl.'

'Is this true?'

Amelia met Gerard's concerned look. 'Yes. Michael has warned me that you are interested only in my fortune many times. I told him that I did not believe you to be so mercenary—and he did tell me that I would be sorry if—' She broke off and shook her head. 'I cannot believe that my brother would try to shoot me like that.'

'He knows that if you marry me he would no longer have a chance of claiming your fortune for himself. I am sorry to say that there are some men who would stop at nothing where a large amount of money is concerned.'

'Michael is a bully—but I am not certain he would murder for gain.'

'At the moment he is our most likely suspect.' Gerard reached for her hand and held it. 'Do not fear, Amelia. You will be protected. I have already set measures in hand to have you watched all the time. I had not thought it necessary while we stayed at Pendleton. I imagined that you might be at risk once we announce our engagement, but my men will be in place by then.' His expression was grave. 'Unless you wish to withdraw in the circumstances?'

'I refuse to let anyone dictate to me!' Amelia lifted

her head proudly. 'Whoever this person is, the threat would not go away if we postponed the announcement of our engagement, Gerard.'

'You are as brave as I imagined.' Gerard squeezed her hand comfortingly. 'I had planned to tell you all this after Christmas. I did not want to spoil the celebrations for Susannah and her guests—but I am afraid that this unpleasant incident will cast a shadow over things.'

'Can you not let people think it was merely a poacher or some such thing?'

'At half an hour past midnight?' Gerard smiled. 'I could try, Amelia, but I doubt I should be believed. We might tell everyone that it was an attempted robbery.'

'That would be much better—and it may even be the truth,' Amelia said. 'You say that you were warned, Gerard—how exactly were you warned?'

'I was sent a doll that had been mutilated. A note in the wrappings said that if I cared for her I must stay away from her.'

'Could that not have meant Lisa?'

'Very few people even knew that I had a daughter until today,' Gerard said. 'Besides, why should I stay away from my own daughter—who could that benefit? She does not have a fortune...'

'No one could benefit from her death. It would in any case seem that I am the target after what happened this evening.' Amelia looked at him steadily. 'It is most unpleasant, Gerard... that someone should wish to kill me for money.'

'It is wicked!' Emily burst out, obviously upset. 'I think he should be ashamed of himself! Oh, do not look at me so, Amelia. It must be Sir Michael behind this monstrous plot. Who else could it be?'

'I do not know—yet I am loathe to think my brother would stoop so low.'

'You think well of most people,' Gerard said as the carriage began to slow down. 'Forgive me for allowing that evil man to get near enough to take a shot at you this night, Amelia. I promise it will not happen again.'

He jumped out as soon as the carriage drew to a halt, helped Amelia down and sheltered her with his body as he hurried her into the house. Once inside, he saw how pale she looked and took her into his arms for a moment, holding her close. Amelia wanted to cling to him and weep, but controlled her feelings. Gerard would not care for a clinging wife. She stood unmoving within his arms and he let her go as they heard the other guests, who had attended mass with them, arriving.

'Perhaps you would prefer to go straight up?'

'Yes, I should. I do not wish to discuss the matter further at the moment. Excuse me, I shall see you in the morning.'

Amelia went quickly up the stairs, followed immediately by Emily. She was conscious of an irritation of the nerves. When Emily tried to follow her into her bedroom, she turned to her with a hasty dismissal.

'Please excuse me, Emily. I would prefer to be alone.'

'Yes, of course.'

Emily looked a little hurt at her tone, but Amelia was in too much distress to notice. It was bad enough that someone should try to shoot her, but to know that they all thought it was her brother who was behind the plot to murder her was lowering. Amelia had suffered much at the hands of her brother and sister-in-law—but murder was too terrible to comprehend.

She took off her bonnet and shawl, feeling glad that she had put on a gown that fastened at the front and told her maid not to wait up for her. At the moment her mind was in such turmoil that she could not speak to anyone.

Amelia slept fitfully and was awake long before the maids brought breakfast to her room. However, she had recovered from her irritation of the nerves and asked that the breakfast be laid in the sitting room. Wearing a pretty new lace peignoir, she went through to the little parlour and found that Emily was already there.

'Good morning, my love. May I wish you a Happy Christmas?'

'Thank you—Happy Christmas to you, Amelia. I hope you will like my gift. It is not much, but was chosen with care.'

'I am sure I shall.' Amelia presented her with an exquisitely wrapped parcel and smiled as Emily gave a cry of pleasure on opening it. Inside was an evening purse made of delicate links of gold, which fastened with a crossover clasp set with diamonds. It was a very expensive gift and reflected Amelia's true regard for her companion.

'This is so beautiful…you are always so generous to me…' Emily's lashes were wet with tears. 'To think that anyone could wish—' She broke off and wiped her hand across her cheek. 'I know you will not wish me to mention it, but I have not slept for thinking of what happened. Had the earl not been so alert you might not be here this morning…'

'You must not let a silly incident upset you. It will not happen again,' Amelia said and opened her parcel. Discovering a scarf she had admired some weeks before Christmas, she went to embrace her friend. 'This is exactly what I wished for, Emily. How sweet of you to remember it.'

'I bought it the day after we saw it,' Emily said and helped herself to some toast and honey. 'Lady Pendleton gave me a lovely scent flask with silver ends last evening, but this purse…it is the most beautiful thing I have ever owned.'

'I am glad you are pleased with it, my love. Has Mr Sinclair given you a gift?'

'No—but I think he has one for me. I believe he intended it to be a ring…' She fiddled with her toast. 'I bought a horn-and-ivory card case inlaid with gold for him, but I am undecided as to whether I should give it to him or not.'

'I am certain that you should exchange gifts with Mr Sinclair, Emily. He is a close friend and I also have a gift for him. You may deliver mine at the same time if it makes you feel better, my love.'

'Yes, I think it would. I should not feel so particular. May I ask what you have bought for Mr Sinclair?'

'I purchased a rather fine diamond stickpin. It has the shape of four hands linking and I thought it might appeal to him.'

'It will be the very thing for him,' Emily said and laughed delightedly. 'He was so very desperate to become a member of the Four-in-Hand Club and he delights in wearing the special waistcoat.'

'I am very fond of that gentleman,' Amelia said with a smile. 'He played his part in the fortunes of both of my protégées. Susannah and Helene have both been lucky. I should be happy to see you settled as well, Emily my love.'

A delicate blush appeared in her companion's cheeks. 'I think I may say without fear of boasting that Mr Sinclair does care for me—but whether he could accept my shame…'

'Emily, that is enough! The shame belongs to the man who forced you, my love. I will not have you hang your head. I was thinking that I would ask you to be my bridesmaid—and, of course, Susannah and Helene will be matrons of honour if they can spare the time from their busy lives—and Lisa must be a bridesmaid also, of course.'

'I should be honoured,' Emily told her and finished eating her toast. 'Mr Sinclair asked me if I would be paying my usual morning visit to the nursery and I said yes. I have a gift for Susannah's son—and also a little ring that I had as a girl, which I mean to give to Lisa.'

'How thoughtful of you, my love,' Amelia approved. 'I bought a doll for Lisa…just in case she was staying here with her father this Christmas. I think I shall come with you this morning—if you would not mind waiting until I dress?'

'I should be delighted. I usually go for a walk after I visit the children, but it snowed early this morning. Not enough to make walking impossible, but I felt…' She floundered to a halt.

'Yes, I understand.' Amelia nodded. 'I too shall be very careful when and where I walk until Gerard has his men in place. It may be as well to remain indoors for the moment—and we may blame the weather for it is inclement.'

'You wish to keep last night's incident as private as possible? I doubt that it will be possible, Amelia. Not everyone will keep it to himself or herself. I dare say the incident will be whispered of, if not openly admitted.'

'Yes, I fear that it may.' Amelia sighed. 'We, however, shall make light of it—there was a rogue near the church who sought to rob us. It is a weak excuse but it will suffice. Excuse me while I dress.'

'There is no hurry. I have something to do first—besides, you have not yet opened all your letters.'

'I have rather a lot of them, but I shall open one or two before I dress.' She looked with pleasure at the pile of letters waiting for her.

One of Amelia's chief pleasures in life was in writing to her friends. It was a good way of keeping in touch with many acquaintances she hardly ever saw. Amongst the cards and greetings she had received that Christmas morning was one from a lady for whom she had profound sympathy. The lady was very much in the position Amelia had been for years, at the mercy of her family. Except that Marguerite had no chance of marriage at all and Amelia might have married if she had wished.

Something must be done for her friend, Amelia thought. A Season in town would not solve Marguerite's problem, but perhaps she could think of some way of getting her away from her family for a while. She wrote a long and cheerful letter and sealed it. It had occurred to her that she would need someone she trusted to help her care for Lisa. Marguerite adored children and she might enjoy helping with Lisa's education.

Glancing at the clock, Amelia realised that it was time she paid her visit to the nursery. Lisa would have had her breakfast and she would be waiting for the gift Amelia had promised her. She hoped the child would be pleased with the doll she had chosen.

Amelia spent a pleasant half an hour in the nursery, playing with Lisa, who had been given several presents, including a pretty doll from her father. Lisa was delighted to have two dolls, especially as Amelia's had curly hair.

'She is like me,' she said and put the doll up against her face. 'Thank you, Mademoiselle Royston.'

'You may call me Amelia. We are going to be friends, Lisa.'

'Papa says you are to be my mama.' Lisa's eyes were large and apprehensive. 'Will you live with us, Melia?'

'Yes, I shall live with you and your papa,' Amelia replied. 'That is why I want us to be friends, dearest. As you grow up, it will be I who buys your dresses and teaches you to be a young lady. You will have a governess, but she will be kind and I shall make certain that your studies include games as well as the dull things.'

Lisa's face lit up, then a shy expression came into her eyes. 'Will you love me, *mademoiselle*?'

'I already love you,' Amelia said and took her into her arms, hugging and kissing her. 'You are a delight to me, Lisa—and perhaps one day you may have brothers or sisters to play with you.'

'I should like that but…Papa will not send me away when you are married?'

'No, of course not. Why should you think that?'

'Nanny told me it would happen if I did not do everything she told me.'

'That lady has been dismissed. I shall choose another nurse to help look after you, and I assure you that she will be kind.'

'I love you,' Lisa said as she climbed on Amelia's knee and put her arms about her neck. 'Nanny hasn't left yet, Melia. I saw her in the garden as I looked from my window. She was talking to someone—a man. I have seen her talk to him before, but she said that if I told Papa she would whip me.'

'She was very wicked to threaten you like that.'

Amelia controlled her anger. 'Your papa has dismissed her. If she has not already left this house, she will do so within a few hours. I dare say your papa thought it would be unfair to make her leave at Christmastide. However, she will not be allowed near you again.' Amelia touched her hair. 'You must always tell Papa or me these things, Lisa, if someone hurts or frightens you—or if you see someone who makes you feel uncomfortable.'

'I will tell you. Papa might think I was telling tales—and gentlemen do not approve of such things.'

'There are times when telling a grown-up the truth is important. If someone frightens you, Lisa— or threatens you—you must tell us. Please promise me you will?'

'I promise.' Lisa slid from her lap as some of the other children came running into the nursery schoolroom. They were all clutching new toys of some kind. 'I must not keep you, *mademoiselle*. Nanny said that mothers only spend a few minutes with children; they are too busy to waste their time with us.'

Amelia smothered a sigh. Gerard had not dismissed that woman a moment too soon!

'When we are all living together, you will spend a part of your day with your papa and me when he has the time. It is true that gentlemen have their business to keep them busy, but I assure you that I shall take you for walks and I think your papa might teach you to ride a pony.'

'Ride a pony?' Lisa's face lit up. 'Truly? Would Papa truly teach me to ride himself?'

'I am sure that he will, as soon as he considers you are ready.' Amelia kissed her cheek. 'I must go now, my love, but I shall ask your papa if he will take us both for a little carriage ride after dinner.'

Amelia received an enthusiastic hug. She was smiling as she went downstairs. As she turned towards the large drawing room where she knew many of the other guests had gathered, she was unaware that she was being watched from the gallery above.

Turning away to return to the room she would have to leave in the morning, Lisa's former nanny, Alice Horton, gave a spiteful smile. The Royston woman was riding for a fall. She had not hesitated to use her position and influence to have Alice dismissed from her position, but she would not see herself installed as the Earl of Ravenshead's wife. There were plans afoot that would prevent their marriage. When *he* had first approached her, Alice had been reluctant to give him any information about her employer or his daughter. However, she had no such scruples now.

He had paid her well for the news that Lisa was to have a new mama very soon. Alice had enough money to see her through the next few months without having to apply for a new position—and if she did what *he* asked, she might never have to work again…

Amelia saw Gerard standing near the window in the large salon. He had been in conversation with Harry, but as soon as he noticed her, he said something to his friend and came to greet her.

'Have you been to see Lisa? Toby told me that he saw you with Miss Barton on your way there.'

'I took her my gift. I had bought her a doll. She received several dolls, but mine had curly hair like hers and that pleased her.' Amelia lifted her hand to her own neat, dark locks. She had allowed her maid to dress it in a softer style and believed it suited her. 'I have made Lisa a promise on your behalf, Gerard. She seemed to think that she must not expect us to visit her for more than half an hour in the mornings. I told her that when we were married I should take her for walks—and that you would teach her to ride a pony. I hope I have not spoken out of turn?'

'Of course you have not,' Gerard assured her instantly. 'I had intended to buy the child a pony quite soon—and I shall certainly teach her to ride it myself. Since we shall be spending much of our lives in the country there will be plenty of time for such pleasures. You must feel free to do as you think best, Amelia. I am confident that your sure judgement will bring many benefits to both Lisa's life and my own.'

'I shall do my best to be the mother she lacks.'

'You will be the best mother she could have—the only one she has known.'

'I am glad you feel as I do,' Amelia said. 'I know that in many families the children are confined to the nursery until they are old enough to come out—but I do not approve of such rigid rules. Naturally, they must study and there are times when they might be a nuisance to guests, but when it is just the family I hope we shall often be together.'

He gave her a look of warm approval. 'You are a constant delight to me. I knew you would be generous towards my daughter—but this is more than I could have expected.'

'I love her. She is a delightful child, Gerard.'

A tiny pinprick of hurt entered her heart, because it was so obvious that he wanted and needed a mother for Lisa. Would any woman have done—or did he feel something stronger toward her?

'Yes, she is.' He smiled and took a small box from inside his coat. 'This is my gift to you for today, Amelia. I shall be sending for the family jewels and you may make your choice of them—though I warn you that they will need to be refurbished for they are heavy and old-fashioned. This is something I thought might please you.'

Amelia unwrapped the box and took out the beautiful diamond brooch inside. It was shaped like a delicate bouquet of flowers and the heads trembled as she took it from its box.

'This is beautiful,' she said and pinned it to her gown. She reached into the pocket of her gown. 'I have a small gift for you, Gerard—it is a mere trinket…' In value, it was a similar gift to the one she had given Toby Sinclair, something she might have given to any member of her close friends and family. Not what she might have chosen had she known they would be engaged by Christmas Day.

He took the box and dispensed with the wrappings, revealing the silver-gilt card case. 'More than a trinket, Amelia. Thank you.'

Amelia shook her head, changing the subject. 'Emily was saying that she would not walk alone, because of what happened last night. I too think it would be best to take care for the moment. I wondered if we might take Lisa for a little ride in your carriage after dinner?'

'I see no reason why we should not go for a drive,' Gerard said. 'As for what happened last night, the matter is in hand. Any strangers seen on the estate will be stopped and questioned.'

Amelia recalled what Lisa had told her about the nanny speaking to a man in the gardens—a man the woman had spoken to before. However, she had no reason to suppose that the man could have anything to do with the incident outside the church. As unlikely as it seemed, Nanny probably had a follower.

Dismissing the nanny from her mind, she smiled as Susannah came up to them. She was wearing the pearl-and-diamond pendant that Amelia had given her as a Christmas gift and the next few minutes were taken up with her delight and her gratitude. By the time Amelia and Gerard spoke again, the nanny had been forgotten.

It was a pleasant morning. Amelia exchanged gifts with several friends, enjoying some music before nuncheon. After they had eaten, Gerard sent for his carriage. Lisa's nurse brought her downstairs. She was wearing a pretty pink coat and hat and had a fur muff that her papa had given her. She was excited to be going for a drive, chattering about the many gifts that she had received that morning.

'I had four dolls altogether, Papa—was I not fortunate?' she said as they went out to the carriage. 'One was broken.'

Gerard's attention was caught. 'A broken doll— who gave you that, my love?'

'I do not know, Papa. I asked Nurse Mary. She said there was no card.'

'I shall have a look at the doll later,' Gerard said. 'It was a shame the doll was broken.' His eyes met Amelia's over Lisa's head.

'I did not mind,' Lisa said. 'I had so many pretty things. I did not expect so many presents. Nanny said it was obscene for one small child to have so many expensive clothes as I have. What does obscene mean, Papa?'

'I think it means that I spoil you,' Gerard said, but his mouth had pulled into a grim line.

Amelia touched his hand. He glanced at her but his expression remained grim.

'I have been spoiled too,' Amelia said and smiled at the child as she touched the brooch she was wearing. She had fastened it to the scarf Emily had given her, and she was wearing a new black velvet cloak she had purchased in London; it had a fur lining and was very warm. 'I was given this lovely scarf and this brooch—do you see how it trembles as I move?'

'Did Papa give it to you?' Amelia nodded. 'It is very beautiful—but you are *très ravissante*, Melia. Papa will be lucky when you marry him.'

'We shall all be lucky to have each other,' Amelia said. 'Look, Lisa—can you see the deer over there? I think they have come closer to the house than usual. I know that Susannah has food put out for them when the weather is inclement.'

'They are lovely…' Lisa said, pressing her face to the carriage window. 'Papa, do we have deer at Ravenshead?'

'I believe not,' he said. 'We might have some brought into the park if you would like that, Lisa.' His face had relaxed. He smiled as he met Amelia's eyes. She nodded slightly, understanding his feelings. The broken doll was worrying, but might simply be a co-incidence.

'Oh, yes, please. I should love that, Papa—and could I please have a puppy…?'

'Is there anything else, miss?' he asked, brows rising indulgently.

'Oh, no, Papa,' Lisa said and put her hand into Amelia's. 'But Melia did say I should tell you anything I wanted.'

'Did she, indeed?' Gerard laughed. 'I can see that I am to be petticoat-led now that I have two beautiful ladies in my life.'

Amelia was pleased that he had managed to put his worries to one side, and yet she sensed a shadow hanging over them.

She glanced out of the carriage window. A light dusting of snow clung to the trees and shrubs, but it was beginning to melt. A pale sun had brightened the day. Shadows might gather in the distance, but for today Amelia would try to forget them and think only of pleasant things.

Lisa was singing a little French song when Amelia took her up to the nursery and handed her back to Mary. The little girl turned to her, hugging her as she took her leave.

'Thank you for my lovely afternoon, Melia.'

'You are very welcome, Lisa. It was a pleasure for me.'

Amelia smiled and left the child with her nurse. The future was looking so much brighter. Children were a blessing and already the ache she had carried deep inside her was easing. She was a mother to Gerard's daughter and in time they would have others of their own.

She hastened to the apartments she shared with Emily, because the hour was late and she would have to hurry if she were to change and be ready in time for dinner. As she entered the little parlour, the sound of sobbing met her. The sight of Emily weeping desperately brought her to a halt.

She went to her at once. 'Emily, dearest—what is wrong?'

'Oh…Amelia…' Emily lifted her head to look at her. 'Forgive me. I did not mean you to see me like this…' She wiped her hand across her face. 'I should have gone to my bedchamber.'

'Do not be foolish. You should not hide your tears from me, Emily. Can you not tell me what is wrong?'

'I spoke to Mr Sinclair when we exchanged gifts,'

Emily said, her body shaken by a deep, hurtful sob. 'He gave me a beautiful sapphire-and-diamond ring and I...told him that I could not marry him. He asked me why and I told him that I had given birth to a child...' She bent her head, the tears falling once more.

'Emily, my love.' Amelia knelt down beside her and took her hand. 'Did you explain that you were forced?' Emily shook her head and Amelia gave her fingers a gentle squeeze 'You should have made that plain. He did not understand the circumstances.'

'He did not give me a chance,' Emily said. She took a kerchief from her sleeve and wiped her face. 'He looked so stunned, Amelia. It was as if I had thrown a jug of cold water over him. He drew back, shaking his head and looked...as if he could not bear the sight of me. I think he must hate me now.'

'Emily! I am certain it was merely shock. He did not understand the circumstances. Mr Sinclair is a gentleman. I do not believe he would have done that to you deliberately.'

'I begged him not to look at me that way. I pleaded for a chance to explain, but he said that he must have time—and then he walked away and left me. It is over. He has a disgust of me now.'

'He was shocked, that is all. I am sure that when he has recovered from his...' Amelia paused, searching for the right word.

'Disappointment?' Emily lifted her head. 'I saw it in his eyes, Amelia. He was stunned, disappointed, even revolted—I think he could not bear the idea that I had been with another man.'

'It must have been upsetting for him, but he may have thought you had a love child, Emily. You must try to understand that he had put you on a pedestal. He may have misunderstood you. He may think that you took a lover. You must tell him the truth.'

'I could not! I do not think I could bear to face him again.'

'Emily dearest,' Amelia said, 'I understand that it would be too difficult for you to tell him every-thing—but I could speak to him. I could explain how badly your family treated you. I am hopeful that once he has had time to think about things he will still wish to marry you.'

'No! Please do not,' Emily begged, a sob in her voice. 'I cannot bear to speak of it.' She jumped to her feet and ran into her own bedroom, shutting the door and locking it behind her. Amelia knocked at the door.

'Emily. Please listen to me. You must not let this destroy you. If Mr Sinclair truly loves you it will all come right. Do not throw away your chance of hap-piness too soon.'

'Please do not ask me to see him. I shall not come down this evening.'

'Emily…'

Amelia sighed as she heard a renewal of wild sobbing from her companion. In the hall downstairs the longcase clock was chiming the hour. She realised with a start that she would be late for dinner. She must hurry and change her clothes. Emily would come to her senses when she had cried herself to sleep. In the morning they would talk about things calmly—and she would have a few words with Mr Sinclair. If he had behaved as badly as Emily claimed, he was not the gentleman she had thought him!

Amelia apologised to the company when she joined them in the drawing room. She spoke to Susannah, telling her that Emily had a headache and would not be joining them that evening.

'I am so sorry.' Susannah was concerned. 'I hope it is nothing serious. Should we send for the doctor?'

'No, I am sure that will not be necessary,' Amelia told her. 'I am sorry if Emily's absence has unbalanced your dining table.'

'As it happens she is not the only guest missing,' Susannah replied. 'Toby Sinclair received a message from home and left us two hours ago. His parents had not joined us for Christmas because Mr Sinclair was feeling a little unwell. He had insisted that his son join his friends, but perhaps he has taken a turn for the worse. Toby seemed in a strange mood. He was abrupt—distant—and that is not like him…not like him at all. Harry thinks that his brother-in-law must be quite ill to send for his son.'

'I am sorry to hear it. Illness in the family is distressing, especially at this time of the year.'

'Had it been at any other time Harry would have gone to his sister immediately, but we cannot desert our guests. Lady Elizabeth is staying with her daughter this Christmas, so Harry's sister will not be completely alone should anything happen.'

'We must hope that it is not serious.' Amelia was

thoughtful as she joined the guests moving into the long dining room. If Toby Sinclair had received bad news, it was understandable that he had left—but he ought to have left a note for Emily.

Gerard came to offer her his arm. 'You look serious, Amelia. Is something wrong?'

'Emily has a headache. I am sure she will be better in the morning.'

'I am sorry she is unwell. I understand that Toby has taken himself off in a hurry—there wouldn't be a connection?'

'Perhaps—but I cannot tell you, for it is not my secret.'

'Then you must keep it.' He paused, then, 'I have spoken to Lisa's nurse and looked at the doll. It is not the same as the one I had sent to me. I believe it may just be a coincidence—I must hope so, otherwise it would be serious. If I believed the child was threatened, I should take her back to France.'

'I think we must talk about this matter. I know your opinion—but I am not sure.' Amelia shook her head as his brows lifted. 'We shall not discuss this tonight. The morning will be soon enough, but I must tell you that I believe your theory about my brother may be wrong.'

'Yes, you may be correct. We shall talk tomorrow, Amelia. We must make arrangements for the future and discuss this other business.'

'Yes, the morning will be time enough. We shall enjoy this evening, for Susannah has gone to so much trouble for us all.'

Chapter Four

Throughout dinner Gerard was very aware of the woman sitting beside him. She was lovely, but more than that she had an air of serenity, a presence that was lacking in so many other ladies. He was not certain why she had accepted his proposal of marriage. Was it only that she wished to be married and felt comfortable in his presence? They were good friends and shared an interest in many things. Marriage to Amelia would, he had no doubt, be pleasant and comfortable whatever the case, but he was not looking for someone to place his slippers by the fire and arrange for his favourite meals to be served. He wanted so much more! He wanted a woman who would welcome him to her bed with open arms.

The scent of her perfume was intoxicating. She seemed to smell of flowers and yet there was a subtle fragrance that was all her own. The sight of her, the way she turned her head, the way she moved, her voice...her smile...all these things set him on fire with longing. He wanted to take her in his arms and make love to her that very night, but was not sure that she would welcome a show of passion.

Amelia's manner gave little away. Her first reaction to his proposal had seemed positive, but since then she had become more reserved. He was not sure why. The incident at the church had been upsetting, of course—but he did not think Amelia would allow that to upset her. She had insisted that she wished to go on with the engagement.

Was it something in Gerard himself that had caused her to withdraw? He knew that his rejection of Lisette the night she had crept into his bed had been the reason for her desperate unhappiness. He had not been able to tell Amelia that he had rejected Lisette's attempt to ask for his love. After her death he had regretted his curt manner that night. He had married her on a whim, indulging his sense of honour and pity—and he had still been angry with Amelia and her brother. Later, when he began to realise that there was only one woman he wanted despite what had happened, he had regretted the impulse that had urged him to wed a woman he did not know or love. However, he had meant to honour his promise, but, in rejecting Lisette when she tried to give herself to him, he had hurt her. He believed it was his rejection that had driven her to take her own life. Perhaps there was more, perhaps he was incapable of making a woman happy...

'Susannah is a wonderful hostess, is she not?'

Amelia remarked, breaking into his thoughts. 'When I recall how anxious she was the first time she stayed here, I cannot believe how much she has matured.'

'Harry seems very content with his family,' Gerard replied. He smiled inwardly, wondering if Amelia guessed how aroused he was when she turned to him and made some intimate remark. It was fortunate that the table hid the evidence of his intense need at that moment. He must think of other things!

Several times since the incident outside the church he had wondered if he had placed Amelia's life in danger by proposing. Harry was aware of his anxious thoughts and had been forthright in his opinion.

'I have no idea who this enemy of yours is, Gerard—but to give in to him would be more dangerous, believe me. If it is Royston, Amelia would be at his mercy, and if it is not...' He shook his head and frowned. 'She would never truly be safe—and nor, my friend, would you.'

'Then we are working in the dark. I have searched my memory for someone I have offended, but I can think of no one—at least, no one who would think it worthwhile to kill Amelia simply to spite me. I am still of the opinion that the plotter is Royston.'

'You may well be right, but Susannah is very close to Amelia. She thinks that Amelia is doubtful about her brother being the culprit.'

'It would be hard for any woman to accept such an idea,' Gerard said. 'I have not tried to impress my feelings on her, but for the moment I can see no other reason for the attempt on her life.'

* * *

Gerard felt Amelia's loss keenly when the ladies retired to the drawing room to take tea. He wished that he could follow at once, but custom dictated that he remain with the gentlemen to drink port and discuss politics and sport. When the gentlemen at last made their move towards the drawing room, Harry invited him to play a game of billiards. Not wanting to offend his friend, he agreed.

They had been playing for half an hour or so when he caught the smell of the perfume he always associated with Amelia and turned to see her watching them. The wistful expression he surprised in her eyes set him wondering. Was she wishing that they might be alone? Did she burn to be in his arms? He realised that despite their long friendship he hardly knew her. Gerard well remembered the passionate girl who would have given herself to him one never-forgotten night—but who was she now? Beautiful, serene, sophisticated, she was surrounded by friends, loved by those who knew her best, envied by many—but who was the woman behind the mask? How did she really feel about their marriage? He wished he knew.

'I came to say goodnight,' she said. 'I must see if Emily is feeling better. I shall speak to you in the morning, Gerard—shall we say at nine?'

'If that is not too early for you.' He inclined his head, then went to her, taking her hand and turning it to drop a kiss into the palm. 'Sleep well, my dearest. I hope you find Miss Barton much recovered.'

'Thank you.' Amelia smiled as she bid both men goodnight and then walked from the room.

'You know that I shall be happy to stand up with you at your wedding,' Harry said and lined up a coloured ball, striking it with the white so that it rolled into the pocket. 'Have you agreed the day yet?'

'We are thinking of a month after the ball at Coleridge,' Gerard said. 'I hope that I am doing the right thing…if I thought I was putting Amelia's life in danger by marrying her…'

'If you have an enemy, we shall find him out,' Harry said and potted another ball. 'I have told my men to be on the lookout for strangers, but I doubt that whoever it was the other night will try anything more just yet. I have been wondering if that shot was just another warning.'

'We cannot even be certain that the target is Amelia…' Gerard frowned, missing his ball. His heart was not in the game. All he could think about was Amelia. He wanted her so badly. He would be a fool to let whoever was threatening her have his way.

Amelia sighed as she went into the private sitting room she shared with Emily. She wished that she might have had more time alone with Gerard that evening, but it was not possible. There were so many guests staying and she was acquainted with all of them; mere politeness decreed that she must spend a little time with as many as she could.

She saw that her blue cloak with the fur lining was lying on one of the chairs. She had told Emily that she might wear it that morning, because the weather had turned so cold and she had her new black one, which was even more sumptuously lined. Emily must have left it lying there. That was unusual, for she was by habit a tidy girl. Amelia's maid knew that she had loaned the cloak to her companion and had left it where it was instead of putting it away as she normally would.

Amelia went to her companion's door and knocked softly. 'Are you awake, dearest? Is your headache still bad? Would you like to talk to me about anything?'

There was no reply. Amelia did not persist; she did not wish to wake Emily if she was sleeping. She knew that it was Emily's heart that ached rather than her head, and she felt annoyed with Toby Sinclair. Really, she had thought better of him! Surely he could have accepted that Emily had had a child? It was shocking, but not the crime some thought it, in Amelia's opinion, especially since Emily had been forced. Toby might at least have asked her about the circumstances. Obviously, he had wanted to get home quickly after the news that his father's health had taken a turn for the worse, but he could have left a note for Emily. To leave her without a word—to run away like a disappointed schoolboy—was not what Amelia would have expected from him.

If he really could not face the fact that Emily had given birth to a child, even though she was forced and not willing, he could have found a way of telling her. To simply abandon her like this was so hurtful. It was no wonder that Emily had taken to her bed this evening. She was suffering from a broken heart.

Amelia went to her own bedchamber. She allowed her maid to undo the hooks at the back of her gown and then dismissed her. She sat down at her dressing table, picked up her brush, but then just stared at her mirror.

She was anxious about Emily. The girl was assured of a position with her for as long as she needed it, but there was very little she could do to help with the pain of a disappointment in love. Amelia had once suffered much as her companion was suffering now. She had not even known why Gerard had gone away without speaking to her or telling her he was leaving. For years she had alternated between distress and disappointment at his desertion, but then she had finally understood that her brother was to blame. Michael had acted in a high-handed, ruthless manner, not caring who he hurt!

He had not been a good brother to her. Indeed, there were times when she had come close to hating him. His last letter had been a hateful tirade about her selfishness towards her family that had left her in tears—but would he truly wish her dead so that he could get his hands on her fortune?

Amelia shuddered at the thought. They had quarrelled so many times, but although she had sensed violence in him he had never actually harmed her—except by sending Gerard away.

Her thoughts turned to the man she had never

ceased to love. She had thought there was something of the man she had known when she was young in him that evening…a simmering passion that had made her catch her breath.

She longed for him to want her, to love her—need her, as she loved and desired him. Was she a fool to believe that their marriage could work? If all he truly wanted was a complaisant wife who would care for his child, he might feel cheated when he realised that she was in love with him.

It must not matter! She knew that a marriage that was not equal in love might lead to hurt in the years to come, but perhaps if she were careful to hide her feelings he need never know. He wanted a companion rather than a wife so that was what she would be. Besides, it would break her to leave him now. If she waited, gave him time to know her, he might begin to feel the passion he had once had for her.

Smiling a trifle ruefully, Amelia went to bed. She might be foolish, but she thought that she had seen passion in Gerard's eyes that evening…

Amelia slept a little later than usual. She was woken by her maid pulling back the curtains and yawned, sitting up and blinking at the bright light.

Glancing at the clock, she saw that it was half past eight. 'Has it been snowing again, Martha?'

'Yes, Miss Royston. It has stopped now, but I believe there was a heavy fall last night.'

'What have you brought me this morning?'

'I thought you might like a light repast in bed

instead of going down to the breakfast room. Since you slept in, Miss Royston—'

'How thoughtful you are,' Amelia said. 'I shall need some warm water at once for I have an appointment at nine this morning.'

'I should have woken you sooner, miss—but you were so peaceful.'

'I have half an hour; it is plenty of time if I hurry.'

'I will fetch the water now, miss.'

'Oh…' Amelia said as the girl turned away. 'Have you seen Miss Barton this morning?'

'No, miss. I went into her room to ask if she wished for breakfast in bed, but she was not there. Her bed had been made, but Miss Barton often makes her bed.'

'Yes, she does, because she is a thoughtful girl,' Amelia said. She broke a piece of the soft roll, buttered it and ate a piece as she poured a cup of the dark, slightly bitter chocolate she liked to drink when she indulged in breakfast in bed. It was not often she did so and wished she might linger longer this morning, but she did not want to be late for her meeting with Gerard.

By the time Martha returned with her hot water, Amelia had finished her roll and her cup of chocolate. She washed hastily and dressed in a simple morning gown that she could fasten herself. For once she left her hair hanging loose on her shoulders, merely brushing it back from her face and securing it with a comb at either side. Since she scarcely glanced at herself, she had no idea that she looked much younger and more like the girl she had been when she first met Gerard.

The beautiful mahogany longcase clock in the hall had just finished striking when Amelia went downstairs. She found that Gerard was waiting for her. He looked handsome, elegant in his coat with three layers of capes across the shoulders, his topboots so glossy that you might see your reflection in them. He was frowning, but as she called to him he turned and smiled. Amelia's heart did a somersault, leaving her breathless for one moment. She truly thought that he had the most compelling eyes of any gentleman of her acquaintance and they seemed very intent as he looked at her.

'Forgive me if I have kept you. I slept later than usual and did not think to ask my maid to wake me. I am normally up much earlier.'

'We have all been keeping late hours at Pendleton. I should have suggested ten rather than nine, but I thought we should be sure of being alone. I have the carriage waiting…'

'We have not been much alone,' Amelia said as they went outside together. 'I have been thinking about what happened the other night outside the church, Gerard.'

'I have thought of it constantly.' His eyes dwelled on her face for some moments. 'We shall talk in the carriage. I would not care to be overheard.'

'Surely here there is no one that would wish us harm?'

'Our friends would not,' Gerard agreed, taking her arm and leading her out to the carriage. He helped her inside and she found that a warm brick had been brought so that she might place her feet on it, and a thick rug provided for her knees. 'I hope you will be comfortable, Amelia. It is a bitterly cold day.'

'I dare say your coachman will feel it, but we shall not be out long.'

'Coachman has his comforts, a warm coat and a blanket, I am sure,' Gerard told her. 'You say that we are safe here with friends and to a certain degree I concur, but servants talk—and sometimes they pass on information for money without realising what harm they may do.'

'Yes, I am sure that is so,' Amelia said. 'I believe someone may have mentioned the fact that we had been talking together—for no one but our close friends know that we are engaged.' She frowned. 'Of course, Lisa knows. When did you tell her you were thinking of marrying me—before or after you dismissed Nanny?'

'I believe it was before…' He stared at her. 'You think Nanny may have heard something and passed on the information?'

'Lisa told me yesterday that Nanny did not leave Pendleton immediately. She saw her talking to a man in the gardens—a man that she had seen Nanny speak to before.'

'Why did you not tell me that yesterday?'

'I did not think it important at first. I imagined Miss Horton might have a follower, but when you said just now that servants talk, I realised that she could have been selling information—perhaps because she had been dismissed.'

'Yes, you are right. I should have forced her to leave the house instantly.'

'It would not have changed anything. If she already had the information…'

Gerard swore angrily and then apologised. 'Forgive me. I should not use such language in your presence, Amelia. I have been careless. I did not imagine that my servants would gossip to strangers.'

'It makes little difference. Our enemy would have heard as soon as our engagement was announced.'

Gerard looked concerned. 'I have wondered if I was wrong to ask you. If I have put your life at risk…'

'If my marriage to you renders me liable to be murdered, then it is best that I am aware of it. This threat will not go away if we deny it, Gerard. We must discover who wishes me ill. There is some mystery here and it needs to be solved.'

'You do not accept that it is your brother?'

'I am loathe to do so. I know that Michael resents the fact that Great-Aunt Agatha did not leave him anything. He has tried to bully me into giving him at least half of my fortune. We have quarrelled because I refuse to do as he wishes. Had my aunt wished him to share in her fortune, she would have left him money. I might have done something for him before this had he behaved in a civilised manner. Perhaps— if you believe it is Michael…' She shook her head. 'No! I shall not be blackmailed into giving him my aunt's money. She would not have wished me to do so.'

'I do not think he would be content with a part of it. If he is willing to murder you, then he wants it all.'

'Well, he shall not have it.' Amelia lifted her head proudly. 'I have my own plans for part of the money—though some must be put in trust for our children.'

'You are thinking of your charity?'

'That and other things. I have helped two young ladies find happiness. I know of at least two more deserving cases...' She halted as Gerard raised his brows. 'You do not approve?'

'I am happy with whatever you choose to do, Amelia. I told you that I did not wish to control your fortune and I meant it.'

'It will be *our* money. I should not dream of giving large sums away without first consulting you.'

'I am not your brother, Amelia. Your fortune is not my first concern.'

'Have I made you angry, Gerard? I beg your pardon. I did not mean to.' She looked at him uncertainly.

'I am not angry, but I would not have you think I asked you to marry me for your fortune.'

'I did not.' She hesitated, then, wishing to change the subject, 'Shall we travel to Coleridge together?'

'Yes, certainly.' He was silent for a moment. 'I have made arrangements for you to be protected—Lisa too. If you feel that my theory is wrong I must think carefully. Sir Michael seemed the most obvious since he would inherit.'

'Have you considered that this person may have

something other than money on his mind—or her mind? I suppose it could be a woman…'

'A scorned mistress?' Gerard looked amused. 'I have none to my credit, Amelia. When I first returned from the wars there was a lady in France, but we parted as friends when I returned to England the first time. There has been no one since.'

'Oh…' Amelia digested his statement in silence. Most gentlemen had mistresses before they married. She found no cause for distress in an old affair. 'Then we are at least certain it is a man. My sister-in-law has no love for me, but she would think murder most vulgar.'

'Vulgar?' Laughter gleamed in his eyes.

'You do not know Louisa. She is very strict—rude when she chooses, but *never* vulgar.'

Gerard laughed. 'She sounds formidable?'

'She would consider murder beneath her—and she would not approve of her husband being involved with anything of the kind. Indeed, if she suspected something untoward she would have a deal to say on the subject.'

'Then perhaps I should look elsewhere for a motive.'

'I cannot think of anyone I have offended other than my brother.' Amelia sighed and looked distressed. 'Perhaps you are right—there is no other explanation.'

'Unless I have an enemy…'

'Gerard?' Amelia's eyes widened. 'Have you thought of someone?'

'Unfortunately, no. I dare say I have enemies, though none I would have thought…there is

Northaven, of course. He may hate me enough to threaten, but to kill you...' He shook his head. 'I cannot think it, Amelia. He might wound me in a duel if he could or knock me down, but truth to tell I do not see him as a murderer.'

'I do not see my brother in that light. A bully—yes.'

'It is difficult. All we can do is wait until *he* shows himself—whoever he is. I have agents who may discover something, but...it might be best to delay the announcement of our engagement.'

'You would give in to him? Surely that way he wins? And if my fortune is his object...' Amelia waved her hand in distress. 'As you say, it is difficult. If you wish to withdraw—'

'Damn it, no! You cannot think it, Amelia?'

'No...forgive me. I hardly know what I am thinking.'

'All I want is to make you happy.'

'Then we shall not allow this person to dictate to us. I dare say there is some risk if we go ahead and announce the engagement but there is risk in any case. At the moment our enemy is merely a shadow. Perhaps when he sees he cannot bully us he will step out into the light.'

'You are both wise and brave,' Gerard murmured, taking her gloved hand to kiss it. 'Now we shall talk of happier things? How many guests shall we invite to our wedding—and do you think we should hold an engagement ball?'

'Oh, I think we shall give a ball on the eve of the wedding. I believe that will be sufficient. Shall we all go down to Ravenshead after the Coleridge ball? I think I should like to see your home, Gerard—and we must discuss what I ought to do with Aunt Agatha's estate. I told you that I thought we should sell some of the property, but she loved that house and I am very fond of the garden...'

Amelia was feeling more settled in her mind when they returned to the house an hour or so after they left it. They had discussed most aspects of the wedding and settled that they would keep Amelia's home and also the house in Bath and Gerard's London house, which was larger than her own. Most of the other property would be sold or let to tenants, and the money invested in some form of trust for their children. However, the identity of the person who was trying to prevent their marriage remained a mystery. She knew that Gerard still felt her brother the most likely culprit, though he intended to set his agents the task of discovering if either of them was being watched. There was nothing more they could do for the moment except be vigilant.

Amelia parted from Gerard and went upstairs to her own apartments to change into a more suitable gown. She noticed that the blue velvet cloak she had loaned Emily was not lying on a chair in the sitting room. She could not recall if it had been there when she left earlier that morning, because she had been in too much hurry. Either Emily had taken it and gone out or she had tidied it away. Perhaps she was in her room now.

Amelia knocked at the door. Receiving no answer, she opened it and went in. As the maid had said earlier, the bed had been made and the room was tidy, as always. The gold purse Amelia had given Emily for Christmas was lying on the dressing table, as were one or two other gifts. It was a little odd that Emily should leave them lying there; she would normally have put them in her dressing case for safety. Amelia had an odd sensation, a feeling that Emily might have done something foolish. Surely she had not run away? Or something more desperate! Chills ran down Amelia's spine as she recalled her childhood friend Lucinda's terrible fate. A few years ago, Lucinda had taken her own life in her desperation—but Emily would surely not be so foolish.

Going to the armoire, she looked inside, feeling relieved as she saw the leather dressing case and Emily's clothes. At least she had not run away. Amelia was certain that her companion would not have left without at least taking some of her clothes and the dressing case. Besides, the girl was too conscientious to go off without at least leaving a letter—and, she believed, too sensible to take her own life.

A little reassured, Amelia went to change her clothes. Shortly after, she paid a visit to the nursery, where she talked to Lisa and some of the other children. She was asked to read a story from a book that one of the children had received as a Christmas gift. She read aloud, taking Lisa and one of the others on to her lap. The others crowded about her, clutching at her clothes and staring up into her face adoringly as she acted out the story for them.

She was unaware that Gerard came to the door and watched for a few minutes before leaving.

It was almost nuncheon before Amelia was able to break away from her audience and go downstairs to join the others.

She was at the buffet table, helping herself to cold chicken, a dish of potatoes and turnips and some green vegetables when Gerard came up to her.

'I saw you just now,' he said. 'It is good of you to give so much of your time to the children, Amelia.'

'I enjoy it. Lisa asked if I would read to her and the others wanted to listen. I believe they enjoyed themselves—and, after all, Christmas is for the little ones, do you not think so? Our Lord was born at this time and it is for his sake that we hold these celebrations.'

'You deserve a large family of your own, Amelia.'

'I hope to have several children—if God wills it.'

She looked up into his face and her heart began to race wildly. The way he was looking at her set her on fire and she wished that they were somewhere else—anywhere that they might be alone. She wanted so desperately to be in his arms, to feel his mouth on hers—but most of all she wanted his love. She felt what was becoming a familiar ache about her heart. Gerard had loved her once, but he had told her that something had died inside him when her brother sent him away and he believed that she had merely been toying with his heart. Would he ever be able to love her as she loved him?

'Gerard—' she began and broke off as a footman came up to them, offering a silver salver to him.

'This was delivered for you a few moments ago, sir.'

'For me?' Gerard frowned and opened the sealed note. He swore softly and then looked at Amelia in some bewilderment. 'I do not understand—this note implies that you are a prisoner. I am to pay the sum of forty thousand pounds or you will die…but you are here…'

'Yes…' Amelia shivered as a trickle of ice slithered down her spine. 'But Emily is not…' She glanced round the room, which was filling up with guests. 'I believe she went out early this morning and, as far as I know, she has not returned.'

'Would she stay out so long in this weather?'

'I cannot think it. She was feeling unhappy. I wondered if she had run away, but her things were all in her room.'

'Who would snatch Miss Barton and demand such a huge ransom?'

'Someone who did not know me well,' Amelia said. 'On Christmas Eve I was wearing a dark blue cloak with fur lining. I had bought myself a new black one for Christmas, and because the weather was so very cold I loaned the blue one to Emily. If she was wearing it when she went out, she could have been mistaken for me.'

'Good grief!' Gerard was astounded. 'We must send at once and make certain she is not in her room.'

'I shall go up myself,' Amelia said. 'She was not

in her room when we returned from our drive. I thought she wished to be alone and did not search for her. I should have alerted you before this, but I did not imagine that she was in danger. Excuse me…'

Amelia left her food untouched as she went immediately in search of her companion. She ran up the stairs. The sitting room was empty and so was Emily's room. Nothing had been moved since Amelia's last visit.

Her maid came from the other bedchamber, carrying an evening dress. Amelia asked her if she had seen Emily.

'No, Miss Royston. I came up to fetch this dress. I was going to iron it for you for this evening. Is something wrong?'

'Emily appears to be missing,' Amelia said. 'Please continue with your work, Martha—but make inquiries as you go. I am worried about Miss Barton.'

'Yes, miss. Of course. I'll ask if anyone has seen her this morning.'

Amelia went back down the stairs. Gerard and Harry were talking together in the hall. They turned to look at her. Amelia shook her head.

'Martha hasn't seen her. Her room is just as it was when I was last there.'

'I have alerted my butler,' Harry told her. 'He will make sure that all the servants are asked for their last sighting of her. If we know what time she left, we may discover how long she has been missing.'

'What can we do?' Amelia asked. 'How long have we been given to find the ransom, Gerard? I do not have that kind of money available, but I will sell some investments—anything I can to recover my poor Emily.'

'We will all contribute,' Harry assured her. 'However, it may be possible to recover her without giving this rogue a penny.'

'I cannot risk Emily's life. She was taken because they thought she was me…' Amelia could not prevent a sob of despair. 'If only we knew who had taken her. I shall never forgive myself if anything happens to her.'

'You cannot blame yourself,' Gerard said and frowned. 'I must confess that I should have been devastated had they managed to get their hands on you, Amelia.'

Amelia's eyes flashed with anger. 'Are you saying that Emily's life is less important than mine? That is unfair, Gerard. She is a lovely person and I am very fond of her.'

'I did not mean to imply that she was less worth saving.' Gerard ran fingers through his hair. 'Of course we shall do what we can, but once they know they have the wrong person…'

'Are you saying that they will kill her?' Amelia was rapidly becoming distraught. 'No! How do we let them know that I will pay?' She looked at him wildly. 'This is all my fault. If I had given my brother what he wanted… Oh, no! It is too much.'

At that moment there was a disturbance at the door and then two people entered, their clothes sprinkled with a dusting of snow.

Amelia looked towards the door and saw her companion. She gave a scream and ran to her. 'Emily, my love! I have been out of my mind with worry! Where have you been?'

'I went for a walk…' Emily sobbed and threw herself into Amelia's arms. 'I was snatched from behind and thrust into a carriage. I had a blanket over my head and I did not know what was happening. After some time, perhaps half an hour or so, the carriage stopped and I was carried into a house. I was left alone in a bedroom. It was a very cold house. I screamed and tried to get out but both the window and door were locked. As they carried me in, I heard one of them say that if the money did not come through I was to be killed…'

'Emily…' Amelia drew back in shock to look at her face. 'How terrifying for you, my love. What happened? How did you escape?'

Behind her, at that moment, she heard what seemed to be a quarrel break out. Turning her head, she saw that the man who had entered the house with Emily was the Marquis of Northaven. From the look of it, both Harry and Gerard were threatening him.

'Please, you must not be angry with the marquis,' Emily cried. 'It was he who saved me and brought me back. Had he not come, I should still have been in that room.'

'Is this true?' Gerard demanded. 'Explain yourself if you please, sir.'

'I think we should speak privately,' Northaven said. He took a few steps towards Emily. 'I am sorry that you were subjected to such an ordeal, Miss Barton. I tried to warn the earl that he must be careful, but I did not expect that they would take you. I understood Miss Ravenshead was their quarry.'

'You tried to warn me...' Gerard frowned as something clicked into place. 'Was it you that sent the doll?'

'Yes. A clumsy trick, I think, but I was not sure how else to do it. I wanted to alert you to the fact that Miss Royston might be in danger.'

'Why did you not say so plainly?' Gerard glared at him.

'Would you have believed me if I had signed my name? Would you have received me had I tried to warn you in person?' Northaven lifted his head proudly. 'I do not pretend to be without vice. I have done many things that I might wish undone—but I am not a murderer, though you persist in thinking me one. If I caused the death of comrades by loose talk, I regret it—but it *was* careless talk, no more.'

'I think you need to do more explaining,' Gerard said. 'Amelia, please take Miss Barton upstairs and see that she is cared for. You might wish to send for the doctor?'

Emily shook her head in alarm. 'I am not harmed. I was frightened, but I am well enough now.'

'I shall take you upstairs, my love.' Amelia put a protective arm about her. 'You are cold and trembling. You shall go to bed with a warming pan and a tisane. I shall sit with you and you may tell me all about it.'

Amelia drew her companion from the room. She would have liked to listen to all the marquis had to say, but she knew that Gerard did not wish either her or Emily to hear all the details lest it frighten them more. They had both had a terrible shock and it was only thanks to the Marquis of Northaven that things were not much worse. Amelia could hardly bear to think of what might have happened.

'Were you far from the house when they took you?' she asked Emily as they walked upstairs together.

'Only in the knot gardens,' Emily told her. 'It must have been within sight of the house, but of course it was very early. I dare say even the servants had not risen.' She gave a little sob. 'I lay awake all night. I was tossing and turning and thought that a walk might clear my head. I had forgot what we said—besides, I did not imagine anyone would try to snatch me. It was you I believed in danger.'

'My poor Emily.' Amelia squeezed her hand. 'You were taken because they thought you were me. A huge ransom was demanded, but I should have paid it, my love. We were trying to think how it could be done when you came in. I could not have borne it had anything happened to you.'

'Amelia! I am so glad you did not have to pay— and I am sorry if you were worried. I did not dream that anyone would try to kidnap me.'

'I dare say they would not had you not been wearing my blue cloak,' Amelia said. 'You must not wear it to walk in again until this rogue has been caught and dealt with, Emily.'

'Have you any idea of who it could be?'

'No, not truly. I suppose you heard nothing?'

'They spoke of someone of whom they were afraid,' Emily told her. 'However, they did not name him.'

'I know everyone thinks it must be my brother and I fear it may be so, though I do not wish to believe it.'

'It is so wicked. I do not know who could do such things.' Emily shivered. 'I was to have been strangled had the money not been forthcoming—but that was after I told them who I was. I believe they realised their mistake too late. They spoke of a ransom note and said that if the money was not paid they would amuse themselves before disposing of me.'

'My love! How awful for you. I am so sorry that you were exposed to such wickedness.'

'It was fortunate for me that the marquis came to get me.'

'How did he know that you had been taken—and where to find you?'

'I have no idea. I did not think to ask. I was simply grateful that he got me out of that house before...' A fit of shuddering overtook Emily. 'I have never been as frightened in my life.'

'I am certain that Gerard and Harry will wish to know where the marquis got his information,' Amelia said. 'Come, dearest, let me help you undress. Martha will bring you a pan filled with hot coals and a tisane. Tomorrow I shall take you home.'

'No, please do not. I want to go to the ball as we planned,' Emily said. 'I shall not let this frighten me—nor shall I dwell on what happened with Mr Sinclair. At one time last night I considered taking my own life, but what happened made me see that I want to live. It will be hard to meet Mr Sinclair again, but I shall bear it.'

'My poor love.' Amelia kissed her brow. 'You are a very brave girl. You must forget Mr Sinclair; if he could not behave in a proper manner, he is not worth breaking your heart over.'

Chapter Five

'Well, I am waiting,' Gerard said. 'I am grateful to have Miss Barton back, but this begs an explanation. How did you know that there was a plot to kidnap Miss Royston and how did you know where to find Miss Barton?'

The marquis made a wry face. 'I thought they had Miss Royston until I got there and realised that they had snatched the wrong lady. I persuaded them to drink some rum to keep out the cold and laced it with laudanum. As soon as they became groggy I snatched Miss Barton and brought her here. *He* will know that I tricked them and I dare say my life may be at risk, but I do not value it so highly that I shall lose sleep over it.'

'You have still not told us how you knew what was going on,' Harry objected. 'And who is behind this business?'

'Don't look at me like that, Pendleton,' the

marquis said. 'If you must know, I was offered money to help capture Miss Royston. However, I believe he sensed that I was not going to do his bidding and so he moved ahead of time. I was told the abduction was planned for when she journeyed to Coleridge.'

'You were offered money—how much?'

'Ten thousand pounds.' Northaven laughed ruefully. 'A pittance, I dare say, when you consider her fortune. A few months ago I might have taken his money. I was in debt and the bitterness inside me was much stronger than it is now. You may thank a lady for that—and, no, I shall not name her.'

'Why did you not come to us—tell us who we have to deal with?' Gerard demanded.

'If I knew his name, I would have told you. He keeps to the shadows and hides his face—though I have seen it since our first meeting. I let him believe that I would help him, learning what I could of his intentions. I have tried to follow him, and I think he spotted me, which may be why he did not trust me in the end. However, I knew where they meant to hold Miss Royston for the first few hours—and I was on my way here early this morning. I had decided that I could not handle this alone and meant to ask you to listen to my story. As I walked towards the house, I saw what I thought was Miss Royston being snatched. There was no time to warn you so I followed them. They had not changed the rendezvous—and, thankfully, his rogues still trusted me.'

'You have no idea of his identity?'

'I know that he calls himself Lieutenant Gordon, but I doubt it is his name—though I believe him to have been an officer, for he has the manner of a military man. However, I do not recall that he ever served with us.'

'It was not Sir Michael Royston?'

'Miss Royston's brother? Good lord, no! I would have known his voice. I played cards with him quite recently.'

'Could he not be in league with this rogue?'

'He could, but not to my knowledge.'

'Why were you approached?'

'He believed that I might want to bring you down, Gerard. He must have heard of our quarrel, which is known well enough in certain circles. His plans for Miss Royston were not simply to ransom her, believe me. Had you paid what he asked, he would have taken the money—and then I believe he meant to despoil her and kill you.'

'My God!' Gerard turned pale. 'He must hate me.' He took a turn about the room, then returned to where Harry and the marquis stood. 'What have I done to him that he should hate me so?'

'Only you can answer that,' Northaven said. 'Have you ruined a man at the tables or taken his woman?'

'No…unless…Lisette—' Gerard broke off and smote his forehead with the palm of his hand, a look of disbelief in his eyes. 'I do not know. My wife…was carrying the child of her lover when I married her. She was honest with me. Lisette told me that he had died and that she was alone in the world. I married her to protect her, but if her lover were severely wounded and then recovered…to discover that she had married me…he may blame me for her death.'

'That may be your answer,' Northaven said, eyes narrowed in thought. 'If Gordon believes that you took her from him, he may wish to take what you love in revenge. Since Miss Royston is wealthy and you have your own fortune, he thinks that he may also have some financial gain from it.'

'But I did not take her from him…' Gerard shook his head. 'When I found her she was close to death. She was lying at the side of the road, bruised and beaten. She told me that some French soldiers had raped her—more than one, I believe. I nursed her back to life and then I married her to keep her safe. She was very ill after the birth, but then she recovered…' He paused, a nerve flicking in his cheek. 'Lisette took her own life. I believe because she wanted more from me than I could give her.'

'Good grief!' Harry cried, shocked. 'I had no idea… My dear fellow. I am so sorry.'

Gerard shrugged off his sympathy. 'I told no one until recently. Miss Royston knows some of it, but not all—and I ask you both to keep my secret. I believe Lisette took her own life because I did not love her.'

'*He* blames you for her death,' Northaven said grimly. 'It is as plain as the nose on your face! This Lieutenant Gordon—whoever he is—*he* blames you for the death of the woman he loves.'

'In a way I am guilty, though I never meant to hurt her. I thought Lisette understood that I had married her simply to offer my protection, but she wanted me to love her. I failed her...and her death has haunted me ever since.'

'I believe you have established a motive, Ravens-head—now you need to know who he really is. She did not give you the name of her lover?'

'No. I never asked; I believed him dead and it did not matter.'

'Does he know the child is his?' Harry asked. 'If so, he may feel that you have stolen her as well.'

'I doubt he knows it,' Gerard said. 'She had not seen him since he rode away to battle some weeks earlier—one of his friends told her he had been killed. She was trying to discover more when she was set upon by those rogues who raped her and left her for dead.'

'Then it is best that Gordon never knows the truth,' Harry said. 'Until you can discover the identity of your enemy, Gerard, you must be very careful.'

'Yes, you are right,' Gerard agreed. He looked at Northaven. 'Are you willing to help us?'

'Of course. You had only to *ask*.' Northaven's eyes gleamed. 'Tell me what I may do for you and I shall do my best to oblige.'

Amelia sat with Emily until she drifted off into sleep. After some tears and a fit of the shudders, she had finally settled. Leaving her to rest, Amelia decided to change for the evening. She was thoughtful as she sat for her maid to dress her hair into the new softer style, caught up in an intricate swirl at the nape of her neck. During one of her crying bouts, Emily's deep sadness at the loss of her child had come tumbling out.

Amelia had comforted her as best she could. She had made up her mind that she would definitely speak to someone soon about employing an agent to make inquiries. It might not be possible to trace the child, and even if Emily's child could be found they might not be able to recover her. She would have a family, perhaps a mother and father who loved her—but perhaps it would be enough for Emily to have news of her daughter.

Amelia would do what she could to find the child, but she would say nothing until she knew whether or not it was possible. Having settled that much in her mind, she went down to the parlour where guests had begun to gather for drinks before dinner. She saw Susannah and several of the other guests but there was no sign of Gerard or Harry.

'They went out earlier and have not yet come in,' Susannah said when Amelia asked. 'Harry told me what Northaven had done. I could hardly believe that he had acted so heroically. He was not always courteous to me in the past—and yet I am not sure that he is black as he is often painted.'

'I owe the marquis a debt of deep gratitude,' Amelia said. 'I do not forget that he once fought a duel with Harry and that you were wounded, my love. However, I do not believe he meant to injure you—and perhaps he has gone some way to redeeming himself by bringing Emily back to us.'

'Oh, I forgave him for that long ago.' Susannah smiled. 'He watched us when we walked from church after our wedding, you know. There was something in his eyes…I think he meant me to know that Harry was safe from him, as he has been.' Susannah looked thoughtful. 'He is undoubtedly a rake and has almost certainly done things that would shock us if we knew the whole—but everyone is entitled to a second chance.'

'Yes, I am sure you are right.' Amelia frowned. 'I wanted to speak to Harry, but it will keep.'

'Is there something I can help you with, Amelia?'

'No, Susannah. I need a man's advice about something, my dear. I had thought to ask Harry, for I believe that Gerard has enough on his mind at the moment—but another day will do.'

'Well, I dare say they will not be long, though Harry told me not to hold dinner.'

'I expect they have some business.'

'I dare say they do. It seems very odd that the Marquis of Northaven is involved; Harry was much against him at one time.'

'Gentlemen are contrary creatures,' Amelia teased. 'They can be at odds one minute and the best of friends another.'

'Do you think we can trust him?' Harry asked as they entered the house, shaking a light dusting of snow from their coats. 'I must admit I should not have given him a chance to speak had he not brought Miss Barton back to us. I should probably have told the footmen to throw him out.'

He went over to the magnificent mahogany sideboard in his library and poured brandy for them both, giving one to Gerard and holding the other to warm it in his hands before sipping.

'At the moment I do not have much choice,' Gerard confessed. 'His tale of a Lieutenant Gordon might be a falsehood, but I am inclined to believe him. Lisette had a lover. She believed he had been killed, but it is possible that he still lives. Men fall in battle and are reported dead and then turn up somewhere…' He sighed with frustration. 'If he went looking for her and heard tales of her death, it would explain why he hates me. He probably thinks I am a monster and that I treated her ill. I gave her everything I could, but she needed so much more.'

'If you could speak to him, tell him what happened…'

Gerard shook his head, dismissing the idea. 'I doubt he would listen. In his place I would want revenge.' He groaned his frustration. 'What am I to do, Harry? How can I marry Amelia, knowing that by doing so I am endangering her life? When I thought she was in danger from her brother it was one thing, but now…'

'You cannot be sure of anything. This tale of Northaven's may be a ruse. He could still be in league with the rogues. Besides, you cannot wish to withdraw? You do not wish to jilt Amelia Royston?

Think how it would look? Susannah would never speak to you again.'

'Of course I do not wish to jilt her! Good God! It is the last thing I want—but if the marriage is rendering her the target of a madman…'

'I can only advise you to wait. We shall see that she is protected, of course. Northaven says that he will try to discover the true identity of this man…get as close to him as he can and then bring you news of his whereabouts. We must hope that he will keep his word.'

'Yes, though, if he drugged the rogues who snatched Miss Barton, Northaven's life could be at risk. Lieutenant Gordon will have him shot on sight.'

'He knew that was possible when he agreed. This may be his way of atoning, Gerard. Even if he did not betray us that time in Spain, it was his loose talk while drunk that led to the deaths of several men. The French knew we were coming. Our mission was secret. Only the four of us knew, for we did not tell the troopers where we were going. They followed us blindly to their deaths—and Northaven did not turn up that morning. He says that he woke too late after a night of heavy drinking and gambling, but I am still not certain I believe him.'

'We sent him to Coventry and branded him a coward and a traitor,' Gerard observed grimly. 'He always swore that he was innocent, but in his heart he knew that his loose tongue was to blame. He provoked you into a duel and would have killed any of us in anger—but I believe he has changed, though I have no idea why.'

'He said it was a woman.'

'If rumour does not lie, he has ruined more than one in his time. *She* must be remarkable if she has reformed him. I am not certain that his story is the true one, but I have no other clues. So far this Lieutenant Gordon has managed to cover his tracks. I have set my agents to looking for him, and I am having Northaven watched too. I do not trust him entirely even yet.'

'Then you must carry on as if nothing has happened. If you change your plans, Gordon will become suspicious. There is no guarantee that he will leave Miss Royston in peace, even if you give her up. If I were in your shoes, I would double the number of men watching over her and Miss Barton and go ahead with your plans.'

'I must make Amelia aware of the danger—but I think you are right. We did not tell many people, but these things get out. To draw back now would look as if we had quarrelled. I shall just have to be vigilant.'

'It is all you can do for the moment. I shall come to Coleridge a few days after you, Gerard. In the meantime I will send some of my grooms with you. I know you have your own men, but they will do better in the shadows. My grooms will be armed and ride with you.'

'Thank you, but I hardly like to involve you in this business, Harry. You have a wife and child to think of and this may be a nasty affair before it is ended.'

'We swore to help each other that day in Spain,' Harry reminded him grimly. 'We survived that day because the three of us defended each other's backs. You were there for me when I needed you—I shall not desert you in your time of need.'

'You believe that all this may be because of Lisette's lover? Someone she knew before you married her?' Amelia stared at Gerard in the moonlight. He had come to her as she was about to go up to bed, requesting that she stroll with him in the gallery. The candles had burned low in their sockets, but the moonlight filtered through the long windows, giving them light enough to see each other's faces. Had it not been for the subject under discussion, it might have been romantic. She did not think that he had mentioned that Lisette had had a lover before this, though perhaps she had not perfectly heard him. 'Gerard—how can that be? I am at a loss to understand. Why should this man blame you for what happened?'

'I do not know. Northaven said that Gordon hates me and I can only think he must be bitter because Lisette died. I told you that she took her own life some months after the birth of her child. If he went looking for her in the Spanish village where we lived and was told that she slashed her wrists, he would be horrified, angry. In his shoes I might want revenge.'

'Why did she marry you if she had a lover?'

'She believed he was dead. She was alone and in desperate need.'

'Lisette died four years ago, Gerard. Why has this man never tried to kill you in all those years? Why now?'

'I have no idea. I cannot even be sure that Northaven is telling me the truth. He could have planned the whole thing to gain some advantage for himself.'

'Surely he would not?' Amelia looked thoughtful. 'There must be some other reason that has kept this man from moving against you, Gerard. Something must have changed. Perhaps he did not know how Lisette died and then discovered it.'

'I wish I knew…' Gerard hesitated. 'You know in what danger you stand. Would you prefer it if I went away? I should still try to discover my enemy, but you would be safer. And in time I could return. It would be merely a postponement.'

'You know my answer. I refuse to hide in the shadows. Besides, he would not be fooled. If this man knows so much about us, he would soon learn the truth. If we let him part us, it would be for ever. Do you want that?'

'No! Damn it, no.'

'Then we have no alternative but to go ahead with our plans.'

'It is odd that he knows where we are. I told only a few people I was coming here this Christmas.'

'Most of my acquaintances knew I would be here,' Amelia said. 'However, I told no one that I expected to see you for I did not know if I should.'

'It is a mystery,' Gerard said. 'I may have been followed, of course. I feel like a blind man stumbling about in the dark. As Harry says, we cannot be certain even now for it is all merely theory.'

'I believe the only way is to carry on as normal and hope that he will make a mistake.'

'You are very brave.' Gerard looked at her gravely. 'I would rather give you up than have your death on my conscience, Amelia—but, as you say, if we give way now it does not follow that you will be safe. I think it is better than we go ahead with the wedding as soon as possible so that I am in a position to take care of you.'

Amelia felt as if her heart had been squeezed. Gerard would rather give her up than have her death on his conscience. How could he say such a thing to her? She would rather die than give him up, but it seemed he did not feel the same way.

Lisette had been desperately unhappy because he did not love her. Amelia could not help but wonder if she were laying up pain for herself in the future. She loved him so very much. Would she one day feel desperate because Gerard was unable to love her? Would she ever feel so alone that she would be driven to take her own life?

No, she had known heartbreak and lived through it. She was stronger than Lisette.

'I am certain there is more to this mystery than you yet realise,' she told him. 'Your enemy knows where we are and what we are doing. He knows all about me. How can that be? We must have a mutual acquaintance. Someone close to us who knows where we intend to be.'

'Yes, that would seem to be the case. I am damned if I know who it is, though!'

'We must both think hard. Since I was the target, you cannot be certain that he is your enemy, Gerard. He might very well be mine.'

'You are sure she means to go to Coleridge?' Lieutenant Gordon asked of the woman he had met late at night in the shadows of a summerhouse. 'If I have men waiting on the road and she goes to another location, I may miss my last chance of surprising them.'

The woman's mouth curled in a sneer. 'Your fools bungled it once. Do you imagine that you still have the element of surprise? No, you lost that when you involved Northaven in your plans. Why did you not ask me? I should have told you that he would not do it. I know he spoke of hating them, but he hated only that they distrusted him—thought him a traitor. He is no angel, but neither is he a murderer. I could have told you had you asked my advice.'

'How do you know so much about him?' Gordon asked, looking at her jealously. She was his second cousin. When they were children they had played together in the meadows. She had given herself to him when she was thirteen. Wild and enchanting, she had had the power to command him, making him her slave, but when he joined the army as a young man he had broken free of her. He had fallen in love, but Lisette had betrayed him. He had searched for her when his wounds healed, and when he discovered the truth of her death he had been devastated. On his return to England some months ago, he had sought his childhood love out, discovering that her power to enslave him had become stronger. 'Is Northaven your lover?'

She laughed mockingly. 'I may once have indulged myself with the gentleman for an hour or so one summer, but I never loved him. You have no need to be jealous.' She laid her hand on his arm, giving him a seductive smile. 'Have I not helped you by telling you where you could find Miss Royston? Have I not helped you to plan your revenge on the man who stole your lover?'

'Lisette was a silly little fool. I was angry when I discovered that he had married her and made her unhappy—but I never loved her in the way I love you. I have always adored you. You are the one who hates him. Or is it Miss Royston you hate?'

'She is nothing to me. I care not whether she lives or dies, but he loves her and so her fate is sealed. You want Gerard Ravenshead dead and so do I—we are agreed on this, are we not?' He nodded, though it was she who had demanded Ravenshead's death as her price—the price he must pay to have her. 'Then there is nothing else you need to know.'

He moved towards her, reaching out to pull her hard against him. His mouth was demanding on hers, bruising and possessive. 'You know I love you. I have hated him for what he did to Lisette, but—'

'You would have let him live?' Her eyes snapped with scorn. 'She cut her wrists…bled to death…and you would let him live? You snivelling coward! I thought you had more courage. Perhaps I should find another to help me.'

'No!' Gordon caught her wrist as she would have turned away from him. 'I will see her dead and he shall witness her death, as I promised you.'

'She must be ravished and he must see it! I want him to suffer. His death is not punishment enough.'

'Why do you hate him so much? What did he do to you?'

'That is my affair,' *she* told him and her eyes blazed with bitter anger. 'I want revenge and I know how to get it. Forget your ideas of ambushing them on the road. They will have outriders and grooms and all will be armed. The rogues you employ will turn tail and flee at the first shot fired at them. No, I have a much better idea. Listen well, because this is what we shall do…'

'I wish that we were coming with you.' Susannah hugged Amelia as they parted. Christmas was over and the snow had cleared, but the overnight frost had turned the ground hard. 'I know that we shall see you at Coleridge, but I am concerned for you on the journey.'

'You must not be, dearest.' Amelia kissed her cheek. 'Thank you for giving us such a wonderful Christmas. Perhaps another year you may come to us.'

'I doubt if the relatives would give up the Christmas visit. It is tradition, you know—but I shall be very glad to stay with you at other times. The *Old Crusties*, as Toby Sinclair calls them, enjoy their stay. I shall be fortunate to get to Coleridge before the day of the ball.'

'You make them too comfortable.' Amelia laughed.

'Well, I must not keep Gerard waiting; I know he is anxious that we should make good time.'

'I shall see you soon. You must write to me as soon as you arrive.'

Amelia laughed. 'You sound like Marguerite. She is always anxious to hear my news. I must write to her again soon.'

Susannah frowned. 'Marguerite? I do not think I know her.'

'No, perhaps I did not mention her to you. We did not communicate for some years following a family tragedy, but then she wrote to me and I learned how miserable her life has become. Since then I have written to her at least twice a month and sometimes more.'

'Is she another of your lame ducks, Amelia?' Susannah laughed teasingly.

'Marguerite's situation is more difficult. Her parents are not poor. Indeed, they have money enough to give her a Season in town if they wish—but they refuse to allow it. Marguerite never goes into company without her mama. She is kept very strictly at home.'

'That is such a shame. Poor girl! What has she done to deserve such a fate?'

'She is hardly a girl. I believe we are of a similar age. She may be a year or so older. Marguerite has done nothing to merit her fate, which is why I feel for her so strongly. Her parents blame her for something that happened to her sister and that is unfair.'

'You must ask her to stay with you,' Susannah said. 'Perhaps you could find her a husband. After all, she is old enough to marry without permission, is she not?'

'Yes, but her father is a bully. I think she is afraid of him. However, I do have something in mind, though I am not sure she would wish to accept. I did invite her to stay with me in Bath, but her father would not allow it at that time.'

'That is so unfair, especially if she has done nothing wrong,' Susannah said and hugged her again. 'She is lucky to have you as a friend, Amelia. I am sure you will do something to help her if you can.'

'I have written to Marguerite with my suggestion. I wrote as soon as I knew Lisa would need a new nanny. Marguerite's parents will not allow her to have a Season in London or Bath, but they may allow her to stay with me in the country to help to care for a motherless child. If Lisa were in her care, I should feel that we could safely leave her sometimes.'

'And you entertain a great deal so she would have company and make friends.' Susannah clapped her hands. 'How clever you are, Amelia! It is exactly the thing. I do not see how her parents could object to such a suggestion for their daughter.'

'Well, we shall see. Marguerite may not like the idea of becoming a child's nanny—but she will live as one of the family and have the opportunity to meet all my friends. In time she might meet someone suitable that she might marry.'

'I do hope it all works out for her,' Susannah said. 'And now you really must go, because I can see Gerard in the hall and he looks impatient.'

'Farewell for now, dearest Susannah. I shall write

to you and you will join us at Coleridge within the week.'

Amelia parted from her friend and went into the hall where Gerard was in close conversation with Harry. He turned as soon as she came up to him, looking relieved.

'We must go, Amelia. I am sorry to hurry you, but I wish to reach Coleridge before dark. We shall change the horses, but we shall not stop for refreshments. Harry's chef has put up a picnic for us and we may eat on the road.'

'Yes, of course. I understand perfectly.' Amelia glanced at Harry. 'You will not forget what I asked of you, sir?'

'The matter is already in hand. I have the details and my agent will deal with it as a matter of urgency.'

'Thank you. I am in your debt.'

Harry bowed over her hand. 'No, no, Amelia. You brought Susannah to me. I shall forever be in your debt.'

Amelia shook her head and smiled as she followed Gerard outside. He looked at her oddly.

'What was that about, Amelia? If you need the services of an agent, I could have arranged it for you.'

'I know and I would have asked, but you have enough worries as it is—and it is a matter for someone else, Gerard. It is not personal and need not concern you.'

'Very well,' he said but there was a jut to his chin, as if it had not pleased him that she had asked Harry to execute her commission.

Amelia was prevented from saying more because Emily was standing by the carriage. She could not tell Gerard that she had asked Harry to see if he could find Emily's daughter at that moment. Besides, though she had been forced to confide the details to Harry, she had done so in confidence and would not speak of it more than she need, even to Gerard.

He looked a little serious as he handed both ladies into the carriage. Amelia wondered if she had offended him and regretted it. She did not wish anything to overshadow their wedding. Gerard's careless words had given her a restless night, but eventually she had told herself that she was being foolish. Gerard cared for her safety, which meant she was important to him. It was foolish to wish for the romantic love of their youth. Had she not already decided that a marriage of convenience would do very well?

She was impatient for their wedding so that they could begin their new life together. This threat hanging over them was unpleasant, but she had perfect faith in Gerard and his ability to protect her. She could not help feeling relieved that he no longer believed her brother had been trying to murder her. Michael would not be pleased when she wrote to him to tell him that she intended to marry the man he had expressly forbidden her to wed. She frowned as she wondered just why her brother was so much against the marriage. He had gone to great lengths to prevent it when she was younger, but Gerard had inherited an estate he had not expected to inherit. He was not as wealthy as Harry Pendleton or Max Coleridge, but he was certainly not a pauper and his estate was free of encumbrances. It was unreasonable for Michael to be so against the marriage now.

Amelia turned to her companion as they settled in their seats. Gerard had chosen to ride behind the carriage for the first part of the journey and the ladies were alone, Amelia's maids following in the second coach with Lisa's nurse and the child.

'Nurse insisted that Lisa ride with them for a while, but I think when we stop I shall tell her to come in with us—you will not mind that, Emily?'

'Of course not. She is a delightful child, intelligent, and seems older than her years, though she is almost five now...' The shadows were in Emily's eyes, though she was no longer weepy and was clearly making an effort to be cheerful.

'Are you sure you wish to come to Coleridge? If you would prefer to go to Bath until I am settled at Ravenshead, I would understand.'

'Of course I wish to come. I am looking forward to seeing Helene.'

'You know that Toby Sinclair may be there for the ball?'

'We are bound to meet in company,' Emily said. She lifted her head; her face was proud though her mouth trembled a little. 'I have accepted that he has rejected me. I am in control of my feelings now, Amelia. I shall not break down again.'

Amelia reached for her hand and squeezed it. It was Emily's hurt that had prompted her to have a search made for her child. If she could arrange for

Emily to visit her little girl now and then, it would be something.

'I think you have behaved with dignity, my love. It is natural that you should weep for your lost hopes. I must tell you that Mr Sinclair is not the man I thought him.'

'I cannot blame him. I should have told him the truth when I first knew he was becoming interested. It was my own fault for allowing him to think me something I am not.'

'You must not think of yourself as a fallen woman, Emily. The fault was not yours.' Amelia saw that her companion was unconvinced. 'I told you of my friend Lucinda, did I not?' Emily nodded. 'Lucinda took her life because she was too ashamed to have her baby. You were braver. I am proud of you, my love.' She touched her hand. 'Now, I have a request to make of you...'

'Anything. You know I am always happy to oblige you, Amelia.'

'Lucinda had a sister. She was a year older than Lucinda and not as pretty. When Lucinda took her life and her parents understood that she had been seduced, they became much stricter with Margue-rite. They refused to let her go to dances or anything where she might be alone with gentlemen. She is taken out only when her mother goes into company with her friends, which is, as you can imagine, a tedious life for a young woman.'

'Poor Marguerite.' Emily smiled. 'I can guess what you mean to ask me, Amelia. You are going to invite her to live with us.'

'I have written to her parents and asked if she may be allowed to live at Ravenshead to help care for Lisa. I am not sure Marguerite will wish to come, but if she does I hope you will make her feel at home with us.'

'Naturally I shall. It is most unfair that she should be denied the pleasures of society just because her sister was seduced...I know just how she feels.' Emily's voice quivered with passion. 'She has been treated most unfairly!'

'Of course you know, dearest,' Amelia said and smiled at her. 'I thought you could help Marguerite to find her way in society again. She may find it a little frightening after so many years of being almost a prisoner in her parents' home.'

'I shall do all I can to help her,' Emily said and looked thoughtful.

Amelia felt a warm satisfaction. Emily would find some ease for her own pain in thinking of others—and perhaps soon both of her friends would find happiness.

In the meantime, she could only hope that their journey would be accomplished peacefully. She could not help but be aware that they were surrounded by grooms, far more than she would normally dream of travelling with—and all of them armed. Gerard and Harry were taking no chances and she could only be grateful for their care of her.

They stopped briefly to change the horses, and, in the case of the ladies, to relieve themselves in private at a good posting inn. Lisa transferred to the main carriage and was as good as gold, perhaps because Amelia had thought to bring along a book filled with bright pictures. The ladies ate a picnic in the carriage and fortunately did not need to get out again at any point. In consequence, they were able to make good time and it was not yet dark when they arrived at Coleridge.

Helene came to greet them eagerly, kissing Amelia and then Emily. She looked radiant and very happy, as she told her friends that she was increasing.

'I believe Max thinks it is a little soon, but he is merely concerned for me,' she said as she led the way upstairs. 'Your rooms are adjacent and there is a connecting door should you wish to use it. I hope you will both be very comfortable with us. I have been looking forward to your visit so much. Did you enjoy yourselves at Pendleton?'

'Susannah made us very welcome, as always,' Amelia said. 'I am delighted at your news, my love. I must tell you that I have a little news myself. I am to be married.'

'Amelia! I am so pleased. You must be promised to the Earl of Ravenshead?'

'Yes. Gerard asked me to wed him at Pendleton and I agreed. However, I fear there is someone who does not wish us to marry and has already tried to prevent us.'

'Amelia?' Helene looked at her in alarm. 'Are you speaking of your brother?'

'Michael does not wish for it. Indeed, he forbade me—but this is someone else: someone who would prefer to see us dead rather than happy. As yet we are not certain of his identity, though we believe he may use the name of Lieutenant Gordon.'

'How can that be? Who would wish to see you dead?' Helene looked shocked.

'We are not certain.' Amelia frowned. 'I do not wish you to worry, Helene—especially in your condition. If you would prefer that we leave…'

'Certainly not. How could you think it? After all you have done for me, Amelia, I would never close my door to you—and I am sure that Max will wish to help Gerard in whatever way he can.'

'Thank you, dearest.' Amelia smiled her gratitude. 'I was sure you would feel that way. We have decided to announce our engagement at the ball.'

'I am so happy for you. I must admit that I thought you might never marry, but now you are to wed the earl and I know you will be content—he is a good man.' Helene turned to look at Emily. 'How are you, dearest? I have thought that you might also have some news for me.'

'No, I fear I have not,' Emily replied, avoiding Helene's bright gaze. 'Besides, I should not dream of leaving Amelia while she had need of me.'

'I could not bear to part with you,' Amelia told her, guessing how much it was costing her to keep her smile in place. Helene would never deliberately hurt Emily and she could have no idea how much her careless remark had wounded her. 'I expect you will have many guests for the ball, Helene—but I hope you will find room for one more. I mentioned Marguerite to you in my last letter, did I not?'

'Yes—and I sent her an invitation, Amelia. I have had no reply.'

'I dare say her father would not permit it. However, I have appealed to her mama to let her come to help me with my stepdaughter. You have not yet met Lisa, Helene. Her nurse took her straight upstairs, as you may have noticed. She is lovely and also a little charmer.'

'I shall look forward to meeting her,' Helene said. 'You know that I once wished to find a position as a teacher in your orphanage, Amelia. Lisa is so much luckier than the children you help, because she has you and Gerard.'

'She will also have Emily and possibly Marguerite to make a fuss of her.' Amelia laughed softly. 'It will be a wonder if she is not utterly spoiled—but she lost her mama when she was a small child and the nanny Gerard employed when he brought her to England was not kind to her. I want her to be content and I think it will be a happy release for Marguerite to come to us. I told her we should be here until a day after the ball and then we shall go down to Ravenshead. If I find the house acceptable, and Gerard assures me I shall, we shall spend most of our time there. We shall visit Bath and London in the Season, naturally, but our home will be at Ravenshead.'

'Will you not miss your home?'

'Perhaps at first—at least the garden. However, I

shall make a garden of my own at Ravenshead. We shall keep my aunt's estate for our second child.'

They had reached the upper floor, which housed the bedchambers. Having seen Emily installed in hers, Amelia looked at her own with pleasure.

'This has been freshly refurbished in the colours I love, Helene.'

'Yes, it has. It was done especially for you—for the best friend that I could ever have.' Helene reached forwards and kissed her cheek. 'You are such a generous person, Amelia. I cannot imagine that anyone would wish to harm you.'

'Well, it may be all a storm in a teacup,' Amelia said and laughed in a dismissive manner. 'Gerard and Harry took great precautions to safeguard us on the way here, but nothing happened. I dare say having made a blunder once the rogue has decided it is not worth the effort to try anything of the sort again.'

Helene was clearly puzzled. Amelia told her about Emily being kidnapped and then restored to them by the Marquis of Northaven.

'He told you that Emily was taken in mistake for you?' Helene was amazed. 'Oh, Amelia—it is almost like when attempts were made on Max's life and we thought it might be his cousin, but in the end it turned out to be his cousin's physician. When someone wishes you harm, it is difficult to know who they are.'

Amelia nodded but looked thoughtful. 'I hope this will not distress you, my love. I wonder if perhaps it would be better if we did not stay for the ball...'

'I should be most distressed then.' Helene lifted her head proudly. 'I was not frightened when that awful man threatened to kill me in order to get to Max…at least only a little and not until it was over. I do not want you to leave, Amelia. Max will help Gerard discover who this wicked rogue is. Gerard helped us—as did Mr Sinclair…' She frowned. 'I had thought that Toby Sinclair might propose to Emily.'

Amelia hesitated, then, 'In actual fact he did at Christmas, but she turned him down.'

'Emily turned down Mr Sinclair? Why? He is perfect for her.'

'She has her reasons, I dare say. It would be best if you did not speak of him to her, Helene—unless she takes you into her confidence, which she may. I know you were good friends.'

'We still are. Emily writes to me once in a while.' Helene looked thoughtful. 'I know she has a secret. I shall not ask you or her to reveal it, but I have seen the sadness in her eyes.'

'I shall tell you only that she had had an unhappy life before she came to me. I too had hopes of Mr Sinclair for her, but it seems that it was not to be. He left the same night and we have not heard from him since.'

'Then you do not know that his father died?'

'Oh, no! That is sad news indeed. I had wondered why he went so suddenly. Susannah told me he had an urgent summons to return, but I had no idea it was so serious.'

'Extremely serious. I know Max had a letter only this morning. Toby gave us the news and said that he was not sure if he could attend the ball. His mother and sister are in great distress. I dare say he cannot leave them immediately, especially for a ball. I am sure Toby will have written to Harry and Susannah, but perhaps the letter had not reached him before you left.'

'No, I dare say it had not, for he would have mentioned it,' Amelia replied. 'It is a sad time for the family and I do not expect that Toby will feel able to attend your ball. Indeed, it would look wrong if he did. I think too that Harry's sister will need him at her side at this difficult time.'

Helene chattered on for a while, but Amelia was thoughtful. She might have misjudged Mr Sinclair somewhat. She had thought him cruel and rude to abandon Emily so abruptly, but if he had received terrible news and then arrived home only in time to see his father on his deathbed, it was not to be expected that he would write immediately to Emily.

'His mother and sister must come first—and of course there will be business to be done. He must be very distressed, I imagine.'

'Yes, very sad. I am sorry that Emily refused him—but perhaps she will reconsider.'

'I should be happy to think she might. However, at the moment I do not think it possible.'

Left to herself, Amelia took off her pelisse and fur-trimmed bonnet. The news about Mr Sinclair's father was shocking. She did not know if his family had expected it, but even so it would have devastated them. Susannah had certainly not expected it. The very fact that Toby Sinclair had intimated that he might come to Coleridge even now made Amelia think that he had not completely given up the idea of wedding Emily. She would tell her companion the sad news, but she would not speculate about Toby Sinclair's intentions.

If he had any he would make them clear himself in time. Amelia's thoughts turned once more to Marguerite. She fully intended to make sure that Marguerite had every chance to meet a decent gentleman—and to help persuade her parents if the chance of a marriage presented itself.

Chapter Six

'Mr Sinclair's father has died?' Emily was shocked and distressed when Amelia told her the news the next morning. 'How terribly sad! I had no idea that he was so ill.'

'I do not believe anyone realised quite how precarious his health was—at least no one outside the family.'

'I thought...how selfish of me to be so upset about my own concerns.' Emily blushed. 'If Toby has been caught up in family problems—' She broke off and shook her head. 'No, I must not allow myself to hope. If he wished to communicate with me he could have sent me a letter.'

'I dare say he may have had too much on his mind.'

'You said he wrote to Helene to tell her the news—could he not have written to us?'

'He could...but perhaps he felt a letter inappropriate. What he has to say to you must be said face to face.'

'You are trying to make me feel better, but you did not see his expression when I told him about my child.' Emily raised her head. 'It would be foolish to imagine that this changes anything. If Mr Sinclair comes to the ball, I shall greet him as if nothing has happened between us, but I dare say his mama will need him with them for some time.'

'Yes, I think you may be right,' Amelia agreed. 'However, you should not give up hope entirely, dearest.'

'It was foolish of me to think that I might marry. My father told me that no decent man would want me and he is right.' The sheen of tears was in Emily's eyes, but she held them back. 'Perhaps we should go down now, Amelia. We do not wish to keep everyone waiting.'

Amelia did not answer. She knew that Emily was suffering, but there was no cure for a broken heart, as she had discovered to her cost when she was younger. Time alone would soften the hurt. She could only hope that Toby Sinclair would not visit Coleridge unless he was prepared to say something of importance to Emily.

'Now that I understand the circumstances I am prepared to make allowances for Toby,' Amelia told Gerard when they walked together in the long gallery later that day. 'However, I think that he might have made an effort to write to Emily—if only to tell her of his father's death.'

'Letters are sometimes too difficult to write,'

Gerard said. He stopped walking and looked at her. 'Think of the wasted years, Amelia. Had I written to you at the time, we might have saved ourselves so much unhappiness.' He reached out to touch her face, remembered sorrow in his eyes. 'If you knew of all the tortured nights I spent thinking of you…longing for you. I should never have let your brother poison my mind against you. I should have known that he lied when he said that you had asked him to send me a message.'

'Is that what he said to you? How dared he? You must know that I would never have done something like that.'

'Afterwards, when I had time to think it over, I began to see that I had been a fool to believe him, but at first I was too bitter. I married Lisette while still resenting both you and Michael, Amelia. And then it was too late…'

Amelia took a step towards him. Her body throbbed with a deep and urgent desire, making her discard her usual reserve. 'You were not alone in your despair, Gerard. I thought that I should never know the happiness of loving…never feel the touch of a lover's hand…because I could not forget you even though others asked for me.'

'That would have been a sin.' He smiled, his eyes warm with laughter. 'I know there is passion in you.' He reached forwards, bending his head to kiss her. Amelia did not hold back, clinging to him, giving herself to him without reserve. 'I can hardly wait for our wedding night.'

'Nor I.'

'Perhaps we need not wait…' Gerard was about to kiss her again when they both heard something. He looked beyond her at a woman who stood watching them from the other end of the gallery. 'We are not alone.'

'Forgive me,' the woman said and came forwards. She was a tall woman, slim with silky blonde hair that was caught back from her face in a severe style, and her gown was a dull grey that did nothing for her complexion. 'Lady Coleridge thought I might find you here. I wanted to let you know I had arrived, Amelia—but I did not mean to intrude.'

'Marguerite!' Amelia exclaimed in surprise. 'My dear friend. I am so pleased that you came. I hoped your parents would permit it, but I was not sure. I have had no word that you were coming.'

'I have not been well. Nothing serious, merely a chill. However, Mama thought it would do me good to have a change of air—and of course she is always willing to oblige you, Amelia.'

'How is your dear mama?'

'Very well, thank you.'

'Gerard—this is Miss Marguerite Ross.' Amelia turned to him. 'I am not sure if you know each other? Marguerite's family lived near my father's home when I was a girl. You may have met her when you visited the area. You stayed with friends for some weeks one summer—Max and one other were also visiting in the district… Marguerite, this gentleman is the Earl of Ravenshead. We are engaged and it is his daughter that I have asked you to come and meet.'

Gerard extended his hand. 'I do not think we can have met. I am certain I should have remembered. It is a pleasure to meet any friend of Amelia's, Miss Ross.'

Amelia realised he was puzzled and explained, 'Marguerite's parents do not go out much in society. I asked her to come and stay with us. I believe she might enjoy helping me with Lisa. I do not think we need another nanny. Lisa has her nurse and Marguerite has often told me that she adores children—is that not so, my love?'

'Yes, indeed that is true, Amelia.' Marguerite did not take Gerard's hand. Instead she dipped a curtsy, her head bowed. 'I am sure we have not met, sir. I am delighted to be here and I hope I may be of service to Amelia and you.'

'I am certain you will.' Amelia smiled. 'You are not to think you are a servant, Marguerite, though I shall of course make you an allowance. It will be a pleasure to me to have you live with us—and I shall always be certain that Lisa is safe in your care.'

'I promise you that the child will be cared for as if she were my own,' Marguerite said. 'I shall not intrude on you longer, Amelia. I merely wanted you to know that I was here.' She turned to leave, but Amelia put out a hand to stop her, giving Gerard an apologetic glance. 'Forgive me, Gerard. I want to make sure that Marguerite is settled in—and to introduce her to Lisa…'

'Yes, of course. I must speak to Max about something. I shall see you this evening.'

'You will excuse us?'

'Yes. Please go with Miss Ross.'

Amelia held out her hand to Marguerite, who smiled and took it. She felt a little regretful as she glanced back at Gerard and saw him staring after them. They had reached a new stage of their relationship and it was a pity they had been interrupted. However, they had a whole lifetime ahead of them and she did want to make sure that Marguerite was comfortable.

Gerard stared after them as they left. He had said that he did not recognise Miss Ross; indeed, he could not recall having met her—and yet there was something at the back of his mind. She had looked at him oddly when he said that they had not met, a flicker of annoyance or resentment in her eyes.

Was it possible that they had met at some time in the past? He knew that any woman might feel offended if a gentleman they remembered claimed not to recall their meeting. The name Ross seemed to ring a chord in his subconscious, but he could not immediately find a reason for it.

He must be mistaken. Had they met before he would surely have remembered. Miss Ross was not beautiful, but she was not unattractive. Indeed, she might look very well dressed in a different style. She reminded him of someone, but he could not place the memory.

It would come to him in time. He gave it up and went in search of Max. He had hoped to spend an hour or so with Amelia, but since she was otherwise engaged, he would seek out his friend.

'You look thoughtful.' Max, Lord Coleridge, raised his brows as Gerard entered the library. 'Has something happened to trouble you? You have not received another threat?'

'No. Though the broken doll was, according to Northaven, a warning and not a threat. As you know, I expected there might be an attempt to hold up the carriage on the way here. It would have been easy enough to make it appear the work of a highwayman. However, we were strong enough to fight off a gang of ruffians and perhaps they knew it...which begs the question: how do they know where we go and what we do?'

'A spy in our midst, you think?' Max Coleridge frowned. 'A servant, perhaps—the nanny you dismissed?'

'She could certainly have passed on information after I asked Amelia to marry me, but I doubt she knew anything of her until then.'

'Do you trust Northaven?' Max asked. 'You told me that he brought Miss Barton back to you after she was abducted—but could that not have been arranged to gain your confidence? A ruse to get close to you?'

'Harry and I thought of that, but we believed him genuine in his desire to make amends. I believe we may have misjudged him. He is by no means a knight in shining armour, but may not be the traitor we thought him in Spain.'

'You say he believed he knew where he might find this Lieutenant Gordon—if that is the rogue's real name?' Max picked a speck of fluff from his otherwise immaculate coat. 'I suppose you have heard nothing from him?'

'Not as yet,' Gerard said. 'Perhaps Gordon will give up his attempts now that he knows we are aware of him.'

'Do you really believe that? If he hates you, as seems to be the case, can you see him just giving up and walking away?'

Gerard sighed. 'If I speak truly, no. I suppose I hoped that he might have decided we are too well protected, but I dare say he will simply become more devious.'

'Exactly. We must remain alert at all times, Gerard. Helene has invited so many guests to the ball that it would be an ideal moment to strike. I shall have the grounds patrolled all night, every night— but I think we should have a man on guard outside Amelia's door at night too, just in case.'

'As long as the ladies are not aware of it. We must dress the guard as a footman or we may alarm the guests.'

'Certainly. I am sure we have enough livery to accommodate your men, Gerard.'

'Would you rather we went home and saved you the bother? It is a lot to ask of you, Max. I should not have brought this trouble to your house.'

'Damn you, Gerard! We swore to be true friends in Spain, to help each other in time of need. If it had not been for you, Helene might have died last summer. You stood by me then and I shall stand by you now.'

'Thank you. Both you and Harry have been the best friends a man could have,' Gerard said. 'I do not know why I am so uneasy. I have a feeling that the danger is closer than we imagine—but I have no idea why…'

'Emily, my love. This lady is Marguerite Ross—I mentioned to you that she was coming to live with us.'

'Miss Ross.' Emily dipped a curtsy. 'I am so happy to meet you. I am Emily Barton—Amelia's companion. I hope you will be happy with us. Indeed, I know you must be. Amelia is the most generous of friends.'

'Miss Barton—may I call you Emily?' Marguerite gave her a nervous smile. 'I am so fortunate that Amelia wrote to Mama. My life has been…less than happy since…' She sighed and shook her head. 'No, I shall not dwell on the past. I am here now and I am looking forward to my duties and helping Amelia where I can.'

'You will not find your duties onerous,' Amelia said. 'Lisa has her nurse. Nurse Mary will continue to care for her clothes and to give Lisa her meals. All I ask of you is that you will read to Lisa, play with her—and perhaps help her to study books I shall provide for her pleasure. She is too young for a governess as yet, but she needs friends. I want you to be her friend, Marguerite.'

'She is an adorable child. It will be no hardship to be Lisa's friend,' Marguerite said. 'She is a fortunate child to have a stepmother like you, Amelia. Most women in your place would not wish to take on the daughter of their husband's first wife. They would employ a strict nanny and stay away from the nursery.'

'The earl has just dismissed one nanny for being too strict,' Emily said with a little frown.

Marguerite turned her gaze on her. 'Has he, indeed? I remember our nanny was very strict. Papa told her she must make sure we behaved ourselves. I dare say it did us no harm.'

'I am sure it did not,' Amelia said, 'but I love Lisa as if she were my own. I intend to spend some time with her myself most days. However, there will be times when I cannot and then I shall be able to relax in the knowledge that you are caring for her. I know my dear Emily would care for her, but she may have other concerns. Emily does so much for me.'

Amelia smiled at her companion. Had it not been for Emily's hopes of marriage she would probably not have thought of bringing Marguerite here, but she was pleased that she had done so. The young woman had been living a terrible life, because her parents had made her suffer for her sister's shame and it was not fair.

'However, you must not think that I asked you here simply to be Lisa's friend, Marguerite. You will live as one of the family and accompany us when we go visiting. Lady Coleridge is holding a ball this weekend. I hope you have a suitable gown?'

'I have not had a new ball gown for years.' Marguerite looked distressed. 'I have nothing suitable. I did not realise that I should need one and brought only a few things with me.'

'We are of a similar size.' Amelia's eyes went over her. 'I think that my clothes may fit you, though you may need to adjust the hems slightly. I have a new green gown that I have not worn. I think it will suit you well, Marguerite.' She glanced at her feet. 'I do not think my shoes will fit, for I have smaller feet than you do. Emily—do you have a pair of dancing slippers that might fit Marguerite?'

'Yes, I think I have a pair I have worn only once. You can try them on and see,' Emily said. 'I shall be very happy to give them to you, for I have several pairs to choose from.'

'You are both very kind.' Marguerite's eyes held a glimmer of tears. 'I do not know how to thank you.'

'When we go down to Ravenshead I will commission a seamstress and a shoemaker. I shall need a trousseau and you may as well be fitted out at the same time,' Amelia said. 'No, do not thank me, Marguerite. I have been very fortunate and it is my pleasure to help others less so. All I truly want is for us to live comfortably together.'

Marguerite dabbed at her eyes with a lace kerchief that smelled of rose water. 'I do not know what I have done to deserve such kindness from you.'

'I was distressed when Lucinda took her own life,' Amelia replied. 'She was my friend. I did not know you as well, Marguerite, but I have often thought of you. Had I realised sooner how your life had changed, I should have done more to help you. I know your mama

refused to allow you to stay with me, but had I appealed
to her personally, she might have done so. I shall write
and thank her for allowing you to come to me.'

'Mama admires you, Amelia. I am sure she needs
no thanks for agreeing to something that costs her
so little.'

'Nevertheless, I shall write to her.' Amelia smiled.
'It will be so pleasant to have your company, Marguerite.' She turned to Emily, missing the odd look
in Marguerite's eyes. 'Will you help Marguerite
settle in, dearest? I am going to sort out a few gowns
that I do not need. I shall bring them to your room
later, Marguerite. You would look well in green or
blue—colours will suit you so much better than that
grey gown.'

'Come with me, Marguerite,' Emily invited. 'I
shall show you the rooms we mostly use here—and
then you may try on those dancing slippers.'

Amelia found six gowns that she thought might
appeal to Marguerite. She chose a green ball gown that
she had never worn, a blue evening dress, a silver-grey
evening dress, two afternoon dresses and a striped
green morning gown. She added a spangled shawl,
two pairs of evening gloves and a velvet evening purse.

She judged that the gowns would be enough to see
Marguerite through their short stay at Coleridge.
Once they were at Ravenshead, she would order new
gowns for all of them.

'Martha, would you take these to Miss Ross's
room, please?' Amelia said when she had finished

laying out the clothes. 'You may take the silver-grey gown first and the others can follow later. I am not sure whether Miss Ross has a gown pressed for this evening, but this one is ready to wear.'

'Yes, Miss Royston. Are you sure you meant to give this ball gown away, miss? It is new and your favourite colour.'

'It becomes me well, but I have many others. My friend was unable to bring much with her and she will need these gowns until new ones can be ordered.'

'Yes, miss. I just wanted to be sure.'

Amelia smiled to herself as the maid took the gown away. She was dressed ready for the evening and she wanted to go down early. She had sensed that Gerard was surprised by Marguerite's arrival and she ought to explain that she had said nothing to him only because she had not been sure her friend would come. She had not expected Marguerite to simply arrive, imagining that she would receive a letter from Mrs Ross in the first instance.

Now that she had a moment to herself, she was at last at liberty to think about the scene in the library with Gerard. He had kissed her and she had not held back. What might have happened had Marguerite not come in at that moment?

Gerard had told her more of his feelings when Michael had him thrashed and sent him away. He had spoken of his bitterness, his longing for her and lonely nights. For the first time Amelia understood how he had felt, realising that his pain had been as deep as hers, if not deeper. He had been hurt and humiliated—her brother's bullies had been too many and too strong for him to fight back.

He had married Lisette while still feeling resentful. She had thought he must care for her but it seemed he hadn't loved her. When he spoke of her he seemed deeply disturbed. He had spoken of Lisette's terrible unhappiness, which drove her to take her own life. He said that he could not give her what she needed…would it be the same when they married? Or had Gerard been unable to love his wife because in his heart he still wanted Amelia?

His kiss had been passionate and hungry. She had felt that he truly wanted her. Perhaps he did love her in his way…

'I trust your judgement completely,' Gerard said after Amelia had explained why she had asked Marguerite to come to them. They had met once again in the library so that they could be alone for a few moments before dinner. A fire had been lit and the candles burned brightly, giving the room a warm, intimate feeling. 'It is a sad thing that Miss Ross should have been treated so badly. I did not remember her when we spoke earlier, but I have been thinking and I seem to recall a young woman with a similar name.' He frowned, an odd, slightly uneasy expression in his eyes. 'Was not Lucinda Ross Marguerite's sister? I think Lucinda Ross was the young woman who killed herself some years ago?'

'Yes, that is correct. Lucinda was in some trouble. It happened during that summer. I thought at one time—' She broke off and shook her head. 'Northaven... I know that he had been to the house a few times. I once saw him flirting with Lucinda in the gardens.'

'Both Harry and I were also invited to some functions at the home of Mr and Mrs Ross—but Harry would never dream of seducing a young woman of good family. Nor would I, come to that, but at the time I could think only of you. It was you I loved, Amelia.' He frowned, hesitated, then, 'I do recall the name, but not Lucinda's face, though I remember meeting her. I might have liked her sister more for I believe I danced with her a few times, but there was nothing more than politeness between us. Indeed, I could not recall her when we met, but she may have changed. That gown and hairstyle are not becoming to a young woman.'

'You do not mind that I have invited her to stay with us for a while? She is not beautiful, but I think she would be attractive wearing the right clothes. I hope that she may meet someone she likes who will offer for her.'

'Playing matchmaker again?' Gerard teased.

'No, for I have no one in mind for Marguerite. I merely wish to give her the chance she has been denied so long. Besides, she loves children and she will be a big help to me.'

'Then I am delighted she has come,' Gerard said and smiled. 'Are you looking forward to the ball, my love?'

'Yes, of course.' Amelia moved towards him, her breath catching as she gazed up at him. 'We shall be able to dance together as often as we wish. Once our engagement is announced no one could lift a brow if we danced all night—though I suppose it might be thought rude to ignore one's friends altogether.'

'I think it would be pistols at dawn if I dared to monopolise you completely,' Gerard said teasingly. He turned his head and frowned, then strode towards the door and threw it open.

'Is something the matter?' Amelia asked.

He turned to Amelia, frowning. 'I thought someone was eavesdropping outside the door. If someone was listening to our conversation, he or she fled before I could discover who it was.'

'Listening to our conversation?' Amelia stared at him. 'Surely not? In this house…who would spy on us, Gerard?'

'I wish I knew.' Gerard's eyes darkened. 'It is foolish, but since we came here I have grown more uneasy.'

'You expected an attack on the road, did you not?'

He nodded. 'We were prepared for it, but it did not happen. Therefore our enemy has something else planned—something more devious and perhaps more dangerous. I have men watching the grounds, Amelia. I can shoot a man who tries to abduct you, but I have a feeling that something more sinister is going on.'

'What are your reasons? What has changed?'

'I do not know, but I trust my instincts. They served me well in Spain and at other times.'

A shudder caught Amelia and for a moment she was afraid of something she could not understand. 'I must confess that frightens me…'

'Won't you withdraw before it is too late? I could go away—take the danger with me, for I feel it is directed at me. However, you may be hurt, because this person will use you to get to me.'

'No! I have already told you nothing will keep me from you. Would you go away and condemn me to a life of solitude?' Amelia demanded. She moved towards him, clutching at the lapels of his immaculate coat. 'Will you let me die a maiden—unfulfilled and regretful?' Her eyes were fearful, desperate. 'Have you no idea of the feelings I have for you—the longings I know must seem immodest in an unmarried lady?'

'My dearest one! You cannot believe me indifferent? You are beautiful. Any man would be grateful to have such a woman as his wife.' Gerard caught her to him, kissing her with a fierce hunger that set her pulses racing. She clung to him, her body melting into his as the raging desire swept through her. 'I would leave you only to protect you, believe me.'

'If you do, I may as well die.'

'Never!' Gerard gazed down into her wild face, a thrill of laughter and triumph sweeping over him as he saw the passion he had always believed was in her. 'I shall not give you up, Amelia—and nothing shall part us for a second time.'

'Do you swear it?'

'I swear it with my life. Only my death will part us.'

Amelia pressed herself against him, lifting her face for his kiss. As he took her mouth, she parted her lips for him, meeting his tongue in a delightful dance of sweet desire. Her body flamed, tingled with the need to know him, to lie with him.

'Gerard, I want to be truly yours.'

'I burn for you, my love.' He smiled ruefully. 'I would we were at Ravenshead. I could come to you there without ruining your reputation, Amelia. Here, I hesitate to abuse our hosts' hospitality.'

'Once we are at Ravenshead we shall not wait,' Amelia said. 'Nothing must part us now, for I could not bear it.'

Gerard kissed her, but this time softly. 'We must wait for the moment, but I agree that nothing shall part us, my dearest.'

Hidden behind a heavy curtain, the eavesdropper sat curled up on a deep window ledge and listened. For a moment it had seemed that Ravenshead had discovered the presence of a third person, but he had gone to the slightly open door, thinking the listener was outside. Seeing no one, he had believed himself mistaken. He was mistaken only in the location. What good luck that quick thinking had prevented discovery the instant they entered the room!

A smile touched the lips of the hidden one. Gerard Ravenshead thought himself so clever, but revenge was close. It was like the taste of honey on the tongue of the person who hated him. A smile hovered. Soon now. Soon the debt would be paid...

Amelia went to bed feeling happier than she had been for years. She could no longer doubt that Gerard felt a strong passion for her. He might not love her as he once had, but he was certainly not indifferent. They would not lack for passion in their marriage. She longed for the time when they would be at Ravenshead…when she could at last become one with him.

She had lingered downstairs for as long as she could, but Gerard had been caught up in a discussion about politics with some of the other gentlemen. He had thrown her an apologetic glance, telling her by means of a look that he longed for some time alone with her, but it was impossible. She knew that they must be patient; in a few days they would leave Coleridge and then…

A smile on her lips, Amelia sat down at her desk and took out her writing box. She opened it and took out some sheets of vellum, then dipped her pen in the ink and began to write a letter. She was not yet ready to sleep and she wished to tell several friends her news, for she knew it would please them.

After she had been writing for some half an hour or so she sanded and sealed her letters, four in all, leaving the one addressed to Marguerite's mother on the top of the pile. In the morning she would take them down to the hall and place them with others to be franked by Max and taken to the receiving office with any other letters his guests wished sent.

Amelia brushed her hair, washed her face and hands and then went to bed. She blew out the candle and settled down to sleep, but her mind was busy and it was a while before she settled. She was resting, but not sleeping, when the sound of her door opening startled her. For a moment she lay listening, thinking that she must be mistaken. She had not locked the door to her dressing room for it was that way the maid entered in the morning, but her maid would not creep unannounced into her darkened bedchamber at this hour.

'Who is there?' she called and sat up in bed, her hand reaching for the candle by her bed. It was a moment or two before she secured it and some seconds more before she could strike the tinder. 'Who are you?' she cried as a dark shadow fled through the dressing-room door.

Amelia lit her candle and got out of bed. She went through the door to the dressing room. The intruder had left it open in his haste and she saw that the door that led from the dressing room to the servants' stairs was also open. Whoever had been in her room must have come and left by that means.

Amelia knew that her own maid would not have reacted in such a way. No other servant ought to have been there at this late hour and would not be on their lawful business. Yet someone had come to her room—why? What were they searching for? Amelia's jewellery was locked away in her dressing case, which she kept by the bed as she slept. A brief glance told her that it was still there and untouched. So what had the intruder been doing?

Amelia felt chilled, because this was something she had not expected. What might have happened had she been asleep? She wondered if she had been meant to die—or was it merely an attempt to rob her? She shivered, feeling uneasy and anxious. Ought she to send for someone? Amelia hesitated, but it was past midnight and she did not wish to make a fuss at this hour. However, in future she would make sure that the dressing-room door was locked—at least until they were safe at Ravenshead. Her maid could knock if Amelia were still asleep when she came, but it was more likely that she would be wide awake!

Amelia returned to bed. She was not unduly frightened now that the door was locked. She would not be disturbed again this night, but the incident had shocked her more than she liked. She would have to tell Gerard about the intruder in the morning—and of course Max would have to know. He would wish to make enquiries amongst his servants. It did not seem that anything had been taken, but it could quite easily have been simply a bungled robbery. He would have to warn his people to be vigilant.

'You are certain that the door to the hall was locked?' Max asked the next morning when Gerard asked him to meet in private. 'Whoever it was came from the servants' stairs?'

'Amelia tried the door leading into the hall and it was locked. She is positive that the intruder came and went by means of the servants' stairs. Indeed, she saw the shadow escape that way, though it was too dark to be certain whether it was a man or a woman.'

'It would be easy enough for anyone to come that way once the servants have retired for the night.

However, I gave strict instructions that all the outer doors and windows were to be secured at night.' Max frowned. 'I am loathe to think that any of my people would do such a thing, Gerard—but of course our guests have brought their own servants.'

'It is difficult to point the finger at anyone,' Gerard agreed. 'We had a guard outside Amelia's room and Miss Barton's room. Nothing untoward was seen.'

'And we have men patrolling the grounds...' Max swore softly. 'Are you thinking...?'

'That the intruder must have come from inside the house.' Gerard nodded. 'Amelia suggested that it could have been an attempt to steal her jewels, but I am not so sure.'

'I dare say she does not wish to think it anything more. It is fortunate that she was not asleep.'

'Very.' Gerard looked grim. 'I have been aware that something had changed, but I cannot put my finger on it, Max. I know only that I am uneasy.'

'What does Amelia feel?'

'She says that her maid must knock if she is not awake. She will lock her dressing-room door at night.'

'She is very composed about this, Gerard.'

'Perhaps too much so for her own good. Amelia trusts everyone.'

'What do you mean?' Max's gaze narrowed. 'Has something occurred to you?'

'Yes...at least it is just a little seed of doubt. Something I cannot quite place...' He shook his head as Max lifted his brows. 'I am not certain therefore

I shall lay no blame, but my instincts are telling me I am right.'

'You do not wish to tell me?'

'Yes, of course. You have the right to know—but you will not tell Helene or anyone else except Harry when he arrives, for I may be wrong.'

Amelia wandered around her bedchamber. She was looking for something, but she was not sure what it was. Her dressing case was there and the contents were intact. Her silver evening purse was lying on the dressing table where she had put it last night before she undressed. What else had she done before she went to bed? Ah, yes, she had written some letters.

The letters were missing. She had left a small pile on the desk. They had gone and she had not taken them downstairs herself when she went down to speak to Gerard earlier, for she'd had other things on her mind. She frowned as the door opened and her maid entered carrying a gown she had pressed.

'Martha—did you by chance take my letters down to be franked this morning?'

'No, Miss Royston. I saw them lying on the desk when I woke you first thing, but I was not certain you wished for them to be sent yet. You would have asked had you intended me to do it for you.'

'Yes, I should,' Amelia agreed. 'It is most odd, for I did not do it myself. I wonder if Emily…'

'Miss Barton did come to your room earlier, miss. I saw her leaving as I came to collect your gown for this evening. It needed pressing and I had taken some other things to be laundered earlier so I returned to fetch the gown and Miss Barton was leaving. She asked if I knew where you were.'

'Perhaps she took them down. I shall ask her later.'

Amelia picked up a book she wished to offer Lisa as more interesting reading than those Nanny Horton had considered suitable and left the room. As she went into the nursery, she saw that both Emily and Marguerite were before her. They were playing a game of Blind Man's Buff with Lisa and another child and the children were screaming with laughter.

Amelia watched, smiling as Marguerite allowed herself to be caught by Lisa and accepted the blind-fold from her hand. She stopped suddenly, as if becoming aware of Amelia.

'Oh, we are playing a game. I hope you approve?'

'Melia…' Lisa cried and came running to hug her. 'Marguerite has been teaching me games and Emily has been playing with us. Have you come to join us?'

'I came to bring you this book. It is a bestiary and there are lots of pictures of animals and birds. I thought you would like to have it—but you may look at it another day. Go on with your game, my love.'

'I would rather look at the book with you,' Lisa said and took hold of her arm, pulling her towards a sofa. 'It is just a silly game and the book is beautiful.'

Glancing at Marguerite, Amelia saw her flush and smiled, shaking her head. 'Now that is unkind,

Lisa—and Marguerite was very good to play with you.'

'Thank you, Mademoiselle Ross—and Emily…' Lisa tilted her head, a beguiling smile in her eyes. 'I like to play, but I like books with pictures best.'

'Well, you have run us ragged and we must rest,' Emily said, laughing. 'Next time I shall bring a picture book, miss.'

Lisa giggled and shot a look of mischief at her. 'I like to play sometimes.'

'You won't get round me that way,' Emily teased. 'Is there anything you need, Amelia?'

'No—oh, yes, one thing. Did you by chance take my letters down to the hall this morning?'

'No. I would not without asking you first. You might not have finished them.'

'But your letters were downstairs earlier,' Marguerite said and looked at Emily oddly. 'I wrote a letter to my mother and placed it in the hall for franking, as Lady Coleridge said I might. I saw a letter from you to Mama, Amelia—and some others. If Emily did not put them there, your maid must have done so. Was there something you wished to alter?'

'No. They were ready to go, but Martha says she did not take them and I did not for I had other things on my mind…' Amelia was about to mention the intruder, but changed her mind. Emily had already suffered a bad experience and she did not wish to make her nervous. 'Someone else must have done so. Perhaps one of the other maids went in to clean and saw them there. Well, it does not matter.' She smiled at Lisa. 'When I was young I used to look at this book with my nanny. I believe you will like it.'

'Let me see…' Lisa pulled at her hand. 'Let me see.'

Amelia smiled and sat down, taking the child on to her lap. The small boy who had also been playing with them looked on shyly until Amelia beckoned to him. He came and leaned against her shoulder, his eyes fixing hungrily on the pictures she was showing to Lisa. After a few moments, both children fired questions at her and she was so engrossed with them that she did not look up for some time. She saw that Emily had gone, but Marguerite was still there, watching, a strange, half-envious expression in her eyes.

Thinking that she understood, Amelia handed the book to Lisa and allowed the children to look through it alone.

'Children are such a blessing,' she said to Marguerite and went to stand next to her by the window. 'I thought once that I should never have my own, but now I have hopes for the future—and already I have a daughter to love.'

'Yes, I dare say the care of a motherless child is as good a reason for marriage as any.'

'It is certainly one reason,' Amelia said. 'Lisa is a delightful child and Gerard did need someone to help with the care of her, but we are good friends.'

'Friendship is more than most find in marriage. Men are always so faithless…though I do not imply that the earl will be faithless to you, Amelia. After all, you will bring him a fortune when you marry.'

'Yes, that is true. I expect to be very happy in my marriage. You should not think that all men are faithless, Marguerite, though I know you think of Lucinda.'

'Lucinda was foolish to trust the man who betrayed her.'

'Perhaps she loved him and did not think further.'

'Perhaps. Can you love the child of another woman?' Marguerite's eyes were watchful. 'Will you not think of her, of his wife…?' She shook her head. 'Forgive me. I should not have spoken to you so, Amelia. It was not my place.'

'Emily knows that she may say anything to me— and so may you, Marguerite. If something is on your mind?'

'No.' She hesitated, then, 'I just wondered if the shadow of…the manner of his wife's death might hang over you.'

'I am sorry for the way she died,' Amelia replied, glancing at Lisa, who was happily absorbed in the book. She wondered how Marguerite knew of Lisette's suicide, because not even Emily knew more than that Gerard's wife had died in Spain. 'It is sad when someone dies tragically but I know that Gerard did all he could for her.'

Marguerite looked as if she would speak, gave a little shake of her head and walked to where the children were still entranced by the pictures of animals and birds. She pointed to some words beneath one of the pictures.

'Do you know what this says, Lisa?'

'It is funny writing. I cannot read it.'

'That is because it is in Latin. It says that the picture is of a parrot...'

Amelia watched for a moment as Marguerite continued to explain what the words meant. She thought that she had chosen well, for Marguerite was obviously good with children. She was surprised that Marguerite should have mentioned Gerard's first wife. It almost seemed that she knew exactly how Lisette had died, and yet Amelia was sure he had not spoken of it to many people. How could a woman he had never met know anything about Lisette's suicide?

Amelia was thoughtful as she went downstairs, but then she realised that Marguerite had not actually said anything directly about the suicide. She must, of course, have imagined that Lisette had died from the fever she'd caught after her child was born. So many women died that way that it would be easy to assume it was so. Satisfied that she had misunderstood, Amelia dismissed Marguerite's words. The look in her eyes was harder to dismiss, for it had seemed to carry a warning.

Amelia dressed that evening in a ball gown of blue satin overlaid with swathes of silver lace. It had a deep scooped neckline that revealed a tantalising glimpse of her soft breasts, and little puffed sleeves. Around her neck she had fastened a collar of lustrous pearls with a diamond clasp that had a large baroque pearl as a drop. On her wrists she wore gold-and-pearl bangles and she had a magnificent sapphire-

and-diamond ring on her left hand. Gerard had given it to her after tea that afternoon, slipping it on her finger himself.

'It fits. I am relieved,' he told her, lifting her hand to kiss the palm. 'I hope you like it, my love. It was commissioned for us. In time I shall send for the family jewels and you may take your pick of them, though I know you have jewels enough of your own.'

'Most of Aunt's jewellery was not to my taste and remains in the bank. She was extremely fond of amethysts, but I prefer pearls—and of course sapphires and diamonds.' She looked at the deep blue of the sapphire oval ring surrounded by fine white diamonds. 'This is lovely, Gerard—perfect. Thank you.'

'I am glad you are pleased.' He reached out to touch her cheek. 'I care for you so very much.'

Amelia admired her beautiful ring as she went down to the ballroom. It was a long gallery that normally housed musical instruments and several sofas as well as music stands. This evening it had been cleared of furniture and the rooms connecting on either side had their double doors thrown wide so that the effect was of one very large room.

In the first room, Lord and Lady Coleridge stood waiting to receive their guests and footmen were circulating with trays bearing glasses of the best champagne. Amelia accepted a glass and went to stand with Helene. She was one of the first to appear, but she could already hear the strains of music coming from the gallery.

'May I see your ring?' Helene asked and ex-claimed over it. 'How lovely, Amelia. Three stones is a shape that suits your hands very well—and I believe you already have a small sapphire-and-diamond cluster that was your mama's?'

'Yes, I do, though the shank is wearing a little thin and I did not bring it with me—for I must have it repaired.'

'That sapphire is such a deep colour,' Helene said. 'I am so happy for you, Amelia. If it had not been for you, I should never have met and married Max. I wanted you to be happy too, and now you are.'

'Yes, I am,' Amelia said and kissed her. She moved away as Emily and Marguerite entered the room, wandering into the far room where flowers from a hot house had been arranged. There were some exotic blooms and the perfume was quite heavy, making her want to sneeze.

'Are you all right, Amelia?'

Amelia heard the voice and turned as Marguerite came up to her.

'Yes, perfectly, thank you. I was feeling a little nauseous for a moment, but I think it may have been these flowers—they have a strong smell, not un-pleasant but a little overpowering.'

'You looked pale,' Marguerite said. 'Are you sure you feel quite well?'

'I shall be perfectly well, but I must not linger near these flowers; they are giving me a headache.'

'Why do you not go out for a breath of air?'

'It is too cold. Besides, I am looking forward to

the ball. Excuse me.' Amelia saw Gerard coming and walked to greet him. She smiled and held out her hands to him. 'You look very handsome tonight, sir.'

'And you look beautiful, Miss Royston.' Gerard's eyes went over her hungrily. 'I see some people are beginning to dance—shall we?'

'Yes, please.' Amelia took his hand. 'I have been longing to dance with you again.'

The slight feeling of nausea she had experienced earlier vanished as he took her into his arms. The dancing had begun with a waltz and Amelia felt that she was floating on air as he whirled her along the gallery and back. She felt such sweet sensation, like being carried on a wave of sparkling sea to the stars, lost to everything, but the touch of his hand against her back and the faint masculine scent of him in her nostrils. She wanted to go on and on for ever.

Too soon the dance ended and almost immediately the guests came up to them to congratulate Gerard and wish Amelia happiness. Everyone wanted to know when the wedding would be and all their best friends demanded to be invited, which Amelia assured them would be the case.

A few of her friends told her that they had gifts for her, but the engagement was a surprise to most and they exclaimed over it again and again. Some of their closest friends teased Gerard and said that he had stolen a march on them and she was swept away to dance with several of the gentlemen. It was some time before they danced together again, but she noticed that Gerard danced once with Emily, Marguerite and Helene.

'I am glad to see you have been dancing,' she told him when they danced the final waltz before supper. 'It was good of you to ask Marguerite.'

'I asked Miss Barton because she was looking sad and had hardly danced at all,' Gerard told her. 'I could not avoid asking Miss Ross because it would have seemed rude. She said that she had remembered me and reminded me of the night we met. Apparently, we danced twice that evening and I fetched her some champagne.'

'Did she remember so clearly?' Amelia frowned. She would have liked to ask Gerard if there was any way that Marguerite could have known that Lisette had taken her own life, but the evening of their engagement was not the moment. 'She has not spoken to me of knowing you—though you told me you knew her sister, Lucinda, better.'

'Lucinda was an odd girl…'

Amelia saw his expression. Something in his look made her spine prickle. 'What do you mean? I always thought her a sweet and gentle girl.'

'Did you, my love?' Gerard's forehead creased. 'I thought something different, but keep your memories, Amelia. I hardly knew her after all.'

Amelia was intrigued, vaguely disturbed. He was hiding something from her. She sensed a mystery, but again this was not the time to inquire further. A niggling doubt teased at the back of her mind, but she dismissed it almost at once. Earlier, Marguerite had almost seemed to imply that Gerard was marrying her for her fortune and that he would be faithless once they were married. Did she know something that Amelia did not? She felt cold for a moment and shivered, then squashed the unworthy doubts.

She raised her head and smiled. Nothing should be allowed to spoil her special evening.

'Are you happy, Gerard?'

His gaze seared her. 'Can you doubt it? I cannot wait until we are at Ravenshead...to be alone with you...'

Amelia felt reassured. He felt something more than friendship for her. She would be a fool to doubt it, to let her thoughts be poisoned by a casual remark.

Turning her head at that moment, she suddenly saw Marguerite looking at them. The look on her face was so strange that it sent a shiver down Amelia's spine. Marguerite looked...angry...resentful.

Why should she look as if she hated to see others happy? Amelia had an uneasy feeling that something was very wrong, and yet a moment later, as Marguerite saw her glance she smiled and the shadows were banished from her face.

Amelia decided that she had been mistaken. Marguerite's expression must have been wistful, not resentful. She was thinking of all the dances and happy times she had missed. After all, why should she resent the people who had given her this chance to enjoy herself? Of course she would not. She had several times expressed her gratitude. It would be foolish to imagine resentment where there was none.

Chapter Seven

Emily came to Amelia as she was standing by the buffet looking at a bewildering array of dishes. Her complexion was pale and there were shadows beneath her eyes.

'Are you not feeling well?' Amelia asked in concern.

'I have a headache,' Emily confessed. 'Would you mind if I left after supper and went to bed? Is there anything I can do for you before I retire?'

'I have all I want. Are you truly ill, my love—or is it because…?'

'I truly have a throbbing headache. I do not know why, for I scarcely ever have them, Amelia. I think it must be something to do with the soap that the maids used for laundering my kerchiefs. I came to ask if I might borrow one of yours this morning, because mine all had a strong perfume clinging to them, which seemed to bring on my headache. The pain has been lingering all day and is worse this evening.'

'I am so sorry. Yes, of course you must go to bed, Emily. If you are still unwell in the morning, I shall have the doctor to you—and I will have Martha launder your kerchiefs with the soap she uses for mine.'

'Thank you…' Emily hesitated. 'I did not touch your letters this morning, Amelia. I just went into your room, saw you were not there and then left—you do believe me?'

'Of course. Why should I not? You have always been honest with me.'

'Someone suggested to me that I had taken the letters and lied to you.'

'Someone…' Amelia's gaze narrowed. 'Do you mean Marguerite?'

'I do not wish to say—but I should be distressed if I thought you believed I would lie to you.'

'Well, you may rest easy, Emily. I know you too well to ever think you would lie to me.'

'Thank you.' Emily's eyes carried the sheen of tears. 'I thought…but I shall forget it. My foolish head hurts so. Excuse me, I must go. Goodnight, Amelia.'

'Goodnight, my love. Ask Martha for a tisane if you wish. I hope you feel better soon.'

Amelia frowned as she watched Emily leave the supper room. She was sorry that her friend was feeling unwell for she had enough to bear. The scent clinging to her kerchiefs was odd, for Amelia had experienced a similar thing in the room where all the exotic flowers had been displayed; overpowering perfumes could bring on headaches, especially if one were in close contact through a piece of personal lingerie.

She would ask Martha to wash all of Emily's things as well as Amelia's for the next few days. Helene's maids must be using something that was quite unsuitable.

Amelia was thoughtful as she ate a little supper. She had hoped that Emily might have something to celebrate this evening, but Toby Sinclair had not been able to tear himself away from his family at this sad time. She supposed that he could not decently attend a ball so close to his father's funeral. He was perfectly correct not to come. Perhaps he would write to Emily—or seek her out when they went down to Ravenshead in two days' time. She put her thoughts to one side as Marguerite came to sit with her and eat a syllabub.

'Are you enjoying yourself, Marguerite?'

'How could I not when everyone has been so kind?' Marguerite's mouth curved in a smile. 'Is Emily unwell? She told me she was going to bed…'

'She has a little headache. I dare say it will pass by the morning.'

'She was pale. I would have made her an infusion to help her had she mentioned her headache.'

'Oh, I dare say she will ask Martha. It is a pity that it should come this evening, for Emily seldom has headaches.'

'Perhaps she has been feeling out of sorts. Someone mentioned that she had suffered a disappointment recently. Heartache sometimes manifests itself as illness, do you not agree?'

'You should not listen to gossip,' Amelia said. 'Besides, I am sure Emily will be better soon.'

* * *

Gerard watched the woman from across the room. Why did he have the feeling that she was not all that she appeared? Her smiles made him uneasy—for she seemed to be saying that she knew something he did not. He was pleased when he saw her leave the room. He wished it was as easy to send her packing altogether, but knew that Amelia trusted her, was fond of her. To voice his suspicions would only bring a cloud to their time of happiness—and perhaps he was wrong.

For the moment all he could do was to watch and wait. He turned as Max joined him, understanding that there was something he needed to tell him.

'A few moments of your time, Gerard—in private?'

'Of course,' Gerard agreed. 'I am promised to Amelia for the next dance, but she is otherwise occupied for the moment.' His eyebrows arched. 'You have discovered something?'

'Yes. It means nothing and yet it might...' Max said. 'One of my footmen was up with a toothache early this morning and he saw something that might interest you.'

Amelia saw Gerard leave the supper room with Max. She frowned, because she had wanted a few moments alone with him. However, on further reflection she decided that what she had to say would keep for another day. She turned as Helene came up to her.

'Emily was looking pale earlier,' Helene observed. 'Has she by chance taken a chill?'

'She says that the perfumed soap your maids used

for washing her kerchiefs gave her a headache. I shall ask Martha to use my soap for her in future since it seems that she is sensitive to strong perfumes, as I am myself.'

'I was not aware we were using strongly perfumed soap.' Helene looked puzzled. 'I shall ask my housekeeper and it shall be changed, Amelia. Some of the lilies used this evening had a very strong scent. I had one pot taken out this morning because it was overpowering.'

'Yes, I noticed the lilies,' Amelia said. 'I should have developed a headache had I stayed near them for long.'

'I shall not use that particular variety in the house again,' Helene said. 'I am sorry Emily was made unwell. I had thought it might be something else.'

'You mean because Toby Sinclair did not come this evening?'

'No…' Helene hesitated, looking slightly conscious. 'Forgive me, Amelia—but I am not sure that Emily likes Miss Ross. I think they may have had words…but I may be mistaken.'

'Emily is always so thoughtful,' Amelia said. 'I cannot think she would take a girl like Marguerite, who has suffered much at the hands of her parents, as she did herself, in dislike. They hardly know one another, after all.'

'As I said, I may be mistaken—' Helene broke off as Marguerite came up to them. 'Miss Ross—have you enjoyed yourself this evening?'

'Thank you. It has been a lovely evening. Amelia

was so kind as to give me this dress...' Marguerite held out the skirt of the green gown. 'It is beautiful.'

'It becomes you well,' Helene said. 'I have seen you dancing several times. I think you have made friends and admirers, Miss Ross.'

'Thank you,' Marguerite said, but did not smile. 'I passed Emily as I went to my room just now, Amelia. I believe she had been to yours. She said that she has a terrible headache. I offered to make her a tisane myself, but she refused me.'

'Emily had no doubt been in search of Martha to ask *her* to make her a tisane, as I advised,' Amelia said. 'Ah, here comes Gerard—I am promised to him for the next dance.'

Amelia said goodnight to Gerard. He had escorted her to her door, seeming reluctant to let her go inside. He kissed the palm of her hand, closing her fingers over the kiss.

'Keep that until we can be alone,' he said. 'Sleep well, my dearest. I trust that nothing will disturb your sleep this evening.'

'I dare say it will not. Martha has instructions to lock the dressing-room door when she leaves the room. Max provided her with a key and I also have one so I do not think anyone will intrude on me again.'

'Max has his footmen on duty all night so you should be quite safe,' Gerard told her. 'I shall see you in the morning, but you will sleep in and I have things to do—so you need not look for me before noon.'

Amelia nodded and went into her room. Martha

came when she rang the bell and unfastened her gown at the back, helping her off with it.

'What is that smell, Miss Royston?' she asked, wrinkling her nose. 'You do not have a new perfume?'

'No...' Amelia glanced around her. 'I had just noticed it myself—it smells like lilies...the exotic ones they grow in hot houses that have strong perfume.' She took a step towards the bed, halting as the smell became overpowering. 'I think...behind the chair...is that a pot of lilies? It is not easy to see, but I believe it must be the source of that smell.'

Martha went quickly to look. 'Now how did that get here? I swear it wasn't here when I came in earlier to turn down the bed. The nasty thing!' She picked it up and went to the door, speaking to someone outside for a moment. 'I've given it to the footman to get rid of. I wonder who could have put that in here.'

'I cannot imagine for one moment,' Amelia said. 'Have a look around the room to make sure nothing else has been hidden and then you may go to bed. I am sure you have become tired waiting up for me.'

'I like to see you when you come back from a ball, miss. Have you enjoyed yourself?'

'Yes, very much,' Amelia said, watching as Martha went round the room, looking behind chests and under tables. 'I am sure you will find nothing else. Remember to lock the dressing-room door when you go out, Martha.'

'Yes, of course, miss. I have kept it locked since you told me. If someone entered your room, they must have a key or they came from the hall. You do not lock it when you leave.'

'Whoever it was must have entered from the hall. Lord Coleridge assured me that we have both keys to the dressing room. I have not been accustomed to locking my doors during the day. I have never needed to before, but I shall consider it in future.'

Before retiring, Amelia checked the door to the hall and the one to the dressing room. Both were locked. She was pensive as she pulled back the top covers on her bed and looked to see if anything unpleasant had been placed between the sheets. They were fresh and sweet smelling, just as Martha had prepared them for her.

The lilies were further evidence that someone was stirring up trouble for her. She had not dreamed up the intruder of the previous night—and there were the letters that no one would admit to having taken down to the hall. She had not bothered to ask Max if he had franked them for her, but she might do so in the morning.

She knew that if she spoke to the footman outside the door, Gerard would come to her, but she did not consider the pot of lilies reason enough to disturb him. Their perfume still lingered and she found it strong so she opened her a window a little to let in some fresh air. It seemed odd that Emily should complain of a strong soap used for washing her kerchiefs and now the lilies…

Amelia's thoughts were confused. Emily would not lie to her, but Marguerite had implied that she had taken the letters—and that she had seen her coming from Amelia's room this very evening. If she had not trusted Emily implicitly, she might have wondered if her companion had played a trick on her.

Why would anyone take some letters? Why would they hide a pot of lilies in her room? Supposing it was all part of a clever plot to make her believe that Emily was lying to her... Amelia dismissed the idea immediately. Someone was trying to unnerve her. Why? Was it to make her so distressed that she called off her wedding?

She thought it must be the most likely explanation. Yet why should anyone want to prevent her happiness? The only person she could think of who refused to accept her marriage was her brother. However, he had not been invited to Coleridge for the ball, because Helene did not like him.

Michael could certainly not be behind the odd things that had happened this past few days—though he might have paid someone to do it, of course. A servant, perhaps?

In another moment she would be thinking that Martha had placed the lilies in her room herself! This was so foolish and she would not think of it any more.

Martha had left a jug of lemon barley by her bed. She poured some into a glass and drank most of it. It was a little stronger than usual, but not unpleasant. She snuffed out the candles and closed her eyes. No one would disturb her sleep that night!

* * *

Martha awoke her by pulling back the curtains the next morning. Amelia yawned as she sat up, feeling that she could have slept a little longer, but as she looked at the pretty enamelled carriage clock she kept by her bed, she saw that it was almost noon.

'I am late this morning,' she said as she sat up and threw back the covers. 'Please pour me a cup of chocolate while I dress. Lisa will think I have deserted her.'

'I looked in twice, miss,' Martha said. 'You were sleeping so soundly that I thought it best not to wake you.'

'I must have been tired. I do not usually sleep this late even after a ball.'

Amelia went behind the dressing screen, washed and dressed in the green-striped linen gown that Martha brought her. She drank her chocolate at the dressing table, while Martha brushed her hair and wound it into a shining twist at the back of her head, securing it with pins.

'Thank you. I shall not eat, because it will be nuncheon very soon. I must hurry to spend a few minutes with Lisa before we are summoned.'

Amelia went up to the nursery. Nurse Mary was folding clothes as the children played with puzzles and books at the table.

'I am sorry to visit so late. I overslept this morning.'

'Miss Ross has been to play with the children,' Mary said. 'Miss Barton usually comes, but she hasn't been this morning. It is the first time she has missed since before Christmas.'

'She had a headache last night. Perhaps she still has it.'

Amelia spent a little time with the children. She promised Lisa that she would return later that day.

'We are going to Ravenshead tomorrow,' she said. 'I shall have more time to take you for walks then, my love.'

'Will you be my mama then? Must I call you Mama?'

'I shall always be your friend,' Amelia said. 'If you wish to call me Mama, you may, but if you would rather call me Melia, you can, Lisa.'

'Nanny said I would have to call you Mama— even though you are not my mother…' Lisa frowned. 'My mother died, didn't she?'

'Oh, darling, yes, she did, soon after you were born. Why do you ask?'

'How did my mama die? Did it hurt her?' Lisa's eyes were dark and a little fearful.

'No, she wasn't in pain. She had been ill for a long time—and she just went to sleep. You shouldn't think about it, Lisa. Your mama loved you and she would want you to be happy.'

'You won't die, will you, Melia?'

'No, my love. Not for a long time.'

Lisa clung to her hand. 'Promise me you won't go away and leave me and never come back.'

'I promise. I may go somewhere for a visit with your papa sometimes, but we shall both come back to you. We love you very much and we shall all be together as much as possible.'

'Thank you for telling me.' Lisa's eyes fixed on her intently. 'I love you, Melia.'

'I love you too, my darling.' Amelia embraced her, then looked into her face. 'Who told you that your mama died?'

'I asked Emily, because *she* said—' Lisa broke off as Marguerite entered the room. 'I want to read my book…' She ran to pick up the picture book, her head bent over the beautiful illustrations.

'Emily is unwell,' Marguerite said. 'She has vomited this morning and I think she has a fever. I believe she may be sickening for something. Perhaps we should ask for the doctor to call?'

'Yes, perhaps we should,' Amelia said. 'I must go, Lisa. I shall come again later.'

Amelia hurried from the room. She felt anxious about Emily. It must be something more than strong perfume on her kerchiefs if she had been vomiting. She would visit her and then make a decision about sending for the doctor.

'I am sorry to be so much trouble,' Emily said, looking pale and wan as she lay with her head against a pile of pillows. 'I do not know what is wrong with me. I was awake most of the night and vomited three times.'

'I am so sorry you are ill,' Amelia said. 'I shall send for the doctor. He will give you something to help with the pain.'

'I never have headaches. I thought it was the perfume on my kerchiefs, but it throbs so and I feel terrible…' Emily put a hand to her head. 'I am sorry to cause all this bother, Amelia.'

'You are not causing a bother. I shall call the doctor and hope that you are well enough to travel in the morning, Emily. However, if you are still unwell, we shall put off our journey for a few days. I have no intention of leaving you behind, my love.'

Leaving Emily to rest, Amelia went downstairs. She was late entering the dining parlour and apologised to the assembled company.

'I am sorry to keep you waiting, but Emily is most unwell—and I slept late.'

'I am so sorry Emily is unwell,' Helene said. 'Have you sent for the doctor?'

'Yes, I spoke to one of your servants, Helene. Emily is too sick to keep food down. I have asked Martha to make her a tisane and I shall go up to her as soon as I have eaten.'

'I could help nurse her,' Marguerite offered.

'It would be better if you stayed away from Miss Barton,' Gerard said from across the table. 'If she *is* sickening for something infectious, I would not wish it passed on to Lisa. Your first duty is to the child, Miss Ross.'

Marguerite's face remained impassive, but, happening to look at her, Amelia noticed that a little nerve flickered at the corner of her eye. She was not sure if Marguerite were angry or distressed.

Amelia frowned. 'I promised to visit Lisa this afternoon, Gerard. Perhaps I should not—unless Emily is merely suffering from an excess of nerves?'

Gerard stared at her for a moment in silence, then inclined his head. 'I shall bow to your good judgement, Amelia. However, it might be best if you left the nursing of Emily to Martha or one of the other maids.'

She gave him a reproving look. 'Emily is my friend. She needs me.'

'You are Lisa's mother now. She should be more important to you. I hope you will not let her down, Amelia.'

Gerard's expression was hard to read, but she thought that he was angry. Amelia was puzzled and a little hurt. How could Gerard think that she would desert Emily when she was so ill? Lisa had her nurse and Marguerite, and if Gerard was afraid of cross-infection then she would simply have to stay away from the nursery until Emily was better.

She did not like his tone or the way his words seemed to imply that Amelia's own wishes must come second to the child's. Of course she would never intentionally let Lisa down, but neither could she abandon Emily when she was so ill.

Gerard had been acting a little oddly recently. Amelia was not certain what some of his remarks were supposed to mean. She would ask him to explain, but for the moment it did not look as if she would have time to speak with him alone.

The doctor visited Emily. After examining her, he shook his head and looked grave, but said nothing until Amelia followed him into the small sitting room.

'She has no physical signs of illness other than the vomiting and the headache. There is no fever and I cannot see any sign of a rash—nor does she have any lumps in her stomach that might indicate an internal problem.' He polished his little round spectacles on a white kerchief. 'Could she be suffering from an excess of feeling, perhaps? Has she suffered a disappointment?'

'Yes, I believe she may have.' Amelia frowned. 'That happened some days ago and she was well enough then, distressed but not unwell. Are you sure there is nothing wrong with her?'

'It is my opinion that she is of a delicate constitution and, as you may know, some ladies go into a decline after suffering a severe setback.'

'I would not have thought that Emily had a delicate constitution.' Amelia wanted to say more, but held the words back. 'Thank you for your time, sir. You may send me the bill.'

'I shall send something that may help with the headache—but I believe she needs a tonic to lift her spirits. Perhaps she should go to Bath and take the waters there.'

'Yes, perhaps. I shall suggest it to her.'

Amelia returned to Emily's bedchamber after he left.

'He will send something for the headache, but I believe one of Martha's tisanes would do as well, Emily.'

'I am not sure, but I think it was the tisane that made me sick,' Emily said. 'Martha brought it to me and I left it beside my bed. I was sleepy and did not drink it then, but later…something woke me. I got up to relieve myself and then drank the tisane. Some minutes later I started to vomit.'

'Martha's tisane could not have caused you to be sick,' Amelia said. 'She has made them for me many times when I have felt a little unwell and they always do me good. It is very strange.'

'Well, perhaps it was not the tisane,' Emily said. 'I feel a little better now, but I shall not get up. I want to be well enough to come with you tomorrow, Amelia.'

'If you are not, we shall delay our departure. I shall not leave you behind, dearest. If you are not completely better once we are at Ravenshead, I shall call another doctor. I would send you to my own doctor in Bath, whom you know and like, but I cannot come with you.' Amelia was thoughtful. 'Unless you would like to go alone?'

'No, I should not. I do not want to leave you. Especially at the moment…while you may be in danger.' Emily's fingers moved nervously on the covers. 'I have not forgotten that it was you those rogues meant to snatch when I was kidnapped—the things they said…' She gave a little shiver. 'You must be careful, Amelia—even when you think there is no reason.'

'I know you care for me, Emily. We must just hope that you are soon feeling well again, my love.'

* * *

Amelia came upon Gerard as she was on her way back from the nursery. She had spent a pleasant hour reading to Lisa. The child seemed much happier than she had at Christmas, though she had clung to Amelia and was clearly reluctant to see her leave.

'You have been to visit Lisa?'

She met Gerard's questioning gaze, looking directly into his eyes.

'The doctor says that Emily may be suffering an excess of the nerves. I am not sure that he is correct, but he says there is no fever. She is not infectious. I have visited Lisa as I promised her. Had Emily been infectious, I should not have visited the nursery until it was safe.'

'Are you annoyed with me for suggesting it?'

'You have every right to protect your child. I know she is important to you.'

'It was not simply that…' Gerard frowned. 'Something odd is going on, Amelia. I am not sure what it is, but I have sensed it for a while.'

'I am not sure that I understand you, Gerard. I know Emily was abducted at Pendleton, but nothing else has happened since then. Unless you know something I do not?'

'There was the matter of the intruder in your bed-chamber.' Gerard hesitated. 'A footman saw a woman leaving the back stairs that evening. She went into the hall and up the main staircase. He did not see her face clearly for it was dark and she had no candle, but he thought she wore a grey gown. He thought it odd that she did not carry a candle and reported it to Max.'

'Perhaps there was sufficient light from the stars.'

'But why not take a candle—unless she did not wish to be seen?'

'You think a woman came to my room—a woman who was not a servant?'

'I think perhaps she might have been your intruder.'

'I was not harmed and nothing was taken.'

'But someone was there and must have had a reason.' He frowned. 'The footman thought it might have been your companion.'

'You cannot think it was Emily?'

Amelia had said nothing to Gerard of the letters taken from her desk or the pot of lilies in her room, because the incidents were merely annoying and not of consequence.

'We only have Miss Barton's word—and Northaven's, of course—that she was abducted.'

'Gerard! How could you?' Amelia raised her brows. 'What are you implying? You do not think that Emily would lie about a thing like that? Why would she pretend to be abducted?'

'At the moment I hardly know what I think. Yet something is nagging at the back of my mind.'

'You must tell me later.' Amelia smiled. 'Here comes Marguerite.' She went forwards to meet her. 'Are you on your way to the nursery? We have good news, Marguerite. Emily is not infectious, but she is far from well. I have told her that we shall not travel to Ravenshead until she is better. Indeed, if she does not recover I may have to take her to Bath to visit my own doctor. However, in that event, you would accompany Lisa to Ravenshead—she needs the comforts of her home about her.'

'I am sad to hear that Emily is ill. Is there anything I can do for her, as she is not infectious?' Marguerite's gaze flicked towards Gerard and for a moment her eyes seemed to spark with an emotion that might have been resentment.

'She would rather be left to rest. The vomiting has passed, but she still has a headache. Besides, as Gerard said, you came to us to help with Lisa, did you not?'

'Yes, of course. I just wish to be of as much help to you as I can, Amelia.' Marguerite glanced at Gerard and for a moment her eyes were hard with dislike. 'I shall not hurt or abandon you.'

'I am sure you would not.' Amelia smiled and kissed her cheek. 'I do not know when Emily will be able to resume her duties. In the meantime, I shall need your help, Marguerite.'

'You know that I am always willing to be of service to you, Amelia.'

Amelia glanced at Gerard. 'I shall see you later, sir. I have a little errand for Marguerite and I must explain what I need.' She turned to the other woman. 'Emily usually helps Martha to pack my clothes, but she is not well enough. Indeed, I believe she may need help herself if we are to leave in the morning as planned.'

She took Marguerite's arm and walked away with her, leaving Gerard to stare after them, a puzzled look in his eyes.

Amelia left Marguerite after giving her the task of helping Martha with their packing. She went to visit Emily, but found her sleeping and, after some thought, made her way downstairs to the parlour where she found some of the ladies sitting taking tea. When the ladies began to disperse, going to their rooms to change for the evening, Amelia had a few minutes alone with Helene.

It was almost six when she went up to change for dinner. Meeting Gerard on the stairs, she begged him not to delay her.

'Martha has had all the packing to do. I asked Marguerite to help her, but I must make sure everything has been done that needs to be done—and if I do not hurry I shall be late for dinner.'

'What are you playing at, Amelia?' Gerard's dark eyes narrowed, intent on her face.

'I do not know what you mean, sir.'

'When did I become sir again? I thought everything was settled between us?'

'Of course it is, Gerard,' Amelia said. 'It is true that I have something on my mind, but…' She shook her head. 'Tell me—have you made any discoveries about this Lieutenant Gordon? Has the marquis been in touch since we left Pendleton?'

'Unfortunately I am no nearer solving the mystery

than I was then.' He frowned. 'As you said, nothing of significance has happened and yet my instincts tell me that the danger is very close.'

'We must all continue to be on our guard,' Amelia said. 'I admit that I should feel more comfortable if this horrid business was over, but until we know who wishes to prevent our marriage, there is nothing we can do—is there?'

'Very little except be alert. If anything puzzles you…any little incident seems odd—you must tell me, Amelia.'

'Yes…' Amelia was thoughtful. 'Tomorrow we shall be at Ravenshead if Emily is feeling well enough to travel. Things may be easier to control then, Gerard. For a while, at least, there will be only the four of us, the servants—and Lisa, of course.'

'What are you thinking?' Gerard tipped her chin with his finger, looking into her face. 'Is there anything I should know?'

'Like you, I have an odd feeling…' Amelia shook her head. 'There is nothing I can put into words. Believe me, I would tell you if I knew what to say. Tell me, if you had an enemy, Gerard, would you wish him to be in the shadows where you could not see him, or under your nose?'

'I suppose it would be best to keep him close. You cannot fight an enemy you cannot see.'

'I imagined you would say that.' Amelia nodded in agreement. 'I think I should prefer that too—but do not ask me to explain.' She looked up at him. 'If I thought I knew the answers to your questions, I would tell you.'

'Then I suppose I must be content to wait.' He reached for her hand and kissed it. 'You are not regretting anything?'

'Certainly not. I am looking forward to our wedding,' Amelia told him. 'Besides, Lisa would be hurt if I changed my mind at this late stage, would she not? And now, if you will excuse me, I must go up for I shall almost certainly be late otherwise.'

She smiled and ran up the stairs, leaving him to continue on his way. Gerard thought she was hiding something from him, but it was not so. There were a few things that made no sense—and a feeling that had been growing on her that someone was lying to her.

The problem was that, for the moment, she could not be certain who had lied and who had spoken truly. She might know more once Helene had spoken to Max.

Gerard was thoughtful after he left Amelia. She had put up the barriers again, shutting him out. He had thought when they kissed that she was truly able to put the past behind them, believing that she still felt much of the passion she had when they were first engaged. Now he had begun to wonder.

Amelia had been giving him some odd looks. She had changed in the last day or so, as if she were no longer sure of her feelings for him.

When she entered the bedroom, Martha was folding some clothes and packing them into a large trunk. She looked a little put out and Amelia guessed the cause, but the maid did not complain, merely coming to assist her as Amelia began to change for the evening.

'The tisane you made for Emily last evening— was it the same as you make for me?'

'Yes, Miss Royston. Just an infusion of herbs and a little honey to sweeten it.' Martha gave her a direct stare. 'There was nothing in it to make her sick. I know my herbs, miss, and I would not make a mistake.'

'Did someone imply there might be a mistake?'

'It was suggested that I might have made the infusion of herbs too strong. There was no mistake, Miss Royston.' The maid frowned. 'But I shan't tell tales so don't ask me.'

'No, I am certain that you did not make a mistake, for you never do.' Amelia smiled at her. 'Tell me, Martha—what do you think of Miss Barton?'

'She is a pleasant young lady and always helpful…' Martha set her mouth. 'And if you are going to ask what I think of Miss Ross…I would rather not say.'

'Oh dear.' Amelia smothered the urge to laugh. 'Was she not helpful, Martha? I thought she would save you having so much work to do since Emily is not well enough to do her own packing.'

'The intention was there, miss—but I've had to unpack and start again or we should never find everything again. I have an order to my work, Miss Royston. Pushing things in anywhere will not do for me.'

'Then I shall go down and leave you to work in

peace. I am very sorry, Martha, but Miss Ross
wanted to be of use and I thought it would be something for her to do.'

Chapter Eight

'I wish I were coming with you,' Helene said as she
kissed Amelia's cheek the next morning. They were
in the hall and Amelia was about to leave. 'Please
promise me to take care of yourself.'

'Of course I shall,' Amelia said and embraced her.
'Was Max able to answer the question I asked?'

'He said to tell you it was three.' Helene looked
puzzled. 'I do not see how that helps you, Amelia.'

'I assure you that it does. It is exactly as I suspected and the answer to a small mystery. Thank
you, my love. You are not to worry about me.'

'I shall try not to—though I would be happier if
I knew what was going on.'

'Nothing that need concern you, my dearest,'
Amelia said and squeezed her hand. 'Truly, it is a
mere trifle. I shall write and tell you everything when
I can. I must go now. Gerard is impatient to be off.'

'You haven't quarrelled with him? He seems…a

little odd. I thought he might be angry about something.'

'I dare say he is merely anxious. I fear we are a little at odds, but that may be my fault. He thinks I am keeping something from him—and, truthfully, I am.'

'Amelia! What are you about?'

'Believe me, there is nothing to worry you, Helene.'

Amelia pressed her hand and went out to the waiting carriage. Marguerite was already inside, clearly ready to leave. Emily was sitting in one corner, looking pale, dark shadows beneath her eyes and clutching a kerchief soaked with healing lavender water. The scent of it wafted through the carriage, but was quite pleasant. Amelia had asked earlier if she would like to stay on at Coleridge for a while, but she had refused, insisting that she was well enough to make the journey.

Gerard gave Amelia his hand to help her inside, but said nothing, his mouth set in a grim line. He moved away as the groom put up the steps and turned to mount his horse. Lisa was travelling in the second coach with her nurse and Martha.

'I fear the earl grows angry, Amelia. He seems impatient to get away.' Marguerite's words broke Amelia's reverie.

'Yes. I believe he wishes to be home by this evening.'

'I wonder that you can bear his ill humour...' Marguerite clapped a gloved hand to her mouth. 'Forgive me. I should not have said that...I am sure it is simply a natural impatience to be home. Yet it is not pleasant to live with a man of uncertain temper.

My father is such a man and I have suffered from his rages.'

'I am sorry for that, my dear.'

'I have learned to accept it, but I should not wish you to be unhappy, Amelia. Many ladies are unhappy in their marriages, I think. Men are so faithless—at least many are.'

'Yes, I believe so.' Amelia was silent for a moment. 'Gerard can seem harsh at times, I know, though he is usually good natured.'

'Yes, of course. I did not mean to imply…' Marguerite looked as if she wanted to say more, but was apprehensive. 'You will bring so much to the marriage; he must surely be grateful. Of course he would never do anything to harm you.'

'No, he would not. Why should he?'

'I meant nothing. My words were ill considered and foolish.' Marguerite fiddled with her gloves, twisting them nervously in her hands and then putting them on. 'I hope I have not offended.'

'I told you when you came that you might say anything to me. If you have something to say about the earl, please do so now.'

'Oh, no…' Marguerite shook her head. 'One hears rumours, of course—but I would never repeat anything I did not know for sure.'

'It is always best not to do so. Perhaps I know the rumour you speak of—concerning his wife?'

'Well, yes, I did hear something about the way she died.' She glanced at Emily, who was holding her kerchief to her nose. 'I am not sure who told me.'

'You ought not listen to gossip,' Amelia said and frowned. 'I hope you will forget it—the earl did nothing to harm Lisette.'

'No? Then it was a malicious lie and I am glad I did not repeat it to anyone.'

Marguerite sat back against the squabs, her expression subdued. Obviously, she felt that she had spoken out of turn. She ought not to have repeated gossip, of course. Amelia was glad that Gerard had told her how his wife died, otherwise she might have wondered.

Marguerite had hinted several times that Gerard might be marrying her because of her fortune. Amelia had not considered it, because he had told her that he was not interested in her money. She did not know why Marguerite seemed to dislike Gerard, but she was afraid there was some resentment on Marguerite's part. At the beginning neither one had been prepared to admit they had met before, though later both had remembered that they had known each other in the past.

What did Marguerite know that Amelia didn't? What was she hinting at when she suggested that men were unfaithful?

Amelia frowned. Gerard had left her without a word that summer. He said it was because her brother had warned him off, but could she be certain he had not left for another reason entirely? He had sworn he loved her that summer, but within a few months he had married Lisette.

Had he truly loved Amelia? Or was the truth that he had never—and could never—love anyone? Was he the kind of man who loved lightly and moved on?

No! It was wicked of her to think such things. She did not know why she had allowed the thoughts to creep in. She would put them from her mind at once.

It was late in the evening when they arrived at Ravenshead. However, lights blazed in all the front windows, for the candles had been lit in anticipation of their arrival. The butler and housekeeper came out to welcome them, and Gerard's servants were lined up inside the house to meet them. Amelia was introduced to them all and then the housekeeper took her, Emily and Marguerite up to their rooms.

'I've put Miss Ross in one of the guest rooms, as the earl instructed,' Mrs Mowbray said when they were alone. 'Miss Barton has a room nearer the nursery. I hope that is acceptable?'

'Yes, of course—though perhaps…' Amelia shook her head. If Gerard had asked for the rooms to be allocated that way, she would not interfere. She had hardly glanced at the hall downstairs, though she had received an impression of marble tiles on the floor and elegant mahogany furniture, but here she was aware that the décor was new and the colour variations of the pale aquamarine she liked so much. 'Have these rooms been recently refurbished?'

'The earl had them done in October, Miss Royston. I hope you will be comfortable here?'

'Yes, thank you—they are everything I could wish.'

Amelia sighed and took off her bonnet and pelisse. She had come straight up to her apartments so had not taken them off in the hall. It was obvious that Gerard had had the rooms done specially for her. She wished that she could thank him in the way she would like, but something warned her that she must be careful.

She was exploring the bedchamber, discovering the space in the large armoire, when she heard something behind her. Turning, she saw that Gerard had entered through the dressing-room door. For a moment she was surprised, then realised that these apartments had been planned for when they married. As long as the key was his side, he could come and go as he pleased.

'Gerard…you startled me. I was not aware that we had adjoining apartments.'

'You do not object? Should I have knocked at the hall door?'

'No, of course not. It will be convenient when we wish to talk.'

'And at other times…' Gerard moved closer. He reached out to touch her cheek. 'We spoke of being together in a special way when we came to Ravenshead? You have not changed your mind?'

'I think we should be careful for the moment.' Amelia saw his quick frown. 'I have good reason for what I do and say, Gerard—but please do not doubt my feelings for you.'

'I do not understand you…' Gerard began, but someone knocked at the door. Amelia gave him a little push towards the dressing room. He went through and closed the door.

'Just a moment,' Amelia called. 'Come in, please.'

The door opened and then Marguerite entered. She glanced round, her eyes absorbing the décor. 'What a beautiful room, Amelia. Did I hear voices? I am sorry if I interrupted something…'

'You did not,' Amelia replied. 'Did you need something, Marguerite?'

'Nothing. I have a very adequate room. I merely came to see if I might be of service to you?'

'Martha will see to my unpacking. I am ready to go down if you are, Marguerite. Mrs Mowbray will have a light supper prepared for us, I am sure. Emily told us that she requires no supper so we shall leave her to rest for the moment.'

'Well, if you are certain I can do nothing,' Marguerite said and turned to leave. 'Just remember that I am always ready to help you. Especially as Emily is not well enough to run errands for you. If ever you are unhappy or in distress, you may rely on me for help.'

'I am sure you will make yourself indispensable,' Amelia told her with a smile. 'I am very pleased you came to me, Marguerite—and I am sure Lisa adores you already.'

'She is a pretty little thing and she has good manners. I dare say she is very like her mother.'

'Yes, perhaps. I suppose you did not know her mama?'

Marguerite looked startled for a moment, then shook her head. 'She was French, was she not? I have few friends, Amelia. You know that it was almost impossible for me to meet anyone after Lucinda…' Her voice cracked on a little sob. 'Mama and Papa broke their hearts when she died. She was so foolish. She should have named her seducer and faced her shame. He might have been forced to marry her. His desertion broke her heart.' Marguerite's eyes flashed with sudden anger. 'If I could, I would make him pay for what he did to her.'

'She would not tell me his name. Did she never say anything to you, Marguerite?'

'She hinted once or twice…' Marguerite shook her head. 'I do not know his name, Amelia—just that it was a gentleman we all knew. Someone who ought to have known better than to seduce an innocent girl.'

'That is a wide field. I was so sorry when Lucinda took her own life.'

'If she did…' Marguerite's eyes flashed with sudden anger. 'How can we be sure that she did kill herself?'

'I thought there was no doubt?'

'I have sometimes thought…' Marguerite hesitated. 'Just before she died she was happy. She hinted that she might have something exciting to tell me soon…and then she disappeared and they dragged her body from the river. Her dress had been torn and…a ring she had been wearing had gone from her hand. I think her lover gave her the ring and…I suspect he took it from her before he…killed her…'

'Marguerite!' Amelia stared at her in horror. Prickles of ice danced along her spine. 'You think her lover killed her—but why?'

'I know he killed her! Even if she had taken her

own life it would have been his fault. He would still have been her murderer,' Marguerite said bitterly. 'She was but a child and he took advantage. I think when she threatened to reveal his name, he pushed her into the river and watched her drown. She could not swim.'

'How can you know that? You do not even know his name.'

'I know most of what happened.' Marguerite lifted her head defiantly. Something flickered in her eyes. 'If I knew his name...I should not rest until he was punished.'

Amelia touched her arm. 'I understand your pain and distress, but hate will not bring her back, Marguerite. You cannot change the past.'

'I have suffered for her stupid lack of morality. If she had behaved as she ought, none of this would have happened. Why did she give herself to a faithless rogue? She ruined her own life and mine.'

'You must try to forget it. You are here now, Marguerite. You will meet my friends and Gerard's. You have every opportunity to find happiness.'

'My parents would not allow me to marry.'

'I think they might if it was a good match,' Amelia said. 'I believe I might be able to persuade them if you found someone you thought you could love.'

'Men are not to be trusted,' Marguerite flashed at her. 'They seduce you with their smiles and sweet words and then they destroy your life. Be careful who you trust, Amelia. Even marriage does not mean you are guaranteed happiness.'

'Are you suggesting that the earl cannot be trusted?'

'His first wife was unhappy enough to take her own life…' Marguerite said and then put a hand to her mouth in horror. 'I should not have said that…now you will send me home. Yet it is true and you should be careful, Amelia. Be sure that he truly cares for you or you may be hurt too.'

'No, I shall not send you home,' Amelia said, looking at her steadily. 'Tell me, do you really believe that Lisette's death happened because Gerard made her unhappy? Are you saying that he was cruel to her?'

'I only know what someone told me.' Marguerite looked at her oddly. 'What do you think, Amelia? Why would she take her own life if she were happy?'

'I know the truth of it and I know it was not Gerard's fault,' Amelia said. 'But perhaps I shall ask him about it again.'

'You should.' Marguerite gripped her wrist. 'For your own sake, Amelia. I should be so sorry if something were to happen to you because of him.'

'You are hurting me.'

'Forgive me. I did not realise what I did…'

Amelia drew away and Marguerite let go of her wrist. Amelia rubbed at it. 'There is nothing to forgive. I know you are thinking of me—but we shall not speak of this again.'

'I am sorry. You have been so good to me. I had no right to speak but I care about you.'

'I know you do.' Amelia smiled at her. 'Do not look so anxious, Marguerite. I am not going to send you away.'

'You are too forgiving,' Marguerite said. 'People take advantage of you. Emily told me what you did for Lady Pendleton and Lady Coleridge.'

'Had I known how unhappy you were, I should have asked for your company before this,' Amelia told her. 'However, it is not too late for you to make a new life. Nothing that has happened so far should make it impossible for you to find happiness—if you can let go of the past.'

Marguerite stared at her in silence. Amelia nodded at her encouragingly, hoping she might respond to the invitation, but Marguerite turned her face away, going ahead of her down the stairs.

Amelia thought she understood why Marguerite thought so badly of Gerard. She was still grieving for her sister and did not trust any man. When she came to know him better, she would realise that she was wrong to distrust him.

Amelia was seated at her dressing table later that night when the door to the dressing room opened and Gerard entered. He went to the hall door and tried the handle, nodding his satisfaction when he discovered it was locked. Amelia stood up. Her hair had been taken down from its customary style and hung loosely on her shoulders, and she was wearing a pale blue lace peignoir over a matching silk nightgown. Her feet were bare. She picked up a perfume flask and dabbed a drop behind her ears.

'Why did you check the door?'

'Because I wanted to make certain we were not interrupted this time, Amelia.'

Amelia saw that he was still fully clothed, though he had taken off his boots. 'To what do I owe the pleasure of this visit, Gerard?'

'I have not been able to speak to you alone for days,' he said, looking frustrated. 'We need to talk.'

'Yes, I agree. I think you should tell me the whole truth about Lisette, Gerard. You told me something, but I do not believe it was all—was it?'

'What do you wish to know?' Gerard's gaze narrowed.

'You told me that you married her while still angry with my brother and me—but did you love her?'

'No. As I told you, she had been raped and was lying by the side of the road, beaten and close to death. I nursed her back to health and then she told me her lover was dead. She was having his child. I married her to protect her and the child—and because I thought I could never have you.'

She gazed up at him. 'I know you said something died in you the night Michael had you beaten, but do you think you can learn to love me?'

'Did I say that to you?' Gerard looked puzzled. 'I felt that way for a long time, but you cannot believe it now? You must know that I care for you, my dear one.'

'I hoped that you might in time…'

'Believe me, you are the only woman I want as my wife.'

'You truly mean that?'

'Yes, of course.'

'Why did you come to me tonight?'

'So that we could talk. Why?' His eyebrows arched.

'I thought you might have come for another reason,' she said and moved closer to him, the scent of her body inviting and tempting.

Gerard looked at her steadily. 'You told me you thought we should be careful—and I have noticed something odd in your manner of late. You asked me about Lisette and I have answered you truthfully. Will you tell me what is troubling you?'

'Yes, perhaps I should,' she agreed. 'But do not expect me to solve the mystery, Gerard. I am concerned because I think… Emily and Marguerite do not truly like one another. Helene noticed it and…Marguerite has hinted that Emily is lying to me.'

'Good grief!' Gerard frowned. 'What has she said exactly?'

'Some letters were taken from my room. I asked Martha, Emily and Marguerite if they had taken them. They all said no, but Marguerite told me she had seen letters in my hand on the salver in the hall. As you know, Max always franks his guests' letters to save their families the expense of some sixpences.'

'Letters…' Gerard wrinkled his brow. 'I can see nothing wrong in anyone taking them down for you. What is strange in this?'

'Nothing—except that one of them must have taken the letters, but none of them will admit it.'

'You have questioned your maid?'

'Yes. Martha would only take the letters if I told her. Marguerite told me that Emily had been to my room that morning. She still denied having taken them—and Max told Helene that he had franked three letters for me. I wrote four.'

'Four…you are certain?' Amelia inclined her head and Gerard pursed his lips. 'Was there anything of value in any of the letters? Were they important?'

'They were thank-you letters for Christmas gifts—and one to my brother to inform him of our marriage.'

'You do not know which one was taken?'

'I cannot know for certain. Max recalled the number, but he would not have remembered to whom they were addressed—but one was to Marguerite's mother, to thank her for allowing her daughter to come to us.'

'You think it may have been the letter that went astray?'

'I do not know…' Amelia hesitated. 'And there were the lilies…a pot of them in my room. Martha noticed the smell and took them away. If we had not noticed it, they might have given me a headache for they were very strong. It was a silly incident—but something Marguerite said has led me to believe that it might have been Emily. Unless…' She sighed. 'It is quite ridiculous. I have wondered if Marguerite wishes to take Emily's place in my affections…and if Emily feigned illness because she is perhaps a little jealous.'

'This is all trivial stuff,' Gerard said. He reached out to lift her chin with his finger. 'You are certain this is all, Amelia?'

'There have been other hints…things said that I felt not quite as I would like, but nothing that means anything. Someone spoke of Lisa's mother dying to her. She was upset until I told her that her mother died peacefully with no pain.' She saw him flinch. 'It would be wrong to tell her the truth, Gerard. I believe she was afraid that I might die or leave her. I told her it would not happen for a long time.'

She said nothing of Marguerite's hints that he might be unfaithful to her. He had told her the truth about Lisette and to question about the summer he had courted her would seem as if she distrusted him.

'Who told her? You should speak to whoever it was, Amelia. Make it clear that you will not tolerate this kind of thing.'

'Emily has been unwell. I shall speak to her when she is better.'

'You think it was Miss Barton?' Gerard's gaze narrowed, became intent. 'Did Miss Ross tell you it was Emily?'

'No. Lisa started to tell me something, but after I explained, she seemed content and wanted to look at her book. To question her would make more of an incident best forgotten. I shall talk to Emily once she has fully recovered from whatever ails her.'

'Perhaps you would do better to let them both go,' Gerard suggested. 'We could find a governess for Lisa—'

'Gerard! They are my friends. I could not be so cruel as to dismiss either of them for such trivial things.'

'Are you sure they are trivial?'

'No more, Gerard.' Amelia reached up to touch his cheek. 'Now you know why I hesitated to tell you in the beginning. Someone has lied to me—and someone said things they should not—but at the moment I can make no sense of it all. Emily's abduction has turned everything upside down. It is easy to start at shadows, to imagine fault where there is none. Besides, if there was something…we need to know the truth, Gerard. To send the guilty person away might mean that we should never be free of this shadow.'

'If I thought either of them meant harm to you or Lisa…' A glint of anger leapt in his eyes.

Amelia placed her fingers to his lips. 'Lisa is safe, my dearest. Why should anyone wish to harm her? Besides, they both love her. I am sure they do.'

'Why should anyone wish to stop our marriage?'

'It could not benefit either Emily or Marguerite. No, I am certain this is just because of a little jealousy.'

'Then we are no nearer to discovering our enemy.'

'I think we may be,' Amelia said. 'I cannot give you a reason, but I feel that things have moved forwards, though why is not clear. Something is at the back of my mind, but I cannot tell you what it is.'

'You are not holding back from me?' Gerard's eyes seemed to look deep into her soul. Wordlessly, she shook her head. He smiled oddly and reached for her, drawing her close so that she felt the heat of his body and the urgency of his need. 'I should not be here. You are too tempting, my love. I want to sweep you up in my arms and carry you to that bed. I want to kiss and know every inch of your lovely body.'

Amelia's lips parted invitingly, her breath sweet and quick. 'You know how much I want to be with you, Gerard—to be yours. I should not deny you if you took me now.'

'I am tempted beyond bearing, but something is warning me that I ought not to take advantage—that I should wait…' His fingers traced the arch of her white throat. He bent his head to lick the little pulse spot at the base of her neck. Amelia quivered, pressing herself against him, her body surrendering to the need inside.

'Gerard…forget the shadows…forget caution. I want to be yours.'

'Supposing something happens to me…if there should be a child…' he warned as he caught her to him; his mouth pressed against her neck, warm and moist as he nibbled gently. She arched into him, melting in the heat of their mutual desire, lifting her face for his kiss. 'Amelia, my love. I want you so much…'

'If something happened to part us, I should have known your love,' she whispered passionately. 'I am not a green girl, Gerard. I am a woman, but I have never known a man's love—never felt the happiness of being one with you. Do not let me go to my grave never having known what it is to be loved, I beg you. If either of us should die before we wed, we should at least have had this night.'

Gerard's resolve melted as she pressed herself

against him. There was a wild, wanton look in her eyes; the barriers were down and he could not resist their mutual need.

He moaned softly in his throat, bending to sweep her up in his arms and carry her to the bed. She smiled up at him trustingly as he lay her down amongst the soft sheets, her peignoir falling open to reveal the sweet swell of her breasts. His body throbbed with the need to have her and he began to strip away his shirt, ripping the fine material carelessly. Amelia undid her peignoir, pushing it back from her shoulders, slipping her arms out so that all she wore was the thin nightdress that did nothing to hide the contours of her shapely body.

Gerard stripped off the rest of his clothing. Amelia's eyes travelled over the lean length of him, his strong legs and arms, his smooth chest and the sprinkling of dark hair that arrowed to his aroused manhood. The sight of his beautiful naked body was shocking and breathtaking, making her quiver with anticipation as he raised her so that he could pull her nightgown over her head and dispose of it with his clothes.

Then he was lying beside her on the sheets. He faced her, his mouth close to hers. He could smell the sweetness of her breath, the light taste of wine on her lips, and the perfume of her hair was intoxicating. His hands stroked down her back, smoothing the arch, cupping her buttocks and pressing her against him. She moaned softly, lips parting for the invasion of his tongue. He sucked at her, tasting her, their tongues meeting in little experimental darts of sensation, seeking, finding pleasure beyond all expectation.

He caressed her back and her shoulders, stroking firmly until she quivered and moaned with pleasure. Bending his head, he sucked at her nipples, taking first one and then the other into his mouth, the roughness of his tongue against them sending jolts of pleasure through her. His hand stroked her thigh. His tongue traced its way over her navel to her mound, and then his hand parted her legs. He stroked the sensitive inner thigh for some minutes, making her pant with endless, aching need to feel his fingers touching her inner citadel.

When he touched her there she gasped, her back arching as the sensation of fierce pleasure shot through her. She opened wide, allowing him to stroke and then to enter her moistness. His mouth returned to hers, kissing her as his body slid over hers, and then the hot, hard probing of his manhood entered her with gentle thrusts, deeper and deeper until he found what he was seeking.

Amelia cried out as he broke through her maidenhead. For one moment the pain was sharp, but then his kiss was taking it away, soothing her. His hands stroked and pleasured, bringing her back to a state of blissful desire so that the moisture ran and she opened, taking him deep inside her. Their bodies moved together in a sensuous rhythm, the almost unbearable sensation making Amelia's breath come in quick gasps and then all at once Gerard gave a shout and she felt his release. She clung to him as the powerful spasm took her, making her cry out and arch beneath him.

After the intense sensations had faded to a pleasant feeling of satisfaction, Amelia turned her face into his shoulder as he lay beside her, still stroking the silken arch of her back. Her cheeks were wet with tears for she had not expected to feel anything as wonderful...as fulfilling as this sweet certainty of belonging.

'I dreamed...' she whispered. 'I dreamed so many nights...but I could not guess at what it would be...so beautiful...'

'You made it beautiful,' Gerard told her. 'I have never loved anyone else...never known such completeness...such happiness.'

'Gerard...' she murmured against his shoulder. 'We are one, together. No one can part us now.'

'I shall not let them,' he vowed fiercely as he lifted himself on one elbow to gaze down into her face. 'You are mine. Nothing and no one can come between us now.'

They held each other, falling asleep wrapped in each other's arms.

Amelia had not drawn her curtains completely. The light of the candles clearly showed the outline of two people as they moved together and embraced.

The woman watched for a few moments. In the light of the moon, which had just moved out from behind some clouds, the anger and bitterness was stamped on her features. So intent on what was happening in that room was she that she did not hear the man approach and jumped as he touched her shoulder. She whirled round, fingers clawing at his face. He gave a shout of alarm, jerking back and grabbing her wrists.

'What do you think you are doing? It is me—Gordon.'

'You startled me. Creeping up on me like that! I thought I was being attacked.'

'Wild cat,' he said and grinned as he caught her to him. He kissed her hungrily, but she pushed him away with an angry cry.

'I told you! Not until I have what I want. Gerard Ravenshead must die.'

'What of her?' Lieutenant Gordon nodded his head at the window. 'You said she must be raped and he must watch. I'm not your man for that…I'll gladly put a ball into his black heart, but she has done me no harm. I've never killed a woman and the idea has bothered me.'

'I wanted her to suffer as someone else suffered, but that no longer matters. Now all I want is that he should see her dead. He must suffer—he must know what it feels like to lose everything.' Her eyes glittered with hatred. 'His death is not enough for what he has done. If you want me, you must take revenge for me—and for yourself.' She smiled at him, suddenly luring him with a look that took his breath. 'I know you want me…but first I need my revenge.'

'You shall have it. I'll kill him for you and willingly,' he vowed. 'I heard that they are to be married soon. Shall it be before or after the wedding?'

She glanced back towards the bedroom window. There was no sign of the couple embracing now. She imagined them lying together...making love. At that moment her anger was so intense that she shook, but she fought the rage, knowing she must not give way to one of her fits. She was so close now—so close to the revenge she craved.

'It must be soon,' she said. 'There is no reason to wait longer. I have been making plans. Where can I reach you if I need you quickly?'

'At the inn in the village. Send a letter—or find a stable lad to bring your message.'

'Meet me here again in one week and then I shall tell you what I plan.'

Amelia woke to find the bed cold beside her. She looked at the indentation in the pillow where his head had lain, touching it, inhaling the scent of him that still clung to the sheets. Gerard had left her before the servants were about, because he was still trying to protect her reputation. She smiled, stretching, aware of how good she felt. The night had been filled with pleasure as they explored each other's bodies, touching, kissing, reaching a place that Amelia had never been. Gerard had told her it was the same for him.

'No other woman has ever made me feel as you do, my love,' he'd told her just before she fell deeply asleep.

She had slept so soundly that she had not felt him leave their bed. Perhaps he had tried not to wake her. Amelia was a little amused at his gallantry for her maid would know when she changed the sheets.

Amelia's blood had stained them, and the masculine smell of Gerard clung to them. Martha would know. She might keep the knowledge to herself, but it would not be long before it became common knowledge below stairs.

Once, Amelia might have worried that her good name might be soiled, but she was too much in love to care. She was engaged to the man she loved and in a few weeks she would be Gerard's wife. Nothing else really mattered...but life went on. She had obligations she must fulfil.

Amelia rose, washed in the water that remained from the night before in the jug on the washstand and dressed in a serviceable gown, leaving her room before Martha arrived to open the curtains. She walked along the passage and up one short flight of stairs to the rooms nearer the nursery. When she reached Emily's door, she knocked and called softly, 'May I come in, my love?'

'The door is open,' Emily replied. 'Please enter, Amelia.'

Amelia went into the bedroom to discover that Emily was already up and dressed, her bed neatly made. However, she was still a little pale and it was obvious that she had not slept well.

'How are you feeling, my love?'

'I am about the same as yesterday. I have not been sick, but my head still aches a little.'

'I am so sorry.' Amelia looked at her anxiously. 'Shall I ask Gerard to send for the doctor, my love?'

'No, I do not wish to trouble him,' Emily said. 'I

am sure it is nothing serious, Amelia. I shall be better soon.' She fiddled with the sash of her gown, pulling at a slight crease. 'I should wish to be of use to you. Is there anything I can do…help you with the wedding invitations? You will have much to do if the wedding is to be soon.'

'I should prefer that you rest as much as possible. I do not like to see you so low, Emily. Marguerite may help for the moment—and you may join me when you are feeling more the thing.'

'I am much recovered—and I would rather help you than stay in my room.'

'Very well. I have drawn up a list. You may look through it with me and see if I have forgotten anyone. When it is complete, Gerard will have the invitations printed and I shall sign them. I dare say you will be well enough to address some envelopes for me. And there will be thank-you letters to friends, for I believe his notice to *The Times* should be inserted any day now.'

'You look so happy,' Emily said and smiled. 'Please do not worry about me, dearest Amelia. This should be a happy time for you—and I shall be well enough in a few days.'

'I hope so, my love. Meet me in the little parlour at the back of the house at eleven, Emily. I am going to visit the nursery first—and then I shall accompany Mrs Mowbray on a tour of the house, but I should be finished by eleven o'clock.'

As Amelia had expected, she found Lisa wide awake and ready to play. She spent a delightful hour reading to her and helping her to draw pictures on her slate. Lisa drew a credible picture of a dog and then looked at Amelia.

'Will Papa remember I wanted a puppy?'

'I should think he might, but if he doesn't I will remind him.'

'You are so good to me! *She* told me he would forget… *She* said that he did not truly love me, because he did not love my mama…' Lisa's eyes were dark with anxiety. 'Papa does love me…he says he does.'

'Who said that to you, Lisa? Was it Emily?' Amelia frowned. 'Was it Emily who told you that your mama was dead?'

Lisa shook her head. She shuffled her feet and glanced over her shoulder. '*She* said if I told you Nanny would come back and punish me.'

'Nanny will never come back. I promised you that, Lisa.'

'But I saw her…I saw her outside in the gardens last night. I saw her from the window. I like to look out at the moon, you see…'

'You saw Nanny? Miss Horton—you saw her here in the gardens last night?'

'Yes. Nanny was talking to a man—and then they both walked away.'

'I shall tell your papa about this,' Amelia said. 'Nanny has no right to be here and she will be sent away. Who told you that Nanny would come back, Lisa?'

Lisa opened her mouth and then shut it as someone entered the nursery, but her eyes flew to

Amelia's face and something in them answered her question. Amelia held her hand and smiled at her reassuringly.

'Papa will not forget, my love,' she said, holding her close to whisper in her ear. 'Whatever anyone else tells you, I shall not let you be hurt or neglected.'

Lisa hugged her, clinging to her as if she did not want to let her go.

'Run to your nurse now, my love. I have other things to do this morning, but I shall return later and we will go for a little walk in the garden this afternoon.'

Amelia turned and greeted Marguerite with a smile. 'You are up early,' she said. 'Perhaps like me you like to be up with the lark?'

'I often rise early. It is the best part of the day. I like to walk before anyone else is about.'

'Excuse me, my dear. I have things I must do this morning...' Amelia said.

Chapter Ten

After completing a tour of the house with Mrs Mowbray, Amelia consulted with her on various things. She was asked if everything was to her satisfaction and if there were any changes to the routine that she would like to instigate.

'For the moment I think I am pleased with everything,' she said. 'However, I believe Nurse Mary needs more help in the nursery. She cannot do everything and I do not want Lisa to be left alone at any time.'

'I thought Miss Ross was to have charge of the nursery, Miss Royston?'

'Miss Ross is part-governess, part-friend,' Amelia said. 'She will spend time with Lisa—but I want another sensible girl to work with Mary. Someone who would know what to do in the event of an emergency. Do you have a suitable girl—or should we employ another?'

'There is Beattie…' Mrs Mowbray frowned. 'She is a good-hearted lass and has eight brothers and sisters younger than herself at home—but she isn't a clever girl. Beattie is very loyal, but she can't help with Miss Ravenshead's studies or anything of the sort.'

'I think Beattie may be just the girl I am looking for,' Amelia said. 'Will you send her to my room in a few minutes, please?'

'Yes, of course, miss. This will be a step up for the girl, Miss Royston. She will be pleased.'

'She must have a rise in her wages. I leave it to you to decide what would be appropriate, Mrs Mowbray.'

'Now that is generous.' The housekeeper beamed her approval. 'Beattie gives most of her money to her mother and this will be a help to them. I think five shillings a month would be fair.'

'Then we are agreed,' Amelia said. 'I am going up to change my gown now. Please send Beattie to me as soon as you can.'

Amelia left the housekeeper and went up to her room.

She had finished changing her gown and was struggling with a hook at the nape of her neck when a knock at the door announced Beattie's arrival.

'Ah, there you are,' Amelia said. 'Could you do this up for me, please?'

'Yes, miss, of course.'

Beattie fastened the hook and then stood before Amelia, her hands clasped in front of her.

'Do you like children, Beattie?'

'Oh, yes, miss. I love them. It's as well I do, miss. Ma has nine of us at home and I helped with the young ones until I came to work here.'

'Then you would enjoy looking after Lisa?'

'Yes, miss. She is a lovely little thing.' Beattie was beaming all over her face.

She was a plump, homely girl with curly hair and blue eyes, but there was something sturdy about her and Amelia could see why the housekeeper had recommended her.

'I am asking you to help Nurse Mary, because I do not wish Lisa to be left alone at any time. Either you or Nurse Mary will accompany her at all times— in the nursery or when she goes out. The only exception is when the earl or I take her out ourselves. Nurse Mary is in charge of the nursery, but if there is anything that worries you at any time, you may ask to speak to me.'

'Yes, miss. I understand,' Beattie said. 'You can trust me to keep an eye on her.'

'Yes,' Amelia said and nodded. 'That is exactly what I need, Beattie…'

Amelia was in a small parlour that overlooked the rose gardens when Gerard entered. She had been going through the list of guests for the wedding with Emily, but when he entered Emily stood up.

'If you will excuse me, Amelia. I shall go up to my room. I have a headache coming on and I think I shall lie down for half an hour before nuncheon.'

'You must not come down for the rest of the day if you are unwell, my love. Something can be brought to you on a tray.'

'Thank you. Martha will make me a tisane and I shall be better soon.'

Gerard frowned as Emily left the room. 'Do you think Miss Barton is pining? I could write to Sinclair if you wish—ask him to explain himself.'

'No. He had his reasons for what he did,' Amelia said. 'I dare say he will come here when he feels ready. Besides, I am not sure that is the reason for Emily's headaches.'

'If she is really ill, we should have the doctor.'

'I shall send for one if she does not improve within a day or so.' Amelia smiled and got to her feet as he came to her. 'How are you this beautiful morning, Gerard?'

'It may have escaped your notice, but it is raining and there is a gale blowing.' Gerard laughed softly and held out his hands to her. 'Yes, it is a beautiful morning, my dearest one.' He took her hands, gazing down into her eyes. 'You have no regrets?'

'None. Have you?'

'You know the answer to that, Amelia.' He bent his head to kiss her softly on the mouth. 'I loved you before last night—but now I worship you, my lovely, passionate woman.'

Amelia blushed faintly. 'I dare say you think me wanton?'

'Deliciously so. I think myself the most fortunate man alive this morning, my love.'

'Oh, Gerard…it was so wonderful…all that I had dreamed of, longed for, for so many years.'

'And so many years wasted.' Gerard frowned. 'I was a damned fool to let your brother send me away. Nothing will stand between us now, Amelia. The only thing that can prevent our marriage is death.'

'And your men will patrol the grounds, Gerard. Are they in place?'

'Yes. I have given orders this morning. Why do you ask?'

'Because Lisa saw Nanny Horton and a man in the garden last night…'

Gerard swore. 'We must have been followed here. I had men riding behind us, some distance apart. None of them reported a shadow. I thought it would take a few days before anyone realised where we were.' His brow wrinkled. 'But why would Nanny Horton be here in the garden? I do not understand.'

'I think I begin to—' Amelia broke off as the door opened and someone entered. 'Good morning, Marguerite. Have you just come from the nursery?'

'Yes. I spent an hour reading to Lisa. She has a new maid. The girl refused to leave the room when I asked her to fetch something. I think she may prove insolent, Amelia. You may have to replace her.'

'Oh, I think not,' Amelia replied with a smile. 'Beattie has been told that Lisa is not to be left alone.' She glanced at Gerard, her eyes seeming to convey a message. 'I think I should reveal something to you, Marguerite. The earl received a warning—a broken doll. We believe this may constitute a threat against his daughter. Perhaps an abduction for a ransom? Therefore I have asked that one of the maids is always at hand. If an attempt at abduction were to be made, you might be overcome if you were alone, but if two of you are there I think she should be safe for one may raise the alarm—do you not agree?'

'A threat to abduct Lisa?' Marguerite was clearly shocked. 'That is terrible, Amelia. How upsetting for you! I understand why you have given orders that Lisa should never be left alone. I do not know how anyone can be wicked enough to threaten a child—and she is adorable!'

'Yes, she is,' Amelia said. 'I think I would prefer to be threatened myself. If anyone harmed Lisa, I would never forgive them.'

'Indeed, no,' Marguerite said. 'How could you?'

'Was there something you needed?' Amelia asked. 'You came in search of me—for a particular reason?'

'Oh… Emily told me that she is unwell again,' Marguerite said. 'She said that she would ask Martha for a tisane. I do not know what herbs your maid uses, Amelia—but some can cause headaches in certain people. However, I find camomile tea very soothing. Would you like me to make some for Emily?'

'Did you ask her?'

'She refused me, but perhaps if I took it to her room…'

'That would be very kind of you, Marguerite. Emily might find it soothing. I do myself.'

'Then I shall.' Marguerite inclined her head towards Gerard and went out, closing the door behind her.

'What was that about…?' Gerard began, but Amelia shook her head. She went to the door and opened it, looking out. Gerard watched her, brows raised in inquiry. 'What are you up to, Amelia? You did not tell me that you had arranged for another maid for Lisa.'

'I should have done so in a moment had we not been interrupted. It was a precaution after Lisa told me about Nanny Horton.'

'But the tale about the doll? We already know that it came from Northaven.'

'I know that—but I wish others to believe that we think it a threat to Lisa.'

'By "others" I take it you mean Marguerite Ross?' He stared at her hard. 'Something about her has been nagging at me, but I cannot think what…' He stopped, his gaze intent on her face. 'You know something—tell me.'

'I am not certain, but I believe that Alice Horton may once have been in the employ of Mr and Mrs Ross…as a nanny when the girls were young. I believe she was dismissed when they were older, but she may have kept in touch with Marguerite…' Amelia paused. 'Marguerite likes to write letters, as I do myself. I think it possible that they have never lost touch.' She looked at him. 'Tell me, how came you to employ Alice Horton?'

'I made inquiries at an agency…and she was one of those who applied for the post. She had letters of recommendation. I checked her last employer and they said she was reliable.'

'I dare say she is in many ways, but too strict for my liking.'

'I do not see the connection.' Gerard looked puzzled. 'You said Marguerite was a friend. You invited her here because you felt sympathy for her plight.'

'Her sister was my friend. After Lucinda died I wrote to console the family. Mrs Ross wrote to me a few times and I responded—then Marguerite wrote to me and told me of her plight. She begged me to say nothing to her mother, because Mrs Ross's health was precarious at that time.'

'None of this makes sense. Why did Miss Ross come here?'

'I believed she came to help us. I know that she has longed for a child, but did not expect to have one. She told me that she had no hope of marriage for she seldom mixed in society and the only gentlemen she met were her father's friends and too old.' Amelia frowned. 'When I invited her here I was not sure she would be allowed to come. As I told you, I wrote to her mother to thank her for allowing it, but now I am sure that letter was not sent.'

'So you think you've solved the mystery of the missing letters?' His brow arched.

'Precisely. I could not see why anyone would want to steal one of my letters. I wondered if perhaps one of them had been damaged and the ruse was to cover up carelessness on the part of someone. I was not sure if it was Emily, Martha—or Marguerite.'

'And now you think it was Marguerite? Why? Why would she wish to prevent your letter to her mother reaching her?'

'I wish I knew. I think Nanny Horton knew we were coming here and perhaps came on ahead. If Lisa is right, Nanny Horton spoke to a man last night in the gardens. I do not know who the man was, but…' She paused and gave him a significant look.

'You are wondering if it could have been Lieutenant Gordon?' Gerard pursed his lips as Amelia nodded. 'It would explain some of the mystery.'

'Yes, it would explain how they knew where we would be. I have been writing to Marguerite for more than a year now.'

'So she knew you were at Pendleton the summer before last?'

'Yes, she did.'

'Damn it!' Gerard took a turn around the room. 'We may have invited our enemy into our home, Amelia.'

'Marguerite would never harm a child.' Amelia frowned. 'If she has come under the influence of this man…'

'You think he has turned her mind…that she has been giving him information? She may be infatuated with him.'

'Perhaps.' Amelia frowned. 'I am not sure if she understands what he means to do.'

'I wish that I understood,' Gerard said in a tone of frustration. 'Everything is speculation. We have heard nothing of Northaven—' He broke off as they heard the ring of more than one person's footsteps in the hall and then the door was opened and Mrs Mowbray entered. 'Yes?'

'Excuse me for interrupting, sir—but there is a gentleman…' She had hardly finished when Toby Sinclair walked past her.

'Forgive me,' he said. 'Amelia—I must speak with Emily. It is important.'

'Toby!' Amelia gave Gerard an apologetic look and moved towards him. They were being interrupted once more, but she could not deny Toby—she knew how important this might be to Emily. 'I am glad to see you here. We were all so sorry to hear of your loss.'

A shadow passed across his face. 'It was expected and yet it was sudden. Father knew he had only a few months, but in the end we thought it would not be quite so soon. Mama was distraught. I could not leave her before this—but I must and will see Emily.'

'Of course you must. Why should you not?'

'I was told that I could not see her because she is ill.' Toby's face was white, his manner desperate. 'I cannot blame her if she hates me—but still I must see her. I know something that she must be told.'

'You have news for Emily?' Amelia stared at him, seeing the excitement, the triumph in his eyes. Her intuition told her what the news must be. 'Did Harry find the child?'

'His agents were able to help point me in the right direction, but I found her myself only yesterday. I would have been here sooner, but the circumstances…and then I heard news that delayed me.'

'You have come to tell Emily that you've found the child?' Amelia stared at him in dawning delight.

'Yes, I am pleased to say I have—but first Harry bid me speak to you, Gerard.' Toby turned towards him. 'He has learned that an attempt to murder Northaven was made three days ago. He was shot in the back, but the assassin's aim was poor and the ball merely grazed his shoulder. Harry told me that Emily was abducted and that Northaven helped her…and that may be the reason why he was shot.'

'Good grief! Has Harry spoken to him?'

'He told me that he would do so today—and then he will come here. He may bring Northaven with him.'

'Thank you for coming to me.' Gerard's mouth thinned. 'This becomes serious…if Northaven was shot because of what I asked him to do, it means they will stop at nothing.'

'Gerard…' Amelia's eyes sought his in concern. 'This is far worse than I imagined. If they would kill the marquis because he helped Emily escape…'

Gerard turned to her. 'Go up to Emily. See if you can persuade her to come down,' he said. 'I would have a few words alone with Toby.'

'Yes, of course.' Amelia glanced at Toby. 'Emily is lying down with a headache, but I will ask her to see you in the front parlour. Tell me, is the news good for her?'

'I hope she will think it excellent.'

'Very well. I shall let you tell her yourself.'

Amelia ran upstairs. For the moment her suspicions must be shelved. She was not sure when she had begun to suspect that something was not quite as it ought to be in Marguerite's manner—perhaps only in the last day or so, or this very morning. Now she was feeling concerned, for though she was certain that the woman would never harm a child, she could not be trusted if she were under the influence of a man who would kill anyone who stood in his way.

She had been unwilling to send Marguerite away until she had proof and had taken the precaution she thought necessary, but this latest news had made her uneasy. If Gerard wished to dismiss Marguerite, she could not deny him.

She paused at Emily's door to compose herself. Emily answered her knock, her eyes suspiciously red.

'Amelia…please don't ask me to see him. I cannot…'

'You would be foolish not to do so, my love. He has come here to see you—and he has something important to tell you.' She saw the doubt and fear in Emily's eyes and touched her hand. 'Do not look so nervous, Emily. I think you must hear what he has to say. It may turn out better than you imagine. I believe he has your happiness at heart.'

Emily raised her head, a glimmer of hope in her face. 'If you think I must see him…'

'Yes, you must. He has done you a service. It was something I hoped to do for you, but Toby has news. I shall let him tell you. Wash your face and go down to him now…' Amelia paused. 'Did Marguerite bring you some camomile tea?'

'Yes, but I poured it away.'

'Good. I expected you would do so. I think you have been suspicious of her from the start. Now tidy yourself and go down to the front parlour, my love. I shall tell Toby you are willing to see him.'

When Amelia returned to the back parlour, she discovered that Toby was alone. He turned to her eagerly, smiling in relief as she inclined her head.

'Emily will come down to the front parlour in a few minutes.'

'I cannot thank you enough,' Toby said and looked awkward. 'I know I have hurt her. You must think badly of me.'

'Your apology must be to her. I trust you do not intend to hurt her again?'

'Not for the world!'

'Then you need say no more to me, sir.' Amelia smiled and glanced round. 'Did Gerard say where he was going?'

'He said he must speak to Max and told me to wait for you here. He said to tell you that he would explain later.'

'Yes, I am sure he will, thank you. Tell me, has the child been well cared for?'

His smile faded. 'I fear she has not been treated as she ought, but she is in good hands now. I left her with my mother, who is preparing to spoil her.'

'Does Lady Sinclair know whose child she is?'

'Mama has been told all she needs to know for now. Excuse me—I must not keep Emily waiting.'

'Of course.' Amelia smiled as he left the room

hurriedly. She had not asked his intentions, but she could only feel that Emily's future was assured. Toby Sinclair had acted in his usual impulsive way. His reaction to the news that Emily had given birth to a child had been one of shock, but the time accorded him by his father's death had clearly brought him to understand what was important. The fact that he had found the child and taken her to his home said all that needed to be said in Amelia's opinion.

She wished that her own affairs might be settled as easily. It would not sit easily with her conscience if she had brought danger to Lisa by inviting a woman she had thought of as a friend to this house. Yet even though her mind was tortured with doubts, she could not imagine why Marguerite would wish to harm any of them. Unless, of course, she had fallen under a man's spell...

Feeling uneasy, she decided to visit the nursery again even though it was well past the time for nuncheon.

As it happened, only Marguerite was in the small dining parlour when Amelia entered it after a brief visit to the nursery. She had discovered Beattie playing a game with strands of wool bound about the child's fingers. Lisa had been perfectly happy, absorbed in the game. Amelia watched for a few minutes and left them to it. Beattie obviously knew how to amuse children. A governess would need to be found in time, but for the moment Lisa was safe and happy.

Marguerite stood up as Amelia entered. 'No one

else has come to nuncheon, Amelia. I sent the maid away for I can serve myself. Would you like me to serve you?'

'No, thank you.' Amelia went to the sideboard where an array of cold meats, cheese and bread with butter and savoury preserves had been laid out. 'I do not wish for very much. Please continue with your meal, Marguerite. I have just spoken to Emily. She told me that the tea you made for her was helpful.'

'I am so pleased. I am sure that it was the tisane that upset her before. Some people are more sensitive to herbs than others.'

'Do you often make tisanes yourself?'

'I made them for Mama,' Marguerite said. 'After Lucinda died, she often suffered with irritation of the nerves. She could not sleep without her tisanes.'

'I sometimes have nights when I do not sleep well, but Martha's tisanes have helped me.'

'I hope she does not use laudanum. It can be dangerous if you use too much. I have known it to kill.'

'No, I think she merely uses herbs.' Amelia sat down at the table with her plate in front of her. 'Is your mother better now?'

'Oh, yes. I could not have left her otherwise.' Marguerite sipped a glass of water.

'I am sure she relies on you, Marguerite. If she should need you, you must not hesitate to tell me.'

'I am sure she will not.' A closed expression had come over Marguerite's face. 'Would you wish me to take some food up to Emily?'

'Oh, no, I do not think she wishes for food at the

moment.' Amelia forked a small piece of ham. 'I know that you love children, for you have told me so often—has there never been anyone you would like to marry?'

Marguerite hesitated. Her eyes did not meet Amelia's as she said, 'There was once someone I liked, but Lucinda ruined my chances. He went away and I did not see him again. Papa would not have allowed it even had he asked me.'

'I am sorry, my dear. That was sad for you. You have had a hard time of it since your sister died.'

'Lucinda was a fool.' Marguerite stood up. 'Besides, men can never be trusted. You should remember that, Amelia. Do not put too much faith in the man you marry or you may be hurt. Excuse me. I must see to some lessons for Lisa. If you need me, I shall be in my room.'

'Yes, of course.'

Amelia ate her solitary lunch. She was not sure whether or not she had driven Marguerite away with her questions, but she had felt it necessary to ask them. It was as she stood up to leave the dining parlour that she heard the ring of boots on marble tiles. She looked towards the door, waiting, expecting Gerard, and gasped as instead she saw her brother enter.

'Michael—what are you doing here?'

'Did you expect me to ignore your letter?' He glared at her. 'You cannot truly intend to marry that scoundrel, Amelia? After all the warnings I have given you…'

'Please, come into the back parlour where we

may be private,' Amelia told him. 'I would be glad if you speak in a softer tone, Michael. If we are to quarrel, it should not carry to the servants. I do not care to have my private business open knowledge.'

'It will be known soon enough if I have my way. This marriage cannot go ahead. I forbid it.'

She led the way into the small parlour she had begun to make her own. It overlooked pleasant gardens and had a French window, which she could have open when the weather permitted, enabling her to walk on to a stone terrace. The room itself was furnished comfortably with wing chairs, occasional tables and a desk where she could see herself writing letters in the future. She might make a few changes, bring some of her personal effects into the room, but for the moment it served very well. A fire had been lit and it was warm despite the bitter cold day.

When the door was closed, she turned to face her brother. His neck was red with temper and she noticed the fine purple lines mottling his nose and cheeks. His temper and his lifestyle had not improved his looks, for he had been handsome as a young man.

'I shall be honest with you. I hoped you would not come, Michael. Let me tell you at once that you cannot change my mind. I do not see why you should wish to. Gerard may not have come up to your standards when he was younger, but he is the Earl of Ravenshead now and his fortune is sufficient for his needs.'

'Can you not see that it is your fortune that interests him now? You are an old maid, Amelia. If he wished for a wife, he might find a dozen young girls to catch his interest. Depend upon it, he wants your money. The man is a scoundrel and not to be trusted.'

Amelia's expression remained unchanged despite his deliberately hurtful words, which were uncannily similar to Marguerite's.

'You are wrong, Michael. Gerard has told me that I may order my fortune as I wish. We shall secure much of it to my children; the rest will pay for the upkeep of my orphanage and be at my disposal if I need it.'

'And you believe him? The man is a rogue. Listen to me, sister—or you may be sorry. I have had a letter informing me that his first wife took her own life because of his cruelty. It was not signed, but I believe it to be true.'

'It is a wicked lie. I know what happened. Lisette took her own life, it is true, but it was not Gerard's fault.' Amelia lifted her eyes to his. 'If you have a good cause for your objection to my marriage, tell me—otherwise please leave me in peace.'

'You have got above yourself, miss. If you had done your duty to your family and allowed me the control of your fortune, none of this need have happened.'

'If my aunt had wished you to control my fortune, she would have left it to you.' Amelia glared at him. 'You have not answered my questions—why do you so dislike Gerard?'

'You will force me to tell you.' Sir Michael glared at her. 'I have tried to bring you to your senses, Amelia. I do not wish to break your heart—'

'Indeed? You had no such scruples when you had Gerard beaten and sent him away.'

'I had him beaten for good reason. I believed—I still believe—that he was Lucinda Ross's lover. I also think that he may have had a hand in her death…that he threw her into the river when he discovered that she was with child. Even then, you were a better match.'

Amelia staggered as if he had struck her, reeling from the shock. 'No! You accuse him of such wickedness to spite us. It is not true. It cannot be true. I shall not listen to your lies. What proof have you that any of this is true?' Her face had drained of colour and she could only stare at him in horror. 'No…it is not so…'

It must be a wicked lie and yet, if it were true, all the things Marguerite had been saying to her would make sense. She had been trying to warn Amelia from the moment she came and found her with Gerard, about to kiss.

'I do not believe it. He could not…he loved me.'

'Damn you, listen to me.' Michael scowled at her. 'I know that I saw them together in the woods some weeks before she died. She was in his arms, kissing him as if her life depended upon it—and I believe that he may have been near the river the day she died.'

'I do not believe you—this is all lies. Gerard could not…he would not…' Amelia shook her head and sat down as her legs threatened to give way. Supposing Gerard had never loved her…that he had seduced Lucinda at the same time as he had courted Amelia? He had married only a short time after their parting. He swore he had never loved Lisette…but was it all lies? Her heart would not believe it, but her mind told her that there must be a grain of truth in her brother's words. Yet still she continued to deny it. 'Gerard was visiting his uncle at that time. Besides, he would not have done such a wicked thing! Gerard would not…' A little sob broke from her. 'He would not…'

'What would I not do?'

Amelia turned her head and saw him standing in the doorway. He was staring at her, his eyes narrowed, angry. 'Gerard—how much did you hear?'

'Only your last words.' His gaze narrowed, moved to her brother. 'To what do we owe this pleasure, sir?'

'It does not please me to visit under your roof.' Sir Michael glared at him. 'Well, I have spoken my piece. I shall not linger.'

'Leaving already?' Gerard barred his way as he would have left them. 'You will oblige me by telling me what you have said to Amelia. I know that you despise me, sir. I would hear your reasons from your own lips.'

'Very well,' Sir Michael said. 'I know your evil heart, Ravenshead. You were Lucinda Ross's lover— and it is my belief that when she told you she was with child, you killed her.'

Gerard's face went white with shock. 'That is a foul lie! How can you make such an accusation? You have no proof. It is without foundation.'

'I saw you kissing Lucinda in the woods—my woods,' Sir Michael said. 'It was the kind of kiss a young woman gives only to her lover—and it is my belief that you killed her when she threatened to tell everyone that you were her lover.'

'Lucinda kissed me once in the woods—that I shall not deny,' Gerard replied, a little nerve flicking at his right temple. He glanced at Amelia. 'I had forgot it, but it came back to me recently. She declared that she loved me and threw her arms about me. I pushed her away and told her not to be foolish. At no time was she my lover—nor did she ever threaten to reveal that I was the father of her child. She could not, for I did not lie with her. Whatever you may have heard to the contrary, I was visiting friends elsewhere when she killed herself. I returned to ask for Amelia's hand—and you were waiting for me, Royston.' He lifted his head, nostrils flared, proud, angry. 'I had no idea of what had happened to a girl I hardly knew until some time later.'

Amelia's eyes were on his face. Guilt mixed with the anger. He was hiding something from her. She felt as if a dagger had been plunged into her heart.

'Do you expect me to believe that?' Sir Michael sneered. 'I saw you together in the woods some weeks before she died. I witnessed the kiss. You did not throw her off immediately.'

'I was gentle with her,' Gerard admitted. 'I may have been flattered for she declared she loved me. I swear that I did nothing to encourage her. She meant nothing to me.' His gaze moved to Amelia. He frowned as he saw she was pale, her eyes dark with horror. 'You cannot believe his lies? You must believe me, Amelia. I was not Lucinda's lover—nor did I kill her.'

'If you tell me it was not so, I believe you.' Amelia's gaze went from him to her brother. She felt bewildered and she was hurting, trying not to believe that Gerard had lied to her. She had sensed there was something he was hiding when he had hinted that Lucinda was not as innocent as Amelia believed. Had he lain with her? No, no, she could not believe such ill of him. It would destroy her. 'You are wrong, Michael…you must be.'

'Why must he be wrong?'

Amelia spun round as she heard Marguerite's voice. She was standing in the doorway, her eyes wild, full of bitterness, her mouth curling in a snarl of hatred as she stared at Gerard.

'Lucinda told me. She boasted of it to me. Everyone thinks that she took her secret to the grave with her—but that is not true. She told me that Gerard Ravenshead was the father of her child and that she would marry him. I warned her that he was not suitable. Father would not have agreed for he hoped then that we should both make advantageous matches. It was only after her shame was known that he told us we would never be allowed to marry.'

'No!' Amelia looked at Gerard; the doubts were in her eyes now. She did not want to believe what Marguerite was saying, but Michael also believed that Gerard was Lucinda's lover—and for a moment she had seen guilt in Gerard's eyes. He had broken her heart once—how could she be sure that he was not lying to her now? 'Please—it cannot be true.'

'I tried to warn you,' Marguerite cried. 'I told you that he was not to be trusted but you would not listen.'

'Damn you!' Gerard moved towards her in a threatening manner. 'You will leave my house, witch. Your sister was a wanton, but I was not her lover. I believe that she did not know the name of her child's father, for she had more than one lover—'

'Gerard!' Amelia moved to protect Marguerite from his anger. 'Do not speak to her thus. Lucinda was my friend. She could not have been as you describe her.'

'You would take her word above mine?' Gerard's eyes blazed with fury. 'I shall not tolerate that woman in my house another day, Amelia. I will arrange for my coach to take her home, but she leaves today.'

'Do not bother to defend me, Amelia,' Marguerite said. 'I was coming to tell you that I was leaving. Mama has need of me.' She turned and walked from the room, leaving silence behind her.

'Well—' Gerard's tone was harsh as he looked at Amelia '—do you believe her or me?'

Amelia was silent. He was so angry...bitter almost. She hardly knew him. This was not the charming man she had fallen in love with. Her tender lover of the previous night had disappeared, in his place a cold and angry stranger. She wanted to believe him, because if she did not her love became ashes—but she had seen a flicker of guilt in his eyes. He had admitted that he had kissed Lucinda.

'Gerard, I…' She faltered, the words stuck in her throat and she could not go on.

'If she believes you, she is a fool,' Sir Michael said. He glared at them both. 'I've said my piece, Amelia. If you choose to marry him now, I wash my hands of you. Do not expect me to attend your wedding.'

Amelia blinked away the foolish tears, looking at him proudly. 'You will always be welcome in my house—providing you behave as a gentleman.'

Sir Michael inclined his head, turned and walked from the room. Amelia moved away, looking out of the window at the view. The rain had stopped and the sky was getting lighter but it was as if a dark cloud hung over her.

'I am waiting for an answer.'

Amelia could not look at him. 'I am trying to believe you, Gerard,' she said, without turning her head.

'Trying!' He took hold of her shoulders, swinging her round to face him. His eyes blazed with fury. 'Good grief! You cannot think that I would ravish a young girl of good birth and then kill her when she tells me she is with child? What kind of a monster do you think I am?'

'She told Marguerite you were her lover…' Amelia drew a trembling breath. 'I know you would not kill her. I believe she took her own life, but—'

'You think that perhaps I was her lover? You think I played with her emotions, took a despicable advantage at the same time as I courted you—and then destroyed her? You believe that I drove her to her death.' Gerard's face was grey with shock, horror in his eyes. 'You swore you did not blame me for Lisette's death, but perhaps you lied? You do think me capable of these things…and Lisette did die because I hurt her, because I could not love her. I am innocent of all else, but perhaps you prefer to believe your friend?' His tone was scathing, flicking her on the raw.

Amelia shook her head. It was impossible to answer. She did not want to believe that Gerard had done the things he was accused of, but the seed of doubt had been planted. She was too shocked, too stunned to think clearly.

'I am sorry—' she began, but was interrupted by the arrival of Emily followed by Toby. One look at their faces was enough to tell the world how they felt. 'Emily…' Amelia wanted to tell her that this was not the time but before she could speak Gerard had walked from the room. 'Gerard…'

Amelia choked on the words. She wanted to call him back, but did not know what she would say if she did, because she was still reeling from the shock of Marguerite's accusation. Had it been only her brother, she would have dismissed his claim, but Marguerite's accusation had the ring of truth. Oh, but she did not want to believe her! She must be lying…

Smothering her desire to weep, Amelia turned to face Emily. She forced herself to smile.

'So, my love—is it all settled?'

'Toby has found my daughter,' Emily told her. Her face was glowing, her eyes lit from within. 'He says she has not been well treated, but she is quite healthy. She was neglected, but not harmed physically. Her adopted parents did not love her, because they had children of their own and they had long spent the money they were given to take her. They gave her up readily and Toby has taken Beth to his parents. He says that his mother will adopt her. I shall be able to see her every day. I shall look after her, love her and teach her to be happy—but her birth will remain our secret.' Her cheeks turned pink as she glanced up at Toby a little shyly. 'He has explained it is for my sake and not because he is ashamed of me…he loves me truly…'

'If you wish it, we will tell the world,' Toby said stoutly. 'But for your sake, my love, it will be better if Beth is brought up as Mama's adopted daughter. No one will think anything of it if you love her—and one day you may tell her the truth if you wish.'

'And does Toby know the truth of what happened to you now?' Amelia asked.

'When I thought about it, I guessed what must have happened,' Toby answered for her, his hand reaching to take Emily's in his own. 'I love her. I should not stop loving her whatever the truth, but when I discovered how she had been treated, I knew what I must do.'

'And how did you discover that?'

'Harry Pendleton wrote to me. He knew how I felt about Emily and once you told him her story, he thought I should be informed. It was simple enough to find the child, for no one had bothered to conceal her whereabouts. Harry's agent met me and told me what he knew and the rest was easy.' He reached for Emily's hand and kissed it. 'I am taking Emily home to Mama. We shall stay for a couple of weeks and then come back for your wedding, Amelia. Emily would not want to miss that for the world.'

Amelia wondered if there would be a wedding. She was not certain how she felt, but she could not cast a cloud over her friend's shining happiness.

'I am very pleased for you both,' she said. 'When are you leaving?'

'Almost immediately. I thought Emily could pack a small bag for now. Perhaps you would have her things sent to her at my mother's home?' Toby said with his customary eagerness.

'Yes, of course. I shall be happy to do so. Martha will see to her packing.' She moved to kiss Emily on the cheek and then Toby. 'I hope I shall be invited to the wedding?'

'You will be the guest of honour,' Emily told her. 'Toby says we shall hold a ball and announce our engagement in a few months from now. We may be married in the summer. It should not be sooner, because of his father's death. Besides, I am going to live with his mama and we shall see each other all the time…' She hesitated, looking anxious. 'You will not need me, Amelia? I know it is short notice, but you have Marguerite to keep you company now.'

It was impossible to tell Emily that Marguerite was leaving under a cloud—or that she might be forced to return home alone. 'Yes, of course. You must not worry about me, my dearest. I am delighted at the way things have turned out for you. I wish you both every happiness.'

'I am so very fond of you,' Emily said and embraced her. 'I would not leave so suddenly, but I know that you are happy and settled.'

'Yes, of course I am,' Amelia said. 'Go and pack your bag now, dearest.'

'My mother is anxious to become acquainted with Emily,' Toby said after she had gone. 'Harry told me that you intended to search for Emily's child. I am grateful, because his agent was able to save me some time in locating the child.'

'She was so very unhappy after you left. I felt I must do something.'

Toby looked a little uncomfortable. 'I did not behave well, but I must admit Emily's revelation came as a bolt of lightning. Had my father not died, I should have returned sooner. As soon as I could, I went to Pendleton and then in search of the child.'

'I dare say Emily will forgive you. She has not been well, but I believe she will soon be better now.'

Amelia left Toby to prepare his curricle for the journey. She went upstairs to her room. Discovering that the key to the dressing-room door had been put her side, she locked it. She sat down on the bed, bending her head and covering her face with her hands.

Amelia did not cry. Her distress was too deep for tears. She did not know how she felt about things at the moment. She had begun the day feeling on top of the world, but a few spiteful words had turned her world upside down. Her thoughts went round and round in her head as she tried to come to terms with what she had been told. She raised her head, a look of determination in her eyes. She must think about this calmly. It would be foolish to give way to emotion.

Michael had been certain enough of his beliefs to have Gerard beaten. He had acted in a high-handed manner to prevent her marriage at that time, but it seemed he had meant to protect her from a man he believed a rogue. He ought to have told her the story and let her discover the truth for herself. Yet perhaps he had acted as he thought best.

Amelia stood up and began to pace the room. The most terrible accusations had come from Lucinda's own sister! Marguerite was convinced that Gerard was her sister's lover. She had not been lying. She truly believed it.

Marguerite had sworn that her sister had told her that Gerard was her lover. The evidence seemed damning. Amelia had always known it was possible that it could have been Gerard who was Lucinda's lover, if only because he was one of several men visiting the area at that time, but, as time went on, she had completely exonerated him. She had believed that Lucinda's lover was Northaven, but then she had begun to wonder if she had misjudged him too. Now two people had told her that Gerard had seduced and deserted Lucinda at the time he was supposed to be courting Amelia. A shudder of horror went through her, for if Gerard were capable of such an act he would not be the man she loved.

No, no, it could not be true! Everything she knew of him denied it. Besides, something was deeply wrong here...

If Marguerite believed that Gerard had seduced her sister and then driven her to her death—why had she come to this house? She had known that Amelia was going to marry him, for she had told her, asked her to come and help take care of his child. Why would she do that if she were convinced of his guilt?

Amelia frowned as she began to revise the theory she had previously held. She had believed that Gerard's enemy was Lieutenant Gordon—that he wanted revenge because of the way Lisette had met her death. She had imagined that he was the instigator of the plot to kidnap her, possibly persuading Marguerite to help him. She had wondered if Marguerite had fallen in love with Gordon. However, if Marguerite had had reasons of her own to hate Gerard...

She would never rest unless she knew the truth!

Amelia decided she would speak to Marguerite before she left. She went along the landing to Marguerite's room, knocked at the door and then went in. She saw at once that things had been snatched from the armoire and from the chest. A stocking lay abandoned on the floor and the gowns Amelia had given Marguerite were lying on the bed—each of them had been torn with a sharp instrument, rendering them useless. The glass dressing-table set had been knocked to the floor and some silver items were missing. The mess caused had clearly been done out of spite. Marguerite had vented her anger on anything to hand.

Amelia felt slightly sick at the sight of such wanton destruction. She was seized with fear and hurried to the nursery. Relief swept over her as she found Beattie playing with Lisa while Mary stood folding a pile of clean linen and smiled as the child laughed. Lisa was safe! Amelia schooled her features to a pleasant smile.

'Have either of you seen Miss Ross in the past hour?'

'No. She came earlier, but not in the last hour,' Nurse Mary said. 'Is something the matter, Miss Royston?'

'Miss Ross is leaving us. I do not want her near Lisa again.'

'I'm glad she's gone and that's a fact,' Beattie said. 'She gave me the creeps—and that's the truth.'

Amelia didn't ask her to elaborate. She accepted that she had made a mistake in asking Marguerite to come here on the basis of a few letters. Had anything happened to Lisa because of her error she would not have forgiven herself. If Marguerite was consumed with hate for Lisa's father, she might well have constituted a danger to the child. Amelia felt guilty for having brought her to the house.

She was on her way back to her room when she saw Emily walking towards her with a bag in her hand and a cloak over her arm.

'I wanted to say goodbye,' she said. 'This is your cloak, Amelia. You were kind to lend it to me, but after I was kidnapped while wearing it I did not wear it again.'

'I do not think I shall wear it,' Amelia said. 'I may give it to one of the maids, for it is warm and comfortable.' She leaned forwards to kiss Emily's cheek. 'I wish you lots of happiness, my love.'

'I am very happy—but a little nervous. Supposing Beth does not like me…?'

'How could that be?' Amelia shook her head. 'She will come to love you, as I have, dearest. Go on now. Toby has his horses waiting.'

'Yes, I must not keep him. I shall write often— and we shall be here for the wedding.'

Amelia nodded and let her go. She took her cloak into the bedroom and threw it over a chair. She glanced uncertainly at the locked dressing-room door. As she did so, she saw the handle move.

'Amelia…are you in there? Open the door please. I would like to talk to you.'

Amelia hesitated. She wasn't ready to talk to Gerard yet because she was not sure what to say to him. Picking up the cloak she had discarded, she put it around her shoulders and went out of her room. She ran down the stairs and left the house by a side door. The rain had stopped and the wind had blown itself out, though the sky was dark and it was very cold.

She did not mind the cold. She wanted some fresh air—and she needed to be alone for a while.

Chapter Ten

Damn it! How could she think him capable of seducing a young woman and deserting her—and at the same time as he was courting Amelia herself?

Gerard was so angry when he left the room that he was afraid he might do or say something he ought not if he remained. When he saw Toby and Emily come in, he had felt there was no other option than to leave, because he could not speak as he wished with them present. Amelia was clearly in a state of shock and distress. He could only hope that she would come to her senses after a moment or two of reflection.

He was in his own bedchamber when he thought he heard sounds coming from Amelia's room. He went through the dressing closet and tried the handle of the connecting door, calling out to her. She did not answer, yet he was certain she was there. Why would she not speak to him?

It was an impossible situation! How could she believe those vile allegations? She could not if she loved him.

Gerard vaguely remembered the scene in the woods near Amelia's home some years previously. He had been on his way to visit Amelia when he met a young woman. She had been visiting her friend, for she told him that she had just come from the Roystons' house. She was carrying her bonnet by its ribbons, her long fair hair loose on her shoulders. The sunshine suited her—her skin had turned a pale gold and she wore no pelisse, her muslin gown clinging to her shapely form.

'I have been visiting Amelia,' she told him, laughing up at him with her soft ripe lips and her blue eyes filled with mischief. 'It is so warm today. I think I shall go for a swim in the river.'

Gerard struggled to recall his reply. It was something like, *'It is certainly warm enough. You should take care, Miss Ross. The river is deep and there are reeds that might catch your skirts and drag you down.'* Yes, he remembered saying something of the sort. The scene was becoming clearer now. He had dismissed it as unimportant, but now he thought it imperative that he should remember exactly.

'I shall not be wearing clothes…' She licked her lips, an invitation in her eyes. 'Why do you not come with me? We could swim and…' Her laughter was husky and seductive. 'Who knows what else we might find to do, Gerard?' She moved towards him, the perfume of roses wafting from her skin. 'I have always thought you one of the most handsome men I know.'

'You should not say such things, Lucinda.' Gerard could not help smiling, for she was a lovely young woman. He was in love with Amelia, but a light dalliance was no sin on a summer afternoon. 'Some men might take you at your word.'

Had his manner challenged her—encouraged her? He had not meant it to, but perhaps he had been at fault for her reply had been swift and bold.

'I should like you to take me at my word…' Lucinda threw herself at him, winding her arms about his neck and pressing herself against his body. He put up his hands to hold her arms and push her away, but she pressed her lips against his in a wild, passionate kiss that shocked him and for just one moment he had responded. He was, after all, a young man with red blood in his veins. 'Take me swimming…lie with me this afternoon…make love to me, Gerard.'

'No!' Gerard had pushed her away as the moment passed and he realised what she was asking. He did not want her. He was in love with Amelia Royston. This wanton girl was beautiful and he had been tempted by her kiss, but now her boldness revolted him. 'Behave yourself! Think of the disgrace to your family if you were seen swimming naked.'

Lucinda laughed mockingly. 'I do not know why Marguerite thinks herself in love with you. You are such a righteous bore, Gerard Ravenshead. I do not want you. I already have a lover and he does not scruple to take me swimming and then lie with me on a summer afternoon.'

She had laughed again and then run off through the woods. Gerard had laughed too, because he thought it the foolish boasting of a young woman who felt herself scorned. He had forgotten it until he heard about the scandal and the shocking tragedy of her death.

He had never spoken to anyone of that afternoon. He had never realised that they had been seen in what must have looked like a passionate embrace. He had certainly never thought it the true reason for the beating he had been given by Sir Michael Royston's bully-boys.

'I do not know why Marguerite thinks herself in love with you.'

Gerard frowned. He had known there was something he ought to remember from the first moment Miss Ross arrived at Pendleton.

He had not even considered Lucinda's words serious at the time. Remembering now, he thought there had been something a little spiteful in the way Lucinda had spoken of her sister. Why should Marguerite Ross have thought herself in love with him? He hardly knew her. They had danced once or twice—three times at most. He had sat next to her one evening at dinner and made polite conversation, but he had hardly noticed her. He had already been in love with Amelia.

His mind turned back to the scene earlier when Marguerite had thrown those vile accusations at him. He had been looking at Amelia, willing her to trust him, to love him as he loved her—but he had seen the doubts in her eyes.

Marguerite's accusations, the way she looked at him, had seemed angry…almost bitter. Why did she hate him? It seemed clear that she must—for why else would she meet Lieutenant Gordon and plot with him? He was certain now that the two had worked together. Gordon must have had his information from Marguerite. Amelia's innocent letters had told her all she needed to know.

Amelia had begun to suspect it even before Marguerite's outburst. She had thought the woman under Gordon's influence but…supposing *she* were the instigator of the plot to abduct Amelia and kill her? It made perfect sense. Gordon might hate him because of Lisette's death, but he had not looked for revenge at the start. Something—or someone—had made him decide that he would punish Gerard through Amelia. If that someone were Marguerite, it explained why she had suddenly arrived at Pendleton.

Gerard felt cold. They had harboured a viper in their midst! His first thought was for Lisa, because she was an innocent, unsuspecting child. Receiving no answer from Amelia's room, he went immediately to the nursery, where he found the same peaceful scene that Amelia had found earlier. His relief was soon overcome with anger.

Damn it! He would not put up with this nonsense. Gerard returned to the master suite and opened the door to Amelia's room from the hall. A brief search told him that she was not there. He left and walked towards the stairs. Down in the hall, he asked the footman on duty if he had seen Miss Royston recently.

'She went out a few minutes ago, my lord. Perhaps a quarter of an hour. I watched her for a moment, because she seemed unlike herself—a little distracted, if you will forgive my saying so. I think she walked towards the lake.'

'Thank you.'

Gerard frowned. He was not dressed for walking. It would take but a moment to fetch his greatcoat. He would follow her and hope that they could settle this nonsense!

The cold air stung her cheeks and eyes, but Amelia pulled the hood of her cloak over her head, determined not to be put off her walk. She knew it was foolish of her to run away from Gerard, because they would have to talk sooner or later. However, she was feeling too raw to face him just yet. Had the accusation come from just one person she might have dismissed it—but both her brother and Marguerite had blamed Gerard for Lucinda's downfall and her death. Until the previous night she had been unsure of his feelings for her, but after their lovemaking she had felt secure in his love. Now all those niggling doubts had come flooding back.

If Gerard loved her, why had he married so soon after they parted? Why hadn't he come to her and told her what her brother had done? Amelia's thoughts went round and round as she battled her tears.

Was it possible that Gerard had seduced her friend

while at the same time swearing eternal love for Amelia? Could he truly be so ruthless...so cold and uncaring? Could he make love to her so tenderly if he were the man her brother and Marguerite claimed?

No, of course not! Now that she could think clearly, Amelia began to see how wrong it was. Gerard loved her. It was true that he had married another woman, and Lisette had taken her own life—perhaps because Gerard had told her that he could not love her. She had exonerated him freely of blame for that—could she not show as much faith again? She must if she trusted her own senses, her own heart—because she loved him.

She still loved him! Despite all the doubts and accusations thrown at him, she loved him. She would always love him. Without Gerard her life would be empty, a sterile pointless existence that would lead to bitter old age.

Amelia frowned. If she accepted that her brother had been mistaken in what he had seen, she must believe Gerard. He had told her that Lucinda was wanton...that *she* had kissed him. It was this that she had found so hard to accept. A light, flirtatious kiss in a moment of fun—yes, that she could accept—but Lucinda a wanton?

Was it possible that she had never really known her? They had been friends, but had Lucinda kept secrets from her? The answer must be that she had, because she had never told Amelia that she had a lover. Only when she discovered that she was with child and confessed to her parents that her lover would not marry her, had she told anyone of her shame.

Amelia wished that she knew the truth. She had always felt sad about Lucinda's suicide…but Marguerite had hinted that Gerard had killed her because she threatened to name him.

No, he would never do something like that! Amelia could not accept that he was a murderer. Everything that was in her protested his innocence. If he was innocent of her death, it followed that Lucinda had either taken her own life in a moment of despair—or someone else had killed her. So if Amelia believed Gerard was innocent of murder, she ought to believe him innocent of seduction and desertion.

She did believe him! Amelia felt the doubts fall away, a weight lifting from her shoulders as her mind cleared. Gerard would not lie to her! How could he after what they had been to one another? She had hurt and angered him because she had not instantly accepted his word. She ought to have known at once, of course, but the accusations had shocked her so deeply that she hardly knew what she was saying. She had had to deal with Emily and Toby, forcing herself to behave naturally, and it was only now that she had been able to see things clearly.

Why had Marguerite come to the house if she believed that Gerard had seduced and murdered her sister?

There could be only one answer. She was in league with Lieutenant Gordon. He craved revenge for Lisette's death and Marguerite wanted revenge for her sister's shame.

Why did she believe that Lucinda had been forced into the river? Amelia had always thought that she must have flung herself from the bridge because she could not face her shame…why did Marguerite think otherwise?

It was puzzling for until now she had never heard anyone speak of such a possibility. Even Mrs Ross had spoken of her daughter's suicide.

'I was angry with her for her foolish behaviour but I would have taken care of her. She had no need to take her own life,' the grieving mother declared. *'Her papa was angry, but I loved her.'*

Amelia recalled the mother's tears. She frowned as she tried to picture the scene that afternoon. She had gone to the Rosses' house to visit and pay her condolences. Mrs Ross had received her alone and then…Marguerite had come in. Amelia had glanced at her face and…she had been so angry…

Angry. Marguerite had not looked as if she were grieving. Her eyes were not ringed with red, as her mother's were—she was angry.

'Marguerite…' Amelia unconsciously spoke the words aloud. 'She was jealous of her sister—and angry…' Why was she so angry? Amelia could not quite grasp the last pieces of the puzzle.

She had reached the lake. She stood for a moment, staring down the steep bank at the dark grey water, which reflected the clouds above. On a summer day it would be pleasant here, but today there was a feeling of isolation as a light mist began to curl across the water. Amelia sighed, feeling lonely, uneasy. Then, as she heard a twig snap beneath someone's foot, she turned and looked into Marguerite's face. She was as angry now as she had been on the day Amelia visited her home.

'What are you doing here?' she asked her. 'I thought you had left?'

'I met someone and we decided we would wait for a while.' Marguerite's eyes flicked past Amelia to someone who had approached from the right. 'It seems we were lucky, Nanny. You said that she would walk out alone if she was upset—and you were right.'

Amelia looked round and saw Alice Horton. She was dressed in a black cloak, the hood covering her head and most of her face—but her eyes were cold, filled with malice.

A sliver of fear ran down Amelia's spine. She was completely alone here, for few were out on a day like this. Even the labourers would hurry home to eat their dinner in a warm kitchen.

'This is private land. You have no right here. The earl dismissed you.'

'Because you told him to,' Alice Horton said bitterly. 'You stole my girl's admirer and then wrote pitying letters to her…asking her to be a governess. She is a lady…better than you…'

'What are you talking about? I have stolen no one's lover.' Amelia stared at Marguerite, trying to make some sense of the accusation. 'Is she speaking about you? I did not mean to patronise you by offering you a place in my household—only to help you find happiness.'

'He liked me before you made eyes at him…' Marguerite's eyes glittered with hatred. 'Lucinda knew how I felt. She laughed at me when she told me he was courting you…but then she stopped laughing.'

Amelia felt icy cold as she looked into the other woman's face. Anger and hatred—and something more…something dangerous.

'What happened to Lucinda? Why do you think she did not commit suicide?'

Marguerite's lips curved in a sneer. 'She could swim like a fish. Lucinda used to swim in the river all the time. She learned when she was five years old. She was always laughing at me because I dare not follow her into the deep water. She had no fear of anything.'

'If Lucinda could swim, why did she drown?'

'She fell from the bridge and hit her head on an iron strut. It was an accident…' Marguerite's eyes looked strange. 'She was laughing…and then she stopped laughing because I pushed her and she fell.' A queer, high laugh escaped Marguerite. 'I shouldn't have told you that, should I? You will guess now and that means you have to die…but it doesn't matter because you were going to die anyway.' She looked at Alice Horton and giggled. 'Shall I push her in the lake? Everyone will think she killed herself because he betrayed her with that slut of a sister of mine. I got away with it once, I can do it again.'

'Now then, pet, you mustn't get so upset,' Alice

Horton soothed. 'Lucinda was a silly girl, but you didn't mean to kill her. It was an accident.'

'Oh, but I did…' Marguerite's eyes blazed. 'I wanted her to die. She boasted that he was her lover. She knew that I loved him. It was why she wanted him. She had the other one—the one who had given her a child—but she wanted *him* too, because she knew I loved him. She always had to have every-thing, but this time I stopped her.'

'Who was the other one?' Amelia asked. She curled her nails into her palms, willing herself to keep calm. She must hear the truth now! 'What was his name?'

'Surely you know?' Marguerite glared at her. 'He was so angry because he saw her with Gerard that he wouldn't help her. He had promised to leave his wife. He was besotted with Lucinda, gave her presents of jewellery. He told her that Louisa was a nag and a scold and he would get a divorce, but after he saw her with Gerard he raged at her, told her she was a slut and he wouldn't see her again. Lucinda told me it all before I—'

'My brother?' Amelia stared at her in horror. Suddenly, it all made sense. It wasn't to protect her that Michael had had Gerard thrashed—it was jealousy, because he believed the woman he loved had betrayed him with Gerard Ravenshead! His hatred stemmed from the belief that Gerard had taken Lucinda from him!

The sickness rose in her throat as she saw it all so clearly. Michael had been Lucinda's lover, not Gerard, but he had seen them kiss. It was just a moment of light flirtation, as Gerard claimed, but Michael had lost his head. He had had Gerard beaten and broken Amelia's heart because he was jealous.

Amelia's head was whirling as she tried to take all the new information in. Her brother had seduced Lucinda. He was the father of her child. He had promised to leave his wife, but then he'd seen her in Gerard's arms that summer afternoon and he had believed they were lovers. Amelia didn't know what had happened that day, but she imagined it was just a piece of nonsense on a warm afternoon—*because of it Michael had had Gerard thrashed and ruined her life. But what had Marguerite done?*

'Did you kill Lucinda because you believed she had taken Gerard from you?'

Marguerite's eyes had gone blank, but now they focused on Amelia once more. 'You stole him from me. I thought it was her, but it was you. She laughed at me and told me he was going to marry you. I flew at her and we struggled and then…she fell and hit her head. I saw her floating with her face in the water.'

'Why didn't you fetch help or try to get her out?'

'I couldn't swim. I'm afraid of the deep water and—' Suddenly, Marguerite's eyes narrowed, became crafty, evil. 'I wanted her to die. I want you to die. Why should you have everything while I have nothing? My father said I would never marry…it was her fault…your fault…' Marguerite advanced on her, her hands going for Amelia's throat. 'If you drown, they will blame him…and he will die too. He will know what it is like to lose everything.'

'No!' Amelia tried to throw her off, but Marguerite was too strong. 'Help me! Help me…'

Alice Horton stood for a moment, seeming undecided, then she pulled at Marguerite's arm.

'Stop this, sweeting. It isn't her fault that you can't marry. You know what your papa said—'

'Get off me!' Marguerite swung her arm back, throwing the older woman off balance so that she fell to her knees. In that moment Amelia struggled free and started to run. Marguerite came after her, grabbing her by the waist and somehow bringing her down. 'You've got to die. You can't live now that you know. *He* was supposed to help me, but he is a weak coward. So I must do it myself.'

Amelia screamed and struggled to throw Marguerite off, but she was very strong. Her hands were tightening their hold about Amelia's throat and she couldn't breathe. Everything was going black and then she heard a shout…several voices shouting. People were racing towards them.

'Damn you! You murdering bitch!'

Gerard's voice! Amelia heard it through a haze of mist, as if she were far away. Several men were shouting and there were the sounds of a struggle. She heard Marguerite screaming and then water splashing, more screaming, shouting and then sobbing. A woman was weeping bitterly.

'Is she dead, sir? My poor little mad girl.'

Amelia's throat hurt, but she struggled to sit up. She couldn't see clearly, but she knew that Gerard wasn't alone. There were other men there…some of them had guns. She thought one voice might have belonged to the Marquis of Northaven, but she wasn't sure, because it was distant, blurred. Everything was going hazy again as she fell back on the damp ground.

The woman was still sobbing. She thought it was Alice Horton. Men were talking, calling for someone to go for the doctor. Things seemed to be going on around her. She was being lifted and carried in someone's arms, but she couldn't see or hear any more…

Gerard stood looking down, his heart wrenched as he saw Amelia throw out her arm and cry out something he could not hear. Her body was drenched in sweat. However many times they changed the sheets she became wet through again and the doctor was worried that her fever would turn to pneumonia.

'If the fever turns putrid, she may die,' he had told Gerard before he left. 'All you can do is to watch over her and pray.'

'Don't let her die…' The anguished words were torn from him. 'If I have sinned, vent your anger on me—let me take her place. I beg you, do not let her die.'

Gerard was not sure who he was praying to, for long ago he had felt that God was a myth, a fairy story. How could a gentle God allow the things he had seen in battle?

Tears trickled down his cheeks as he bent over Amelia and kissed her damp brow. 'Live for me, my darling,' he whispered. 'Live for me. I cannot bear it if you leave me…forgive me…forgive me…'

His expression was wintry. This was his fault. If he had spoken to Amelia earlier she would not have gone out alone. He should have made her believe that he'd had nothing to do with Lucinda.

Amelia opened her eyes to see a woman bending over her. The mist cleared for long enough for her to see that it was someone she knew…Susannah. She tried to speak, but the words wouldn't come. Her throat hurt too badly and every part of her body ached. Susannah touched her hand, a tear sliding down her cheek.

'You've been so ill, dearest,' she said. 'You had a fever, The doctor said it was a putrid infection of the lungs. We thought we were going to lose you. Gerard has been out of his mind.'

'Marguerite…' The word was a harsh whisper.

Susannah gripped her hand. 'Do not worry, dearest. She can't hurt anyone again. Her father has agreed to have her sent to a secure place where she will be properly cared for as long as she lives. He says he should have done it years ago, but her mother would not have it.'

'Not dead? I thought…' Amelia sighed.

'No…she tried to drown herself, but the Marquis of Northaven pulled her out of the lake. Gerard met him a few minutes earlier as he left the house to search for you. He had brought news and they were talking as they walked to the lake—and then they saw what was happening. Some of Gerard's men were already racing to your rescue, but he was the first to reach you.'

'She wanted to kill me…' Amelia's head was spinning as she tried to remember. 'She was so… strong…'

'She was ill, Amelia. Northaven has discovered the truth from Lieutenant Gordon. She is his cousin and he has always loved her, though he knew she was wild even as a girl. Miss Horton has told us more. As a child Marguerite was prone to tantrums. That is why they had a strict nanny for her. When she grew up she seemed better, calmer, but when Lucinda became pregnant their father started to forbid the girls to go anywhere—and Marguerite had become moody. She sneaked out at night, walking in the woods alone and she was prone to bouts of melancholy. Mr Ross suspected that she had killed her own sister and decided that she ought never to marry, though he was too proud of his good name to admit it to the world.'

Amelia closed her eyes for a moment. 'She was the one who planned all this, the abduction of me that went wrong and the rest…wasn't she?'

'Lieutenant Gordon says that she persuaded him; she said that he had to abduct you and kill you in front of Gerard—and then kill him. Only then would she give him what he wanted from her. He believed that Gerard was responsible for Lisette's death and agreed, because she had bewitched him, manipulated him—but in the end he couldn't go through with all the things she asked of him. When Northaven accused him of trying to shoot him in the back, he broke down and confessed that he had taken a pot shot at him, but swears it was more in the hope of scaring him off than killing him.'

'You mean the marquis forced him to confess?' Amelia's head was clearing a little. She sat up with Susannah's help and sipped a little water. 'I wonder why Marguerite decided she would kill me herself.'

'It was an impulse. You were in an isolated spot, alone—and she took her chance. She was always a little unstable...her nurse knew it. She said that both the Ross girls were inclined to be wild at times, but Marguerite got much worse after Lucinda's death. Perhaps it was her guilt because she killed her.'

'Poor Marguerite...'

'Do not pity her, Amelia.'

'I can only feel pity for her despite what she did.'

'Alice Horton was resentful because you had her dismissed, but when Marguerite tried to kill you, she attempted to stop her. She might have agreed to help with an abduction for a ransom, but she drew the line at murder.'

'Did she?' Amelia's brow wrinkled. 'I cannot remember...'

'You have been very ill, Amelia.'

'Did they send for you?'

'As soon as I heard what had happened, I was determined to come. Helene is here—and so is Emily. She put off her visit to Sinclair's. We all love you, dearest Amelia.'

'Helene should not be worrying over me. She must take care of herself and her baby.'

'We haven't let her nurse you. Emily and I have done most of it—and Martha, of course. Everyone wanted to do their best and Lisa has been crying for you. Gerard has been here much of the time, but today he had to see some people. Lieutenant Gordon has made a full confession. They are deciding what should be done with him—whether he should be sent abroad or given up to the magistrates.'

Amelia nodded. She closed her eyes. She was so very tired.

'Thank you for explaining…but I think I should like to sleep now.'

'Yes, of course,' Susannah said and kissed her cheek. 'Go to sleep, dearest. You will soon begin to feel better now…'

'Well, it is over,' Harry said as they sat together in the library. 'I am of the opinion that Gordon has learned his lesson. When he discovered that Marguerite had murdered her own sister, I thought he would be sick. The look of revulsion on his face tells me that he will not be drawn into such an affair again.'

'I still think he should have stood his trial,' Max said. 'You were too lenient with him, Gerard—he was behind the attempted kidnap on Amelia and the abduction of Miss Barton—and that shot outside the church at Pendleton, though he says it was no more than a warning.'

'The shot might have been meant for me. Amelia suffered no ill effects and Emily was returned unhurt thanks to Northaven. I have a great deal to thank Northaven for…and I believe we all owe him an apology.'

'Not certain of that,' Harry objected. 'His careless talk was almost certainly to blame for what happened in Spain.'

'Yes, I am sure it was—but he did not deliberately betray us and we ought to show some mercy. I let Gordon go because he is genuinely remorseful. Besides, it was Marguerite who planned it all. He was merely her tool.'

'I hope you have forgiven yourself too.' Max laid a hand on his shoulder. 'Lisette had been through a great deal, losing her lover, the rapes and then giving birth. Her mind was disturbed when she took her own life.'

'And I refused her when she asked me for love.' Gerard looked grave. 'Perhaps that is why I am being punished. If I lose Amelia…'

'Ridiculous!' Harry said. 'You cannot blame yourself for what happened to Amelia the other day. She invited that mad woman into your home.'

'If she had not, I might not have been there when she needed me. She could have been attacked at any time…perhaps months after we were married.'

'Amelia will pull through,' Max told him. 'She is surrounded by people who love her, and they will all do whatever they can to help. Just give it time, Gerard.'

'Yes, I know—thank you.' Gerard forced a

smile. 'You are the best friends a man could have at such a time.'

Gerard said no more. It was impossible to explain that he was afraid that when Amelia recovered her senses, she would not wish to marry him—that she might still believe the lies Marguerite had told her.

Amelia was dreaming. She was in the water and something was dragging her down. When she looked beneath the surface, she saw the eyes of a dead girl staring at her. Then the girl's skinny claws reached out to pull her to the bottom. She could feel the air draining from her lungs…

'Amelia…' A gentle hand shook her shoulder. 'It's just a nightmare, my love. I am so sorry she hurt you. Please forgive me.'

Amelia opened her eyes. For a moment she could not focus, but then she saw Gerard. His face were pale in the candlelight and tears were wetting his cheeks. He was crying…for her. She lifted her hand as he bent over her, touching his face.

'Don't cry,' she said. 'I am better now, Gerard…' She shuddered as she remembered. 'It was just a dream…just a horrid dream.'

Gerard sat on the edge of the bed. He reached for her hand, holding it as if it were made of fine porcelain. 'When I saw what Marguerite was doing I was so afraid. I thought I might be too late. My men had held off because they did not realise what she meant to do. She was your guest, not a stranger, so they hesitated and then it was almost too late.'

'How could anyone have guessed what she would do? I had noticed small things that seemed odd, but I thought she was merely suffering from melancholy because of the life she led. Indeed, I suspect that her father may have pushed her over the edge by depriving her of her freedom.'

'She tried to kill you, Amelia. You were lying there so still... I thought you were dead.' His voice broke with emotion.

'I think I almost was,' Amelia said with a wry smile. 'If you had not come...you and Northaven and the others... I owe the marquis an apology, Gerard. I once thought he was responsible for Lucinda's death, because I thought him her seducer—but now I know that he is blameless. I know who seduced her and then left her to face her shame alone.'

'He is a rake and more, but he is blameless in this instance.' Gerard's gaze narrowed. 'You do not truly think that I...?' Amelia shook her head. 'Then who...?'

Amelia reached for his hand. 'Before she tried to kill me, Marguerite told me it was Michael.'

'Your brother...but he accused me...the morning he came here—he accused me...'

'Of seducing her and then deserting her. Yes, he did—and he drove us apart, Gerard—because he was mad with jealousy. He was besotted with Lucinda. I see it all so clearly now. Things I should have noticed when she came to the house. She pretended to visit me, but it was Michael she wanted to see. He bought her things...promised to divorce Louisa—and then he saw her kissing you. In his rage and disappointment he blamed you. He loved her, still wanted her even though they quarrelled. If she had not died, he might still have kept his word to her in the end. She may have known it in her heart. She did not take her own life.'

'You are sure Marguerite was not lying?'

'It all makes sense, Gerard—and Michael changed after that time. Before Lucinda died he was not so bad tempered. He has become worse over the years. He does not care for his wife or she for him. He is a disappointed, bitter man.'

'Lucinda kissed me. I may have let her for a moment. It was a summer day and she was pretty that day, lit up from inside—but when she wanted me to lie with her I said no. At no time did I encourage her—or Marguerite. I hardly saw either of them. I was in love with you. You do believe me?' His fingers tightened around hers.

'Yes, I do. I think that was why Marguerite wanted to kill me. In her rage, she told me that Lucinda laughed at her, told her that you would marry me—and she went for her. It may have been an accident, but in Marguerite's mind she killed her sister. I think it played on her conscience. Her father had made her a virtual prisoner and she dwelled on her wrongs. You did not want her, so you became Lucinda's murderer though she knew she had done it—but she wanted to punish you. When she suspected we were likely to marry it made her angry and somehow she persuaded Lieutenant Gordon to help her.'

Gerard nodded. 'Alice Horton came to see me this morning. She apologised for what happened and told me that a couple of months ago Marguerite's mother was taken by a stroke and can no longer speak. Because his wife was so ill, her father allowed Marguerite to help with the nursing. She took some of the sleeping draught the doctor had left for her mother and put it in her father's ale—and then she left the house to come to us. He had no idea where she had gone. She had to take the letter you wrote to her mother—if her father had known where she was, he would have come after her.'

'I suspected that something must be wrong at her home when I realised she must have taken the letter. I feel so guilty,' Amelia said. 'She might have harmed Lisa.'

'How could you know what was in her mind? Besides, she did not hurt the child. Alice told me that Marguerite desperately wanted a child of her own. I think if Marguerite had succeeded in her plans to be rid of us, she might have spirited Lisa away. We found silver from her room at Ravenshead and also some diamond earrings of yours, Amelia. No doubt she would have taken whatever she needed before she disappeared with my daughter. Imagine what might have been Lisa's fate then…living with that woman…growing up as her child.'

'It does not bear thinking of!' Amelia closed her eyes for a moment. Gerard's fingers tightened over hers. She looked at him. 'Forgive me. I had no idea that she was unstable. Her letters were so sad…so pitiful…'

'The work of a clever if deranged mind. Her father may have suspected that she had killed her sister, but no one could prove it. She had brooded on her wrongs. When Gordon came home from France and went to visit, he told her about Lisette and how she died. She saw her chance to take revenge on me.

'Gordon was angry, but he had no thought of murder until she prompted him. He says that he resisted at first, but she was too strong for him. He had loved her since they were children, and she knew how to make him do her bidding. He wanted her, but she made him promise her that he would kill us both.'

Amelia shuddered. 'And I invited her to come here.'

'You could not have known what was in her mind.'

'What will happen to Lieutenant Gordon?'

'He is to live abroad. I have given him a letter of recommendation to a plantation owner in Jamaica. I met Jacques in France and he offered me help if I should go there.'

'Should Lieutenant Gordon not go to prison?' Amelia looked at him steadily. 'Many would seek revenge, Gerard.'

'I think he has suffered enough. He lost the woman he loved.'

'Does he know that Lisa is his child?'

'No. Perhaps it was harsh, but I thought it best for her to stay with us. She could not be more loved than she is now.'

'I am glad—for her sake. You are her true papa, Gerard.'

'Yes, I am—and you are her mama. We shall both love her and care for her, and she will remain our daughter even when we have children of our own.'

'Yes, we shall always love her.' Amelia smiled. 'Can you forgive me for doubting you even for a moment? I am so sorry, Gerard. I should have known, but I was stunned…I could not think clearly. Once I had time to let my mind clear, I knew you were innocent of all their accusations.'

'Can you forgive me for letting you walk into danger? You were close to death, Amelia.'

'That was entirely my own fault. I had completely forgotten everything else when I left the house. Besides, it is over—it is over, isn't it?' She lifted her eyes to meet his anxiously.

'Yes, my dearest. I am certain it is.'

'Then there is nothing to stop our marriage—is there?'

'Your brother…shall you tell him what you know?'

'I shall tell him all of it, Gerard. You were blameless. His jealousy and anger were misplaced. I think he may have blamed himself for Lucinda's suicide, because he told her he would not help her after he saw her kiss you—and he may find peace in the knowledge that she did not jump into the river because of his harshness. Perhaps he can find peace at last, and it may be the saving of him.'

'Yes, he may find some comfort in that,' Gerard agreed. 'He may still not forgive us—either of us.'

'If Michael wishes to remain a stranger to me, it is his choice. He may apologise and put an end to this feud if he wishes—if not…' Amelia shook her head. 'I cannot condone the way he behaved with a young woman he knew to be my friend. Besides, he made me so unhappy when he sent you away, Gerard. I have you and Lisa and all my friends—why should I need anyone else?'

Amelia stood at the church door, her arm resting lightly on Gerard's. The bells were ringing out joyfully and a large crowd of friends and local people had gathered outside to watch the bride and groom leave. Rice and dried rose petals were showered over them as they ran for the carriage.

Once inside out of the bitter February wind, Gerard drew her to him, kissing her softly, his hand moving at the nape of her neck. His eyes seemed to search her face.

'What is it?'

'You are happy? Truly happy?'

'You know I am. How could I not be on such a day? We are married and we have our friends about us. I have all that I ever wanted.'

'Your brother did not attend the wedding.'

'No, but my nephew, John, did—and he brought me a gift from my brother.' She touched the simple but beautiful baroque pearl that hung from a fine gold chain about her throat. 'This is the pendant my mother wore when she married. Michael sent it to me. It is the closest he could come to an apology.'

'Your mother's…' Gerard nodded. 'I wondered why you chose something so simple, though it is a fine pearl.'

'Mama's jewellery was divided between us after she died. Michael was allowed to choose first. He realised afterwards that I would have liked the pendant and he told me I should have it on my wedding day. Sending it for my wedding was a symbol of forgiveness…an olive branch. I wore it to show I had accepted his offering. I shall have many occasions to wear the diamonds you gave me, my dearest.'

'You hardly need diamonds,' Gerard told her and kissed her once more. 'Whatever you wear, whatever you do, you are lovely inside and out, my darling Amelia.'

'I love you so much…'

'I am the luckiest man to have found you.' Gerard took her hand as the carriage drew to a halt outside the house. 'Only you would have asked that Lisa should accompany us on our wedding trip to Paris. You are a pearl amongst women, Amelia. Your brother's gift was appropriate.'

'Thank you for being so understanding. Most men would hold a grudge after what Michael did…but you don't…do you?'

'I may never forgive him completely for what he did to us. It truly broke my heart and I wanted to die. I was reckless on the field of battle in the hope of death. However, I want you to be happy, Amelia. I know it would not suit you to cut your brother or his family entirely. I dare say I can greet him in a civil manner if it comes to it, though we shall never be friends.'

'It is enough,' she murmured as the carriage door was opened and a groom let down the steps. 'We must not keep our guests waiting, Gerard.'

* * *

Gerard watched as his wife moved amongst her friends at the lavish reception they had given. He felt a swelling of pride as he saw the way people greeted her. She was liked, respected and loved by everyone here. Known for her generosity, her dignity and her character, she was a truly great lady and he felt privileged that she was his to love and protect for the rest of their lives.

'Father wanted to come, you know.' Captain John Royston spoke from behind him, making Gerard turn his head. 'He is often bad tempered and lets his tongue run away with him—but he was upset when he heard what happened. Amelia looks well enough now, though.'

'Thankfully, she has made a full recovery,' Gerard said. 'You may tell your father he may visit us in Hanover Square when he chooses. I dare say Amelia will wish for a ball when we go to town next Season. I should be pleased to see him and your mother and brother—and you, of course, should you be on leave from your regiment.'

'Thank you. I'll make that known to my father.' John offered his hand and shook on it, then he nodded and moved away.

Harry Pendleton came up to him. 'So we are all three wed,' he observed. 'I think we have done well for ourselves, Gerard. There was a time in Spain when I believed none of us would ever see this day.'

'We were lucky to escape with our lives.' Gerard's mouth formed a grim line. 'And we have all had our troubles since. However, I believe we can all look forward to a more peaceful future.'

'With Napoleon safely tucked up in his island prison, I dare say England will be at peace—and I think the same may be said for us.' Harry looked thoughtful. 'I wrote to Northaven and thanked him for the part he played in this last affair, Gerard. You were right—the past is gone and should be forgotten.'

'It was harder for you to forgive, because of what happened to Susannah, but, from something he said when we talked, I believe that when he saw her fall with his ball in her shoulder it changed him. I dare say, given the chance, he may lead a better life in future.'

Harry shrugged and then grinned. 'Susannah wanted me to write the letter. It is amazing what we do for love, Gerard.'

'Indeed, I agree with that,' Gerard said and laughed. 'Excuse me, my dear fellow, but I believe they are about to play a waltz and I should like to dance with my wife…'

Amelia turned in her husband's arms. She thought he was sleeping and she smiled as she traced the line of his mouth with her fingertip. Sometimes he could look stern, forbidding, but in sleep he looked younger and at peace, very like the young man she had first fallen in love with so many years ago. The previous night, he had made love to her passionately, hungrily, but with such tenderness that she had wept tears of happiness. She bent her head to kiss his lips softly and found herself caught in an imprisoning embrace.

'I thought you were asleep,' she said and smiled down at him.

'Were you trying to take advantage of me?' His eyes mocked her lovingly.

'Foolish man…' She tried to pull away but he moved swiftly, rolling her beneath him, gazing down at her. Her hair was loose and tumbling about her face in disarray, her skin pearly pink and smooth as his eyes feasted on her sweetness. 'Gerard…it is almost time to get up.'

'This is our honeymoon and I may not leave this bed for a week.'

'Is that a threat or a promise?' she teased, touching his beloved face. 'I think I should be quite happy to stay right here for as long as you wish.'

'I shall take that as an invitation,' he murmured huskily, bending his head to suck gently at her nipples, which peaked at his touch. 'You are so beautiful, my love. I think I can never have enough of you.'

Amelia moaned softly, her body arching, tingling as he stroked her, coming vibrantly alive as the desire pooled inside her. She ran her hands over his back, loving the satin feel of his skin, the hardness of toned muscles. His maleness felt hard and hot against her inner thigh as he sought the sweet moistness of her femininity, entering her with a deep thrust that made her cry out with pleasure.

They moved together, slowly, taking their time as

their bodies matched and met in equal need—a need that took them soaring into realms of pleasure known only to true lovers. Carried and tossed by raging passion, they ended on a far shore where the soft sea spray kissed a sunlit breach and the scent of blooms wafted on a warm breeze.

'I am in paradise...' she murmured against his shoulder, tasting the salt of his sweat. 'I am truly happy, Gerard.'

'We are both in paradise then,' he murmured and smiled down at her. 'For I am in a place I never thought to be.'

Amelia lay back, content to feel him lying beside her. She thought that he had fallen asleep or perhaps he was just pretending again.

'I was thinking,' she said. 'We have so much, Gerard. We must find a way to share some of our good fortune. I realise that I made a mistake with Marguerite, but there is a young woman I know who really does need a little good fortune. Her name is Jane and I thought we might give her a Season in town this year.'

Gerard did not answer. He must truly be asleep this time. Amelia smiled. Somewhere within the house she could hear a longcase clock striking. She felt sleepy, at peace with herself. There was no hurry for anything. When they returned to England, she would write to the young woman and invite her to stay with them at their house in Hanover Square...